Scion of a Swan

Scion of a Swan

AGE OF SHADOWS: BOOK 1
FOURTH EDITION

A. R. STERN

Fourth edition October 2025
Cover design by AmbientPixel Design
Edited by Steven Noll

Library of Congress Control Number: 2025919798
ISBN: 979-8-9928426-2-3 (paperback)
ISBN: 979-8-9928426-3-0 (ebook)

Published in the United States of America by Between The Stars Publishing LLC

www.ar-stern.com

To those who tell you that you can't...
You can.

Thank you to those who have supported me from day one. Your love made these ideas a reality.

The Compendium of Magick

Crimson – The shade of conquest and allure. Wielded for success, power, enchantment, and irresistible attraction.

Red – Born of flame and fury. Invoked for anger, lust, harmful intentions, bindings, and curses.

Orange – A color of veiled charm and hidden dominance. Used in glamour workings, luck, and summoning what lies beyond mortal sight.

Yellow – Bright with creativity and the quickening of the mind. Strengthens confidence, intellect, and clairvoyant sight.

Pink – Gentle yet potent. Governs love, fertility, and the fortification of bonds.

Green – The heart of protection and stability. Drawn upon for manifestation, healing, love, wealth, and fortune.

Blue – *A tranquil current. Called for serenity, truth, dream work, and rites of death and rebirth.*

Indigo – *A bridge to the Otherworld. Neutralizes hostile magick, affirms truth, and wards against slander.*

Purple – *The mind's fortress. Strengthens spirit, sharpens thought, shields against harm, and deepens dreams.*

Violet – *The highest sorcery. Connects to the Higher Self, the elements, and the spiritual currents of protection and power.*

Prologue

A delicate trickle of blood drips steadily from his nose. A small reflective pool has formed in the dip of the floorboards of the bedroom. Desmond stopped trying to slow the bleeding long ago, back when he first arrived in this hellscape. The edges of his nostrils are caked in drying mounds of it, but he no longer tries viciously scrubbing at the red stains on his skin. Even if he managed to scour his skin clean, it would often grow raw, and it wouldn't take long for fresh blood to take the place of the old. Cleanliness is a privilege he no longer has.

This bedroom is a facsimile of his in the real world. The bed feels and appears similar, but his real blankets are a steel gray, while these are a lighter tone of silver. The window is nothing more than a frame nailed into a wall with maroon curtains bordering it; his real bedroom has a real window with steel blue curtains that pair with his bedsheets.

This bedroom has no closet and the desk is the same matte black with shelves and drawers to hold books and casting tools. His altar of magickal ingredients and tomes from countless years of collecting is vacant from its usual spot. Sometimes he thinks he can see the phantom flicker of where they are supposed to be, but the vision fades the second he stands to grasp them in his trembling hands. Magick doesn't work here, either. That's how he knows this place isn't real.

This new reality is an illusion he can't grasp. A world where the laws of the physical world doesn't just bend, they fracture into a new dimension. Whatever place he now resides in is a hellscape, personalized just for him. Nothing is real. No one is safe. None of his senses can be trusted.

A knock sounds from behind, startling him enough to swallow a clot of blood. Three slow knocks. Desmond doesn't bother glancing back. He knows what is expected of him. He hadn't always started out in this room, but as of late, this has been his starting point each time he wakes, right before death can sweep him free.

That's another thing Desmond learned quickly. He can't die. Unless he is already dead, in which case this torment will never cease. He tries not to think about that.

He's lost count of how many near-death experiences he's had since arriving wherever *here* is. Desmond has become intimate with death's grasp, brushing tantalizingly close and breathing in a sigh of relief at the whisper of peace. His serenity splinters when he wakes in this fake bedroom, or in a prison cell, or a hospital bed, forced to live another moment in this nightmare. Once he had woken while completely submerged in a pool sputtering, coughing, and wheezing for air. It wasn't until he managed to drag himself from the pool that he had realized he had been choking on blood, not water. There was always so much blood.

Swiping a hand against the constant drip from his nose, he smears the stain against the clean sheets of the bed. When he woke for the very first time, his nose hadn't bled permanently as it does now. His body also hadn't constantly ached. He hadn't felt nearly as exhausted, yet the fear was there from the start. Fear has always been a constant companion, but now the fear has a dull edge to it. When the pain was heightened or something began stalking him, that's when the fear sharpened. Until then, it's a blunt ache he hardly noticed anymore.

The first bed he'd awoken in was in a hospital. He had sat up and attempted to recall how he'd arrived there. He remembered Beltane and talking to Daire and seeing her unorthodox friends. After that he could recall little else. It was as if his memory had been wiped clean. He had called out for a nurse, a doctor, his mom, anyone, but no one came. After pacing the room and checking the bathroom, he had decided to check the hall.

That's when the fear had sunk its teeth in. He had been wearing only a hospital gown, and the moment his hospital door shut behind him, the lights had turned off. He'd padded down the hall on bare feet calling for help. When he'd finally heard a nurse respond back, relief washed through him so hard he thought he'd pass out. But when Desmond followed the voice into a different room with flickering fluorescent lights, he had immediately noticed the glass shattered on the floor and the silence in the hospital. No other patients were found as he checked each room, and the hospital lacked the expected bustle. It felt abandoned and *wrong*. It was as if everyone had been plucked from the building, leaving it as an empty and discarded shell.

When Desmond had arrived at the room the nurse resided in, glass crunched into his heels and fear lodged in his throat. There was something there, and it wasn't human. It was ivory white and so tall it had to hunch so as not to hit the ceiling. It was emaciated, and Desmond could count each of its ribs. Hip bones jutted like knives through the milky flesh as its joints threatened to punch through the thin skin. Its knees were unnaturally long and skinny with little muscle visible beneath paper flesh. Four arms connected with knobby joints and spindly fingers protruded from its abdomen. Where the elbows creased, there appeared to be a fine webbing, similar to a spider's web, that frayed and thickened with movement. Its face had no eye holes, not even sockets, but instead had the paper flesh covering it with two slits for a nose in the center of its face. A gaping maw was filled by a forked tongue the color of a plum and two rows of serrated teeth stained red.

But when it spoke, it sounded human.

It sounded like Aubrie, his mother. "My Dessy," it purred with a slow tilt of its head. "You must rest. You must heal." It had reached its clawed fingers toward him, to hold him still so he could not run. Desmond had stumbled away, tracking blood as he moved further from the nightmare. "I am your mother," it had growled with a flick of its sinuous tongue, "and you will obey."

Tiny bits of glass bit into the soft arch of his feet and slicked the floor as he ran. It never caught him, though several times he could feel the hot decay of its breath through the thin sheet of gown.

Desmond had slipped through an open door and slammed it closed, only to find himself in a different hell. He had been standing outdoors in a field of sunflowers, a warm sun pelting his skin. He still wore the hospital gown and his feet throbbed from the embedded glass. Ahead had stood Daire, watching him with those bewitching eyes of hers. Her onyx hair was braided over one shoulder with her typical unamused expression on her lips.

Her eyes weren't quite right: the amber had appeared too gold and the blue had appeared almost purple. Her tattoos also hadn't been correct with some missing entirely from her body while others she bore he didn't recognize. The closer he'd looked, the more about her had seemed wrong. Her arms were to long, her legs were to bowed. Instead of her typical haughty and ambivalent expression she wore whenever she looked at him, something hungry and sinister had snaked across her face.

"Des," she had said with a rough and gravelly voice, "I can save you. But first you must follow me."

With no other option, he had followed her. She led him to a grove of trees. He stayed standing in the sun, and when she stepped into the shadows, her skin began to melt, her muscle sloughing from the bone. It happened within seconds, her flesh and blood pooling and bubbling at her feet until she was nothing but bone with a black glow emanating from within her core. Her organs held solid; her eyes unsettling without lids to cover their bulge, her heart thumping steadily beneath her breast bone, intestines curled and slimy above her hips. A walking nightmare.

"Desmond," she said, reaching out her skeletal hand. "You can never leave. You're mine."

A knock sounds behind him and snaps his recollection of his first moments in Hell. A second and a third knock follows with an echo that resonates in his bones. Desmond snorts and licks his mouth when a fresh splatter of blood coats his lips. That memory feels like decades ago. He can't keep track of each horror he encountered. Sometimes it's his mother trying to trick him, other times it's his friends, Roman and Luca. It always ends in one of two ways; either the Mimic chases and attacks him until he is a breath away from death, or it begs for his help, only to be brutally and gruesomely maimed in front of his eyes.

It hadn't taken long for him to realize he couldn't trust anything. Any person he saw is a facade, a monster hiding behind a mask. Even the animals and plants weren't always safe. He had been eaten alive by a swarm of rats when he couldn't escape a prison cell he had been locked in. Another time he was cut to shreds by literal blades of grass.

He can trust nothing about his surroundings.

And he always feels like he's being watched. No matter his location, the feeling of being hunted never ceases. Even if he is truly and utterly alone, as he is now, sitting on his bed in his room, he senses it watching him. It never shows itself. No, that's what the creatures are for. Somehow he knows they are not what is controlling this place. The creatures are simply a pawn in this hellscape game.

But he still isn't sure what the endgame is.

Standing, Desmond crosses the distance between him and the closed bedroom door, his feet dragging through the puddle of blood and smearing a trail as he goes. His stomach clenches in memory, knowing whatever is beyond this door isn't an escape, only another sadistic means of torture. The fear bubbles in his throat and he spits out a lump of bloodied saliva. Before the fear can make him falter further, he grips the handle and wrests the door free of the frame.

The moment he steps over the threshold, a cool breeze has him shivering, and he absently wipes away the blood tickling his lips and chin. He stands in a courtyard lined with symmetrical, hulking trees. Their leaves are eerily vibrant green and seem to glow in the mists blanketing the yard. A path leads through the center of the evenly spaced topiary. Desmond gazes skyward to find a sky thick with cloud cover. It appears to glow a soft gold, as if the sun is just beyond, trying to poke through but unable to.

Ahead is a towering building three stories high with barred windows and an overwhelming sense of dread rockets into his chest. Thick swathes of lichen coat the first floor of the building, its green claws tracking its way up to the second, yet unable to reach the third level. The air smells sweet and welcoming.

"Welcome to Hell," he whispers to himself and starts down the path. He shoots a wary look over his shoulder, unsurprised when he spots only a locked and barred wrought-iron gate. The door he entered through is nowhere in sight.

At least nothing is chasing him yet.

He passes the first set of trees, giving them no more than a once over before continuing. As he passes the second set, he slows and his heart plummets as he sees a body swing from one of the larger branches over the pathway. The face is bloated and pale with the head cocked at a sharp angle from a broken neck. He recognizes the face instantly. Luca has been dead for a while.

He continues down the path, leaving a trail of blood dripping from his nose as he goes. The next tree he passes has Roman hanging from it. His eye sockets are black and barren from where his eyes have been removed.

The next pair of trees has a body hanging from either side of him. On his left hangs Sabrina, Daire's cousin, though he hadn't known her well, he enjoyed her company. Red stains streak down her cheeks like tears. Her hands are tied behind her back as she swings from her broken neck.

Klowbi hangs to his right, and this time a whimper presses against his lips. Her freckles are smeared with dirt, her auburn hair dull and knotted, and her body spins in a lazy circle. Her spiraling creates a ring of blood beneath her as it spurts from where her arms should have been. Desmond glances around, trying to locate her missing limbs. He liked Klowbi. She wasn't born into the world of magick, yet she had meshed with it well. Daire had been so fond of her. He can recall several happy memories from the sabbats they'd often celebrate together. Seeing her mauled on his behalf spurs bile from his throat.

There is nothing he can do about it now. It isn't the first time he's seen her dead, or his friends, or his mother. He's seen them killed thousands of different ways, and their screams all sound the same. Whether they are gutted, burned, stretched, doused in acid or any other creative form of death, by the end he can't tell the difference between the screams.

The last set of trees is closest to the stairs leading to the building. Both are empty. Glancing up to the barred windows, a pale face flashes for a moment before disappearing into the depths. He can't make out who it is, and the urge to follow keeps his feet moving up the stairs towards the massive steel doors. He learned the hard way that if he refuses to move, something else will encourage him to. Moving on his own accord is better than the alternative.

The heavy doors aren't coated in lichen like the rest of the building, appearing clean and well maintained. He pushes forward to find they move easily. Behind him he hears movement and he freezes in his steps.

"Des," a voice croaks, followed by another. "Don't leave us."

Without looking, he knows the voices are coming from the bodies that twist in the trees. Dead lips speaking dead words. *They're not real. Keep moving.*

"We are real," a voice he thinks is Luca's croaks.

"Save us," Klowbi wheezes.

"Don't leave us to die," they speak as one.

Ignoring their haunting pleas, he walks into the building and lets the door swing shut behind him. A long hall, illuminated by speckled lights, appears never-ending with faint light replacing creeping shadows. The same sweet aroma from the courtyard is even stronger indoors. It makes his stomach churn. It reeks of honey and iron.

A continuous and rhythmic drip from his nose marks his path as he cautiously stalks down the dim hall. His footsteps echo across the tile and a cold sweat beads his brow. Exhaustion is already making his bones ache. A moment of rest sounds like unobtainable bliss, even for an hour. He can't recall the last time he could just breathe or rest his eyes. There is always a looming threat hidden within the confines of this reality and letting his guard down equals only torture.

Though he has no inkling of how long he has been stuck in limbo, he knows his mental capacity has been slipping the longer he stays. It's becoming difficult to discern reality from illusion, if he is truly being followed or if the paranoia has sunken so deep it can't be shaken. Is he hearing nails scraping the inside of the walls as he progresses, or is that just the groan of pipes? Are those a flicker of eyes in the darkness ahead or merely the strain of exhaustion from his eyes creating shapes that aren't there?

The first door Desmond encounters is barred and locked with a small window that can be closed for observation with a steel slat. Whimpering is audible through the heavy steel. Casting a wary glance towards the ever-growing hall, he slowly approaches the door. The whimpering has grown louder, a constant mewl of pain, he realizes. Fingers smeared with blood and grime, he slides the observation slat open.

The cell is small with only a bed housed in the center of the room pressed against the back wall. Sitting on the bed is a woman with a sheared head staring into her lap, her legs raised to her chest revealing bare skin. She's wearing nothing besides a thin sheet that hangs loosely from her gaunt shoulders. Abnormal, bulging masses pulse over her flesh, the masses an unsettling obsidian that are stark against her pale complexion. Some are small, no larger than a pinky nail, while others are the size of a tennis ball. They cover her like a pox, marring her delicate skin. Her legs and thighs, arms and hands, throat and cranium are dotted with the pulsating lesions. Beneath the thin sheet, dark masses can be seen covering her abdomen, her breasts, her shoulders. She's lathered in them.

Cringing at the sight, he pulls away, peering down the hall to ease the anxiety roiling in his belly. Finding the hall unchanged with the lights flickering overhead, he returns his gaze to the girl in the cell. Her head is lifted as she stares directly at him. Her face is covered in black pustules. Half her face is blotted with abscesses and covers an eye. She grimaces and her lips are speckled with them. Her lips move, but she's too quiet for him to hear from this distance.

He observes her from behind the safety of the reinforced steel. Growing tired of watching her, he moves to continue down the hall when she lets out a gasp and cries out in pain. Desmond's stomach clenches, and his heart rate increases at her outcry. He turns to look back at her, morbid curiosity begging him to seek out the source of her pain.

She pitches forward onto the bed as her hands clasp around a twitching bulge on her abdomen. She cries out again, her voice sounding muted in the small space, and she tears at the sheet and tosses it to the side despite being completely naked underneath. One of the largest black masses is writhing against her flesh, her hands cupping the tender flesh.

"Help me," she whines and glances at the observation window while another cry of agony rips past her throat. "It's coming. Oh God, please kill me."

Tuning out her pleas and increasing screams of anguish, Desmond watches as the black mass hisses and a goo oozes out, dribbling past her fingertips and staining the skin around it gray. A thick drop lazily makes its way past her navel to pool in the bowl of her pelvic bone. When she screams again, her head is thrown back. She sounds beastly, her cries guttural and harsh. Desmond watches with macabre fascination as the masses on her body continue to pop and ooze, and it isn't until her screams don't relent and become a constant crescendo that he finally sees small spider-like beings emerge from the bursting bulbs on her flesh.

There are hundreds of them poking through the black masses and crawling over her skin. Her screams are hysterical. She's batting frantically at her skin in an attempt to brush them away, but they are an unstopping tide. Her skin looks like it's moving of its own accord, a gray outer layer floating atop her pale complexion. The creatures are crawling into her mouth and clogging her nose, which turns her screams into choked spasms. Her eyes are wide, and Desmond watches in horror as the legs pluck at her orbs and climb into her ear canals.

The wave of creatures doesn't stop and are beginning to fill the room. The girl spasms and claws at her throat, revealing thin strips of red welling where her nails dug into soft flesh. Her eyes are no longer visible from the creatures invading her body. Though her screams are still managing to punctuate her wheezing, they're raspier than before. Her body seizes and locks, limbs flailing and body twitching, until all he can hear are the scrabbling legs of the creatures.

Frantic, he shuts the observation slide and steps back. He checks his body for any of the spider creatures or black lumps. Finding none, he hurriedly starts down the hall, hearing three knocks ricochet off the reinforced door behind him.

Desmond jogs down the hall as fear grips his throat. The taste of blood slides down the back of his tongue, comforting in its consistency. Above he hears something rattling in the vents, and the image of some creature hunting him sets his feet moving faster down the flickering hallway.

A door bangs open and he slows just enough to peek inside. Carcasses hang on meat hooks and a cool chill brushes the heat from his cheeks. A girl with empty silver eyes hangs in the center of the room by her feet with a metal trough below. A black silhouette approaches from behind the body. With a flash of silver, a red slash blooms across the dead girl's throat, emptying the contents into the trough beneath. The silhouette grins with thorns for teeth.

Desmond bolts down the hall in a panic. Another door opens as he nears, and this one emits maniacal laughter followed by the clanking of chains. Just as he passes the threshold, a hand shoots out and nearly grabs hold of his arm. A strangled cry escapes past his lips as Desmond stumbles to evade the hand's reach. Inside is what used to be a person with chains around their ankles and throat.

They have no eyes, the skin being stretched so tight across the sockets it doesn't dip like it should. The mouth is abnormally large and saliva dribbles from its gaping jaw. Its abdomen is cut up, revealing all the inner workings of the human body. The heart is still pumping, the lungs still compressing, though there is no blood, the remaining veins throb with non-existent life.

"Knock, knock, knock," the creature growls. A high-pitched shriek of laughter follows. It lunges at Desmond, only to stumble from the weight of the chains, salivating through razor teeth at the blatant terror visible in his eyes.

Desmond starts running again, both from the monsters residing in the rooms he passes and from the creature following closely above in the vents. Each time he looks up to mark where the creature might be, he finds nothing but a smooth ceiling. Not a pipe or vent in sight.

No more, please, no more. His lungs ache and the constant fear and adrenaline rush is making his skin vibrate. He can't remember the last time he ate or when he slept. His body shouldn't be functioning. He should be *dead*.

"Desmond," a feminine voice echoes around him and his footsteps slow. No doors remain, and the screams and banging have ceased. "Desmond, why are you running?"

"Who's there?" he rasps and wipes a cold hand against his nose, smearing blood.

"Child, you know who I am. I've been watching over you this entire time." The voice is soothing and melodic. It makes his stomach churn.

"Please," he begs, ashamed of his voice cracking and the sound of his vulnerability. "Let me go or let me die."

"It isn't time," she says, and within a blink, she is standing an arm's reach ahead. She has his mother's face, but her eyes are milky white and instead of his mother's natural red hair, it shimmers black with iridescent red.

"Time for what?" Desmond asks, staring at the pale skin of the creature in front of him. Despite her mostly human appearance, he knows nothing here is truly human. They are all *other*.

She smiles, her plump red lips glistening. "Follow, child," she croons, turning quickly on her heels and padding down the hall without a sound. Desmond treads several paces behind, deciding it's safer to continue forward than turning back the way he came.

She leads him down the twisting and twining hall. It isn't until his head brushes the ceiling that he realizes it's lowering the further into the building they walk. She still appears upright, but Desmond is having to duck his head and shoulders to avoid grazing them above. He is almost bent sideways, his knees bearing the brunt of his awkward gait, when she stops and turns abruptly to face him.

"It is almost time to make your choice," she says and pushes open the door that he swore was a wall moments before. She walks through without waiting for his response. He follows her, straightening and releasing the tension and aches kinking in the muscles of his back.

When he gazes around his new environment, he finds himself back in the courtyard. Desmond turns around to find the unnaturally sterile steel doors he had passed through earlier. Ahead is the same path leading through the pairs of trees except the bodies have been removed. At the

11

furthest tree from the door stands the woman who stole his mother's face. She smiles at him warmly. A tight coil of anxiety knots in Desmond's belly.

The woman gestures to come closer. He takes one step and warily glances at the trees. It wouldn't be the first time a humanoid hand had emerged from the bark to grasp him, or have the cobblestones beneath smolder and burst into an untamable wildfire. Even the breeze mussing his hair sends a breath of dread down his spine.

"Desmond," she croons gently, "it is almost over."

Steeling himself, Desmond manages to cross the path and avoid the trees with no issue. His heart hammering in his chest feels as if he will lose consciousness if it beats any harder. He stands staring down at the woman, her hair reminding him of smoke and fire, destruction and renewal.

"Come here," she encourages, opening her arms. Without thinking, he steps closer into her embrace. Her smile broadens and thins her red lips.

"Do not shy from me, child," she whispers. Despite the fear telling him to turn and his instinct screaming to back away, he can't find it in himself to listen. He's exhausted from running, from being in a constant state of panic and fear, dreading the next moment of pain. He doesn't want to keep going. He wants it to be over.

Desmond wraps his arms around her as if she really was his mother. His grip tightens on her, breathing in her familiar scent and clenching his eyes shut. A part of him knows this will likely end in near death, but he is beyond caring. He can't recall the last time he had been touched by a loving hand, a tenderness he barely remembers from a life so long ago.

So when she starts to thread her fingers tenderly through his hair, massaging the nape of his neck and rubbing his back, all the tension releases in his body. Tears fall freely, mixing with snot and the constant stream of blood from his nose. Her heartbeat is slow and methodical, an easy beat to lull himself to sleep to.

"Are you tired?" she whispers against his hair.

Desmond nods his head, uncaring as his defenses crumble. Staying in this state of relief is a blip of heaven he thought he'd never experience again. At least here he can pretend he is safe and doesn't have to fight the fear and exhaustion anymore.

Desmond doesn't notice when she loops something around his throat. Nor does he notice as her skin begins to morph from white to a void-like oblivion. It isn't until she stops stroking his muscles and massaging the back of his head, exactly how his mother used to do when he was upset or afraid, that he pulls back.

"Knock, knock, knock," the voice is deep and jarring, borderline inhuman.

Her face is a black void, and the eyes are an even darker abyss he can't find the end or beginning of. The warmth radiating from her is gone and is replaced with a coldness that burns his skin. Her mouth smiles, and inside are thorns for teeth.

An onslaught of terror freezes him as he stares into the depthless eyes and chasm of a maw. Hanging from the thickest branch, the noose around his throat tightens, his feet thrashing for purchase. His jugular jars and bruises at the sudden impact, the oxygen seizing from his lungs while the panic of adrenaline prevents him from fumbling for escape.

The creature grins and grasps the sides of his head as his vision darkens and fades. His muscle spasms weaken as his nails that had been clawing at the bind around his throat sag by his sides. The entirety of his vision is lost to the infinite eclipse and the echoing of the creature's last words.

"Knock, knock, knock."

Chapter 1

Today marks the significance of an otherwise seemingly mundane day.

Beltane is today. A time of union and growth. Of fertility. Of life.

It has been over six months since her passing and today I'm returning to the Wiccan community. Reinstating my prowess to those who doubt me, my ability, my Craft. Even with her gone, my magick has heightened, invigorated by the thirst for truth.

With an adept twirl of my fingers, yellow threads of magick flare. I wend them between my fingers, tossing the energy from palm to palm, the pulsating magick humming in my grasp. Snapping my fist closed, it fizzles and soaks into my skin before returning to its source.

As a Delacroix, we are the only witches who can see magick in its purest form. Even those who've practiced the Craft for decades are not blessed with our ability. Mom would tell me stories when I was a child about our world of magick, and when I'd ask how only we can see its magnificence, she would smile and lean close, whispering that our ancestors were gifted centuries ago with the sight. It runs in our blood and the heterochromia that colors our eyes is a condition of our abilities.

I huff in irritation, rubbing my hands where the magick once was, and peek out the window. A few people pass by along the sidewalk and several patrons sit on the patio of the Black Cat Diner. If I listen close, I can make out the faint clatter of forks scraping against plates below the floorboards. Living above where we work has its perks, even if the walls are paper thin and the odor of grease permeates the carpet. The quaint town of Melas may be small, but the diner is a staple in the state of Oregon.

There's still no sign of Klowbi. *Of all the days to be late, you choose this one.*

I'm already dressed in a form-fitting black dress, my midnight hair plaited, my amber and blue eyes darkened with eyeliner, and a silver belt adorned with runes around my hips. A palm-sized maroon silk bag hangs from the belt with rose quartz, garnet, and hematite inside, each chosen purposefully: rose quartz for calming energy and harmony; garnet for purification and cleansing of things in disorder; hematite for protection and reflecting negative energy. Stepping back into this world means keeping all forms of magick within reach.

It feels strange knowing I'll mingle amongst my fellow witches and Mom won't be one of them. I'll never again see her dance before the flames of magick, teasing Dad about his scruffy beard he can never tame, and getting drunk off mead while rehashing memories that occurred long before I was born.

Forcing the dark thoughts down, I tighten my braid so my hair won't obscure the moon phase tattoos along my collarbone. Mom loved my tattoos, namely the rune wheel inked on my hand and the black swan along my forearm. She rarely condemned my decisions even if I made the wrong one, a stubborn trait she'd sown in my upbringing.

I purse my lips and stalk across my bedroom. We'll be cutting it close if we make it on time even if Klowbi shows up now. At least it gives me time to craft a protection spell while I wait.

Shuffling a few hand-me-down spell books from my desk, I manage to locate an empty mason jar. Clear quartz, a swan feather, rosemary, sea salt, and white clover are added inside, along with a quick note to protect from the malevolent before sealing the lid with black wax. With little effort, I press a flare of lime green magick into the jar. It swirls within the glass and soaks into the contents. I slip the jar beneath my bed as the magick settles.

Most of the population doesn't realize that magick is real. They snicker at us witches and humor us with questions of our belief, nodding along with unconvinced expressions even when there is proof of a spell's success. It saddens me that so many people could alter their lives for the better if only they'd apply their intentions into a spell. Instead they'd rather live their lives in denial of the freedom and possibilities magick can offer them.

Mom and I had plans to travel the world together so we could share the wonder of the Craft and heal those with wounds too great to mend on their own. But that dream died with her.

I've just stepped into the hallway of our two-bedroom apartment when the front door swings open. Klowbi is shucking off her shoes, her hair a wild mane of auburn knots, cheeks flushed red and spotted with freckles. She stumbles into the hall and skids to a halt with a sheepish grin. Her cheeks are an even brighter red at finding me watching her.

"I know I'm late," she begins, slinking past me and into her room. She glances over her shoulder, already shedding her jeans and top. "I'll be ready in less than ten."

"Make it five and I'll skip the part where I lecture you."

Klowbi pouts and kicks the door closed. It takes less than three minutes before she opens it again, now dressed in a rose pink dress. It's a simple design draping to her knees and when she twists it flows around her legs. The sleeves puff from her shoulders in a lighter film of pink and the waist is a chiffon accentuating her curves.

"Beautiful choice," I comment, elbowing into her room.

"It feels too tight."

"It's form fitting. It's supposed to be tight."

"Maybe I should wear something different," Klowbi murmurs, pulling at the material along her waist as she stares into the full-length mirror.

"No time and no need. You look fabulous." Leading her by the elbow, I direct her to sit on the psychedelic quilt with the Wiccan symbol embroidered as the centerpiece. "Let me do your hair."

Pots of flowers and herbs line nearly every spare inch in her room. A hanging pot of devil's ivy pothos suspends near the open window. Dozens of bottles and vases fill her room with a variety of plant life, some dried, some alive, and everywhere in between. It keeps the musty mildew smell of the apartment from festering, and fresh spell ingredients are a bonus.

Klowbi fidgets with a few seashells, another bountiful item in her room. She's been collecting them since she was young, though she hardly embraces the ocean since her injury. A small stack of herbology and gardening books are on her nightstand, and her hairbrush sits beside them. I snag it and twist so I'm sitting behind her, my feet tucked beneath me.

"Stop fidgeting," I chide, brushing through her hair. It catches on a few knots, but she doesn't complain as I meticulously work them free. Her posture is rigid, her fingers worrying.

"Sorry," she murmurs, clasping her hands tightly in her lap.

"Why did you get home so late?"

"I lost track of time. I'm sorry," she apologizes again. She starts chewing on her thumbnail and I clear my throat. She immediately stops, her hands settling tightly in the material of her dress. "Could you weave flowers through my hair?"

Without acknowledgement, I grab a handful of flowers displayed along her nightstand in varying shades of blue, yellow, and purple. I section off thick tresses and begin weaving the flora through her braid.

"Are you okay?" Klowbi lilts, her voice severing the silence.

"Yes."

"Do you think you're ready?"

"I'm ready, Bambi. It's about time I came back."

"I'm happy you've decided to attend the sabbat. I know this won't be easy, but I'll be here." Klowbi offers as I weave her auburn locks around a purple bloom.

"I know. It'll be hard with Mom gone, but I can't continue avoiding the community. They need to see me." Being secluded to my grief and anger had pushed most of the Wiccan community away. Klowbi had tried convincing me to join the festivities previously, but it had felt too wrong, too real, too much. Only now do I finally feel ready. Beltane was Mom's favorite sabbat, and it felt like a slight to her memory if I didn't join in the celebration. In remembering.

"I'm proud of you, Daire." Klowbi whispers.

"Thank you, Bambi," I murmur, embracing her from behind.

"I miss her, too."

"It doesn't feel real most days," I admit. "I still wonder if we could have done more. If we had used a different spell, if we had caught it sooner, if we asked for help from a different deity, then maybe things would have been different."

"You can't keep getting hung up on the what ifs," she says gently. "You still have the good memories like when you would make dandelion cookies or her mentorship with the Craft. The bad doesn't negate the good."

I stew in my thoughts as I finish her braid before tying it off, and Klowbi shifts to sit beside me. Her fingers twirl the bracelet on her wrist. Three small pink flowers are embedded in a chain of gold, a gift from her mother Elaine. They've always been close, and rearing Klowbi as a single mother with little to her name tested the boundaries of their relationship. It's one of the few lavish items Klowbi owns, not just a piece of jewelry, but a reminder that the gift of love is an invaluable thing.

We sit in silence as Klowbi fidgets with her bracelet. She sighs and looks at me, her teeth worrying at her lower lip. Her brows are pinched together as if debating her next words.

"Yes?"

She looks down into her lap before inhaling. "Did you ever figure out how she died?"

"No."

"Oh."

"It wasn't mundane. I believe it had something to do with the Craft or perhaps the Otherworld. It's the only logical explanation." I had spent months prior to Mom's death scouring for an answer. Dad and I found little to nothing with our efforts. Our grief found little reprieve without knowing what took her from us. It's still buried within my heart, corroding the small moments of joy I manage to cling to.

"We don't have to discuss it now. I just wanted to know if you ever found out more," she mumbles while awkwardly rubbing her neck, her shoulder, her waist.

"It's fine," I reassure her. I stand and offer my hand to her. "We should get going."

Klowbi smiles and I hoist her to her feet. She follows me to the entryway and I'm grateful she hasn't pushed for more details. Mom's unknown cause of death is still a sensitive topic even several months after the fact. I think it always will be. How could anyone let go of someone so soon, so unexpectedly?

Shoes in place and appearing better than I have in months, I step outside and lock the front door, following Klowbi to our car. I glance into the windows of the Black Cat Diner, a dozen tables occupied with laughing patrons. I turn away before a grimace steals across my face and enter the car. Upon confirming we have the necessities, I start down the road, going faster than the legal speed limit due to the time crunch.

"I'm so excited to come with." Klowbi claps her hands enthusiastically.

"I can tell."

"You're excited too, right? It can't only be me?"

"I'll be more thrilled once I have several glasses of mead in my belly."

"That's the spirit!"

"You're too giddy for your own good."

"You're too morose for mine."

"Touché," I huff. "Dad will be there."

"Good, he'll be happy to see you."

"It will be nice to see him after so long. And for a happier occasion."

After the first month of Mom's passing, I had spent most of my time with Dad and Karma's Knot, my parents' coven. Their company kept the heartache at bay, never allowing a moment of sadness to trickle through. They kept us busy with laughs and creating new memories, or

19

Marc pranking the others, often to Aubrie's detriment. Desmond and I found it hilarious.

Desmond had stuck through the worst of it with me. He had been my anchor when I wanted to disappear into a sea of sorrow. Oftentimes when the laughter and voices became too much, we would sneak away and sit outside in comfortable silence. We hardly spoke, and if we did, it was only out of necessity. Mostly we would practice the Craft or watch the sky, his hand firmly in mine so as to ground me.

But once reality slunk back in, everyone had to resume their lives, leaving Dad and me to fend alone. He tried to comfort me, but I adamantly pushed for silence and solitude. Magick aided my anger more than conversation. Astral projection lulled my grief.

Klowbi fidgets with the radio and breaks my reverie. If I keep to this pace we will arrive before dark. The sun is starting to set, settling along the tops of the trees, and haloing the world in gold.

"It's been so long since we've done something together." Klowbi comments with a content sigh. Her hair appears scarlet from the gold of the sun. Her smile is genuine in her gentle features.

"I see you all the time," I huff with a bemused smirk.

"We live together. That doesn't mean we're hanging out."

A stretch of silence has me twisting my swan pendant between my fingers. I cast a glance at Klowbi, her fingers pulling at the mesh of her dress or dancing along the silvery scar tissue on her palm and forearm. Her excitement doesn't melt away her anxiety. Something is bothering her.

"Tonight will be fun," I begin, hoping to coax her into conversation.

"It will," she says dreamily. "I was worried how much longer you'd refuse to leave the apartment." Her eyes are tight as if waiting for a terse dismissal.

"I needed time." My tone is curt and bordering on defensive. I exhale and try to soften my words. "Thank you. For being patient with me."

"Always, Daire. I'm always on your side," Klowbi replies, her smile blooming gold. Her gaze flickers to the road and her expression falters as her fingers brush the scar tissue again.

"What is it?"

"Huh? Nothing. I don't know what you mean." Klowbi answers, cheeks flushing.

"You haven't stopped fidgeting since you came home. What's bothering you?" I demand, my gaze leveling onto hers before drifting to the backroads once more.

"You won't get upset?" she murmurs meekly.

"If you answer my question, I won't be."

"Fine," she sighs sharply. Her hands clench tightly in her lap before stilling. "I'm not the only one on your side. The others are too. They miss you, Daire."

I straighten, white-knuckling the wheel, before I force them to relax. "What are you proposing?"

"We should invite them to Beltane. I think it would be a good beginning. A fresh start," she answers with conviction.

My first reaction is to roll my eyes and dismiss her suggestion, but I stop myself and mull it over. She wants the rest of the group to join us, to be together like we used to before Mom died. When Klowbi wasn't at home or work, she visited the others while I isolated myself in the pursuit of magick. I hadn't seen them since after the funeral, preferring the comfort the Craft provided over the sympathetic expressions of friends who tiptoed around me like I was made of glass. It had been months since I'd spoken to them besides a few texts they sent that I hadn't bothered to respond to.

"Alright," I concede.

"Wait, really?"

"Yes, tonight is as good as any."

"Thank you, Daire!" Klowbi laughs. She pulls her phone from beneath her thigh and has it to her ear before I can reply.

My eyes stay on the road while Klowbi is distracted on the phone. I haven't seen a single car since we started along the backroad. It's desolate without even any roadkill to be seen.

A dark splash of movement ahead has my hands jerking the wheel. A cold sweat of fear brushes my brow, my tongue leaden and tasting of iron and rot. My gaze locks on the being standing alongside the road. It's entirely black with no discernible features. Unnaturally still. Not even the wind brushing the tall weeds or golden light from above alters the caliginous shape.

Shadow People.

I thought I had banned them from memory and evicted them from my mind. When I was a child they were everywhere. They followed along the streets, stalked me through school hallways, and lurked around corners. Mom taught me how to protect myself with spells and incantations that her mother had taught her when the Shadows wouldn't relent. Eventually the Shadows kept their distance and, year by year, I saw less and less of them. I had nearly forgotten about their existence with how long it's been since my last encounter.

Until today.

Glancing in the rearview mirror, I stare where the Shadow had been. There's no sign of it, only weeds tossing gently in the breeze and a dusty dirt road to mark its place.

Klowbi is chattering on the phone, oblivious to the black cloud hovering over my heart. I inhale deeply and try to calm my mounting panic. Shadows aren't abnormal. It likely felt my magick and was drawn to the source out of instinct.

I won't let one measly Shadow ruin my mother's favorite sabbat. Today is for remembering Mom. For my friends and my dad.

For me.

Chapter 2

Music drifts from the festival, the bass drum reverberating from my chest down to my toes. The aroma of heavily spiced beef and lavender hovers in the air like a thick, welcoming mist. Smoke from the bonfires sweetens the wind when blows it our way. We are barely past the entrance of the festival and already I feel like I'm home.

As is tradition, the walkways are lined with tiki torches that cast dancing shadows along the trails. My stomach twists at the strange jagged flicker the flames cast. I swallow and force the memory of the Shadow deep into my mind. The fear incited with the sighting of a Shadow is merely childhood trauma manifesting itself. It's irrational. Shadows can't hurt you physically, but they can do everything in their power to frighten you into thinking they can.

"Do you smell that?" Klowbi says from beside me and redirects my thoughts. She lifts onto her tiptoes, closing her eyes and tipping her chin skyward as if it will enhance the smell. The setting sun has her skin glowing burnished gold.

Swiveling on my heel, I shift my thoughts and gaze to the sight of the long tent set up to the right of us. The canopy is bright yellow with stripes of reds and greens. Bouquets of dandelion, jasmine, primrose, and rue cover the poles of the tent. Shimmering lights hang from the exterior, looping from the outside towards the interior, giving off a soft glow. Inside are several long rows of tables, and I know from experience they are stacked high and plentiful with libations and a veritable feast.

There's a family piling plates high with food, their half dozen kids sneaking sweets and giggling with each treat added to the pile. Despite the sexual connotations of the festival, it was a favorite among families to bring the kids along to enjoy the activities of Beltane, allowing them free roam and fun for the night.

A smile splits Klowbi's face at the sight. "It smells like heaven."

"I keep forgetting that you don't come to every festival."

Klowbi brushes a few free strands of auburn hair from her face. "I wish I could come every time. The food here is better than any state fair."

"So is the booze, but not that you would know," I tease with a smirk.

"I can drink here. It's not like anyone will care," Klowbi says with a pout. "And the best part is," she exclaims, leading the way down the path the tiki torches illuminate, "it's all free."

"More or less. There's a lot of donations and sacrifice that goes into each festival."

"Well, it's free tonight."

The flames of the massive bonfire, situated roughly in the festival's center, tower above the crowd, swirling and serpentining vibrant oranges, whites and blues. Witches dance around the flames, several are stripped nearly of all their clothes already, singing and twirling in sync with the flames.

Klowbi stops to watch and fidget with her dress, plucking at the chiffon on her waist. "It's so beautiful," she murmurs with wide eyes.

"It is, isn't it?" This wasn't just a festival, it was a spiritual celebration. A sanctuary where witches can freely be themselves without the burden or societal constraints of normal life.

"It's incredible that nothing bad happens." She walks a tentative path around the crowd circling the fire.

"Like people falling and burning alive? People taking advantage of each other because they're intoxicated?" I snort. "Not all witches have clean consciences, but we all know the consequences of wrongdoing. No one can escape the fallout for harming others. They'd never be allowed back to the festival or welcomed in the witch community."

Klowbi slows to admire a woman dancing with a dress strap slung off her shoulder, her movements smooth and hypnotic, as if she was being whispered the choreography from the fire itself. "It would be exile to harm someone else," Klowbi says and glances at me.

"Yes, but it's a good deterrent. It keeps people safe." I grab Klowbi's left hand and lead her from the fire to where the music is emanating.

"And very comfortable."

"Yes, that too. Being here is liberating, without the worry of societal expectations and the idiots that come with it."

Shrubs and flowers in dozens of different colors sprout sporadically across the grounds. The festival grounds are never burdened by human touch that can't be erased later; they are an open expanse of land that the witch community tends to with forests surrounding it. The festivities occur in the middle of nowhere, country roads and nature on all sides, remote and distant from civilization. The stars are actually visible at night, so close I could imagine plucking one straight from the heavens.

A stage is positioned opposite the festival tents, providing ample space for dancing without overpowering conversations. Not to say the band isn't loud; the bass can be felt through the ground and is a welcome sensation.

Paths lit by torches weave throughout the entire grounds. As we walk, we pass the area where games are set up. Though this has little to do with Beltane, it keeps people entertained. Several games of cornhole are ongoing with squeals of laughter and cheering erupting from the participants.

The maypole, an important symbol of Beltane, stands as the main focal point of the festival, towering above everything. Ribbons of green, blue, red, yellow, and purple are woven around it at all different heights so that anyone who wishes to twirl with the ribbons to embrace the spirit of Beltane can. Streamers of colors twined with flora ripple in the gentle breeze.

The maypole symbolizes fertility, the female and male energy combining as one. Beltane is meant to be the celebration of all life, and before it became modernized, was a very scandalous holiday due to its meaning. Sex was common in celebration, though here it isn't nearly as prevalent.

Mom loved Beltane, even more so when she conceived me during the sabbat. She loved all the colors, all the bountiful food and surplus of drinks. She loved all the music, the flowers, the closeness of being with Mother Earth. She loved being close to Dad. They'd dance all night, and if they weren't dancing they were embracing; kissing, hugging, holding hands. My parents were proof true love did exist, a pure and perfect match. Mom wanted to have more kids, but the Delacroixs have fertility issues, and she counted her blessings having conceived at all.

The memory makes my heart ache, invisible hands twitching around my heart until the pulses feel tight. This is my first Beltane without her here. And Dad's. I haven't been scanning the crowds as we're walking, too overcome with elation from feeling at home again and embracing the smells, the colors, the music, the people.

"Let's find Dad," I murmur into Klowbi's ear. She nods and we follow the trail of torches back towards the entrance of the grounds.

Klowbi stops and points to the games. "Let's check if he's here," she says and walks off without waiting for my response.

I sigh and follow her. Dad rarely lingers by the games. In the past, he normally could be found dancing my mom around by the stage, or they'd be meandering near the endless mead at the food tent. Mom always wore her brightest yellow dress and Dad would wear his honeycomb gold button-up to match her.

I focus my gaze on the faces we pass, searching for Dad's lop-sided grin. Teens with their younger siblings are playing a round of cornhole. I stop short as I spot Klowbi speaking to a group of familiar faces. Desmond catches sight of me and steps from the crowd.

"Daire," Desmond greets and opens his arms wide, a drunken grin plastered to his face. "It's good to see you made it."

The smile I return doesn't meet my eyes as I close the gap between us. "Likewise. It looks like the drinks are treating you well."

Desmond lifts his cup and takes a sip. "Looks like you could use one."

"Haven't made our way to the tent yet," I reply and glance to where Klowbi is chatting with Desmond's friends. Her scarred hand is staying close to her side and she's standing at an angle to keep it from view. She glances over her shoulder and wiggles her eyebrows at me before turning back to the others. I huff in amusement at her antics.

"I'm willing to share just because I'm that great of a guy," he teases, grabbing my attention again. Desmond holds out his Solo cup and he nods at my hands in encouragement to accept his offer.

"It seems the booze hasn't affected your modesty."

The sky has melted into a deep purple and a bottomless cobalt, enhancing the brightness of the undulating flames from the tiki torches. My eyes rove over Desmond and I can't help but admit if he wasn't so arrogant maybe there could have been something between us.

He knows the power his presence holds when he enters a room, the gravitational pull of his charisma like an unrelenting black hole. His grin captivates and his blue diamond gaze is heavy with the weight of his undivided attention. A sculpted jaw, good bone structure, and hair the color of oil that soaks in the light paired with his charm plagues whomever is sucked into his radius of hubris. His talent with magick is one to be reckoned with. As much as I hate to admit it, it's mesmerizing how easily he crafts a spell or potion, watching how pure and effectively he works his magick provides an aurora borealis for my all-seeing eyes.

"My modesty is as solid as stone," Desmond replies with a chuckle.

He reaches out to touch my hand and hesitates a hair's breadth away from my inked skin. Dropping his hand, he shifts his feet so I'm blocked from his friends' and Klowbi's line of sight. Fire pops and hisses in the torches, and it appears as fire and ice in his somber gaze.

"Daire," he whispers my name as if it was a spell of its own. "I'm glad to see you here with us."

"Thank you, Des," I say softly.

His smile is conspiratorial, a moonlit conversation filled with unspoken words. "I'm relieved to see the magick spark hasn't faded from you. The sabbats haven't been the same without you."

27

I raise my brows and step in closer to keep our conversation quiet from the crowds. "You thought I'd leave the Craft?"

Desmond shrugs, the liquid in his cup sloshing over the sides and down over his fingers. "I had faith you were biding your time until you felt strong enough to return. Some presumed you would step away from the Craft."

A snort escapes my lips. "Who the hell was saying that?"

He glances over my shoulder, skimming past the surrounding bodies until they fall on me again. He towers a few inches above me and I hate the fact I have to tilt my head to look into his eyes. His breath is warm and sweet when he leans in. "No one important. I told them once you returned that if they kept up those rumors they'd have warts for weeks."

"They'd have warts for months, and I'd make sure they'd be painful."

He grins and the drunken tilt to his lips is back. "People are intimidated by you, but there were rumors that you would follow the path of your Aunt Mayve and Sabrina."

"They should watch their tongues before they start speaking ill of me or my family," I growl with a bitterness rising in my chest.

Aunt Mayve and my cousin Sabrina are outcasts within the community. They have the same sight as any Delacroix, but they treat their gift as a curse. Aunt Mayve turned her back on her magick long ago, forcing her daughter to do the same, and the community has shunned them for their disrespect of the Craft ever since.

There are few within the community whose opinions I value, and Desmond is among them. Luca and Roman, two of Desmond's closest friends, I've known for years and they often stay clear of the rumoring witches. Karma's Knot, my parents' coven, are the only other opinions I care to take to heart, which happens to include Des's mother Aubrie.

Aubrie and Mom grew up together thick as thieves. Their coven was a part of my life since before I was born. Desmond and I became very familiar with each other at a young age. We trained together, we learned what each colored candle meant, which herbs were used for fortune spells, how to create protection jars, and how to use runes and sigils in our magick.

As we got older, we began to compete to discover who was the better witch. We were evenly matched over the years, but our friendly childhood competition morphed to something less innocent. Des wasn't trying to trump me with knowledge, instead he was trying to craft complex spells so I could witness the magick happen in front of me. He was trying to impress me with his prowess, not best me.

When Desmond's child-like gaze and innocent competition morphed into his diamond stare and grand gestures, his motives were blatantly romantic then on.

"I don't mean to incur the wrath of a Delacroix," Desmond drawls and lifts his hand as if to surrender.

"You're safe tonight, Rivera," I tell him. He smiles again and my lips curl to copy his.

"The night is still young, Delacroix. There might be mischief yet." He winks before his expression sobers and his gaze softens. "How are you faring?"

A cool breeze pops goosebumps along my arms, reminding me of the empty space where my mother should be.

"It's different," I admit.

Desmond lifts his cup again, and this time he grabs my arm. His touch is careful, his fingers cool against the inside of my wrist, and he places the cup in my hand. "You need this tonight more than I do."

A breathy laugh escapes and I raise the cup to my mouth to concede. "Blessed be."

He chuckles and I feel the warmth from his breath on my cheek. Taking a long drink, I savor the sweetness of the honey and the afterbite that follows. Des watches me with kind eyes, a smirk gracing his lips.

Behind Desmond, Roman is smiling and letting loose a booming laugh. Klowbi's soft giggle floats on the air afterwards, and my heart warms knowing she's being treated with the respect she deserves.

I lift the Solo cup to my lips and find only droplets greet my tongue. I hand his cup back, though he doesn't seem to notice I finished off his drink.

My attention returns to Desmond and his brows are furrowed with a deep crease sitting between his eyes, a familiar look from growing up together. He's twisting the empty cup in his hand and I snap my fingers in his face so his stare sharpens on me.

"What are you thinking about that has that look on your face?" I shift and rub my arms from the cool night air.

"What look?" he asks, but he keeps twisting his cup and the furrow hasn't completely gone.

I huff and turn to leave. "Fine, I have other people to see tonight."

His hand grabs my wrist before I can step away and I can't help the smirk that brushes my lips. "So there is something," I murmur, raising my brows expectantly.

"I've been practicing some unconventional magick." Desmond leans in, his voice quiet amongst the bursts of laughter and drone of music around us. "I know that you aren't a stranger to it either."

"What type?" I press, taking a step closer. His hand brushes mine and I'm sure from an outside perspective we look like a lovestruck couple.

Desmond grins. "Some would consider it dark, some would say gray." He leans down so his lips are brushing my hair. "I've been dabbling in red." His breath is searing against my skin, his words a hot brand in my eardrum.

Blood magick.

I step back so his lips aren't so close to mine. Desmond's eyes are bright and the blazing heat from his touch lingers on my wrist. I narrow my eyes at him. "How long?"

"A little over a month. I'm good at it, too," he replies and tips his cup to his lips. He frowns, glancing into the cup before shooting me a glare when he finds it empty. I shrug and he sighs, holding it at his side.

"Why—"

"Daire!" Klowbi calls and walks the few feet where Desmond and I are talking. Her expression is too amused and I shoot her a warning glare. "Let's head to the tent to meet up with the others."

"Sure," I say and point an accusing finger at Desmond. "We'll finish this later."

Desmond laughs and shakes his head. "Of course we will. I'll find you, Black Swan." His eyes flicker to my swan tattoo on my forearm before meeting mine. "Save me a dance."

I turn and snag Klowbi's good hand and we start down the lit path back towards the entrance. Klowbi glances over her shoulder towards the group as Desmond, Luca, and Roman wave at our departure. I roll my eyes when she bumps my shoulder and giggles.

"What?"

"You and Desmond were getting along really well." She squeezes my hand as if that would make me talk.

"I haven't seen him in a while."

"Don't lie, even when you haven't seen him in a while you're usually only seconds away from slapping him." I feel her staring at me and I cave, turning to meet her rosy-cheeked smile. "Did I see you two share his drink?"

"I think you're seeing things."

"Then I definitely imagined him touching you."

"Yes, you did. You should lay off the hallucinogens."

"He's not that bad."

"He's horribly arrogant."

"He's madly in love with you."

"He's madly an idiot, then."

"I don't understand why you never gave him a chance. You two would be an adorable couple."

I shake my head, Desmond's words still echoing. Klowbi practiced minor facets of magick that I've taught her over the years. When I had tried teaching her darker magick, it had led to an argument that ended in me apologizing and promising not to practice that type of magick around her. I've learned not to mention anything about it since.

If she knew Desmond had taken up the darker aspects of the Craft, I'm sure she wouldn't be nearly as thrilled that I was allowing him to grace me with his companionship tonight.

"He's like a brother to me. Also I've never enjoyed the idea of being a lovesick puppy." My hand tightens around hers as we weave through a group of witches. The bonfire's glowing orange and white flames are above the crowd, shadows of smoke curling into a star-speckled sky.

"Clearly it wasn't that bad; he called you 'Black Swan' and you agreed to save him a dance." Her hand slips from mine as the crowd thins, our strides marching to the distant bass of the band. "And you didn't even threaten to curse him."

Had it been any other time, I would have, I think bitterly, yet the intrigue of his admission makes me wonder what pushed him towards blood magick. He knows of my practices, but he never openly expressed interest in it. What changed his mind?

"You know it's my nickname; it strikes fear into the hearts of mortals." I say with a dramatic flick of my fingers.

Klowbi rolls her eyes. "May we be spared the Black Swan's wrath," she teases. "You didn't deny him a dance though. You know he's going to come find you later."

"I'm not worried," I dismiss and follow the path of torches.

Klowbi falls quiet as we walk, her head perking each time the band starts up or a shrill laugh breaks the concrete drone of the crowd. She seems lost in thought, her gaze darting from one moving target to another. I'm thankful for the break in conversation. I can't shake the image of Desmond practicing blood magick. There are countless depths to that type of Craft. How deep has he gone with it? With his talent, he could quickly master the basics. I hadn't considered checking his hands for cuts or scars. I didn't notice a ridge on his palm when he touched me, but I was more concerned with the idea of being touched than focusing on what his flesh felt like against mine.

Most witches, especially in our community, are not tolerant of the practice of baneful magick, nor the generalization of black magick. Those raised with a traditional Wiccan outlook believed in the Rule of Three which was meant to deter those practicing the Craft from utilizing darker elements of magick for selfish needs.

Three familiar faces pull me from my thoughts. Dad is standing with his back to us, but I can recognize his honeycomb button-up at a glance.

His hair looks to be a ruffled blond mess atop his head, and from his heavy-footed posture, he's surpassed the buzzed stage.

The other two men are turned towards us, hovering near the food tent with faces well lit. Marc, Dad's best friend from childhood, has a cup in hand and his hair is even more of a disaster than my dad's. Not surprising, considering Marc is always a spontaneous wild card and one of the remaining eight in their coven.

Thayne towers above them both. He wears a checkered red button-up which compliments his umber complexion. He reminds me of a gentle giant, his smile soft and considerate, whereas Marc's grin is toothy and chaotic. Thayne is also part of the coven, and a close friend of my mom's. Thayne collects books of all types, most commonly anything involving witchcraft or the Otherworld. His library is enviable, hosting enough information to be entertained with knowledge for decades.

Thayne spots us first and his smile broadens. Marc and Dad follow seconds later, both of their drinks sloshing with their unsteady balance. Dad has a pink glow to his cheeks, his face devoid of tension or the unrelenting sadness that never quite disappeared. I feel the knot in my belly loosen as relief overwhelms me seeing him so lighthearted.

"My girls," Dad shouts as he shoves his cup to Thayne and greets us with tight hugs and warm kisses to the tops of our heads.

"Hi Dad," I say once he releases his hold on us. His eyes are bright with shoulders loose and head held high, the night breeze ruffling his hair and carrying the scent of smoke. I turn to Thayne and Marc, both smiling and looking just as giddy to see us.

"Come here." Marc beams and wraps me in a tight hug. I feel some of his drink splash my arm before I manage to slip from his grasp. "It's nice to see you two here."

"It's nice to be back among familiar faces," I reply and give Thayne a hug as well. His smile is sweet as he turns to wrap Klowbi into an embrace.

"I'm glad you two came," Thayne states, his smooth baritone sweet as honey.

Dad is holding his drink heavily tilted in his hands, a thin trickle passing over the lip. "When did you two get here?"

"A little while ago, we've been making our rounds," I reply and glance at Klowbi. Her braid is coming loose and the flowers I delicately placed are starting to unravel.

"We ran into Desmond," Klowbi adds in, "and he was very welcoming."

Dad huffs a laugh. "I imagine that he was." He looks at me and raises a brow, giving me a knowing look. It's not exactly a secret how Desmond feels, or the lack of romantic feeling I reciprocate in return.

"You two look parched." Marc observes, and jabs a thumb in the direction of the tent behind them. "You should be six cups deep by now!"

"We haven't had a chance to grab drinks yet."

"I'm hungry," Klowbi adds, standing on her tiptoes, trying to catch sight of the feast.

"And I could use a drink." I step forward again and give Dad a kiss on the cheek. "We'll see you later, we have some friends to find."

He nods and presses another kiss on my forehead. "Friends? Is it who I think it is?"

"Yes, it's been too long since I've seen them."

Dad rubs my back, lessening the pang in my heart enough for me to get my bearings and push down the unforgiving ache. "Have fun, my little swan."

I lift a hand in goodbye before grabbing Klowbi's good hand and leading her towards the tent. "I'll see you all later."

I catch a glimpse of the three of them waving as we walk away.

"Don't do anything I wouldn't do," Marc calls from behind.

"Horrible advice," Thayne comments wryly.

"Only because I'm much more fun than you."

Klowbi and I enter the tent. The delicious scents of rosemary roasted chicken, herb roasted potatoes, and strawberry honey cake makes my stomach growl. The food has been picked over as the night has progressed, but there are piles of beef kabobs skewered with peppers and soaked in garlic butter. Plates are piled high with honey fritters and bannocks; the story goes that eating a bannock on the day of Beltane will grant the person abundance and prosperity. Dishes of strawberry rhubarb jam are sitting

34

next to the breads and sweets. The table of desserts is lined with cherry pies and rhubarb crisp, along with trays of fruits served with sides of honey, slices of gouda, brie, and goat cheese.

People are milling about the tent, grabbing generous helpings of the food that remains. Klowbi grabs a plate and starts to layer it with potatoes, beef, and honey fritters. I go to the table stacked full of drinks and grab a cup of mead and a cup of May wine. Klowbi is milling around by the edge of the tent and dancing from one foot to the other while carefully balancing her plate piled high with foods of Beltane.

"I see an empty picnic table. Hurry up!" she shouts before vanishing back into the night.

I take a long drink from the cup filled with May wine, the herbal flavor complimentary to the bitterness of the wine. It makes my stomach warm as it settles. My steps falter as I step back into the darkness, my eyes adjusting to the light of the torch flames. I follow Klowbi's steps and see her plate hurriedly dropped to the wood before she takes off running. Klowbi is waving her hands in grand gestures while leading a group of three back to the table, cheeks bright and her tone filled with excitement.

"Look who's here!" Klowbi enthuses, gesturing to the three people around her.

Alko towers above our group. He makes his younger sister, Xuan, look miniature by comparison. He wears jeans and a steel blue zip-up sweater with black cuffs. His slanted eyes appear like black holes except for the reflection of the flames in them, and his hair is as dark as the night sky above. His long fingers are pulling and twisting at his hair, his head swiveling as he passes the massive crowds. As he approaches, his face relaxes and the hand he was using to fuss with his hair raises to wave at me.

There are rings on his fingers, each cast with glamour magick. It looks like he's wearing several items coated in magick. The silver necklace he wears exudes a mist the color of orange neon against the night sky. The rings on his left hand spur undulations of yellow and green vibrating in the air, trailing his fingertips as he waves. His right hand pulses blue, brightening and dimming in time with his breath. The area around him has an undertone of orange.

Xuan wears an oversized burgundy sweater with black jeans. Her hair is in a ponytail, the gentle swoop of her bangs covering her almond eyes. She is the smallest of our group, but she has a vicious mouth. Xuan and Klowbi are walking together, leaving a sour taste in my mouth.

Xuan practices magick like us, but her main focus is magick of the Otherworld. It's the one type of magick I try to avoid and prickles my skin in an air of wrongness.

Another sip of May wine dislodges the heavy rock in my belly. Alko nods at me before his eyes drift to the tent beyond. Xuan plops down onto the bench connected to the table and starts nibbling on a honey fritter, licking the greasy sugar from her fingers. I look past them both and warmth surges within my chest as I lock gazes with Niko. His eyes are just as striking as I remember. They are a deep forest green in the dark. A color that magick should be, the kind that roots you to the earth and holds your mind present.

"This is delicious," Xuan notes and snags another from Klowbi's plate.

"There's a lot of people here," Alko grouses softly and takes a step closer to his younger sister.

"This is going to be a perfect night." Klowbi takes a seat next to Xuan. She grabs a kebab and tears a chunk of beef from the skewer. "Help yourselves; there's food and drink."

"Such a kind hostess," I mutter with a chuckle. Klowbi beams at me and focuses her attention back on Xuan and the mound of food.

Niko stands in front of me. His hair is tamed and curls upwards away from his eyes, but it's already wanting to break free from the gel he used to burst into a wild mess. He's wearing a gray short sleeve with a skater logo plastered across it and he has on his nicest pair of jeans that has a tear at the bottom hem. The hole in the knee reveals his skin covered in scabs.

He smiles and his eyes are a forest caught on fire. I take another sip of my drink and realize it's empty. I frown. "My glass is empty."

"Good to know you have your priorities straight," Niko says and the sound of his voice makes my throat tighten.

I struggle in a breath. "Care to join me to find a replacement?"

"I thought you'd never ask." Niko turns around and starts walking backwards. "We're getting refreshments."

"Don't get distracted," Klowbi shouts around a mouthful of beef.

Alko shifts in his seat and I see the shadow of a smile on his face. "Bring enough back for everyone."

Niko waves his hand at them and turns to walk in step with me. "On it."

Seeing Niko after so long, I forgot how sharp his cheekbones are, the hollows even darker with the snaking shadows of the torchlight. I catch a whiff of familiar herb and I shoot him a glare, attempting to catch sight of his hypnotic eyes. "Are you high, Niko?"

"Well, it's nice to see you too after so long. I'm glad to see you are alive and doing well. Oh, me? I'm doing just splendidly, thanks for your concern." he quips with a toothy grin. I continue glaring. "Sheesh, Daire, I'm not high right now."

I nod and squint as we walk into the lights of the tent. I glance to where my dad had been standing and am relieved to find the space empty. I grab two cups of mead and a glass of May wine for myself, careful not to spill. Niko walks up beside me, and in the light his hair appears a sandy brown, his skin pale.

"There's food if you're hungry," I say watching him collect three drinks as well.

He shrugs and faces me. "I'm more thirsty than hungry." Niko's eyes rove over me and the corners of his lips twitch. "You look good."

I huff. "Thanks." He looks a little rough around the edges. His eyes are red and, even though he said he isn't high, I'm sure he was smoking earlier today. But it's better than the alternative. "How have you been?"

"Can't really complain. Doing the same shit I always do, getting high and eating way too much food." He flashes me his signature grin and I realize how much I missed it. "You look good," he repeats.

I smirk. "You said that already."

He lifts the hand with one drink in it and lets it hover at his mouth. "There's a lot I want to say that I'm not sure I should." He takes a sip and grimaces. "You like this stuff? Is it even alcohol?"

I laugh and start heading back to the table where the other three sit. As I pass the bouquet wrapped around the tent poles, I take in a deep breath, enjoying the strange combination. "It's supposed to be sweet. There might be beer you can have instead."

"I'll drink it, I just won't enjoy it," Niko mutters and takes a begrudging sip. He smacks his lips together, his attention on me. His eyes say more than his lips, and my stomach tightens at the embers of hope burning in his gaze.

The others greet us with a chorus of whoops and cheers as we hand out the drinks. My new drink is already half gone and I cherish the warmth in my center, the soft hum in my head. I smile and the tension coiled in my belly loosens.

Alko has finally sat down and is munching on roasted potatoes. Xuan and Klowbi are sitting elbow to elbow stealing bites of food around their conversation. Niko sits beside Alko and they scoot over to make room for me. I glance at the empty seat next to Klowbi and sit beside her so she's between Xuan and I. I pretend not to see Niko's eyes lower and his subtle frown.

"Isn't this place beautiful?" Klowbi asks and takes a deep swallow from her cup of mead.

Alko sniffs his cup and takes a tentative sip. "This is good," he comments.

Niko raises his eyebrows and eyes his own glass skeptically. "Are you sure we're drinking the same thing?"

"This place feels very powerful." Xuan scans the crowds, her eyes hovering on a few people. "That man, the one with black hair standing further from the crowds," Xuan says and I follow her gaze. "His aura is very bright, very fierce. A furious red."

"That's Maddock," I tell the others. "He's part of the coven. His sister is as well. My parents have known them for a very long time."

"I recognize him. He's a bit stubborn," Klowbi comments and takes another drink.

"He's an ass, but he's alright if he likes you," I say.

Niko grins. "I know someone else like that."

I shoot him a glare. "Too bad that someone doesn't like you."

"One of these days I'll get you to admit it," Niko croons.

I roll my eyes and take several large gulps of my wine.

"I really missed this," Klowbi adds.

"The bickering?" Alko asks.

"The constant glares?" Xuan offers.

"The desperate attempts?" Alko teases.

"Ouch," Niko mutters.

Klowbi giggles and twirls a fraying piece of auburn hair around her finger. "Everything feels normal again." Her cheeks flush and her eyes are bright with both hands clasped around her cup.

Xuan is studying our group and I catch her attention. Her lips quirk and her eyes are black in the dim lighting. "As normal as witches can be."

"Is that cup taken?" Klowbi asks, gesturing to the unclaimed cup sitting in the center of our table.

"Go for it." Niko pushes it towards her.

"Yes, please." Klowbi simpers and snags the glass.

I raise my brows. "Is that your second?"

"Isn't that your second?" Klowbi counters. "I'm enjoying myself."

"Clearly."

Klowbi downs her drink before jumping to her feet and climbing over her seat as she watches the growing crowds and listens to the deep croon of guitar in the distance. "I want to dance," she says, bouncing up and down.

"Now?" I ask, glancing at my empty glass.

"Yes, everyone up!" Klowbi claps her hands, barely able to contain her excitement.

We all stand and let Klowbi lead the way through the crowds. The band is playing across the festival grounds, the beat heavy and making my bones vibrate. My teeth chatter with each step closer, and the heat from the crowd beads sweat on my forehead. Xuan is following a step ahead of me with the boys trailing behind us.

The majority of the festival goers are by the stage area, dancing, swaying, singing. The shadows between the gaps of bodies look darker and my breath hitches. My pace slows and I hesitate as the memory of the

Shadow returns. They don't like hiding amongst us, not so close to the living, yet the fear doesn't abate. It's of no comfort imagining that they aren't in the crowds, but rather standing silent and patiently waiting in the darkness of the trees, at the edge of the forest, where they can see us but we can't see them.

A hand brushes my arm and I jolt, reeling back from the touch and taking several steps back to distance myself. Niko is standing beside me with his hand raised. He furrows his brows. "Are you alright?"

"Yes," I hiss, glancing to where Klowbi's rose hue dress disappears in the crowd. "I'm fine," I add and take off after her fleeting form.

Klowbi and Xuan are standing towards the back of the crowd along the edge. Klowbi's twirling in her dress with flowers falling from her messy braid. Xuan picks up a yellow flower that's fallen to the ground and nestles it behind her own ear as she twists Klowbi to the music. Klowbi's face lights up seeing the three of us emerge from the crowd. She grabs my hands and we start to step, swing, and spin to the rapid tune. A laugh escapes me as the fear drains from my limbs, and in the corner of my eye, the others attempt to dance too.

Klowbi leans in and bops her head in Niko's direction. "You know, this sabbat is a scandalous one."

I roll my eyes. "I'm well aware."

She grins and swoops a flower from the ground, this one a gentle blue, and tucks it in my hair. "I bet Niko would really appreciate the history lesson."

In response, I playfully shove her; she bursts into laughter before twisting away to dance with the rest of the group. I sway to the melodic beat of the drums and the thrum of the guitar and let the vibration guide my movements. I close my eyes and bright pops of light and color burst behind my lids, tinted red from my blood. When I open them, my gaze finds Klowbi grinning at me, her eyes trailing into the crowd and back. I follow her gaze and find Desmond shuffling his way through, diamond eyes locked on me.

"You did promise," she teases.

"Don't remind me," I mutter. Niko is watching and his gaze flits over my shoulder. His face hardens at Desmond's approach, his mouth a firm line of disapproval. My heart aches at the sight, but Desmond snags my hand and twists into my view before I can placate Niko.

"I hope you haven't forgotten our dance," he croons and his thumb brushes the skin of my hand.

My gaze narrows. "Under the condition we resume our previous conversation."

Desmond nods, a knowing glint in his eyes. "Of course."

He leads me away from my group. I refuse to look over my shoulder at them, knowing I'll see the bitter flare in Niko's eyes. We pass a few of Desmond's friends we saw earlier, Roman and Luca among them, with haughty grins on their faces. I hardly repress the urge to scowl.

He stops once we are a safe distance from anyone who might overhear. He turns to face me while my fingers roam to his wrist and twist his palm open. My heart lurches at the sight of a fresh cut that goes across his thumb, thin and neat from a sharpened blade. I clutch his hand to hide the wound as we sway to the music.

"Do you use your own?" I begin with an accusatory tilt of my head. His hands fall to my waist, and I rest my arms on his shoulders, the sweet smell of mead on his breath.

He shrugs. "So what? You use your own as well."

"I've practiced for years," I counter, flicking the back of his head. He winces and glowers at me. "You haven't been practicing for more than a month. Idiotic."

"I've been careful."

"If you were careful, you'd still be using these spells sparingly," I hiss. His hands are firm against my waist and I silently swear to crush his foot if he gets any lower.

"I haven't done a spell against anyone. No karmic chaos, as you put it," he teases. "I can already tell the difference in the magick. The spells are much more powerful. I can almost feel it."

That's what I'm afraid of. I bite my lip before asking, "Who else knows?"

"Just you."

"How'd you learn?"

"I have a couple books."

"No one else showed you?"

"Nope."

"Don't lie to me, Desmond."

"I swear on my blood I am telling the truth." His eyes are sharp, glinting like silver ice in the dark. I search his face for his tell, a flicker of his lids or a tilt of a brow, but his face is relaxed. He's telling the truth.

Or he's a better liar than I remember.

"If I find out you're lying, I'll punch you."

His smile flashes bright. "You never disappoint."

"Why did you decide to practice? You never showed an interest before. You even tried to talk me out of it!"

His smile fades and he looks away. There's heavy contemplation in the tense lines of his face, the way his jaw is clenched, the tightness around his eyes. He inhales and returns his eyes to mine. "I had a dream."

"A dream?" I ask skeptically.

"Or a vision, I'm not really sure," he admits with a shrug.

"What'd you see?" Our steps are in sync with the music and his fingers drum along my lower back, incessant.

"I was doing a spell. I could see myself muttering an incantation, there were thirteen white candles surrounding me in a circle and I was writing a sigil with blood and ink on parchment. Then I burned the sigil." He closes his eyes and his lids flutter before opening them again. His pupils are dilated and I see the solid beat of his heart in his throat. "I tried ignoring the dream, but it returned every night. No matter what I did, I was subjected to it for weeks. Finally, I decided to recreate it. Daire..." His voice is so raspy, it grates my bones. "I've never felt so powerful."

"What sigil?" I ask softly. "Blood magick can last a very long time. It's extremely hard to break the spell once completed. If you aren't careful, you could damn yourself with the consequences."

"I've done my homework." His voice is heavy. "The sigil meant 'appearance'."

"Appearance of what?"

"My power, my true magick," he says simply. "It worked. I've never been so successful with the Craft. It works perfectly to my whim." His grin is suffocating.

The music stops and I release him and take a step back. The band announces they are taking a break and people start to disperse. Desmond watches me and I'm not sure what he's expecting. Praise? Blood magick isn't evil, it's just powerful and damn near permanent.

What Desmond described is different, unnatural. A random spell comes to mind in a dream, one of blood magick which he had no interest in until the dream came to fruition. A spell with a stray intention is dangerous and stupid. Any magick requires decisiveness and a firm goal in mind, especially blood magick.

"I have to get back to my friends," I finally say. His smile cracks, shatters, and those damn diamond eyes chill my blood. "Be careful, Des." I nod to his thumb. "A pinprick of blood will suffice." I turn and stride through the crowd, determined to get away from the ache in my bones, from Desmond and his glass shard eyes.

"Daire," he calls, but his voice is lost amid the crescendo of the crowd.

It takes some searching, but I spot my group sitting along the edge of the grounds. The bonfire is still raging and casting gold light amongst the crowds. As I walk by, I sense the subtle heat of the flames fighting the chilling air. Alko smiles at my approach and Klowbi waves me on frantically. Xuan is laying down watching the stars and lifts her arm in acknowledgement. Niko glares my way and turns his back before facing the forest instead.

"You found us." Klowbi pats the grass next to her.

"You doubted that I would?" I ask and sit down beside her. We form a half circle, Xuan and Niko on the edges and Klowbi, Alko, and I in the middle.

I reach for my spell bags at my hip and slip the hematite from the pouch and grasp it tightly. Closing my eyes, I focus on the energy through my palm, absorbing its essence for protection and reflection of negative energy. The ache in my bones begins to subside and I sigh with relief. The stone warms as I clutch it between my fingers.

"The band was good," Klowbi offers into the silence.

"It was," Alko agrees.

I don't say anything on the subject. My dance with Desmond was the last thing I wanted to address. Or his confession of practicing blood magick.

"What is everyone doing?" Alko queries, looking over his shoulder at the witches sitting down in small groups. Some have pulled out bags, presumably with spell ingredients, others have closed their eyes and are sitting still, while some speak softly and stare intently at the fire or stars.

Klowbi shifts so she's staring at the sky. "Magick."

"Some take the time to craft spells, others enjoy the serenity of being surrounded by so much energy in such a pure state," I explain and stare at the stars. They glitter and shift and it reminds me of how small I am. It makes me smile.

I survey the crowds, lingering on a group sitting close to the forest's edge. My breath hitches as my lungs forget how to breathe and the tightness in my chest barrels into me. There's tingling in my hands and the icy fingers of warning trail down my spine.

A Shadow darker than night has its sights fastened on me. The temperature drops several degrees as a shiver rattles my spine.

"Daire?" Klowbi whispers and follows my gaze.

"Daire." Xuan is sitting up, her voice dragging me back to reality. "What do you see?"

I blink and point in the direction of the Shadow. "There."

But it's gone.

"There's nothing there," Xuan says slowly and exchanges a look with Alko who has gone pale.

"It was there," I mutter, staring at the empty space. Xuan sees Shadows too. With her gifted connection to the Otherworld, she's familiar with the realm more than most. How did she not see it?

"What was there?" Xuan asks.

"I don't like this," Alko whispers. He's pulling at his hair and a few strands float to the grass.

I stare at Xuan and shake my head. "I thought I saw—"

"Holy Hell," Klowbi squeaks, wide eyed.

The Shadow stands only mere feet away from our group. Its black eyes shine with a vicious hunger similar to that of a predator stalking prey.

"Is that a...?" Klowbi whispers and her hand finds mine, squeezing it desperately. "How can I see it?"

Alko shifts so his back is to our group. "I don't like this. We should leave."

"That's fucking terrifying." Niko's voice is loud in the eerie pause of the night.

Two more Shadows stand amongst the tree line with their attention directed at us. I blink and two more pop up along the forest, then four, five, seven. The soft, peaceful murmur amongst the grounds turns into a thick and heavy silence. The Shadows are frozen between groups of witches, an oily black stain against a canvas of unity.

Within seconds, dozens of Shadows loom in the festival grounds. The beautiful aurora of colors from the magick has trickled to darkness, and the only light is the bonfire and the dying torchlight, yet it doesn't reach the Shadows. A dark void unafraid of the light.

I've never witnessed so many Shadows at once, even at a Wiccan festival, even as a witch.

The Shadows lurch forward, charging at whomever is closest to them with a growl reverberating in the still night air. A cluster of Shadows rush towards a group of witches, and they shriek and scatter with a desperation in their movements. As if breaking the trance, screams fill the air along with the heady scent of fear. Shadows take chase as witches scramble towards the safety of the light. Tiki torches are knocked over from scrambling limbs, and as the Shadows pass, the fire snuffs out without an ember left to flicker.

The fear tastes like blood in my mouth.

My eyes dart to the Shadow still watching us at the edge of the forest. It takes a slow step forward as if basking in our fear. I push myself to my feet and grip the searing hot hematite stone in my fist, channeling my magick, and swallowing the fear burning in the back of my throat. My instincts are screaming at me to run, but I hold fast even as my hand trembles. My friends stand to their feet as we press our backs together.

"Negativity that invades this sacred place; I banish you away and back to rest; Beings spent for evil and bane; I cast you now whence you came; Far away I send you this hour; The attempt to harm go no further."

The Shadow halts and a shimmering purple wall erupts between my group and the stalking Shadows. They snarl and pace the length of the barrier, but make no attempt to breach it as they hiss their frustration into the sky.

Around us are the beginning of protection chants being spoken as magick barriers sprout from the ground. Groups of witches stand with talismans in their fists as they aid their fallen, purple bolts spearing in the direction of approaching Shadows. The chanting drowns out the chittering and hissing of the enraged Shadows until dozens of voices form into one.

The Shadows flicker and begin to dissipate into echoes of themselves before melting into the night. A few stubborn Shadows snarl and slash at the barriers until a stray bolt of magick strikes at the head of one, sending it scampering backwards and darting into the forest.

This wasn't supposed to happen. Not my first festival after Mom's death. Shadows never act aggressive like this, and I've never seen them gather in great numbers with a goal to ambush.

Where's Dad?

The thought jars me and I risk a glance around the festival. Purple barricades are flickering out now that the threat has vanished. It's too dark to see the faces of anyone around me besides my group. Everyone appears pale, except Xuan who has a blank expression. Alko looks as if he's ready to faint.

"Let's go home," Klowbi whimpers. Her eyes are shining and her lips tremble.

"What just happened?" Niko asks incredulously.

Xuan's tone is surefire. "Something inherently baleful. It's best we leave."

Alko stands there, shaking his head and pulling his hair. He doesn't speak.

"Daire, come on, I want to leave," Klowbi whines as her eyes dart to the forest back to me.

"What about Dad?" My body feels leaden, my energy sapped.

"He is fine, I'm sure," Xuan answers. "We need to go."

Klowbi grips my hand, pulling me gently away from the terror the Shadows have planted around us. "Fine, let's go." I open my palm to the cooling hematite and drop it into the pouch at my waist as I return my attention to my group.

"I have no idea what just happened," Niko remarks, following Xuan and Alko through the crowd.

"Me either," I mutter and allow Klowbi to lead me from our fading barricade. Purple flecks are flaking to the ground, absorbing back into the earth. A lone Shadow towers at the forest's edge and its eyes flash bone white as a thorny smile transforms its face before it disappears too.

I grit my teeth and call on my magick, a hard glint in my eyes as I take in the destruction the Shadows created.

I vow upon my mother, Fay Delacroix's grave, the truth I will forever seek. Ancient magick I wield in stride to avenge the witches reaped. By Earth, Wind, Fire, Water, and Soul I will pay the toll of the entombed. So mote it be.

A surge of power rushes through me, making my blood sing. My head buzzes with the delicious taste of magick coating my tongue. When I exhale, sharp tendrils of red barbed with orange dance on the wind before absorbing back into the Universe.

Once I believed there was balance in the world.

I was wrong.

My new truth is this: I will be the world's reckoning.

Chapter 3

The bedroom door is closed and the window is open, allowing in the late afternoon sunshine. I'm sitting cross-legged on my bed with my Book of Shadows on my lap with pen in hand. Several other books are scattered on my bed: two different Wiccan spellbooks, a book on blood magick, another on black magick which involves hexes and curses, and one on dark and unusual Wiccan history and phenomena.

I've been scouring and attempting to cross reference the books for several days since we returned from the Beltane festival. Anything relevant or deemed even semi-important I've noted down in a dedicated section of my Book of Shadows which filled up barely half a page. The strange encounter with the Shadows at the Beltane festival appears to be a one-off situation because no matter how many books I've read, nothing even remotely compares to what occurred. Even searching the internet for stories led to fake websites filled with experiences from "real people" that couldn't be backed up with proof. All my leads turned into dead-ends.

Which still didn't answer my question as to what happened at Beltane. Was this another breed of Shadows, a more intelligent metaphysical being? Or were the Shadows being influenced by something else?

They're evolving no matter the root of why. I haven't seen a sign of a Shadow since that night, but the dark corners of my room made my fingers go cold, and when night came the darkness was suffocating. When the wind whistled through the trees, I can't discern if it's the branches scraping together or the strange, inhuman hiss the Shadows made that night.

I sit back and rub my eyes. I haven't found anything worth noting over the last several days of research. Sleep comes in bursts and I haven't been able to sleep a full night since the festival. I'm uncertain if my magick is warning me not to rest in such a vulnerable state, or if my body is too taut with stress to give me a reprieve of dreamless sleep.

The blood magick book is sitting open. When I get frustrated researching the Shadows, I try researching the blood magick that Desmond had described to me. I couldn't find the exact spell he had recounted, but there were similar ones. It worries me that I can't find the identical spell. It's possible he utilized chaos magick to get the results and used blood to strengthen and make the spell permanent. But Desmond's sudden interest in blood magick feels wrong. He followed the Wiccan tradition and didn't dabble in dark magick. He would walk the line between traditional magick and unconventional, but he never crossed it.

I crossed that line long ago. Blood and dark magick call to me like the others don't, save for chaos magick. There is something freeing in the wild abandon these spells offer, the constraints traditional magick keeps one tied too irrelevant when calling on such a powerful force. There are few limitations and no doctrines to follow when choosing to walk this path of the Craft, unlike most witches who choose to walk the path of light, I find myself most comfortable in the dark.

Desmond has confided to me that the path I walk has never called to him. He's dabbled in chaos magick and I've assisted him with incantations focusing on this type, but never once has he shown interest in the other two. Nor have I ever heard of a spell manifesting from a dream as Desmond experienced.

The symbol that was presented to him he claims meant appearance. I did a few quick searches of sigils and runes to see if anything matched.

Nothing stood out as a possibility, and Desmond's expertise should have let him identify the symbol immediately.

Sigils are trickier, some are common and used often, but most witches that use sigils in their magick create their own personalized ones. There are several ways a sigil can be crafted, and there isn't a way I know of to trace it back to its original creator or meaning.

Even with Desmond's personal intentions implied and manifested onto the sigil with his blood, the final outcome wasn't guaranteed. He didn't create the sigil himself, something else did unconsciously. Whatever the originally intended meaning of the sigil is wouldn't be completely influenced by Desmond alone. Which meant the true outcome is unknown.

"Idiot," I growl and slam the blood magick book shut.

My phone rings and shatters the silence. Dad had called briefly after we fled the Beltane festival to assure we were safe. He'd promised to call again once the damages had been assessed, but after several days of no word I'd begun to worry.

"Hi Dad."

"My sweet girl," Dad answers. My smile is instant hearing his voice, the sweet comfort it brings. "I'm happy to hear your voice. I was so worried."

"I was worried about you too," I tell him and push the books into a pile on my bed. I lay down, closing my eyes so I can focus my mind on him.

"Are you alright? You and your friends weren't hurt, were they?" Dad asks, and his voice sounds heavy, rough.

I open my eyes and stare at the ceiling, anxiety coiling in my belly. "We're fine. It's been uneventful since the festival."

I hear him sigh over the phone. "Good. At least you're alright."

My heart quickens, and suddenly the heaviness of his voice is crushing. "What happened?"

His breathing sounds loud over the phone. "A few were hurt when the Shadows appeared. I'm sorry I didn't call you sooner. I stayed to help with clean-up and care for those that were injured. Everything was a mess—"

"Dad, who got hurt?"

"Daire," he begins and I hear a soft, feminine voice in the background. "Desmond is in a coma."

"What?" I say and sit up straight. A book slides from the bed and hits the floor. "How?"

"We don't know what caused it. It's only speculation at this point."

"Is it because of the Shadows?" I ask before I can bite my tongue.

The silence on the other end of the phone is an answer enough for me. "Desmond will be hospitalized for a while. Tests are being run to check for internal damage." His voice is quiet, and again I hear the feminine voice.

"How's Aubrie handling it?"

"Not well, as you can imagine. I'm staying with her for a few days to help out. I'll be in touch with you when I can."

"Alright, Dad, don't overwork yourself."

"I'll be alright. Talk soon, little swan."

The call ends with a click when he hangs up.

Desmond is in a coma. Doctors would conduct numerous tests, perhaps repeating those that were done on my mother during her illness, but I sensed they'd find nothing. Whatever ailed Desmond wasn't something a medical degree could diagnose.

Despite Dad's silence, I have a hunch the Shadows are somehow involved with Desmond's coma. He had been fine the night I saw him. The new aggressive behavior of the Shadows has to link to Desmond unless the blood magick he performed affected him in a way he hadn't been expecting. The magick could've lured the Shadows to Desmond since they have an instinct to stalk whatever radiates the most power.

The first Shadow I saw that night was on the way to the festival, and it was for only a second. Besides seeing a Shadow for the first time in years, there wasn't anything discernibly different. But the first Shadow to appear at the festival was also the last to leave, and I swear I saw its eyes flash white before it disappeared. And it appraised me with that gods forsaken thorny grin.

I jump at the knock on my door and it creaks open to reveal Klowbi. She's wearing yoga pants and a pastel pink top. She strolls in, glancing at the books piled on the bed, before stooping down and picking up the fallen book and examining the cover. She frowns and sets the black magick spell book on the pile and plops down on the mattress.

"Work sucked," she announces. "It was busy and a customer spilt their drink all over my shoes."

"That's unfortunate."

She frowns. "What's wrong?"

"Dad called," I say and explain the conversation to Klowbi. I slide the pile of books closer to me and begin to stack them. I wasn't getting anywhere with my research today, anyway.

"Poor Dad. So, what do you think happened to Desmond?"

I glance at the open page in my Book of Shadows and close it with a sigh. "The timing seems too perfect with the strange behavior of the Shadows and Desmond falling ill. The hospital is running tests." I reply with bitterness coating the last sentence.

"You don't think they'll find anything, do you?" Klowbi asks, repeating my thoughts. We've been around each other for too long to not know what the other is thinking. I shake my head. "Do you think it has to do with the Shadows?" she whispers, as if speaking it too loud would call them into being.

"It seems like a reasonable guess. I've never seen Shadows act that way. Or seen so many in one place at one time. It doesn't feel right." I stack my Book of Shadows on the pile and walk across my room to arrange them back on the shelf.

"I've never seen a Shadow until the Beltane festival," Klowbi shifts so she's watching me. Her freckles are bright against her flush cheeks. "Why can I see them now?"

I face Klowbi with my back leaning against the bookshelf. "Hard to say. Shadows are visible to those who practice the Craft or have a connection to the Otherworld, like Xuan. Some Wiccans and witches view seeing a Shadow as a rite of passage. Shadows often appear at Wiccan festivals, gatherings, and places with abundant energy and magick." I shake my head and rub the frustration from my eyes. "But to see that many at once is unheard of. It just doesn't happen."

"Why were there so many?"

"I don't know. It's possible the Shadows are only seen when they choose to be seen. Perhaps an abundance of magick compelled them to reveal themselves." I speculate, but doubt worms its way into my tone.

Klowbi leans back on the bed and swings her legs, a frown on her face. "Shadows aren't supposed to be aggressive, though, right?"

"They shouldn't be able to physically attack us, either. Yet they did."

Her brows furrow in thought. "Could it be because you've been in the Astral Realm too much? Maybe that influenced them somehow."

"No, the correlation seems unlikely." I wave my hand dismissively.

"Well," Klowbi drawls, sitting up. "You've been there a lot lately. Just because you haven't seen the Shadows doesn't mean they aren't there."

I twist my swan pendant between my fingers. "Maybe, but I've been astral projecting for years. I think I would have seen one if they were."

"Just an idea," she says meekly.

A pang of guilt twists my heart at Klowbi's dismissal. "I'll pay closer attention next time," I amend, taking a seat beside her.

She nods and bumps her shoulder with mine. "What about demons? Could they have been the cause of the attack?"

I shake my head. "Demons are violent and malevolent beings, but they can't walk in our world freely. Not how spirits and Shadows can, anyway. Demons have to be summoned in order to enter our plane and they need a vessel or transcendental boundary to keep them tethered. They have rules they have to follow, otherwise humanity would have been massacred centuries ago."

"I suppose that's a small comfort," Klowbi says halfheartedly. "They weren't spirits either. Unless spirits can transform into Shadows?"

I mull this over, tapping my pendant in thought. "Interesting theory, but I don't think so. Spirits are souls from once living people. Some have the ability to harm or haunt if they died with unfinished business or severe trauma, but most are benevolent and only want to help the living." I lower my hand from my pendant, drumming my fingers on my thigh. "My best theory on Shadows is that they are multi-dimensional beings. It's why we know so little about them. I don't know of a way to capture a Shadow to study it since they don't follow our world's rules."

"I'm sure there are answers for what happened. We will figure it out." She lifts her head and a smile blooms across her face. "Could we hang out with the others tonight? I think we could use a little relaxation."

I huff. "So that's what you came in here for," I tease. "Sure, Bambi, let me finish up then we can leave."

"Thank you," she chimes and jumps to her feet. "I'll be in the living room."

I wait until she leaves before checking beneath my bed. My protection jar is still sealed, which means nothing has attempted to harm me, whether it be an unknown entity or an unwanted spell. I sigh with relief and leave my room. I shut the door tightly and place a protection sigil on its surface. A green trail follows my finger as I trace the sharp lines and swooping curls. When I finish, I step back and admire my work. The green is vibrant and glimmering.

"Ready?" I hear Klowbi call from the living room.

"Almost." Stepping up to her closed bedroom door, I trace the sigil again. Once in place, I head to the living room where Klowbi is standing at the kitchen counter. "Let's go."

"They're ordering pizza," Klowbi says as we step into the hallway.

"Fine with me," I tell her and toss her the car keys. "Go start the car. I'll lock up."

"Don't be long."

"I believe it was you that was late last time we left."

Klowbi smiles sheepishly. "Actually, take all the time you need."

"That's what I thought," I mutter as she descends the stairs. I secure the door, wiggling the knob for added assurance. Calling on my magick again, I trace a stronger, more complex protection sigil on the front door. It's an electric purple, similar to the barrier I had crafted on the night of the festival. The sigil hums as if alive and settles my nerves. Hopefully, it would be enough to keep my paranoia at bay.

Rede of the Wiccan

Being known as the counsel of the Wise Ones:
Bide the Wiccan laws ye must,
in perfect love and perfect trust.
Live and let live, fairly take and fairly give.
Cast the Circle thrice about
to keep the evil spirits out.

To bind the spell every time,
let the spell be spake in rhyme.
Soft of eye and light of touch,
speak little, listen much.
Deosil go by the waxing Moon,
sing and dance the Wiccan rune.
Widdershins go when the moon doth wane,
and the Werewolf howls by the dread Wolfsbane.

When the Lady's Moon is new,
kiss thy hand to Her times two.
When the Moon rides at Her peak
then your heart's desire seek.

Heed the Northwind's mighty gale;
lock the door and drop the sail.

When the wind comes from the South,
love will kiss thee on the mouth.
When the wind blows from the East,
expect the new and set the feast.
When the West wind blows o'er thee,
departed spirits restless be.

Nine woods in the Cauldron go,
burn them quick a' burn them slow.
Elder be ye Lady's tree;
burn it not or cursed ye'll be.
When the Wheel begins to turn,
let the Beltane fires burn.
When the Wheel has turned at Yule,
light the log and let Pan rule.

Heed ye flower bush and tree,
by the Lady Bless'd Be.
Where the rippling waters go
cast a stone and truth ye'll know.
When find that ye have need,
hearken not to others' greed.
With the fool no season spend
or be counted as his friend.

Merry meet and merry part,
bright the cheeks and warm the heart.
Mind the Threefold Law ye should,
three times bad and three times good.
When misfortune is enow,
wear the Blue Star on thy brow.
True in love ever be
unless thy lover's false to thee.
Eight words ye Wiccan Rede fulfill:
An' it harm none, do what ye will.

Lady Gwen Thompson

Chapter 4

"Drinks are in the fridge."

The potent aroma of marijuana reaches me the moment we enter the home. I hear Niko and Alko in the lower level of the condo, the sound of the game they're playing drifting up from the stairs. Xuan stands in the kitchen drinking a fruity seltzer. Her hair is in its usual ponytail. Her dark eyes follow us as we walk forward.

"The boys have been gaming all day." Xuan explains and rolls her eyes.

Klowbi opens the fridge and grabs us both a beverage. She slides mine across the countertop and I pop the top and take a sip. The fruity carbonation makes my nose tingle. "That explains the smell."

Xuan's mouth twitches in a semblance of a smile. "You know Niko, he has to be smoking *something*."

There are worse things he could be smoking. At least weed and cigarettes are legal in Oregon. It's an improvement from his past habits.

"Did you order the pizza?" Klowbi asks.

"It'll be here within the hour," Xuan replies.

The living room has a gray sofa and a recliner facing the TV. A few of Alko's personal paintings are hung up throughout the house. There's one of the beaches in town with massive capsizing waves the color of burnt stone, with dark, wet footprints in the sand leading into the hungry waters. The sky is a strange silver purple with a blood red moon hanging in the sky, turning the water closest to a strange hue of crimson. Every time I see that painting I wonder what spurred his imagination to paint something so ominously beautiful.

There are a few others: a black cat crossing an empty street under a lamplight painted of acrylics, a watercolor piece of an owl atop a human skull, a pastel portrait of a carnival grounds at night with fireworks in the sky. There's fading remnants of the glamour magick Alko used on the paintings, an orange glow emanating from the medium.

A few signs of Xuan's Craft are sitting out in the living room. A poppet with pins sitting straight up and skulls, bones, and feet of dead animals are arrayed neatly on a shelf along the wall. The recognizable hum of the magick is hard to ignore. Xuan is talented with her skills of conversing with the dead, but it's a different type of magick, with a heavy, bitter energy. It raises the hair on the back of my neck.

"You think they'll let me play a round?" Klowbi pipes up, her eyes focusing on the stairs.

Xuan nods. "I'll make sure they do."

Klowbi smiles and shuffles over to the stairs with her drink clasped tightly. She looks over her shoulder. "Are you coming?"

I take a big swig of my drink. "Yes, right behind you."

Klowbi disappears down the stairs. Xuan steps around the counter to stand beside me. "Niko might not be very welcoming."

"Why is that?" I ask coolly. Xuan is shorter than me and has to tilt her head to meet my gaze. Her coal-black eyes are hard as she scrutinizes me.

"Don't act oblivious." Her mouth twists sourly. "You know why."

I frown and continue towards the staircase. "There's nothing between Desmond and me." I noticed Niko's dismissive demeanor the night of the festival after I had danced with Des. Even if I didn't see it as a romantic gesture, everybody else did.

"I'm not the one that needs convincing," she retorts, pushing past me to descend the stairs. Despite my irritation, I follow without a remark.

The smell of weed grows stronger as I descend into the lower level. Alko is setting up a new game while Klowbi fiddles with the controller so it fits comfortably in her scarred right hand. Niko is sitting on his bed and packing a bowl. He glances up, his eyes shimmering emeralds in the dark. He averts his stare and takes a sip of his beer, grunting in acknowledgement.

Xuan claims a spare rolling chair by the bed while Klowbi settles next to Alko on the ground, their backs pressing against the bed for support. The only available options are the bed or sitting on the floor. Despite Niko's cool demeanor, I take a seat next to him. He stays quiet, but he doesn't distance himself from me which I take as a good sign.

"What game are you guys playing?" I ask.

"A racing game. I almost beat Niko last time we played," Klowbi says. "I'm going to beat him this time for sure."

Niko chuckles next to me. "The moment you beat me is the moment I quit smoking."

"Is that a bet?" Klowbi teases.

"Not one I'm willing to shake on," he mutters and lifts the freshly packed bowl into the air. "Dibs?"

"You can have greens," Alko replies.

Niko lights the bowl and inhales, the earthy scent puffing from his mouth afterwards. He's careful not to blow it directly at anybody before passing the bowl to Alko. He takes a hit before offering me the bowl, which I shake my head to decline.

"No one else?" he asks, grabbing the bowl and watching the smoke curl.

"Not everyone enjoys being high," Xuan says with an unamused tone.

"I enjoy getting other people high, though," Niko shoots back with his familiar grin.

"I think I'm getting high from the smell already." Klowbi coughs and fans her face. Her cheeks are flushed with a smile.

"It's one step closer to converting you," Niko declares, before hitting the bowl again.

There's a bookshelf lined with bongs, larger pipes and bowls, and trays which he uses to roll the herb into blunts. It's an impressive collection consisting of dozens of different colors and styles. I notice another poppet doll, black and a mix of green on the shelf, also with pins sticking from the body. A gift from Xuan, most likely a poppet of Niko to protect and heal.

His skateboard and longboard lean against the wall in the room's corner, and several skater posters are plastered randomly throughout the space. A tapestry displays a naked woman smoking from a bong with a pot plant and galaxy-colored smoke above her head. A very Niko choice.

I turn away from the decor and find Niko watching me. I hold his gaze and he doesn't flinch or rear back. I drink him in, noting every detail. His skin doesn't look nearly as gaunt over his bones, his cheekbones not as sharp, and despite the mess of hair on his head, he looks handsome.

"Damnit!" Klowbi shouts and all our heads turn to stare at her except for Alko. "You're cheating."

With a victory burn-out on the screen, Alko declares, "No cheating, just skill."

"Cheater," Klowbi repeats with a frown and hands the controller over to Niko.

Alko puts his controller down in exchange for his beer. Niko exits the game and puts music on in the background, turning it down to background noise. He leans back on the bed and drinks from his can. "So, has anything exciting happened since last time?" Niko asks nonchalantly.

"If you're meaning the Shadows, then no, I haven't seen any since that night," I reply and everyone stiffens. I can practically feel the shift of energy in the room.

"That was the weirdest night of my life, and I've had a lot of weird nights," Niko comments.

"Have you guys experienced anything since then?"

Xuan rolls her chair to face the group. "I've spotted several Shadows lurking along the boundaries of the house. They cannot cross the wards, so they don't linger long."

"For now," Niko mutters. Alko glares at him from the floor, but says nothing.

"Are you going to tell them?" Klowbi speaks softly, her voice fragile.

"Tell us what?"

I sigh and take a drink of my seltzer. I was planning on telling them about the phone call, but I wasn't prepared to tell them so soon. Niko was warming up to me again and I didn't want to shatter that.

"I got a call from Dad," I mutter and tap the can in my hands. Everyone's eyes are focused on me, intent. "A few people were hurt that night. And Desmond was one of them. He's in a coma. No one knows how or why it happened."

Xuan's expression is carefully masked, and I can't read her reaction. Alko's eyes, wide and frightful, mirror the expression he had that same night. Niko's face tightens, but he doesn't avert his gaze when Desmond is mentioned. He rolls his neck and takes another drink.

"Anyone familiar with something like that happening before?" I ask.

"No," Xuan answers, her tone morose. "Shadows shouldn't be capable of such things."

"Hold up," Niko blurts. "I've hardly seen these Shadow things before. I don't have magick in my veins or paranormal ancestry, so why could I see them this time?"

"I've never seen them either," Klowbi adds. "The whole thing is weird. It gives me the creeps."

Niko scoffs. "Obviously, there are Shadow People walking around putting real people in comas."

Klowbi glances at me, her head tilted curiously. "Daire's been doing a lot of reading since the festival. Books on a bunch of different topics."

Everyone turns to stare at me and I straighten my spine as my frustration mounts. "There's no harm in reading."

"What books?" Xuan asks bluntly.

Klowbi's face scrunches in thought, her nose wrinkling with the effort. "A book of Wiccan history and phenomena and spell books." Her face twists into a frown. "Black magick and blood magick."

"You all know the type of Craft I practice. It's no secret," I say in an attempt to dispute any accusations. It was true they knew I practiced other forms of magick, but I never confided in Klowbi that Desmond had a newfound interest in this Craft.

"Why were you researching those books?" Xuan's voice is near emotionless, and the weight of her accusation has my magick flaring in outrage. Sparks of red burst from my fingertips and I feel the numbing tingle where the magick lands on my skin.

"I thought that if there was a spell or ritual that could influence the Shadows, maybe there was a way to reverse it or protect ourselves." I lie with a dismissive shrug. "Hence researching those books. I haven't found anything of use though. Nothing I didn't already know."

Xuan's lips tighten into a thin line as she surveys me with dark eyes. My stomach twists at her probing stare, but I meet her gaze, confident she won't sense the lie. I wasn't about to tell them Desmond's secret, not yet. I wanted to learn why he had this strange dream of practicing blood Craft. Maybe the correlation between the blood magick and the Shadows was a coincidence.

Hardly. Quite a well-timed coincidence if it was.

"That makes sense," Klowbi says and breaks the tension. I try not to show my relief.

"I will never understand," Niko mumbles and shakes his head.

"What if there's something else influencing the Shadows," Klowbi offers and looks to Xuan. "Could it be the Otherworld?"

Her head tilts slightly, nearly imperceptible, and it reminds me of a feline. "Not likely," she replies softly.

"There's nothing off kilter in the Otherworld?" I push in disbelief and set the can I was drinking from aside.

"Nothing pertaining to the Shadows." Her eyes flicker to mine and I my magick spikes at her calculating gaze.

Niko chuckles, oblivious to the tension between Xuan and I. Our gazes shoot at him, and despite our glares, he laughs harder. His eyes are red from smoking and his grin is wide.

"What?" Xuan and I snap simultaneously.

He coughs a few times, takes a sip of his beer, and chuckles. "Out of all the people I could have befriended, I choose the ones who see dead people and cast spells."

This elicits a snort from Alko and a giggle from Klowbi. We glare at the three of them and Klowbi shrugs. "He's not wrong."

"He has good taste in character," Alko says. It's the first thing he's said since the Shadows were brought up.

"You're an idiot," I grumble and he offers me a brilliant grin.

"It's worked for me so far." Niko chuckles.

After a brief pause, Klowbi suggests, "What if..." I resist the urge to cover her mouth in case more scrutinization is cast my way. "What if astral projection could affect the Shadows?"

A huff escapes me before I can catch myself. "I already told you it doesn't work that way."

Klowbi hangs her head, her hair falling over her eyes. Guilt crushes my heart from snapping at her.

"Astral what?" Niko asks.

"Astral projection," Xuan clarifies. "It's an out-of-body experience where consciousness can function without the physical body through the Astral Plane."

Niko's face lights up. "Oh, I've heard of this. Some say when they hallucinate they can see their body without being *in* their body. They can fly through space and stuff."

I cringe. "More or less, but it's far more complicated than hallucinating so hard you can suddenly astral project."

"I know that," he contends sharply.

"Aren't there layers to the Astral Plane?" Klowbi asks.

"There are hundreds of levels to it, but most stay on the basic plane, or ground level. It's the easiest to get to and to stay manifested in," I explain. "The lower levels take less skill to project to, but it still requires mental discipline. The higher the level you ascend to, the more difficult it becomes to stay projected in."

"And much more dangerous," Xuan adds. I catch the briefest look of warning on her face before she turns away.

"Why is it dangerous?" Klowbi queries with her attention on Xuan.

"It can be unpredictable for those who aren't well-practiced in the skillset," Xuan answers, her voice heavy with caution. "The realm is energy based, composed of both your energy and the plane's. It changes and adapts based on what is on the level of the plane, but it can also attract other beings."

"What does that even mean?" Niko remarks, his eyebrows quirked in question.

"It means," I begin slowly, as if speaking to a child, "each Astral level has a different energy that can manipulate our energy or attract something else. While the plane's energy remains constant, our perception of it can vary with each entry."

"The Astral Realm can manipulate our energy?" Klowbi asks in awe.

"Yes, which is why it is best to never test your limits once you know them, to avoid unnecessary risks," Xuan cautions.

"As long as you are in control of your energy and confident in your skills, then you have very little to worry about," I counter with a cool glare at Xuan. Her lips twitch, unamused, but she keeps further argument to herself.

Niko glances between the two of us with a smirk on his face. "Sounds like a challenge to me."

"Don't take this lightly," Xuan advises, her eyes darkening. "The Astral Realm is not to be trifled with. It is an unknown thing that cannot be manipulated. There are beings that reside in that realm that cannot be explained, nor should they be confronted."

Klowbi leans forward and her chestnut eyes alight with interest. "Beings? Like monsters?"

Xuan shakes her head. "Monsters, no. They only seem monstrous because they are not common to us."

"Astral wildlife," I offer. "The initial lower levels are mostly harmless and curious. The higher energy levels you enter, the more aggressive and menacing creatures will appear."

"Sounds like a video game," Niko comments beside me.

"A video game you don't want to lose," I say. "Even though the Astral Plane is energy based, a projector can still come to harm, just not the same way here."

Xuan nods her head in agreement with me, a rarity for the two of us. "Still very dangerous regardless of which skill set you possess, even more so if ignorant." Her eyes dart to mine and I resist the urge to lash out with a tendril of magick.

"What kind of creatures?" Klowbi asks.

"Shadow spiders are common," I reply before Xuan can answer. I ignore Xuan's black-hole gaze and stay focused on Klowbi who is listening with unhindered fascination. "Shadow spiders are curious beings and sometimes they follow you back to your body, but they can't physically harm you. It's happened to me before. They hang out in the room that was projected in, usually for no longer than an hour, then return to the Astral Plane. The one that followed me was the color of Shadows, and it kept creating webs in my room. When I touched the webs, I could feel and see it sticking to my fingers, but it wasn't really there. The spider eventually faded, as did the webs. Nothing remained to prove its existence except what I saw and felt."

"The spiders are the least of your worries if something follows you back," Xuan says gravely. "The Astral Plane must be respected and never be taken advantage of."

"Entering the Astral Plane does not mean one is taking advantage of it," I growl as a burst of red flares from my fingertips, curling into talons.

"In moderation there is no harm," Xuan amends and stands so she is above me. Even with her delicate frame, I sense the fight in her aura, the bitter taste of her magick. "Moderation that you do not have."

My fingers flex and talons twist and lengthen from my nails, morphing and curling into tendrils. The red magick hums as if it's a live wire, twirling and coiling around Xuan. My magick bristles around hers and it flares and heats my blood with a sudden burst of power. I smile at her, reveling in the euphoria of it. "I have control, and that is more than enough."

66

"Are there other creatures," Klowbi continues nervously, "like Shadow People?"

My concentration fizzles and my tendrils fall, withering away at Klowbi's question. Did she really not believe me when I told her I've never seen one in the Astral Realm? Xuan glances at me, her face unreadable. She flicks her wrist as if to work out a kink, and my magick scatters and dissipates completely. Xuan can't see magick, but she's more connected to it than anyone in our group besides me. She must have sensed the power surge and was able to shatter the rest of the magick I was controlling. Did she sense the other moments when my magick began to grow and heat with dissent, or was this a coincidence she warded off my remaining magick?

"It's possible they can reside in the Astral Plane. They are not of this plane, or seemingly any other," Xuan answers. She shifts a few steps away so she's standing closer to the stairs, further from me.

"So entering the Astral Plane a lot shouldn't affect the Shadows?" Klowbi pushes and risks a glance at me.

"Hypothetically no, it shouldn't. I'm unaware of a direct correlation between Shadows and the Astral Plane." Xuan's voice is void of emotion, strictly factual.

"I want to learn."

"No," Alko barks, his voice sudden and sharp. "No, I don't think that's a smart idea."

"Why?" Klowbi pouts. "Daire promised to teach me."

"It's too dangerous right now," Xuan speaks quietly, the gentleness in her tone towards Klowbi shocking compared to her usual cool, apathetic demeanor towards me. "Because we don't know for sure if the Astral Plane does have a direct influence on the Shadows, distance is the safest option. At least until we know more."

Alko nods. "No more astral projection. It's too dangerous."

"Someone's jumpy," Niko teases. "I don't even know how to astral whatever, so no worries here."

"Promise you'll teach me once this is over?" Klowbi pleads and reaches for my hand across the bed. Her doe eyes are full of hope, so innocent.

67

"I promise," I tell her and grab her hand and squeeze. My heart twists at the promise and a wide smile crosses her face, stunning and blooming.

"I'm willing to wait a little longer," Klowbi says with a vigorous nod.

Xuan turns to me. My frustration flares in sync with my magick as it coils at my feet, taking the shape of a viper, its detail-less head rearing back as if to strike. Xuan's eyes flicker to my feet then slowly meet my gaze, a near imperceptible shake of her head. Niko's attention flicks from me to Xuan and the magick ignores his presence. It's solely focused on Xuan. I brush my knees, sending the magick away and curl my fist around my magick to dampen it. My heart buzzes from the sensation, the static tingle bouncing in my belly as it tries to find release.

"Take a break from astral projection. The visits have been too frequent," Xuan demands, and her glower doesn't falter.

My heart sinks as the others try to take away my only safe haven from this reality. Astral projection was a tool I used before Mom fell ill, but after her death I spent as much time away from this world so I could find peace in a new one. Blood and dark magick wasn't enough to mute the grief or fury after losing my mother, so escaping into the Astral was the one place I finally felt whole again.

And now they want to take that away from me.

"It won't be forever," Klowbi adds, "just until things start to get better."

What if they don't get better?

I force the thought from my head and nod reluctantly in agreement. "Fine, temporarily, I'll give it a break," I concede.

Xuan doesn't thank me for agreeing, nor does she even acknowledge my response. She turns to Alko, not missing a beat. "I'm going to get the plates. Pizza should be here soon."

Alko stands from the floor and helps Klowbi to her feet. She smiles and glances around the room and slings an arm around Alko's waist, too short to reach his shoulders. "I missed this."

"The dark, weed-infused scent of Niko's room?" Alko asks.

"The snarky, asshole remarks from Alko?" Niko offers.

Those two never shut up.

"No," Klowbi laughs and gestures to our group. "This, I missed *this.*"

"We did too," Xuan says, and the briefest smile crosses her face.

I raise my eyebrows and glance at Niko, who has an impish grin and is packing another bowl. "I missed you too, Klowbi," he says and bumps my shoulder. "You too."

I smirk at Niko. "I tolerate you."

"That's progress." He grins with a glimmer in his eyes.

I chuckle and shake my head, though despite my differences with Xuan, I did miss the rest of the group. Alko and his quiet creativity, Niko with his constant humor and cheeky attempts at romance, and Klowbi with her heart of gold and careful thoughts. Xuan was cunning and calculating, but she was formidable in her talents, a threat in the wrong situation, an ally at best.

"Pizza's here," Xuan announces from the base of the stairs.

"But there wasn't a—" Niko pauses when he hears a knock at the door. He watches incredulously as Xuan walks up the stairs. "How the hell does she do that?"

"Magick," I mutter.

Chapter 5

After dinner, I step outside to get away from the voices inside. Before the door shuts behind me, I hear Niko complaining about all the olives on the supreme pizza and how disgusting it is that Alko eats them in handfuls. Klowbi is laughing the entire time and exchanging inside jokes with Xuan. It all feels too normal.

It feels wrong.

The loneliness sweeps in suddenly, the sudden jerk of reality that Mom is dead, Desmond has fallen into a mysterious coma, the Shadows have become a dangerous threat, and Xuan apparently has more magickal skill than I realized. The invisible hands squeeze my heart and my lungs, and it makes me wince as my breathing roughens. I exhale slowly and lift my chin to breathe in the deep, starlit sky. The moon is haze behind the clouds and the stars that peek through glimmer softly.

Xuan's emergence of power and control bothers me. How could she sense and dissipate my magick? For the nearly five years I've known her, she's never shown a sign that she could manipulate my magick. Perhaps subtly, but not to the extreme ability she showed tonight. It was as if she had taken temporary control over my gift. No witch, not even Desmond or my parents, had the ability to dissolve my magick like that. They could overpower it with their own, but that battle was about strength and will. Not anything like Xuan did; it was as if she erased it entirely.

And now they're taking away my freedom to astral project based on a fearful whim that the Shadows could be linked to the Astral Plane.

Bullshit.

The air cools my heated skin and cascades goosebumps down my arms. The streets are barely lit by the street lamps and trees groan with the wind. Long shadows stretch across the expanse of the road and I pray they are the only ones I see tonight.

I hear the front door open and close followed by footsteps behind me. I brace myself, expecting it to be Niko with a new barrage of his futile romantic quips or Xuan's brooding accusations. Instead a warm hand brushes against mine. Our hands tentatively take hold of each other. My thumb brushes against the missing gap where a pinky should be and the bumpy flesh of scar tissue that dresses her palm all the way up to her elbow.

"Why are you outside?" She's staring at the few stars that are visible.

I take in a deep breath of night air, willing the tightness in my lungs to release. "I needed to be alone."

"I get it. It's a lot to deal with at once," Klowbi acknowledges and squeezes my hand. She lowers her gaze to the street, her auburn hair falling into her face. "I'm sorry about earlier. I didn't mean for you and Xuan to fight."

I shrug. "It's fine, Bambi."

"I didn't expect her to be so serious about not astral projecting. I truly wasn't trying to take that away from you," Klowbi says with a sadness in her doe eyes. "I'm sorry."

Turning towards her, I grasp her other hand tightly in mine. "I know you didn't mean it. Let's just hope this passes."

"Thanks, Daire."

I release her hands and turn to watch the stars again. More clouds have moved in overhead. The darkness feels heavy, damp. My heart aches as a memory of stargazing with Mom comes to mind.

"Remember when all of us made a nest of blankets outside in the backyard? We had so many blankets and pillows stacked around us. Mom and Dad would lay in the nest with us pointing out constellations." I reminisce with a warm smile. The memory makes my heart ease and my insides warm. "We ate so many cookies that night."

"My stomach ached after that," Klowbi laughs.

"Then the stars started to fall, first one, then several, and then sudden-ly..." I sigh breathily at the memory. I was young and had never experienced anything like a meteor shower. I exclaimed the stars were coming to meet us. The brilliant flaring tails of the meteors blazed against the midnight sky the same color as my hair. Dozens lit up the night. We had laid in silence watching them, and it was the sweetest moment of peace.

"I remember that. It was a beautiful night."

I smile despite the sickening ache in my heart. Even with Mom gone, at least I still have sweet memories of her, of us as a family. "It really was," I murmur and tear my gaze from the heavens. "So, what did you come out here to ask me?"

Klowbi's face reddens and her freckles are bright on her skin. "How do you know I wanted to ask you something?"

"I know you, Klowbi."

"Oh, well," she starts with a nervous laugh, "can we stay the night?"

"Dinner wasn't enough?" I mumble and return my eyes back to the stars.

"Please," she begs, glancing at the door where laughter emanates from within. "It's been a great night. We haven't had a night like this since..."

"Since before Mom got sick," I finish for her. Klowbi bites her lip but doesn't disagree. I know Klowbi spent time with them without me and how important it is to her to have our group back together, even if it was a mere semblance of normalcy. I roll my eyes at her pouting lower lip. "You really want to stay?"

She nods her head emphatically. "Yes."

"Fine, we can stay the night." I cave and turn back towards the house.

"Thank you!" Klowbi cheers and nearly knocks me off my feet with her hug. She pulls away with a blooming grin and a child-like gleam in her eyes. Seeing her so happy finally gives me the breath I need and the stranglehold on my lungs fades. "Come on!" She drags me back inside by my hand.

We return downstairs to where the others have disappeared. Alko and Niko are sitting on the floor smoking another bowl with console controllers in hand. Xuan is sitting in the same chair from earlier, watching them with a bemused expression. Klowbi sits on the bed and I take a spot next to her with my hands fisted in my lap in hopes of keeping better control of my magick.

"Best two out of three," Niko goads with an exhale of smoke.

"Challenge accepted," Alko answers and inhales from the bowl.

"You know I'll win," Niko gloats with an arrogant grin, his teeth flashing in the dim room.

"Your arrogance is your fault."

"I think you mean confidence, and it will bring me victory," Niko remarks as they start the race.

"I play the winner," I declare and both of them dare a look over their shoulders before returning their gaze to the screen.

"You dare challenge me?" Niko says.

I huff. "You haven't won yet."

"And he won't." Alko replies, taking first place in the race.

"It's only just begun." Niko drifts directly into a corner and places himself near last. "Damnit."

"You know what I was just thinking about," Klowbi ventures.

"Considering no one here reads minds," Niko offers, "then no, we wouldn't know."

"How do you know I can't?" Xuan croons.

"Because if you could, I think you'd have killed me by now," Niko mutters.

"I'm still contemplating if I should," Xuan remarks with a glimpse of a smile.

"The moment I cross you is the day I stop smoking weed," Niko promises.

"What's that supposed to mean?" I chime.

"It means it won't ever happen," he says.

"Go on, Klowbi," Alko interrupts.

"I was thinking," Klowbi reiterates, "I know it's only May, but we should all go to the Summer Solstice festival."

"You mean the one we go to every year?" Niko asks sarcastically.

Klowbi grins, ignoring his comment. "Yes, it's like attending a reunion. It's where we all met. How we became friends."

"Such fond memories," Niko says with a dreamy sigh. "The first time I heard Daire speak to me. I believe you called me, and I quote, 'a selfish, pompous asshole without any regards to anyone but yourself.' I have been enamored ever since with your words. Spoken like poetry."

I roll my eyes. "You trampled Klowbi's flower crown."

"By accident."

"You were going to walk off with nothing but a lame apology."

"At least I apologized."

"Only after I confronted you."

"Yes, and then you harshly chastised me in front of the entire crowd."

I chuckle, remembering how dumbstruck Niko was that night. Niko had stood there frozen, mouth agape, eyes wide, and unspeaking when I had launched my verbal assault for upsetting Klowbi and crushing her flower crown. I'd be lying if I said I didn't enjoy the look on his face. "Unsurprisingly, Klowbi came to your rescue before we left you standing there."

Niko's cheeks burn and he shakes his head, his sandy hair swaying with the movement. "It was one of my most embarrassing moments."

"You looked ridiculous," Alko agrees with a chuckle. "We were watching the entire exchange."

"And you did nothing!"

"We laughed, that's something."

"Asshole."

"Idiot."

"You walked back to us looking so ashamed," Xuan recalls. "I don't think I'd ever seen you look so guilty before."

"Yeah, well, it makes a difference when you're scolded in front of dozens in public." Niko grumbles.

I arch a brow and lean over to the edge of the bed near Niko, close enough that my breath tickles his ear. "So you felt no remorse until I confronted you?"

Niko shivers and he shifts away, his eyes darting between me and the screen as if he couldn't decide which he needed to pay attention to. "Well, I did, but you rubbed salt in the wound."

"Clearly it didn't sting that bad." I sit back up. Klowbi gives me a knowing look and giggles.

"You brought us new flower crowns though," Klowbi offers.

"That was my idea," Alko adds. Niko shoots him a glare and punches him on the arm. Both of their race cars crash into the wall.

"It was my money though," Niko counters and glances back at me, his emerald eyes sparkling. "I saw how impressed you were with my chivalry. You were captivated by my courteous nature."

"Hardly," I grumble.

Klowbi laughs, the sound bright and sweet. "You asked if we wanted to watch fireworks with you, too. I remember Xuan and Alko watching us."

"I was surprised you let him talk that long," Xuan quips to me.

"So was I," I admit.

"I thought you'd deny me after all the kindness I did for you," Niko says with dramatic flair.

I lean forward and flick the back of his head, and he winces, rubbing where it connected. "You mean after the inconvenience you put us through?"

"I bought you both ice cream," Niko argues, completely discarding the race and looking at me directly.

"That was my stipulation since Klowbi wanted to talk with you guys." I huff and cross my arms.

"You coerced me into it."

"You had to bribe us to join."

"Touché."

Klowbi playfully pushes my arm. "It's as if it were fate," she says wistfully, peering around the room at our ragtag group.

I ignore the false idea of fate influencing our paths. There was no fated path I'd willingly walk with Mom dead. Fate is a figment.

"Wish it could be more than friends," Niko grumbles.

I stir the ill thought from my mind. "What?" I ask, leaning forward.

"Nothing," he covers quickly.

Alko delicately sets the controller in his lap. "Looks like I won."

"I still have a chance," Niko says with a glance my way.

"Arrogance only gets you so far," I tell him.

"Shut up," Niko grumbles as they restart.

Xuan peers our way, her gaze unreadable, before standing. "Let's leave them to their game, Klowbi. How does a movie sound?"

Klowbi nods and forces back a yawn. "A movie sounds more entertaining than the boys yelling at a TV. Daire, are you staying with them?"

I mull it over before refocusing on the boys. "Go ahead, I'll mediate."

Klowbi shrugs and follows Xuan up the stairs.

"Still plan on playing the winner?" Niko asks, shifting closer to the screen.

I sidle up to the edge of the bed where they are sitting on the floor and sit with my legs hanging. "That's what I said." The second race is significantly faster than the first. With just two laps remaining, Niko maintains the lead.

"Are you still working at the diner?"

"Yes, nothing has changed in those regards," I tell him.

"The cinnamon rolls are delectable," Alko comments.

"Drop by and I'll make sure a few get sent your way."

"Free of charge?" Alko asks with a smile on his thin lips.

"I can make it happen."

Niko shouts and pumps a fist in the air. "Hell yeah, I won!"

"We tied," Alko corrects, "you didn't win."

"Winner plays me anyway," I say, "so you will still lose."

"Competitive, I like it." Niko smirks, starting the third race.

While Alko and Niko battle for first place to decide who faces me, we talk about the small changes in our lives. Alko strives to make a living by selling his artwork. Niko still isn't sure what he wants to do with his life, but he's keeping his nose clean, so he's content with the minimum. I try to avoid all questioning and the topic of Mom, directing the conversation back to them when they pry. Eventually the conversation goes quiet as they vie for first place. They are within a placement of each other, the lead switching rapidly, until Niko drifts ahead, cuts off Alko and manages to cross the finish line first.

"Damn it!" Alko barks and tosses the controller from his lap.

"What were you both telling me? That arrogance only gets me so far?" Niko says mockingly.

Alko shoots him a glare. "Cocky asshole."

Niko offers a grin and rolls his shoulders. "Thank you."

Alko straightens his spine and hands me the controller he had discarded onto the floor. "Kick his ass."

I grin. "Gladly."

"Whose side are you on?" Niko complains.

"Not yours," Alko says.

"Clearly."

"I'm heading to bed, though," Alko stands and his obsidian hair is a mess covering his eyes. "Goodnight."

"Later."

"Night." He walks up the stairs, exchanging a subtle look with Niko before disappearing.

Niko makes his way onto the bed beside me and he shifts so we aren't touching. He clumsily grabs for the bowl. He looks at me through his lashes and a crooked grin sharpens his features. "You want a hit?"

I shake my head and fiddle with my necklace, my fingers tracing the pentagram above the swan in smooth and decisive movements. "You know I don't like smoking."

"We both know that's not entirely true," he pushes, and his grin is wicked. My heart stutters in my breastbone at the sight and I have to look away to focus myself. "You don't smoke recreationally like me, but you dabble. I've seen it with my own two eyes."

"Your two eyes are sadly mistaken," I reply with a sly smile of my own.

His vivid, verdant eyes are dilated and I realize this is the first time in months that Niko and I are alone. My magick purrs and brushes against my skin like a content cat. Now that the others have left, my defenses are crumbling against him as my magick craves to be closer to him. As I long to be closer with him.

No. We tried that before and, despite the magnetic pull I feel towards him, it isn't enough to ignore the fact our lives are too vastly different to ever blend harmoniously. Even if he makes my heart skip and my stomach flutters with butterflies and my magick wants him more than anything else I've ever known.

Niko flashes me a grin that leaves me defenseless. "You'll find I can be rather convincing when I want to be," he says with a deep growl and takes a hit of the bowl. He offers it to me and I glower at him as the smoke pools from his mouth. "Just one."

"You're an ass," I tell him with my heart thumping wildly and accept the bowl. I take one inhale, watching the embers flare to life, and hand it back with a cloud drifting from my lips.

He chuckles. "That wasn't so bad, was it?"

I shove him and we both laugh. My walls are crumbling like they do every time we're alone, and the tension eases from my bones. My magick hums on my palms, a fine pink webbing blooming between my fingers. I shake my hands out and watch them tangle, twist, and soak into my palms again.

We've only been alone for a few minutes and my magick already wants him.

I turn away from him with a blush heating my cheeks and focus on the game. "So, how are things with your family?"

Niko straightens and his striking grin falters. "Nothing's changed."

"When did you last speak to them?"

He doesn't say anything at first, his features normally so relaxed and humorous are now tense, guarded. He looks at me with a darkened gleam. "It's been a while," he admits with a shake of his head. "It's for the best."

"What about Nadene? She admires you."

"She's too young to understand," he mumbles and grabs for the bowl. "Just drop it." He lights the bowl, exhales, and his lips purse and I wonder if he still tastes the same. "How's your dad?"

I rub the warm plastic of the controller and will my heart to calm. "He's fine, considering."

"And how are you, considering?"

"I'm fine." My magick quiets at his questioning and it slithers through my veins in waiting.

"Right," he says doubtfully. "Have things gotten easier after...?" Niko trails off and he does a circling hand motion to finish his sentence.

"I don't think 'easy' is the correct term, but things have been more manageable. It's still hard, and I'm still angry, so damn angry..." I run my fingers through my dark locks and study the tattoos on my arms, the intricate line work of runes on my right hand. All of it reminds me of Mom, of what she was, of what I had, of what I lost. I swallow and curl my fingers into claws as a score of red bursts from my fingertips and streams into my palm. It flickers and crackles like fire, the strange sensation sending my flesh to heat and itch, but I don't shy from the uncomfortable sensation. I push more of my magick into it and the flames roil between red and crimson.

"Are you doing it?" He gestures at my palms.

I smile at the foreign heat flickering across my face. "Yes," I tell him. "Are you still frightened of it?"

Niko swallows and shakes his head, the bowl of weed forgotten in his hands. "It's a little intimidating." He leans forward as his eyes focus on my palms. "What do you see?"

"It reminds me of flames," I say and lift my hand, curling my fingers so the flames engulf them, too. The strange itchy heat forces me to catch my breath as I study it. "Red and crimson."

"Those colors never seem to mean anything good," he mutters and leans away with a note of disdain.

"It's all intention." The flames light his face and sharpen his features. "Red, probably for anger."

Or lust, I am around Niko.

"Crimson for power," I add.

Also could be love and enchantment. The magick is just as attracted to him as I am.

"Why anger?"

"I'm always angry, Niko. I've merely learned to utilize it instead of allowing it to destroy me."

I watch my words sink in as understanding dawns on his face. "Does it hurt?" He lifts his hand to touch my palm, his fingers barely a hair's breadth away from touching the glowing flares. He stops and pulls away, rubbing the back of his neck as I gape at the muscle flexing in his bicep.

I silently chide myself and allow the magick to creep higher. "No, but it itches like fire does when you get too close. As if it's clawing at my skin, trying to climb the rest of me." I clasp my hands together and douse the flames. When I display my palms, there's no trace of anything being there.

"It's crazy."

"Careful what you say," I tease. "I just might curse you."

"I don't think you're crazy," he clarifies, "but the fact you are literally magick is."

"Anyone has the potential, it's a skill like any other. The more you practice, the better you'll be."

"I'll pass." He turns towards the screen again and my hope plummets at his dismissal. "Do you still practice the other magick?"

"You'll have to be more specific."

"The black and blood magick." He spits it out, succinct and harsh to my ears.

I straighten at the crudeness of his tone. "Yes, but I'm skilled in that Craft."

His silent nod ends the discussion. He readies the game, and before starting it he turns to me. He looks uncertain, and he takes a few breaths before finally breaking the silence. "How do you feel about Desmond?" he

SCION OF A SWAN

asks and a blush paints his high cheekbones. "About him being in a coma, I mean," he corrects quickly.

"Niko," I say and his eyes light at the sound, "you know I don't have feelings for him. I empathize with Aubrie; her only son is in a coma from unknown means. But Desmond is family to me. I care for him and I want him to wake from this." Familiar sadness douses any remaining happiness I felt earlier as I sink into the dark spiral of my thoughts.

"Alright, I believe you." He intently study the loading screen of the game.

"Can we start the race now? I think it's time I kick your ass," I tease in an attempt to shake the depressing mood. I shift closer to the screen, closer to Niko.

He chuckles, and a smile splits his face. "Prepare to lose."

"Shut up," I say and the race begins.

The silence is no longer uncomfortable, and I embrace the gentle waves of the high. I'm in the lead of the race, but I overcorrect on a turn and crash my car, allowing Niko to get ahead. I groan in frustration, feeling sleep itch my eyes, and admire Niko while I wait to respawn. Even though he's skinny, his muscles flex beneath his skin, and I imagine his slim fingers adorned with cuts and gashes from skateboarding brushing my cheek as he holds my face. I blink the sudden thought away and notice the pale band on his right ring finger. My stomach jolts at the empty sight. I survey the stand beside his bed, searching for the ring, but find nothing. He bumps my leg and my attention lands on him.

"You've respawned," he tells me, and I hear the foreign sound of worry in his tone.

"The ring," I mutter, and half-heartedly begin driving my car again.

"What? Oh," he says sheepishly and touches the bare skin. His eyes dart from me to the screen, flashes of emerald in the dim light. "I haven't worn it for a while."

I nod solemnly, unable to nullify the bitter ache in my heart. "Understandable."

81

"I still have it," he states roughly, his voice thick. "It's in the night-stand." He nods his head in its direction with his attention still on the race. "It was too much of a reminder..."

It barely makes the raw pang ease knowing he still has the ring I gave him. Why would he continue wearing it after not speaking for months? I had brutally and knowingly discarded him from my life, even if it was temporary. The ring was a callous reminder of me, of the whisper of what we once were.

Of what we still are.

I'm barely paying attention, severely in last place, and Niko's car crosses the finish line. "You win," I tell him as my car finally rumbles across, ending the race. "I blame the weed."

"The more you practice, the better you'll be," he teases, quoting me from earlier. I glare at him and set the controller down, absently tracing the runes on my hand as my heart aches in my chest. His fingers brush my wrist and glide to my fingers. His touch firms, as if making up his mind, and he grips both my hands in his. I can't stop my breath from hitching or the aphrodisia of his touch sparking my magick to life in ribbons of pink and crimson around our clasped hands.

"Daire," Niko begins and pauses. His emerald eyes search mine as admire the rapid pulse in his throat, the shallows of his cheeks, the sharp lines of his jaw. He lets go of my hands, my magick sputtering and unravel-ing with the disappearance of his heated touch, and he grabs for the bowl instead. "I'm really glad you came over."

"Me too," I murmur, my words hollow. My heart is hollow. The ache in my chest heaves and the invisible hands squeeze my lungs, never gone for long. "I should go to sleep."

"Yeah, it's late," Niko agrees, and the tension is palpable. "Don't be a stranger."

I stand and face him, force a smile. The double meaning of his words, innocent from the outside view. *Don't disappear.*

"Goodnight, Niko," I say and head up the stairs.

"G'night." His attention flits back to the screen, to the bowl, to his hands, anywhere but at me.

The living room flickers with light from the movie still playing on the TV. Klowbi is asleep on the couch, a blanket cocooned around her. Her hair is already a knotted mess, an auburn curl draped across her nose that floats with her breath. Both Xuan and Alko are out of sight, seemingly retired to their own rooms. I head to the recliner, grab a blanket, and settle into the cushions. I can't discern the title of the movie Klowbi has picked, yet I can tell it's a paranormal horror mystery. It's towards the end of it, and with the weed in my system, I feel myself drift off, the voices and screams of the movie following me into the dark.

When I open my eyes, my breath hitches at the sight of the ocean, forever sprawling into the horizon. A jagged cliff drops into the depthless waters, swashing against the bedrock far below. The familiar scent of briny waters teases my nostrils, intrinsically tied to the ocean.

Within a stone's throw away is a sentinel of pines leading into a forest. The expanse between the forest and the cliff's edge is filled only with threads of grass. It would be a peaceful scene if it weren't for the crumbling ledge to my left and the fall that would plunge into frigid ocean waters.

The ocean, upon another glance, has turned a dark blue bordering on black, no longer the welcoming sparkle of sunshine dancing on the waters. A gust of wind shoves me closer to the edge, the sky edging a turbulent gray with storm clouds on the horizon. The pines croak, and a scream of terror pierces the air. It's male, high pitched and filled with unspoken horrors.

I follow the source of the scream, treading carefully across the bare slip of land towards the towering trees when an invisible force stops me. It's as if I've hit a barrier of glass barring me from approaching. My hands press against the force, flattening against nothing. I follow the invisible line, and again am met with resistance. A line drawn in the sand where I can look, but I cannot cross.

A murder of crows take flight from the depths of the trees, screeching their unease to the winds. I hold my breath, my heart beating loudly in my ears, as the branches of the trees seem to part to reveal a boy clawing his way from the darkness.

He's limping terribly, a trail of blood painting his escape route. Filthy black hair falls over his eyes, his mouth twisted into a grimace as he crosses the threshold of forest to barren earth. The trees at his back cackle through mouths made of bark, their branches bending with forked limbs slashing and stabbing where the boy once stood. He barely misses a switch to his side as he stumbles and falls, pulling himself further from tenebrosity.

I watch in muted horror as gleaming eyes stalk from within the pall of the forest, howls and snarls echoing off the cliffside. The boy pulls himself to his feet, his back to me, and my eyes drop to the jagged gash along his calf, lightning down to his heel. Blood cakes his jeans and pools in the footprint in the dirt.

I cup my hands around my mouth, and with a mighty breath, I call, "Hey! Over here!"

The boy freezes, his body shivering rigid as he limps in a circle. Our eyes meet for one second, then two, and he keeps swiveling, searching for my voice. My fist knocks on the barrier, my eyes watching the bleeding boy. The barrier is keeping me hidden, a bystander of the nightmare unraveling in front of me.

And then I recognize his familiar diamond shard eyes as he limps closer to the precipice. I scream for him, praying to the gods for him to hear me, that together we could break through the barrier and I could save him. But Desmond keeps walking, his head snapping back and forth in search of my voice even though I'm only a quick sprint from wrapping my arms around him, from protecting him from the monsters lurking in the dark.

I call for my magick, hoping that with it I can smash the barrier, but I feel nothing except the sweat on my palms. I bang my fists on the barrier, my voice grating raw as I watch Desmond with fear etched across his features as he peers over the ledge, then looks past me, and his gaze falls on the dark masses emerging from the forest. They take their time as they pull from the darkness, massive slinking shapes born of midnight and brimstone, glistening fangs and beady eyes burrowed in their heads.

"Daire!" Desmond cries, his voice catching on the wind. He stumbles backwards closer to the edge, his shoulders shaking, tears slipping down his cheeks. "Help me!"

I scream for him, my fists bloodied as I slam against the barrier. It holds fast, my efforts are nothing but a minor inconvenience. Ragged breaths shred my lungs as the black beasts from Hell snicker and snarl, circling Desmond so there's nowhere to run. I feel the desperation crackling in the air, taste the fear prickling my tongue, my heart near shattering my ribs, and watch understanding dawn on Desmond's face. The acceptance and defiance written in the hard line of his lips and furrow of his brow.

"Find me, Daire," Desmond calls softly and he dives off the cliff, the creatures scrambling after him a moment too late.

I jolt awake, my hands around my throat. Sweat has pooled along my back and trails down my face. Breaths come in jagged bursts, and I scan the room where Klowbi is still passed out on the couch, the TV on sleep mode. The sun is peeking through the blinds and I hear the faint songs of birds outside.

Desmond was there in my vision. It was no dream, this was too real, too terrifying, for it to be imagined. Wherever Desmond's conscious lay, it was far from our reality. I couldn't reach him, couldn't save him from the monsters born of darkness, but he could hear me. Somehow he knew I was there, clawing to save him.

It wasn't too late for him. There had to be a way to bring him back. And I would find it. I'd save him before he had to jump.

I sit up and run my hands through my hair in a meek attempt to shake the terror from my bones. Closing my eyes, I will myself to calm and breathe slowly, opening them again and focusing on my magick. Relief washes over me when it responds and I sag into the recliner with a sparkle of purple glittering on the palms of my hands.

I don't bother going back to sleep. I sit in silence and focus my attention purely on my magick, my power, my strength. The one constant in my life that can't be stolen. I set my jaw and manipulate my magick into an arc that I bounce from one palm to the other.

And I make another spell, another vow.

Power I seek and revenge I crave. My magick will protect and send my foes to the grave. So mote it be.

Chapter 6

A week has passed since I last saw Xuan, Alko, and Niko. My nightmare vision hasn't recurred, and the Shadows have made themselves sparse. It's as if they've disappeared, seemingly lost interest since the night of Beltane.

Their sparsity hasn't eased the paranoia or terror since that night. I half expect to leave my room and find a Shadow patiently waiting across the street for me. The nightmare lingers each time I search for sleep, and the fresh fear that Xuan can control my magick, paired with the unknown of what happened to Desmond, leaves me irritable.

I had been debating if I should confide in Klowbi about Xuan's ability to disperse my magick along with the nightmare when I saw Desmond jump from a cliff, but images of Klowbi going to Xuan immediately haunted my mind. I couldn't trust that she would keep things between us. Secrets were better kept with only one mouth.

Frustration boils inside as I come up with more questions than answers. I need guidance, and since Mom isn't here to help, I turn to my deity instead.

Herbs and crystals lay on my altar along with candles, incense, bones, water, several types of dirt, and any other miscellaneous spell ingredients I might need. My ritualistic tools are displayed near the stitched penta-gram: the athame—a ceremonial dagger, a chalice, and a wand that I use only for intensive ritual work.

Standing in front of my altar, I bless the offerings I've laid out for my goddess Lilith. I offer a rose and slices of dark chocolate in hopes she'll lead me to answers.

With the offering complete, I grab my phone and pull up Dad's number. I rub at my swan pendant and I stare out the window of my room as it rings. The sun is high in the May sky as a lady walks her golden retriever on the sidewalk. A few customers are sitting on the patio of the Black Cat and their laughter floats towards my window.

It takes five horribly long rings before Dad answers the phone. The exhaustion in his voice tightens the building anxiety in my chest. I should have made more time to help him and make sure he was alright.

"Hi, Dad," I say into the phone, my heart thumping rapidly.

"My little swan," he says and a smile blooms across my face, "how are you?"

"I'm fine. I miss you."

"I miss you, too. Everything fine with you still?"

I nod, even though he can't see me. "Yeah, things are fine here. Are you doing okay?"

Dad sighs and the weight of it crushes my heart. "Aubrie isn't doing well, but she's managing better. I haven't been home in days and I'm sick of eating hospital food. I'm pretty sure the meat there isn't actually meat at all."

I can't help myself and laugh at his humor. "I'm not envious of your dining options."

"If it were my choice, I'd be eating steak and lobster every day for a month."

"Good choice." I turn from the window and glare at the blood magick book on my shelf with ire building in my veins. "How's Desmond?"

There's a pause, then quietly, "There hasn't been much progress. The doctors confirmed there's no internal bleeding, he has no broken bones and doesn't seem to be in pain. He has brain activity, but he shows no signs of waking up. It's as if he's been completely removed from our reality."

I have innumerable questions for Dad and countless theories to discuss. I hold my tongue, deciding to ask him in person. "Dad, would you mind if I came to visit for a few days?"

"Of course not, Daire. You are always welcome at my house. Is everything there alright?" he asks with concern lacing his tone.

"Yeah, everything's fine here. I need a break from Melas, and I can assist you at home."

"I'll be home tomorrow morning before visiting Aubrie at the hospital later that afternoon. She would appreciate you visiting. Seeing Desmond might be beneficial for you, too."

In case he doesn't make it.

I shake the thought from my head. "I'll be there tomorrow morning before you leave for the hospital again."

"I'll see you tomorrow," Dad says.

"See you tomorrow."

I hang up the phone and pull up Klowbi's number. She's visiting her mom for the day. Our conversation was clipped before she left, but she invited me with her anyway. Ever since Mom died, I couldn't find it in myself to accept her offer. Klowbi only has her mom and her father has been out of the picture from the beginning. Her dad is why she moved from California to Oregon to begin with, that and the shark attack she experienced as a child.

If it hadn't happened how it did, maybe we wouldn't have ended up as neighbors. She told me once that the thought of us never meeting scares her more than sharks do.

I text Klowbi, telling her I'll be leaving in the morning to visit Dad alone. She responds instantly, telling me that she'll be home before dinner so we can spend the evening together. I smile and text her to pick up more wine for the evening.

Setting my phone aside, I head to the kitchen to grab a glass of wine before packing my things for the next few days. Regardless of the uncertainty ahead, I plan to indulge in a buzz before all hell breaks loose.

The sun has been up in the sky for several hours by the time I arrive at Dad's. The kitchen window is propped open and inside Dad is bustling around. As I walk closer to the front stoop, I smell lasagna wafting through the open window. The path up to the house is lined with blooming pink and purple rhododendrons and brilliant gold black-eyed susans. A few of Mom's old lawn ornaments are hidden amongst the blooms; a small garden fairy, night-glowing spotted mushrooms, plastic gnomes with their colorful caps hiding their eyes.

I knock on the cabin door. I understand why Dad moved here after Mom died. It's peaceful and serene with no mechanical beasts prowling the streets. It's exactly what Mom would have wanted if she were still here.

The front door opens and Dad greets me. His hair is a blond mess atop his head, his beard scruffy and in desperate need of a trim. His eyes are darkly shadowed, but a genuine smile crosses his face and his mahogany eyes glisten as he pulls me into a hug. "My sweet girl," he mutters softly into the top of my head.

"Hi, Dad," I say and return the hug, burying my head into his shoulder. The joy of feeling like a kid again, believing Dad can fix everything, rushes through me and shoves out the dark clouds in my mind.

He pulls away, then examines me from head to toe. "You look great, Daire, I'm a bit of a mess. I cooked lasagna so Aubrie wouldn't have to keep eating hospital food," he explains and leads me inside. "I haven't had time to tidy up. Things have been less than ideal."

The kitchen is a disaster. Pots, pans and unwanted vegetable remains scatter across the countertops and pile in the sink. Stacks of paper are strewn about the kitchen table haphazardly and mysterious splatters coat the counter and cabinets. At least the place doesn't stink; it still holds the cabin smell with the scent of lasagna wafting through the air.

"It's fine, Dad, you've been busy." I dismiss, waving him off.

"I have to clean up this mess and haven't had time to change clothes."

"Dad, I'll take care of the kitchen. Go clean up."

"Are you sure?" he asks, but the relief on his face is evident from my offer.

"Yes, and take your time. Your beard needs a bit of a trim."

Dad smiles and his eyes crinkle. "You don't like my haven't-shaved-in-a-week look? I thought it made me look younger and more hip." he teases and attempts to comb his fingers through his beard.

I chuckle. "Go clean up. I can handle things out here."

Dad places another kiss on my head. "I'll be quick."

"I'm not worried."

I methodically start wiping down the countertops and scrubbing stains from the surfaces. I pile up the vegetable ends for composting, wash the dishes, and cover the lasagna for easy transport. The shower is running in the background, and I'm happy that Dad can have a moment of peace.

It doesn't take long to have the kitchen looking tidy, so I start rummaging through the mounds of paper piled haplessly on the kitchen table. The first few envelopes I pick up are bills and I stack those aside. The spam mail I pile into another corner of the table. I begin sorting through news articles, and pause when a picture of a Shadow peeks out from underneath the weekly paper. I pull it out and discover more articles and stories about the Shadows underneath. Glancing over my shoulder to be certain Dad is still in the bathroom, I scrutinize the articles, skimming each one for any tidbits of information.

The first few pages I skim are stories of people who have encountered Shadows. One person said they experienced something watching them while trying to sleep, and when they opened their eyes, a Shadow was peering at them from the doorway. Another states that as a child, the Shadows were a daily occurrence and they would stand against the wall or hover in doorways, observing. Someone else said a Shadow hovered in an art room at a school, and when the student noticed it, it waved before disappearing. The stories were harmless, with only one Shadow seen at a time, unlike Beltane.

I grab another article that states Shadows only manifest when people believe in and fear them, making the apparitions appear. Another study suggests that the Shadows are only hallucinations caused by lack of sleep, drug use, or a symptom of mental illness. Another article claims that the Shadows are interdimensional beings and the reason that we perceive them as purely black silhouettes is because our brain cannot process what we see properly and attempts to fill in the gaps, thus the Shadows have no discernible features. It continues to theorize that, because they are not truly from this dimension, they can bend reality to a degree. Children are the most susceptible to the Shadows because their unblocked minds become targets.

I flip through more pages and my attention catches on a photo of a Shadow in a top hat and faint suit outline. Below the photo it reads *The Hat Man*. The article says this Shadow in particular is considered a more demonic entity that feeds from fear and negative emotions. Multiple witnesses claim when they encountered the infamous Shadow, the fear was so paralyzing that even breathing became difficult. The entity is considered a parasite, showing itself to mainly children or those suffering from extreme trauma, and uses this as its source of energy. A few anonymously claim the Hat Man attacked them and left bruising and shallow cuts during an attempt to be rid of the Shadow.

Nothing states how other Shadows act when around the Hat Man. Was it possible that Shadow behaviors change when around a more baneful being? Could it control or influence the lesser Shadows to its will?

I whirl around as the door shuts, pressing my back to the table to face Dad. His hair is combed neatly, his beard no longer a ratty, blond nest, and with fresh clothes he looks like the familiar happy go-lucky father I've grown accustomed to. He smiles at me and his gaze flits to the articles I had been scouring, his amusement fading. "Doing some light reading?"

I take a step from the table and shrug. "I was organizing and it happened to catch my interest." I tap my fingers on an article with the Hat Man plastered to the front. "Do you think that's what happened? Is there a connection to the Hat Man?"

Dad shakes his head and stalks to the table, pushing all the articles into one unorganized pile before turning to look at me. "I'm not sure, but it's something I've been looking into. There's so much conflicting information

I can't tell what's true and what's fictitious." He scratches at his beard and narrows his eyes at me. "Do not mention this to Aubrie. She has enough stress to contend with already."

The warning is clear and I nod my head. The feeling of déjà vu makes my head light; this is what we both did when Mom got sick, researching anything and everything that could have provided a probable cause for her demise in a desperate hope for a cure that didn't exist.

"I won't mention it. How long have you been searching?"

"Long enough," he says briskly. "Drop it for now. We can talk about this later." Dad assuages and turns from me, snatching his keys sitting on the counter. He glances around. "Kitchen looks nice. Grab the lasagna, we have to go."

I don't ask again and I follow obediently, grabbing the lasagna still cooling on the stove. I accompany Dad outside as he unlocks his car. The sweet scent of the rhododendrons tickles my nose as I walk past. I slip into the passenger seat and guard the lasagna in my lap as he backs down the driveway.

The drive lasts about an hour and my thighs ache from the heat of the pan on my lap. I try to keep the conversation light, avoiding the topic of Shadows, of Beltane, and of Mom. The closer we get, the harder it is to speak, and eventually I fall silent. The invisible hands dig into my chest until my breaths feel shallow and light, and my heart is pounding so fervently it hurts. The memory of Mom in the hospital haunts me, and the scent of alcohol swabs and disinfectant, of fresh bandages and muffled screams, is a stain on the pleasant memories that remain of her.

As the hospital comes into sight, it looms above the other buildings, burdensome with its dying insides. It's not the same hospital Mom died in, but it might as well be for how much good the doctors did. Countless memories surface of pulling into the hospital parking lot, silently slipping through the halls to Mom's room, and the tight smiles and tentative nods from the nurses as we pass. Always the same empty promise. "She's doing better." Always the same weary warning. "She had an episode."

A hospital is a living graveyard.

Losing Mom nearly destroyed me. Her absence has left an ever-aching black hole, a silence that cannot be filled, a space left forever empty. The idea of losing Desmond hurts more than I thought. It would break something inside me and I worry the shattered pieces would fill with an unknowable, all-encompassing darkness.

Soundlessly, I tread after Dad through the parking lot, past the hollow smiling nurses in the halls, and into the elevator. With us stands a woman just slightly older than me, silent and anxious, her red eyes downcast and hands wringing. The doors open and Dad steps out, so I follow. The floors are too pristine, the smell of antiseptic makes me want to gag, and I hear a patient moaning in another room.

I try not to recall Mom's moans of pain, or her screaming.

We come to a door that looks like all the others, and Dad softly raps his knuckles against the wood. "Come in," a voice rasps from the other side.

Shutting the door behind me, the room looks just like Mom's. There's a small bathroom, two chairs sitting along the wall, a TV mounted so the patient can view it, and the hospital bed where Desmond lays. Desmond is hooked to a machine that monitors his vitals; heart rate, breathing, blood pressure, intracranial pressure, and cerebral perfusion pressure. A tube is strung through his nose and EKG wires are stuck to his chest. An IV is hooked to his arm and a catheter is peeking through. He looks like a vodou doll, cushioned with needles and tubes and wires.

Aubrie sits in a chair closest to Desmond. Her face is pale and eyes sunken as if she hasn't slept in weeks. Her usually vibrant red hair looks dull and snarled in a messy bun atop her head. Even her eyes appear muted, the same diamond eyes Desmond has.

Unceremoniously, I offer her the lasagna. She offers a broken smile before she looks back at her comatose son. "Thank you for coming, Daire. You can put that on the chair."

I slink past Dad and set the dish down, glancing between Dad, Aubrie, and Des. "Your father has been a great help these past few weeks." Aubrie says solemnly.

"I'm just helping out family," Dad replies.

Back when Mom first passed, I remember the members of Karma's Knot taking shifts visiting us. Marc was around the most, but Aubrie and Desmond graced us often. Des did his best to comfort me, despite my threats. He did what he could to distract me and make me laugh, but when the laughs sounded empty and sadness swelled in its place, he held me. Not in a romantic way, but in a way so I wouldn't fall apart, so the nothingness stayed at bay.

Aubrie smiles and brushes a few dark locks of hair from Des's face. "The doctors don't have any answers. Despite their extensive tests and samples, their only recommendation is to wait for his possible self-recovery."

"Did he have any broken bones or punctures?" I ask, my voice sounding unnaturally loud in the sterile silence.

"Daire," Dad admonishes.

Aubrie waves him off. "Dallan, it's fine. She's as much family as my own blood. They grew up together." She looks at me and I feel small in the depths of her sorrow. "Strangely enough, no, he had no broken bones, no punctured lungs, no torn muscles, no bruised heart. His brain activity is as normal as it can be." She looks away, her eyes flickering over Desmond's still face. "Sometimes he will get nosebleeds or strange bruising will appear." She gestures to Desmond's hands which are spotted with dark blue bruising.

"What do the doctors say about that?"

"Some of them say it's a delayed trauma response or a possible bleeding or blood disorder." Aubrie sighs and places a hand to her temple. "Up until that night, my son was healthy. Yet here he sits, unresponsive in a damn hospital room with no answers forthcoming from the entire team of doctors working on his case."

The weight of her words makes me stagger, and I sit down before I lose balance. The similarities to Desmond's situation and Mom's is uncanny. Dad and I had identical pleas when it was Mom in that bed instead of Desmond. The fear leaves a bitter residue on my tongue.

"Aubrie," Dad says gently, placing a hand on her shoulder. "Deep breaths. Desmond is still here, and as long as he's here, there's hope."

"Don't they say people in comas can hear you?" I blurt.

Both of them look at me and exchange looks. "That's what the doctors claim." Aubrie mutters.

I stand from the safety of the chair and approach until I'm beside Desmond. Gently, I grab his hand and close mine around it. His skin is soft and warm, and I feel a wave of relief. A morbid part of me expected his skin to be cool to the touch, like he was already dead. I run a thumb over the top of his hand, tenderly over his mysterious bruises. His face is wrought with pain, his eyes are tight, and his lids flutter restlessly. His mouth is slightly agape, his face thinner from the two and a half weeks he's been hospitalized.

"Desmond," I begin, pushing through the embarrassment of Aubrie and Dad watching, "you've always been a thorn in my ass. You make everything a competition, and most days I want to slap you." I feel Aubrie staring at me and hear Dad chuckle quietly. "But you are family, you are *my* family, we are witches, we are magick, and whatever this thing is, you can best it. Everyone misses you." I bow my head. "I miss you."

"You are a brilliantly talented witch and clever and infuriatingly charming. I know I give you hell and I'm not going to stop now. Fight this and come back to us. If you really can hear me, you can hold this over my head for the rest of our lives, but you have to come back." I have to stop and inhale deeply to center myself. Heat sears behind my eyes and the persistent pulsing pressure in my chest from unshed tears leaves my throat tight. Crying means he's gone, but he's not gone. I lift my head and lean over to kiss his cheek. "You'd be elated to see I kissed you of my own accord. Don't get used to it."

"Come back to us, Des." Aubrie places a kiss to his other cheek, then his forehead, his hand. "We all love you."

The three of us sit in silence, heads bowed, each lost in our own thoughts. The possibility of losing Desmond terrifies me. We did everything together as kids and even as we got older we had each other's backs. Even if I wanted to tackle Desmond to the ground and slap the stupid out of him, I'd have fought anyone who hurt him. Losing him isn't an option. I'll do everything in my power to make sure he wakes up.

And I'll slap him as soon as he comes to.

A sudden knock on the door startles everyone, all eyes snapping towards it. An older man, gray at the temples, enters with a stethoscope around his neck. He wears all white, clipboard in hand, and takes in our little group before offering his most sympathetic smile.

I want to slap him too.

"Desmond has some visitors," the doctor observes in a frail voice. "I'm assuming you are his girlfriend?" he asks, addressing me.

I shake my head, glancing at Desmond as if even the idea of us being together would have him jolt awake. "No, we're family."

He nods. "Just as well." The man looks at Aubrie. "I would like to touch base with you on his condition..."

"Go ahead, they can hear it as well," Aubrie answers, back straight and eyes sharp.

"Good news is his vitals are strong and there seems to be no recorded brain damage. We want to try a few more scans on his brain and a few more blood samples to test for any underlying problems due to his strange bruising and nosebleeds." The doctor says as he reads off the clipboard. "I'll go over the logistics privately with you."

Aubrie nods and her attention strays back to her son. "And if the tests don't provide answers?"

"Then we keep doing what we're doing. He's young and healthy, so the likelihood of him waking up is very high."

I grit my teeth and look back towards Desmond. That's nearly the exact same words the doctors treating Mom kept saying. She was healthy for her age, and no amount of tests or blood samples could provide an answer or a cure. Yet she slowly went insane and died alone in a hospital bed. She hardly recognized any of us by the end.

Desmond can't share that same fate.

"Thank you," Aubrie says tonelessly.

The doctor drums his fingers on the clipboard. "The nurse will be by shortly to check Desmond's vitals and reactions." He turns to me. "Nice meeting you." He nods to Dad once before exiting, the door closing behind him.

"Thank you both for visiting. It means a lot." Aubrie smiles and gestures to the cooling lasagna. "And thank you for bringing some real food, Dallan."

Dad smiles. "Of course. It should taste better than whatever they serve here."

"I've no doubt." Aubrie sits back and rubs her eyes. "I'll be alright. I'll call with updates or if I need another real meal."

"I'll visit again in a few days," Dad promises before turning to me. "Ready, Daire?"

"Almost," I say and grip Desmond's hands tightly between mine. I exhale and focus my magick so it cocoons around him. A tingle warms my hands, and between my fingers I see a gentle green glow. It cascades and wraps around Desmond, slinking up his arms, his shoulders, down his back, and up to his head until he is glowing.

By the gifts of Earth; By the power of Cernunnos, Heal the heart beneath my hands; Mend the mind lost in chance; Hear my call; Blessed Be.

I watch the green glow flare and spark, heating my hands, before sizzling out and settling beneath Desmond's skin. When I remove my touch, the dark bruises he once had have faded to yellow. I hold my breath and watch his lids flutter, willing his eyes to open, for him to jerk awake and make a stupid remark about how I had kissed him. But he doesn't open his eyes. He still lies comatose.

I stand and Aubrie catches my hands. Her eyes are bright, hopeful, and it makes my heart hurt. Hope can be dangerous. Hope can kill.

"Thank you, Daire," she whispers, her attention solely on Desmond.

I have no words. I lean down and place one more kiss on Desmond's cheek. Dad squeezes Des's shoulder. Without another word, we leave the hospital room. As soon as the door closes I think I hear Aubrie sob, but I don't turn around. I keep walking.

I don't remember the walk to the car. I don't know how far down the road we get before I finally realize we left. Dad is listening to the radio turned low, his fingers tapping the tune on the steering wheel.

"I thought it would work," I murmur.

"Hmm?" he asks, glancing at me.

"I did a healing spell on Desmond. I asked for Cernunnos's aid. I thought it would work."

Dad sighs and squeezes my shoulder reassuringly, just as he did Desmond. "It did work, Daire. You healed his bruises. Who knows, maybe Cernunnos did hear your call and he needs more time."

"What if Desmond doesn't have more time?" I choke out, the tightness in my chest arduous.

"Desmond is just as stubborn as you. He will be okay." Dad comforts, but I'm not sure if he's saying it because he means it or if he's saying it because he's scared he doesn't.

"I hope so."

I can't lose him, too.

A few minutes pass and I feel Dad's worried gaze flicker from me to the road. Finally, he says, "So, I was planning on us making dinner together like the good 'ole days, but I don't want to cook again. How about we get takeout?"

"I agree only if we get Chinese."

"Deal."

The hour drive back to Dad's goes quickly and we pick up dinner on the way. We share the wontons on our way home and Dad turns the radio up loud enough so I don't have to think about Desmond. Or Mom.

Once back at Dad's, we sit in the living room and dish up the fried rice and orange chicken. The food is still hot and I eat greedily, my eyes drifting from my plate to the discarded articles still on the kitchen table. I lean into the couch and watch Dad help himself to seconds before speaking.

"So, how long have you been researching?" I ask nonchalantly and take another bite of rice.

Dad chews, eyes me cautiously, and swallows, his gaze drifting to the articles. "After Beltane."

"So you think it's the Shadows, too?"

"It's only a theory. The doctors haven't found any answers and the timing is too coincidental to dismiss." Dad takes another bite. His gaze is distant.

"I think it has something to do with the Shadows. What's the Hat Man?"

Dad sighs and lowers his fork from his mouth. "From what I've gathered, he is a Higher Shadow. He shows more intelligence than the others and he seems to have more power. I haven't had much time to research thoroughly, but if he's capable of causing physical injury, he may also have the ability to influence brain injuries."

"A Higher Shadow? Like Higher Demons?"

"In theory, yes. It seems they possess a cleverness unlike the average Shadow, a unique ability or physique that sets them apart."

"Is it even possible for a Shadow to manipulate humans so severely? If the basic Shadows can harm physically, what does that mean for the Higher Shadows?" The realization of the disaster hits me. If all Shadows have suddenly acquired the ability to physically interact and harm in our world, it would affect not just witches, but everyone. It would be as if an invisible barrier keeping them at bay never existed.

"Exactly. It's not much, but it's something."

"There could be others though? Different types of Higher Shadows."

Dad shrugs. "I have the same knowledge as you, Daire. I don't see why not, though. We know very little about Shadows in general, not to mention their types or capabilities."

I spread the rice around on my plate. Even if it was the Hat Man which caused Desmond's coma, it didn't explain the vision he had pertaining to blood magick. I've never heard of a Shadow that could manipulate the human brain and cause visions or brain trauma without blunt force. Hallucinations weren't uncommon, especially when between consciousness and unconsciousness. Demons were more likely to cause severe hallucinations and psychosis, but not comas. Typically they want their host awake and alive so they can be influenced and controlled.

There are parallels to Desmond's condition and Mom's. For both, the doctors have no physical ailments diagnosed, but where Mom was conscious and sinking deeper into psychosis, Desmond is unconscious and unresponsive. Mom, towards the end, became violent towards others and herself. Desmond has no way to interact with us, yet mysterious bruises and nose bleeds are appearing without a sign of physical force. It's possible it could be a side effect of a spell or hex. But both sicknesses happened suddenly and without warning.

Except with Desmond there's a possible lead as to why, which means there's a chance to reverse it.

It makes sense why Dad is so determined to help. Where we failed to cure Mom, saving Desmond would be redemption. It's a second chance.

We finish eating dinner with small talk and watching TV. I clean up our mess in the living room and wander into the sunroom where Dad has a massive bookshelf and his desk. Photos line the walls. There's several from back when Mom and Dad had first met, dates that followed, their wedding day, and then baby pictures of me, family photos, some with me and Klowbi. I pick up a framed photo of Mom and Dad wearing casual clothes, a sunset behind them, and Dad's arm is around Mom's waist. He's smiling down at her, oblivious to the camera, while Mom has the widest grin on her face, her head tilted towards Dad with one hand on her round belly. I smile and hug the photo to my chest.

I flip over the photo to find the picture's date. Instead of numbers, there's a small note tucked neatly in the lip of the frame. I unfold the paper and recognize the handwriting immediately; it's Mom's. As I read the first few lines, I realize it's a love letter Mom wrote to Dad.

"She gave me that letter the day the photo was taken," Dad explains from behind. I start and turn to face him. He holds out his hand and I offer him the letter. He takes it gingerly, as if the paper will crumble to ash, and reads it, a tender smile crossing his face. "I never expected to find such a beautiful woman to build a life with. Then here she is, the love of my life, pregnant with you. Life truly was bliss."

"You both look so happy," I observe, admiring the photo.

"We were. That woman was a lot to handle, but not once have I regretted starting a life with her, even after she was gone." He smiles sadly and looks at me. "I miss her every day. Our love surpassed all others I've known. After having you, seeing you grow up, I knew no matter what happened I made the right choice."

"I miss her so much," I whisper. The pressure behind my eyes burns and I inhale sharply to swallow my tears.

"I know, my little swan," he says and pulls me into a hug, kisses the top of my head. "But your mother would be so proud of you. You are so much like her and it's the greatest gift I've ever received, being your father."

I smile and hug him tighter. I hug him until the sorrow is a dull throb and I step back. Dad's eyes are glistening, but he smiles and kisses my forehead. "Alright, no more sadness." He gently takes the photo from my hands, tucks the note back in, and hangs the photo back up. "I'm going to lay down. You have free roam of the house."

"Goodnight," I say and give him one last hug before he leaves.

"Goodnight, Daire. You know where your room is?" He stops at the threshold.

"Same room it always is."

"Sweet dreams," Dad offers one last smile before heading to bed.

I tread to the kitchen and grab a mug from the cupboard. I set water boiling on the kettle and measure out peppermint leaf, damiana leaf, mugwort, and cinnamon before combining them in a mug. I pour the boiling water into the mug and add honey for sweetness and wait for the tea to cool and the flavors to steep. I watch the steam roil above, my fingers tentatively touching the ceramic.

This is a basic recipe for astral tea that helps with astral travel, among other benefits like insomnia and dreaming. I used to drink different teas when I was learning how to astral project to help me focus and master control.

I know I promised not to astral project until the strange phenomena with the Shadows calmed down, but seeing Desmond in the hospital doesn't sit right with me. The doctors found nothing, and the Hat Man lead isn't a guaranteed answer either. With the very little information Des confided in me regarding the blood magick and his vision, I have no idea where to continue looking. There are too many unknowns. But maybe there's an answer elsewhere.

Gaining astral insight outweighs my broken promise. And anyway, unless I tell them, they'll never know. Saving a life justifies a small lie. Surely there are greater betrayals.

I grab my mug and slink quietly through the hall down to the guest bedroom. I turn the lamp on beside my bed as the door clicks shut. Changing into a baggy shirt and sweatpants, I sit cross-legged on the bed and gingerly sip the tea. The warmth is welcoming in my belly and the flavor is comforting after such a dark day. I drink until nothing but tea leaves remain. Setting the cup down, I shut off the light and sink into the covers. I close my eyes and focus on my breath, relaxing my muscles, melting my bones.

And I wait.

Excerpt from Daire's BoS

Casting Magick in Astral Realm

Like most things pertaining to magick, intention is everything, but even more so in the Astral Realm. Magick will be instantaneous in the Astral Realm due to the constant pure energy source. But casting is much more dangerous because of this and cannot be hidden behind a false agenda. Any spell cast will reflect the caster's intention regardless of any outside influence. The only variable that is placed higher than intention is instinct. Even if the caster has fine-tuned their control over their magick, instinct will override this in order to protect the caster. Just like the body will have involuntary muscle spasms or reflexes our magick functions in a similar way. The caster's magick will respond accordingly in order to protect the wielder based off of instinctual threat. It is not understood as to why, just that it will.

Chapter 7

The feeling of flight in the Astral Realm is unparalleled to the physical world. It is smoother than bird flight, but harder to control. It's easy to get lost in the worlds, the creatures, the bizarre sensations and the eccentric, wild energy that makes up the Astral Realm. Only the brave and open-minded can explore this hidden realm beyond reality. Logic-reliant individuals find it nightmarish, while those who appreciate the nameless revel in paradise.

Daire careens expertly though the basic areas, or ground level, of the Astral Realm. She sees the house where she and her father lay in bed, the dirt roads snaking through the hills to the cabin, the forests and, as she ascends, the neighboring towns sparkling with cars dotting the everlasting darkness. She's soaring faster, shooting through the atmosphere so the towns look like small bubbles of light rather than life-size towns where people reside. The strange rush takes her nonexistent breath, since she does not need to breathe in the Astral Realm, as she breaks into space. The moon is bright and speckled with a strange blue hue. The stars are magnificent as they shimmer and sputter; the sun spitting flares of light that curl back into its mass.

She closes her eyes, bracing herself, and with a jolt her feet find purchase. The Astral level recognizes her, accustomed to her energy wrapped in its own.

She knows she's projected herself to the second level of the Astral Realm, one of the easiest levels to manifest and stay present in. This level is where she first began to train and test her abilities. A simple task now to bring herself here, when once it took severe concentration.

Daire smiles and opens her eyes. The relief of returning to boundless existence is indescribable. A home away from home.

Massive columns of rock jut from the ground, spiraling so high the tops cannot be seen. They are cocooned in vegetation at the base with a strange yellow hue to it. The vegetation climbs up the colossal pillars, growing sparser the further up it crawls. Trees the size of skyscrapers reach only a third of the way up the rock formations, seemingly dwarf-size in comparison. The pillars themselves are squared, each one with four jagged sides with the texture of bark and the density of bedrock.

Blues and grays bleed the sky, the same abnormal yellow hue fogging over. There is no apparent sun, or stars, or unnatural astrological phenomena. There are no clouds, but a gold mist hangs in the air, leaving golden droplets on the looming trees and dampening the pillars. The ground gives beneath her feet, the grass covered in golden dew, the dirt the color of bronze.

Daire brushes her fingertips on a bare patch of pillar and looks down to see her fingers covered in the thick, golden dew. She turns in a circle, but everywhere looks the same, with towering cliffs, spiraling vines and trees, and aurelian dew coating the surfaces. After many years in the Astral Realm, she's observed its tendency to recreate Earth with peculiar twists. Even knowing it isn't Earth, she has a sense of familiarity and comfort without distorting the wonderment of the level. But the higher the level, the more bizarre and unpredictable the world becomes.

Picking a direction at random, Daire begins to walk. Although the Astral Realm lacks physicality, it still exhibits reactions. She can feel the dense dirt compact beneath each step, or the light wind that whistles through the columns carrying a perfume of sugar and rot. The flowers can be plucked from the ground and water can still make things wet. Despite not requiring oxygen, Daire habitually breathes and could potentially drown if submerged in water, unless she remembers that physics don't apply. The Astral Realm is a mind game, a carnival of tricks.

It takes only a moment for a paradise to become a nightmare.

"Hello, old friend," Daire says tenderly, brushing a palm against a fern at the base of a pillar. As if in response, the wind responds with the scent of sugar overpowering the rot. She wipes the gold residue on her hip where it leaves a shimmering stain.

She smiles at the embrace. Daire believes that the Astral Realm is a sentient being, though difficult to understand. Perhaps not living, but it can respond without a conscious and exist without a body, react and feel like a creature. The energy embodies everything and interacts through the world, not limited to only one thing but an infinite everything.

Daire continues walking through the forest of pillars, eyes trailing up and searching for the tops, only to find them distorted and misted in gold. An indistinct whisper floats on the wind, sending goosebumps down her arms. The words are unclear and muted, yet there's a certain desperation that has Daire pivoting in a circle, searching for the source.

A shadow of movement on the bedrock pillars slows her pace. Clinging to the rock with eight spindly legs is a sand colored spider. It's lowering its bulbous body into the tree cover, a glitz of gold shimmering on its back and the tips of its legs. Looking closer, she finds an even larger spider already nestled in its spider-silk web. Even from where she stands, the spiders are imposing with their size, considering she can see the pincers speckled with dew drops and note the calculated placement of each of its legs tipped with razors. They had to be at least as large as a human adult, if not bigger, and undoubtedly craftier.

Despite knowing that the spiders can not physically harm her, she takes a few steps back from their web. Pain is different here too. Astral wildlife can't inflict pain on the projector, though the more intelligent and conniving creatures might try to take chase or force fear onto their victims. Vulnerability arises when the projector's mind begins to crack for the few seconds it takes to connect with the physical body. During that brief time, astral wildlife may return to the physical world and have the opportunity to inflict pain onto the projector. Daire, in all her experience, has yet to meet a creature strong and determined enough to cause true pain. Many creatures she encountered were curious and passive, but caution was still necessary in a lawless world.

The whisper is louder this time, a mixture of plea and frustration without words. Daire freezes and closes her eyes, summoning her magick to heighten the sound. A squelching echoes, followed by a masculine grunt of pain. Her eyes snap open, jogging towards the thread of sound, afraid to believe who she's hearing. She knows that voice, the baritone unmistakable, and the image of him jumping from a cliff with the Shadows snapping after him fills her vision.

A beam of light catches Daire's peripheral among the vegetation, and instinctively her magick flares, shooting off a purple scythe in the general direction. It goes short and the blade-like curve of the spell buries itself into the ground, leaving a massive gash. The bronze soil hisses and steams from the impact, a few ferns within range sizzling and curling from the purity of magick. Daire winces and shakes out her hands. She curses and attempts focusing on the whisper, clinging to the hope that it is Desmond, but there is nothing except silence.

Daire steps forward with caution towards the light's origin, stopping at the dirt gash. A Fayrie flutters from its hiding spot, a creature consisting a white glowing orb as its body with feathered beads of light in the shape of bird wings. It hovers for a moment observing Daire. She offers her hands, palms up and flat, to the Fayrie. Its light shimmers, the remaining dew surrounding it reflecting the creature's light, before it darts forward and sits in her hands. Its body is warm and her skin tingles where it sits, and despite seemingly being made of light, she does not wince while staring at it.

An unbidden laugh escapes her lips, startling the creature. It jolts upwards a foot before floating back down and settling back into her hands. Several more orbs of light with fluttery wings emerge from the thick branches and ferns. They float lazily around her, their wings gently brushing her arms and face and sending warm currents through her. "Hello, little ones," Daire murmurs. "I suppose you don't happen to know whose whispers I heard on the wind?"

Unable to communicate, the Fayries flicker and flutter around her, a few taking turns sitting on her shoulders. Another Fayrie attempts to join the first one already there. Their wings crisscross, amplifying the light, and her fingers tingle from the intensity of the creatures. Daire gently tosses one in the air, letting it float back to her hands, then tosses the other up until it rests in her palms. She bounces them back and forth, and besides a few bursts of hectic wing flits, they don't try to leave.

She tosses the Fayrie, lost in their mesmerizing light and bliss, when a piercing scream splits her reverie, louder than the previous whispers from before. Agony weaves within the shriek, her own vocal cords feeling as if they've been dragged over hot coals. Daire stumbles, the Fayrie fleeing into hiding, and the screaming cuts off with a jagged bleat.

The scent of sugar and rot is suffocating, her lungs spasming with the effort to inhale past swollen vocal cords. It feels as if she's the one shouting despite the sound being distinctly male.

Daire whips around, willing for the screaming to reappear if only to reassure herself he isn't dead. "Desmond," Daire rasps into the rotting wind. "Where are you?"

A static clings to her skin, teasing her tongue, and her vision darkens until all she sees is a disheveled figure crouching behind a metal chair banded with leather straps. Rivulets of blood roll down his forearm where his middle and ring finger have been severed. Sweat plasters his ink black hair to his forehead, his pulse hammering in his throat.

"Desmond!" Daire gasps at the sight, reaching out to pull him to her.

Desmond stiffens, his head swiveling in her direction just as a chuckle of death drapes across them, leaving verglas in its wake. "Don't let it see you."

Ice clings to his lashes, rimming them in glittering silver. "What is it?" Daire shifts to peak around the chair, and Desmond lashes out with an arm blocking her path, her eyes connecting on the missing digits still pumping blood.

"It is Hell," Desmond's diamond eyes lock on hers, shining with a newfound dread and hardened by weeks of torment. "It's a beast of the void, heralding ruin. It is Death."

A rumbling shakes the vision and the image of Desmond flickers, the frost coating his skin like sweat. A breathy growl layered with razors has Desmond cowering lower behind the metal chair.

He leans closer, his lips tinting blue from the climbing frost. "Never let it catch you. Never let it find you." Desmond stares at her with despondent diamond eyes, his lower lip trembling, and pushes her as a shadow figure looms behind Desmond, its eyes flickering like hellfire.

"Desmond!" Daire screams, grasping for his hoarfrost skin, and finds herself clutching air. She swivels, seeing only towering pillars of stone and golden dew coating her skin where the frost once clung.

Sugar and rotting wind shifts around her, and she wills her magick to send her back to Desmond. Focusing her energy, she sends tentative tendrils out in echoing vibrations in a desperate attempt to find him.

There is no scream in her head, no blackening vision, no death rattle of a demon stalking just beyond the horizon.

A static traces her tongue and there's a pull on her magick, as if something is beckoning for her. It is unlike the transition she felt when materializing next to Desmond, and it doesn't hold a demented aura like the Shadow with hellfire eyes. This feels like power, but one of benevolence and familiarity.

"I sense you," she growls as if issuing a threat to the newfound energy.

Daire exhales and closes her eyes, peeling herself from the Astral back to her body. The wind lifts, and the sharp flavor of static and storm overwhelms her. Daire reaches out with her magick, a flash of Desmond's doomed expression and bloody features burning in her mind, and a sense of dread that this is her final goodbye to her coven brother.

Chapter 8

After I returned home, the following days blurred together. Stuck in a mindless routine of working long, arduous hours at the Black Cat Diner, and often scheduling doubles to make up for my lack of hours over the past few weeks. Between waking before the sun, and laying to rest long after the moon has risen, I had little time to dive back into my research.

The memory of Desmond haunts me during the day and follows me into the night. His diamond eyes diluted with fear, the blood staining his skin, and the missing fingers on his hand felt like I was staring at a stranger. The terror that laced his words hung heavy in my mind, echoing repeatedly with a silent, suffocating dread.

It's a beast of the void, heralding ruin. It is Death.

The looming entity with hellfire eyes showing itself moments before Desmond pushed me from his side saved me from a fate certainly worse than death. He was stuck in a nightmare with no way to wake up from it. Resignation had lined his handsome features, as if accepting there would be no rescue.

Yet I saw a twinkle in his eyes, as muted as it was with pain and horror, when I appeared at his side, a sliver of hope rising to the surface. He was fighting as best he could, but he couldn't best this monster alone. I am his only hope for salvation.

Guilt gnaws at my insides from breaking the pact of not astral projecting, and knowing full well I will return as soon as I can in search of Desmond. If I can talk to him, glean as much information as I can, then I can tell the others what I've uncovered. They will be livid that I've gone behind their backs, but it's for good reason.

If I could talk to Desmond again, I could ask him more about the blood magick he had practiced and the sigil he had used. I could help him unmask this entity haunting him and bring him back.

"Daire." A familiar voice shatters my reverie. I turn, swiping the fatigue from my eyes and plastering on a fake smile only to find Klowbi standing in front of me. Her attire is covered in grease from helping out in the kitchen, and her smile is filled with genuine concern. "Are you alright? You seem really distracted lately, like you're here but not here at the same time."

I shrug off her worry and shake my head. "I could use some relaxation, but I'm fine, Bambi. Promise."

She eyes me and her concern melts away into one of her blooming grins. "Well, I was thinking, maybe after our shift we can go to the beach? I'll place an order with the kitchen to ensure it's ready when we're set to leave."

"Sure, it's a nice enough day for it." I say, glancing out through the windows. The sun hangs high and bright in the azure sky and the cool breeze balances the heat. Not warm enough for swimming, but perfect for sitting on the sand and listening to the ocean.

"I'll let the kitchen know." Klowbi peeks at the clock and I realize our shift is over. "I'll be up to change in a second. Meet you in the car?"

"Don't be late," I tease.

Klowbi heads towards the kitchen to place our order and I head into the break room. I clock out, rush upstairs, and enter our apartment before any customer can call for me. I splash my face with cold water in hopes of washing the weariness from my eyes then change into ripped black jeans and a soft gray sweater, plait my hair into a half french braid, and throw on a pair of silver boots. Grabbing my bag with runes and pentacles on it, I slip my Book of Shadows inside along with a handful of hastily written notes, articles on Shadows and phenomena, my book on blood magick, and two stones; obsidian and clear quartz.

With everything in hand, I start for the door, but pause to check beneath my bed. My stomach knots painfully as I lean down to search for my protection jar. Relief floods me finding it still whole. A part of me had feared that it would be shattered after entering the Astral Realm.

Satisfied, I shut my bedroom door and make for the exit without another look. As I make my way down the stairs, Klowbi passes, her face flushed. She stops and smiles at me, gesturing down to her clothes. "Let me change real quick."

"I'll meet you in the car," I say, then continue downstairs. I unlock my silver Honda and get in, throwing my bag in the backseat. I start the car and turn on the radio, listening to whatever station comes on first. I sit through two songs when Klowbi comes running up to the car with a takeout bag from the Black Cat Diner in hand.

"I have food," Klowbi announces, getting in and slamming the door.

I look her over once and glare. "You're wearing the same sweater as me."

She grins. "My sweater is pink." Klowbi gestures to her shirt with a giggle that could bloom flowers. "Now hurry, I'm hungry and want to eat at the beach."

I start driving, grateful that the beach isn't far with how delicious the greasy food from the bag smells. We pass the familiar shops; our favorite pizza place with red and white checkered awnings over the windows; the family owned coffee shop with the patio filled with patrons; a colorful park filled with dozens of kids running with giant grins on their faces and bubbles floating through the air.

Pulling into the beach parking lot, I barely have time to park the car when Klowbi jumps out and snatches a blanket from the backseat. She bounces from one foot to the other, blanket and food in hand, peering over her shoulder towards the sand and crashing waves.

"Hurry, Daire," she whines, holding the food up.

"I'm just as hungry as you are," I mutter with a roll of my eyes. I snag my bag from the back and lock the doors and follow Klowbi through the sand. We walk away from the busier portion of the beach before settling on a quieter section of sand. Klowbi lays out the blanket, plopping down and handing out our food before I have the chance to sit.

"I needed this." I pull my food into my lap and watch the squealing kids running to and from the water. I have my bag resting against my hip, an arm hanging over it protectively. I open my takeout and find fish and chips. I shove a few fries into my mouth and sigh. "Thank you."

Klowbi nods as she takes a bite of burger, a dribble of grease tracing down the side of her lip. "Yes, you did." she mumbles through a mouthful of beef.

"I'm surprised you remembered my meal."

Klowbi's eyes widen, her hand going to her chest in feigning insult. "I'm hurt you'd think I'd forget."

We sit in comfortable silence together, munching on our meals. The ocean is an angry blue gray as the waters lash the beach. Those who dare swim struggle as waves drag them down. Even the gulls give a wide berth to the tide.

"Are you alright?" Klowbi asks while chewing on a fry.

I nod and lick the grease from my fingers. "Yeah, I'm fine."

Klowbi gives me a doubtful look. "You just seem off ever since you got back from visiting your dad."

Shrugging, I take a bite of fish so she has to wait for my reply. A flash of Desmond cowering sears my lids, and I blink several times to clear the image. "It's been a stressful week."

"Is it Desmond?" she coaxes gently. The wind is blowing her auburn locks across her face, a few hairs sticking to her lips. She swipes them away, watching me intently. I don't answer and take another bite of my food, my hunger ebbing.

"It is. How's he doing?" She massages her hand and her eyes tighten at the pressure.

"No better than before. He's still not showing any signs of waking up and the bruises and bleeding aren't stopping." I stare at the food in my lap and set it aside. I ate half, but talking about Desmond curdles my stomach, knowing where he is while I sit comfortably in the real world. I shift and cross my legs, swinging my bag onto my lap and pulling out my notes before transferring them to Klowbi. "Dad said he thinks it might relate to the Shadows."

"The Hat Man? Who's that?" Her eyes flick back and forth as she skims the pages and my sloppy handwriting.

"Another Shadow, more powerful than the ones we saw at Beltane. Dad thinks there might be a correlation between the Hat Man and Desmond." I point out a few other articles with my notes written in the margins. I'm careful not to show her my new notes I'd written after returning from the Astral and my theories on the entity hunting Desmond. "This article made it sound like there are several other types of Shadows. I didn't have time to research further for validation."

Klowbi glances up and returns my notes. "So you think it was the Shadows?"

"So does Dad. The timing of Beltane is too coincidental, don't you think?"

She nods slowly, her lips thin. "Do you think it was the Shadows we saw or the Hat Man?"

"The Hat Man seems more powerful, increasing the likelihood it was him," I state, observing a seagull approaching our blanket. I frown and wave my hands, making it jump and hobble off before circling back to Klowbi's side of the blanket.

"I never saw a Shadow at Beltane with a hat," Klowbi recalls, her eyes fluttering to the seagull. "I only saw the usual ones."

"It doesn't mean he wasn't there."

"Neither does it mean that he was," Klowbi counters and grabs a fry and tosses it to the gull. It caws and picks it up, ruffling its feathers and taking flight to eat in peace. "How do you know it was a Shadow? Perhaps it was a demon or some other entity."

After seeing the entity in the Astral, I can't rule out that it isn't a demon. It was monstrous and ghastly, and demons could take many forms. Even though I'd seen only a glimpse, it resembled more of a Shadow than any demons I'd researched. Yet I've never seen a Shadow with eyes of fire nor as malignant as this entity. The demon theory holds weight, since it isn't residing in the physical world and instead inhabiting the mind, it would have more freedom to do as it pleased.

"Demons typically need to be summoned and temporarily tied to our world in order to exist physically. If it were demons that attacked on Beltane, someone there would have had to summon it. Or there's possession, but the host has no control over that and the signs of possession are incredibly difficult to hide." I frown and twist my pendant between my fingers. "Based on that, it makes sense that the attack on Beltane was caused by Shadows. However, I've never heard of anything like this happening."

"Maybe the Shadows are evolving?" Klowbi offers while nibbling a fry. She tosses the end to a curious gull hopping by.

"Maybe." I mutter and glance at the other books in my bag.

I reach inside and glide my finger across the spine of my blood magick spell book. I hadn't told anyone about Des's vision or his new thirst for blood magick. Klowbi wasn't a fan of that type of magick, but she respected other practices of the Craft. Maybe it was time I let her in.

Klowbi tosses more of her fries to the gulls. A smile is on her lips and her cheeks are rosy from the wind. She looks at me and her smile falters, her brows furrowing. "What's that look for?"

Making up my mind, I pull out the book and offer it to her. Some pages are tagged with peeking sticky notes. "I wasn't completely honest about what happened with Desmond the night of Beltane."

Klowbi stares at the book as if it might bite. Tentatively, she grabs it and begins to skim through where I had left bookmarks on possibilities of the magick Desmond used. "How is this relevant?"

"That night, Desmond confided in me and said he had started practicing blood magick."

Klowbi's lips tighten, but she nods and looks at me from the pages. "That doesn't sound like him."

"No, it doesn't. He said he had a vision. He was doing a spell, though from his description, it sounded more like the beginnings of a ritual. Weeks passed, but the vision persisted until he made it a reality."

Klowbi swallows and glances at the book in her lap. Her face has paled, her freckles stark along her cheeks and nose. "What was his vision?"

"He lit thirteen white candles and wrote a sigil in blood before burning it. I should have asked about the sigil's appearance. That would have been helpful." I lean over and flip to a page covered in sticky notes with different runes and sigils drawn across them.

Klowbi traces a finger over several sigils before looking back at me. "What did the sigil signify?"

"He said it meant appearance, but all the sigils I searched with the similar meaning didn't give the impression of something sinister. He saw it in a vision. Who knows if that's what its true power meant." I watch as a gaggle of seagulls, now finished with their portion of fries, come forward again. I raise my hand and flick my wrist in their direction. A webbing of red shoots from my palm and they squawk and scatter, taking off further down the beach. A feather shakes loose and sits in the sand. Klowbi gives me a disapproving look but doesn't comment.

"Do you believe the vision is significant?"

"My instinct says yes."

Klowbi hands me the book back and I close and return it to my bag. "What if he was unknowingly summoning something? Maybe that's why you can't find anything. It's not about Shadows or blood magick."

I stiffen from Klowbi's insight as realization dawns.

"You're brilliant, Klowbi!" My excitement wanes and I drag my fingers through the sand. "I know very little about the Otherworld. If it were to be a demon or something worse, I wouldn't even know where to begin looking."

Klowbi straightens, her face brightening. "We could ask Xuan. She's knowledgeable with demons and spirits. She could help narrow it down."

"You think she would reach out to the Otherworld to help us?" I ask skeptically. Xuan is the last person I want to get involved with Desmond's wellbeing and her magick leaves a bitter taste in my mouth, especially knowing she can manipulate my power. The idea makes me grimace.

"Yes, she would help. I'll call her tonight. I planned on going over there this weekend."

I avert my attention as my stomach twists from the sudden excitement in her eyes at the mention of her. "Fine," I say begrudgingly, imagining Desmond screaming in pain, and I wince. "It's worth a try."

"Perfect. She won't mind," she assures, giving me a playful bump of the shoulder.

I force a smile, realizing she's misreading my hesitation. "Hopefully we can find answers," I croon. "You and Xuan seem to be really close."

Klowbi grins and nods her head without missing a beat. "We get along really well. We have this connection, an unspoken bond. She's super sweet." Her cheeks flush as she speaks and I doubt it's from the wind.

"I'm glad." It takes all my effort to keep my voice light and hide the venom in my tone. My magick spurs and heats my belly. I fist my fingers to keep my magick in check.

Klowbi massages her hand, her fingers flexing and twitching at the pressure. "Are you in pain?" I ask and lean closer to gauge her aches.

"It aches," she admits, lifting it between us. "My orders today were heavier than normal. I think I put too much strain on it."

"Here," I grab the clear quartz and obsidian from my bag. I hand her the chunk of smooth obsidian and gently fold her fingers over it. I grip the quartz in my left hand and I cup my right over hers. I'm careful as I touch her scars that I don't apply much force.

"Quartz amplifies and channels magick; obsidian heals." I call on my magick as warmth emanates from where I touch her scars, and a river of blue snakes along the tissue.

"My phantom pains worsen when a storm is coming," she says absently, watching our hands. "Similar to when joints ache when a storm is near."

I nod and focus my attention on our hands. The warmth increases and the blue is getting brighter, thicker, like glowing vines suctioning and wrapping around her hand. I feel her muscles relax and notice her fingers are no longer twitching against mine.

"Daire," Klowbi says and my gaze flickers to her face for an instant. "Thank you for telling me about the vision Desmond had. You can rely on me. I want to help you and Des. So do the others." I stay quiet and my eyes drift back down to focus on healing her aches. "Can you promise me something?"

"Of course, Bambi."

"Promise me you won't keep secrets from me. That if something happens or you need help, you'll tell me." Klowbi sounds desperate, her voice tiny.

This time I keep my gaze on hers and her wide doe eyes fill with concern. She reminds me of a child with her innocence and her compassion. She loves so openly without thinking of the consequences, not considering that people lie or inflict pain on purpose. She always seeks the best in people, even when they've given her every reason not to.

"Of course," I assure and force a smile. The smile is empty and my heart pangs with guilt. "You're my best friend."

Klowbi's attention shifts down to our hands. "Thank you."

I'm not sure if she's thanking me for healing her hurt or for my hollow promise. I release her hand and sit back. The blue healing slowly fades and sinks into her scar all the way up to her forearm. I offer her the quartz, which is now swirling blue on the inside; remnants of the magick that it was channeling and enhancing. I open up her fingers and switch the obsidian with the quartz. "It has some healing magick in it. Next time you are in pain, grip it in your fist and focus your energy on it. Or use it in a spell. It should help."

She nods and squeezes the quartz in her hand before slipping it into her pocket. I put the obsidian back in my bag. It's warm from her grip.

"It doesn't hurt anymore."

"I'm glad, Klowbi. You shouldn't have to hurt."

This isn't the first time I aided in her pain, but she rarely asks when it bothers her. On the hard days, I've caught her holding back tears from the phantom fire with her convinced a tooth is still lodged in her flesh. In those moments I wish I could go back in time to stop her from ever walking into the ocean, to protect her like she should have been back then.

Even though I'll do near anything to protect her, my list of secrets continues to grow and my guilt along with it. There are answers in the Astral I'm certain that will help me save Desmond. If I come clean about projecting, she'll try to stop me from returning and hinder any chance of rescuing Desmond from the same fate as Mom. If he's taken from me, I'll never forgive myself for not protecting him too.

Chapter 9

"This might not even work. This is a waste of time." I grouse as we walk up to the front door. The outside porch light is on as the sky ripples into pinks, oranges, and purples.

Klowbi jabs me in the ribs and side-eyes me. "You don't know that. It's not going to hurt anything," she replies and offers one of her warm smiles. "And if we don't discover an answer, it doesn't mean it was a waste. We'll know where to look next."

"I don't like it," I mutter and knock on the door.

"I know."

The door swings open and Xuan nods to us with a flicker of a smile on her face before stepping aside to let us pass. "Come."

Klowbi leads the way and Xuan shuts the door behind us. A prickling feeling has my skin itch, and I fumble for my pendant at my throat. I trace the pentacle with my fingers, clutching it in my fist.

"We will be in my room," Xuan states. Her dark hair is in a ponytail and a few stray locks frame her face. She's wearing a cream and pastel sweater and baggy sweatpants, unnervingly normal clothes for conversing with the Otherworld.

I follow Xuan down the hall into her room. Her door is ajar and the faint scent of smoke greets me. Candles are the only source of light, and they cast ominous shapes dancing along the walls.

"Where are the boys?" I ask as I meander about her room.

Klowbi studies a demonology book she plucked form the bookshelf. Xuan stands by her soot colored bed, her expression reticent.

"Boys' night," Xuan replies. "They went to the bar."

"Not surprised," I mutter and survey her room.

The bookshelf is filled with books about the paranormal, spirits, demons, vodou, and several types of magick. Decorating the empty spaces between books are strange talismans; chicken feet, mystic amulets that undulate like a water current, tokens with veves emblazoned on them, stone figures with grotesque features that are borderline human, and a case with foreign symbols on it large enough to house a dagger.

Along the windowsill sit several potted plants. I recognize one as the rose of Jericho which aids in communing with spirits and protection against negative energy, amongst other benefits. Bird skulls, fangs, snake spines, paws, and even the skull of a canine sit atop a desk. Resting amongst the skulls are several vials filled with unknown minerals and liquids, appearing dark red, almost black, in color. Candles flicker by a set of bones, giving the impression that something still resides within. A boline with a finely sharp blade and a bone handle sits beside the skulls. I lean in closer to examine the curved blade and note that a feline has been engraved into the handle.

"A gift," Xuan offers as an explanation and gestures to Klowbi. A smile brushes her almond eyes before falling guarded again.

I frown as Klowbi studies an array of poppets of all different colors lined up neatly along a shelf. "That's from me," she adds beaming, nodding to the boline, and walks back towards us.

My stomach twists at the admission. "It's beautiful," I say and turn to the table with three chairs surrounding it. The candles are beginning to melt and drip wax. Only paper stacks and a pen on the table, nothing unusual.

Xuan nods in acknowledgement and motions to the chairs. She sits facing us with the candlelight dancing in her dark eyes.

"You aren't using the board?" Klowbi asks and points to the Ouija board carefully stashed away on the bottom of the bookshelf. She goes over and sits in one of the chairs and I follow behind. My spine is rigid, and when I meet Xuan's gaze, I can't see the whites in them.

"No, I don't need that," she says dismissively with a secretive smile, "but it helps coax certain spirits." Xuan's gaze flits between us before she tips her head in thought as if she's making up her mind. "Let's begin." She touches the paper sitting between us. "This will be used for the spirit if she needs it."

"She's going to write to us?" I ask dubiously.

"If she needs to. She will speak to me and I will relay it to you. It's good to have multiple sources for communication," Xuan explains, her tone clipped. "I have only a few requests before I reach out to my contact. Firstly, respect the spirits I commune with. They are witnesses to your words and actions. Any backlash is of your own accord. Secondly, no magick while I commune with the spirits. Too much potent energy at once can confuse and ire them. Thirdly, speak to them as you would anybody else. Just because they are dead does not mean their existence is naught. Questions?"

I hold my tongue at Xuan's accusation that I'd use my magick during the session. I was acquainted with the risks and provoking a spirit was far from my intentions. Sucking in a breath, I imagine holding my magick in a sealed box and locking it away until after the session. The feeling of separation leaves a hollow ache in my chest, but risking it to come loose during the session would be much worse.

"Who are you contacting?" Klowbi pipes up beside me. I gape at her, unable to hide my surprise. She seems intrigued by the prospect of communing with the dead. Her eyes, even in flickering candlelight, gleam with fervor and I wonder if this isn't the first time she's spoken with the dead.

"Farah," Xuan answers. Her expression softens and her eyes appear to lose the harsh glare they always hold as the tightness around her mouth lessens. There's a fondness towards the spirit.

The name sounds familiar, but I can't recall where. Klowbi brushes a stray hair from her cheek and clasps her hands on the table as she wiggles with excitement in her seat. "I like Farah."

"And she likes you," Xuan confirms, looking between the two of us. I frown, realizing that I'm the one with less knowledge on who we're conversing with. "Ready?"

Resigning myself to ask for more details about Farah later, I huff my answer. The sooner it's over, the better. My magick coils in my belly with anticipation that boils my insides.

"I'm going to reach out to her," Xuan explains quietly and closes her eyes. Her lids flutter incessantly and her fingers twitch on the table. Suddenly her eyes fly open and she inclines her head, watching us. It reminds me of a feline. "She's here. You may ask."

Klowbi and I exchange glances, and I decide to take the lead. "Hello Farah," I say aloud, "I'm Daire. We need your help, if you're willing?"

Xuan glances to her left, and I follow her gaze. I see nothing, but I feel a strange coldness to the air, a distinct taste of bitter sour coats my tongue. My magick squirms as it tries to acclimate to the sudden shift in the air.

"She says hello. Proceed with your questions."

"Have you noticed anything strange in the Otherworld? Anything that feels off?" I stare in the direction of Xuan's gaze and frustration rises in my cheeks. Feeling that something is here and unable to see it is a new level of helplessness.

Xuan sits quietly for a moment as she studies the empty space before shifting her attention back to us. "Farah says she hasn't noticed anything severely profound, but the energy in the physical realm feels different." She pauses and looks to the left. "Elaborate."

Silence as we wait for her reply. The candles flicker and I notice the flames are smaller than before we started as if starving of oxygen.

"She perceives a newfound heaviness and resistance in our world like something is pushing back." Xuan frowns, her brows furrowing with thought.

"Is that abnormal?" Klowbi asks.

"Spirits often need to establish a connection to our world for communication. The more a spirit practices, the simpler it becomes. However, the initial attempts are typically difficult due to their unfamiliarity with manipulating our world." Xuan tilts her head in the general direction of Farah. "Farah and I have been communicating for years. In theory, there should be minimal resistance, but it is extensive. The higher the resistance, the more energy we both have to expend to stay connected."

"So, there is *something* affecting the Otherworld," I reiterate, and touch my pendant. "Is she able to determine what is causing the push-back?"

Another pause. "She can't tell for sure, but whatever it is, it's dominating."

"How long has there been resistance? Has it changed?" My magick is still humming in my veins, but it feels calmer than it did earlier. Apparently it doesn't feel as threatened by Farah's presence.

"Over the last several years, resistance has risen gradually, almost indiscernible. Within the last seven months, it has increased more rapidly. Similar to a power surge, in layman terms." For the briefest second, something flashes across her face before falling still. Most likely the darkness playing across her face, morphing her expressions.

"Is it possible it's the Shadows manipulating the Otherworld somehow?" I ask.

Xuan sighs and shakes her head. "No, she doesn't think it's the Shadows. The energy doesn't match the signals they normally give off. The energy source is strong, persistent. Hypnotic even. The Shadows are normally quiet. Not nearly as intrusive as this."

I swallow and pinch my pendant harder. Is the entity haunting Desmond even a Shadow or is it worse than I thought? If we're up against something more malevolent than a Shadow, or even a demon, will my magick even be enough to save him?

"Hi Farah," Klowbi begins in greeting. "Could it be another spirit?"

"Doubtful," Xuan says immediately, glancing to the left, then returning her gaze to Klowbi. "Farah agrees with me. Definitely not another spirit."

Klowbi turns to look at the empty space. "Could it be a demon?"

It looks slightly ridiculous seeing her speak to the air. Though I suppose it's just as ridiculous being able to see magick. At the thought, a flare of magick shoots through my veins and I tense. Something is pulling at my energy and pressuring it to react despite my efforts to soothe it. I grit my teeth and try to focus.

"No, demons tend to give off a foreign energy with obvious baleful intentions. The energy she feels does not stray towards one idea of good or bad, it merely is. It's the existence, the intent of survival for the energy." Xuan pulls at her bottom lip, frowns, and drops her hand.

"What does that mean for us?" I ask, failing to keep my frustration at bay.

"The energy will do whatever it takes to thrive. Like a lion, hunting is necessary for survival, not out of spite. Similar concept, the energy will do what it takes to survive." Xuan's gaze flickers to the flames, which are now little licks of fire on wicks. "The prey perceives the lion as a threat. The energy simply follows its instinct; survive. Even if that means disrupting our world."

"Disrupt our world?" Klowbi whispers beside me and picks at a thumbnail.

"Do you mean it can hurt us?" I ask into the empty space, dread thickening in my throat. "What does it need to survive?" I can't hide the desperation in my voice. Whatever this creature is its hunting us as an energy source which means Desmond could be caught within its snare.

"Daire," Xuan warns and narrows her eyes at me.

"Is it trying to hunt us?" I ask as my magick sparks and a crackle of scarlet red burns the tips of my fingers. Tiny candle flames flicker before consuming the entire wick. The flames are massive as they threaten to burn a few stray wisps of my hair, and I lean away from the searing heat. Hot wax starts to coat the table, appearing like melted flesh from bone. I squint against the sudden blaze in the darkness to allow my eyes to adjust.

"Daire!" Xuan shouts. The slanted black pools of her eyes are glaring into mine. Her eyes dart left and she gasps. Her jaw clenches and she closes her eyes, her lids fluttering fiercely, but when she opens them again, the concern is impossible to ignore. "Something's wrong," her voice is tight. "Farah isn't here."

"What's going on?" Klowbi whimpers beside me.

"Where is Farah—"

Xuan's voice is abruptly silenced as the desk jolts and pounds on the floor. The legs tremble from the force, and the sound of splintering wood breaks the panicked silence. Papers and pen fly into the air as if taken by wind with several pieces ripping and twirling downwards to the floor. A piece catches light and begins to curl and smoke as the fire eats at it. My magick thrums hard in my veins and dark spots spatter my vision. Streaks of red bounce between my fingers and palms and it feels so potent my muscles ache from holding onto the power spiraling inside.

The fire from the candle wicks are scorching and climbing in height. The wax is melting at an extreme rate as it oozes over the desk. A strange sensation of being watched settles over me, my skin prickling. I turn back to the desk as wax dribbles to the floor, and a shape takes form in the molten wax.

A surprised squeak escapes from Klowbi as the three of us watch an invisible finger drag itself through the blistering liquid, creating one long continuous shape. An unintelligible voice slinks through my mind as terror lodges in my throat, my magick smoldering in my palms. I watch in muted fascination as a symbol takes form in the wax before every candle goes out in a puff of smoke. The overhead light sparks to life and I wince.

The intense burst of energy, along with the muttering voice, fades with the smoking candles. A tremble shakes my bones despite the sensation of being watched having fled with the ominous presence. My magick coils defensively in my fists, waiting for my command.

I stare at the strange symbol, captivated by the mystery it brings. Klowbi pushes away from the desk to stand in front of the closed door, her eyes wide with fear and arms crossed over her chest. I lift my gaze to find Xuan glaring at me and I return the hostility.

"What was that?" Klowbi asks breathlessly. She's pacing back and forth across the room, keeping her distance from the table. Her eyes stray between us and the wax.

"I sensed your magick spike," Xuan growls through clenched teeth. "I warned you no magick."

"I kept my magick under control around Farah," I snarl back. "My magick didn't spike until the fire ate the candles. It was reacting to whatever else was here with us."

"You have no control," Xuan spits out and closes her eyes, jaw clenched.

Klowbi stops pacing and turns to us, sliding a piece of paper beneath her foot. "If it wasn't Farah, then who was it?"

Bending, I snag paper and pen that had been tossed to the floor. I hastily attempt to recreate the image hardened in the wax onto the paper. My mind whirls with the new evidence. The creature in the Astral haunting Desmond, the strange discordance in the Otherworld, the new violent tendencies of the Shadows, and the entity that intervened during the seance must be intertwined. This entity *wants* to prove it is watching us and that it's powerful. And maybe it will lead me to answers.

"It could be the foreign energy in the Otherworld."

Klowbi frowns and brings a finger to her lip, tearing at the nail. "It felt wrong."

I huff and my attention flits between the wax and the paper. "That's an understatement."

"Farah is back," Xuan blurts, attaining attention from us both. "An external force pushed her aside to claim her connection. She didn't have any warning before it dragged her back and forced her out of the connection with me. Something extremely powerful, unlike any energy source she's encountered."

"Shouldn't you have sensed it, then?" I accuse and stand to my feet. I slip the paper into my pocket to research later. "Shouldn't you feel the energy shift if connected to the Otherworld?"

"I sensed your magick first, and by the time I realized there was something else with us instead of Farah, it had already connected with me," Xuan says cooly, her eyes a black puddle of venom.

"Does Farah know what it was?" Klowbi interjects. Her meek attempt at keeping us from blaming one another.

"No," Xuan answers stiffly. "Not completely, but she thinks what-ever it was has been influencing the Otherworld." She pauses. "The entity drained her energy switching with her. She's too weak to stay connected."

"Is she alright?" Klowbi asks and I'm surprised her concern is so genuine.

"Yes, she'll be fine," she says and turns her back to the corner. Xuan stands and faces me, the animosity a tangible thing between us. "You broke my rules."

"It was a defensive reaction to the being *you* welcomed into the session." My magick burns in my core, starving to lash out at her hostility. My fists are clenched, nails digging into the flesh of my palms. "The biggest concern should be what the hell replaced Farah."

"Even I felt the shift," Klowbi adds and her face flushes red when we both turn to face her. "It felt like something was watching us. The air felt heavy, too."

"Too much concentrated power," Xuan answers. "Probably a mix of Daire's magick and the entity's."

"And yours," I snap with vehemence. "You use magick to commune with the spirits."

Xuan tilts her head as if sizing me up and narrows her slanted coal-black eyes. "I do, but not nearly enough to cause such a substantial disturbance."

"This 'substantial disturbance' is not me. My magick did not cause this." I gesture to the wax symbol. "The entity that pushed out Farah did. Do you think it's trying to communicate with us?"

"Or manipulate us," Xuan suggests cynically. "Those symbols could mean many things. It's best to tread carefully if you plan to utilize it."

I scrutinize the wax symbol in an attempt to burn it into my mind. It looks like a strangely written "m", with two crisscrossing lines con-necting the middle and the last line leaving sharp angles instead of the traditional curve.

"Regardless, it reached out to us. Which means it could do it again," I say with a slip of excitement.

"Daire," Xuan warns, stepping forward. "Do not go out seeking this entity."

"Xuan, this is a huge discovery. This is the lead I've been searching for," I contend, placing my hand on the hardened wax.

"This discovery cost us. This entity knows where I live now, putting Alko and Niko at risk," Xuan quips, and each word hits me with brute force. "And it knows who you and Klowbi are. It'll be much easier for it to find us."

I glance at Klowbi, whose face has gone pale, her freckles harsh against her skin. Steeling myself, I meet Xuan's accusing gaze. "Then let it come. I'll be prepared next time."

Xuan gapes at me, exasperated. She opens her mouth to respond, but a door slams, making us all jump and turn to face her closed bedroom door. Hurried footsteps approach and the door swings open, revealing Alko's terrified face and a baffled Niko behind him.

"What happened? Are you guys alright?" Alko strains, barging into the room before anyone can answer. I watch as his fear turns into understanding as he surveys the room. The scattered papers, our shocked expressions, the melted stubs of candles, and the wax symbol engraved on the desk. As his eyes land on the wax, his expression hardens into fury and he turns to me. His normally careful and kind eyes reveal unbridled fury. His jaw clenches. "You need to leave. Now."

I stare at him, unable to form words to explain what really happened. I've never seen Alko angry like this. He's seething. "Alko—"

"Don't." His voice sends an involuntary shiver down my spine and I take a step back.

"Hey, everything's fine, right? No need to be dramatic and kick them out," Niko interjects and pops his head into the room. I smell booze on his breath.

Alko shakes his head, his eyes never straying from me. "Get. Out."

"We'll leave," Klowbi mediates from behind me. She grabs my arm and begins to lead me out the door. "I'm sorry," she whispers as we pass by Alko. Alko's expression softens when it lands on her, but as I pass his jaw tightens. Niko looks at me and shrugs. His eyes appear glazed, probably from the alcohol.

We pass through the living room and hear the others speaking softly in Xuan's room, but we exit the front door before I can make out any words.

I hadn't realized from the chaos inside that there was thunder roiling in the tumultuous air. The winds are brutal, whipping my plaited braid, and the rain is coming down in torrents. We both scramble for the car, slamming the doors shut and shivering from the rainstorm. A flash of lightning arcs across the sky, the thunder that follows rumbling my breastbone.

I back out of the driveway and head towards home with the windshield wipers whipping as fast as they can. The raindrops sound like hail pinging on the roof of the car.

"I knew it was going to storm," Klowbi murmurs in the passenger seat. When I don't respond, she sighs and swipes a stray raindrop from her cheek. "Don't worry about Alko. He's never been thrilled with the idea of the Otherworld. It makes him anxious."

"How did he know?" Another bolt of lightning breaks the dark sky. The thunder shakes my bones.

"Farah, most likely." I give her an incredulous look. "Oh, I guess you probably don't know," she amends sheepishly. "Alko is connected to the Otherworld too, just not as strongly as Xuan. He can sense and speak with spirits, too. He just doesn't like it."

"So Farah probably told Alko something was wrong when she lost contact with Xuan. That makes sense. Why does he hate the Otherworld?"

"I don't think he hates it. He respects it, but he's afraid of it, too." Klowbi gazes out the window with a pout to her lip. "I don't really know why. I never pushed the subject, but that's my guess."

"Alright, so what's the story about Farah?"

Klowbi glances at me with arched brows. "I didn't realize you didn't know about Farah."

"The name sounds familiar, but that's about it."

"You remember Juna, right? She would take care of Alko and Xuan as kids. Farah is her daughter. She died while volunteering in Haiti." Klowbi picks at a hangnail and winces when a well of blood breaks the surface. "I don't know all the details. All I know is after Farah died, she reached out to Juna and Xuan to comfort them. She's been in contact with Xuan since then."

"I remember Juna. I met her once," I say, recalling the older Haitian woman. She reminded me of a loving grandma with clever eyes and a talent for vodou magick. My magick hisses at the thought.

Klowbi yawns and rubs her eyes. "She's sweet, if not a little old-fashioned."

We sit in silence for a few moments. I'm mulling over the night when Klowbi pipes up again. "I'll talk to them about tonight once they calm down. They're upset now, but they'll understand. I'm sure of it."

"Thanks, Klowbi," I reply with a half-hearted smile. My stomach twists when Alko's seething expression fills my head. I'm used to Xuan's accusations and our constant bickering, but having the calm and collected sibling turn his ire towards me sinks my heart deep in my chest with shame.

And now they're keeping secrets from me. Does Niko know that Alko can commune with the dead? He's known Alko far longer than Klowbi or I. He probably does. So why, after five years, did this never come up, even in passing?

I glance over at Klowbi, whose head is pressed against the glass, her eyes closed. My shame lessens seeing her peaceful expression. I have to protect her from this tangle of lies and secrets I'm weaving. If the entity comes for me, let it, but I will fight until my last breath if it ever directs its violence towards her.

Another bolt of lightning cracks the obsidian clouds, igniting the entire sky. When my gaze falls towards the road I jolt and resist the urge to slam on my breaks as our car rushes towards the Shadow standing in the center of the road. My heart lurches into my throat as we barrel towards it and its eyes flash white, a thorny smile painted on its lips, before it disappears into the haze of the storm. A shiver steals down my spine as we pass where it once stood, my tongue sandpaper against my teeth.

Klowbi hasn't moved and is oblivious to the Shadow encounter that has my blood racing. Purple threads of magick pulse from my fingers, climbing up my arms until I curse and shake the mana off.

I grit my teeth as anger overtakes the fear. I won't cower as it picks off my friends. Next time I see it, I'll be ready.

Thunder rumbles overhead as lighting cracks the raging sky. And this time, I smile.

Excerpt from Daire's BoS

The Fifth Element

Everyone is familiar with the four elements; water, air, earth, and fire. Very few know there is a fifth. It is everywhere, everything, all encompassing and yet it cannot be seen nor touched, it cannot be tasted or heard. It just is. It is the balance of all beings, the invisible tether that binds it all into one. It symbolizes the unknown, the eternal cycle of life and death, to feel what isn't, to comprehend what won't ever exist. It weighs heavy on all our shoulders and yet it's the only solace in this plane of existence. And without this fifth element nothing could exist as it is, perhaps nothing would exist at all. It is in all things, forever infinite, and in this way I suppose that makes us all infinite in its wake.

Chapter 10

The next morning I wake for my shift at the Black Cat Diner as if nothing had happened the night before. The note with the rudimentary drawn symbol sits in my Book of Shadows. I drew it over and over in the book, hoping for a hidden recollection to emerge. I scoured the pages in a vain attempt, praying Mom had alluded to the image, but I found nothing.

Once we arrived home, Klowbi went straight to her room. I retired to mine, but my thoughts were too loud and filled with Shadows to sleep so I read through every book with a codex of sigils and symbols in search of the meaning of the image drawn in wax. I don't remember passing out, but I woke to sheafs of paper all scrawled with the symbol.

The symbol feels familiar like a fragment of a memory I can't quite place. I need to talk to Desmond and figure out what he knows which means returning to the Astral Realm. It feels like ages since I last saw him soaked in fear-sweat and blood. It's only been two weeks, and if it feels like ages for me, I hate to imagine how tortuous the time is for him.

"Daire." A deep voice jolts me from my thoughts as I swivel on my heel. "I need you to focus. You're almost finished with your shift, then you can daydream to your heart's content. But I need you to do your job."

"I'm sorry, James," I say and rub my eyes. "I didn't sleep well last night. Just tired."

"Sleep once your shift is over," my boss says gruffly. His thick black beard moves as he speaks, and he turns to walk away before stopping and looking back over at me. "If it slows down, I'll let you off early, but do your job until then." He scrubs a hand over his bald head and walks back to the kitchen.

"Yes, sir," I mutter after him. I head over to a dirty table and stack the empty dishes and half drank cups onto a tray while hastily swiping crumbs from the table with a wet rag. If I can make it through the last part of my shift without any issues, I'll have a few days off to focus on research. Luckily it slowed down after lunch, so my chances are high I can escape early.

Behind me, I hear the front door open and close. I keep my back turned, hoping another waitress or server will help whoever walked in so I can focus on cleaning the tables. My job or not, I can only stand so many stupid customers before I have to leash my tongue.

"Ma'am," a male voice says directly behind me. I grit my teeth and straighten my spine, taking a few extra long breaths to push away my frustration and plaster on a fake smile.

"Yes?" I say as sweetly as I can, but the forced pleasantness is obvious even to me.

"You look like you're enjoying yourself." Niko comments with his familiar Cheshire grin. "What's a guy gotta do to get some service around this joint?"

"Ask nicely and you'll find out." I frown at the longboard propped against his leg and give him a knowing look. "You better not ride that in here. I'm already on thin ice with James today."

Niko glances around as if already guilty and shrugs. "I'll be sneaky."

"How kind of you," I mutter, grabbing the last dirty dishes from the table. "Did you come here for me or for food?" I ask and find myself lost in his emerald eyes. My magick flutters with the sensation of butterfly wings along my skin and tear my gaze away, willing my cheeks not to flush.

"Let's start with a chocolate milkshake and an order of loaded fries and see what happens from there," Niko answers and nods at the barstools. "I'd like my favorite waitress to cater to my every whim as well."

"Yeah, you don't ask for much, do you?" I huff, arching a brow and walking with him. Cigarette smoke wafts from his clothes. My nose wrinkles and I try to mask my grimace.

Niko takes a seat on one of the red stools, twisting back and forth. "Never. So where is Maddie?"

"Maddie's back-up for the kitchen today. Why do you care?" I slip the dirty dishes through the window to the kitchen.

"I want to see my favorite girl. Give her a little love so I can get a little something too." Niko wiggles his brows suggestively and I gawk at him in disgust. "I'm kidding, Daire!" He bursts into laughter and I roll my eyes as my cheeks flame. "But if I don't get extra whipped cream free of charge on my milkshake, you're not getting a good tip."

"You're an ass," I say and suppress an amused smirk. I gather the ingredients and toss them in the blender, grateful for the raging blender to halt any of Niko's teasing. I pour the concoction into a tall glass and make sure to give him a towering wall of whipped cream and a cherry before sliding it to him.

Niko takes a sip and smacks his lips in clear satisfaction. "Delicious," he says, twirling the straw. "You got time to chat?"

"Not long. I told you my boss isn't pleased with me." My eyes flit to the office doorway as if expecting him to be leaning against the threshold watching me.

"Tell him I was an extremely needy customer that wouldn't leave you alone." Niko drums his fingers on the counter. There's a pale band of skin on his ring finger still and my heart lurches at the sight. A part of me had hoped he'd be wearing it again.

"He recognizes you."

"Then he knows you're not lying. I'm very needy."

"That's the understatement of the decade," I grumble, leaning against the counter. "So, what brought you here? It's not an easy trek on your longboard."

"It's not that bad of a ride, and it's a nice day out. I needed to escape the house." Niko shifts on his stool and pulls at a stray lock. His sandy hair is covered with his maroon beanie and he's wearing what I deem his stoner sweatshirt, the one with thick, coarse threads in black, red, green, and yellow.

"I'm surprised they didn't put the house on lockdown."

Niko takes a long sip of his milkshake, offering me a half smile. "A little paranoia never hurts."

"A little?"

"I can see both sides." The bell behind me rings, signifying that an order is ready. I turn and grab a plate of loaded fries from the window and slide it to Niko. He grabs a handful and chews, chasing it down with his milkshake.

"If you came to lecture me, I'll give you a to-go box and kick you out." Reaching for a wet rag, I viciously scrub the countertops around Niko. My knuckles are white from my grip and my magick pulses with my mounting frustration.

I sense Niko watching me. He doesn't say anything so I lift my eyes to meet his gaze. I swallow my anger as best I can and lessen my grip on the rag. Even my magick softens and calms into a gentler thrum in my heart.

"I didn't come to lecture you." His voice is placid, and he hesitates before continuing. "Xuan explained what happened after you and Klowbi left. She said that your magick flared and then the entity appeared and ripped Farah away. She was adamant that your lack of control is what put everyone in danger—"

"My magick flared *after* the entity switched places with Farah. My magick was fine around her, comfortable even."

"I believe you," Niko says genuinely, and from the sincere look in his eyes, I believe him. My defenses soften again, and I suck in a breath and nod for him to continue. "I've been around you for a while, and with your power, you have control. The night of Beltane proved that much."

"Thank you."

He nods and shovels a few more fries into his mouth. "For the record, I wasn't there when it happened, but I argued in your defense. I reminded

Xuan she knew the risk of reaching out to the Otherworld, and helping you with whatever it is that you're doing. The blame is not solely on you. She wasn't happy, but she didn't deny it either. She was upset that she allowed something like this to slip past her."

"And Alko?" I set the rag aside.

"High emotions and being under the influence of alcohol," he explains with a breathy laugh. "He was still in bed when I left this morning. Complaining he had a headache."

"Poor guy. I imagine they aren't pleased with me still."

"I'd keep my distance for a while if I were you. Give them time to cool off." Niko finishes off the last of the fries, licking the grease from his fingers. "From what Xuan told me, whatever entity did connect with you during the session is dangerous. She made it sound like it might try to reach out again."

"It's possible."

"Xuan mentioned a symbol was left behind. She said you wrote it down before leaving."

"Yes, I did. I presume she's not pleased about that either, is she?"

"No, she wasn't. She's concerned you're going to go looking for it."

I don't answer.

"Are you?" Niko's brows raise.

"I'm going to figure out what the symbols mean, but I'm not going to attempt to summon it." I cross my arms and chew my lip. I'm starting to wonder if Niko came of his own accord or if Xuan sent him as the messenger.

"Do you have it with you?"

"No," I snap, "so you can report that back to Xuan." I snatch the empty plate the second he takes the last fry and slide it through the window to the kitchen.

"I'm not her spy," Niko growls and my insides flutter. His jaw is set defiantly and the hurt of my accusation burns in his emerald eyes. "I wanted to see you." He takes in a sharp breath and looks down at his nearly empty glass. He reaches for his pocket and pulls out a pack of cigarettes, pauses, and slips them back into their usual place. Niko reaches for his longboard and spins the wheels with his scarred fingers. "I came here to ask you on a date, actually."

I sputter for a moment, my blood racing in my ears. My magick purrs and brushes against my skin, urging me to accept. I open my mouth then close it as my fingers fiddle with my pendant.

"You look surprised," he teases, the mischievous glint back in his eyes.

"You caught me off guard," I manage after finding my voice. "When is this supposed date?"

"You have to say yes first." He smirks. My cheeks flush as his features sharpen and I drink in his devilishly handsome features.

This is a bad idea. I should say no.

"Sure," I say before I can bite my tongue. "Yes, I'll go on a date with you." A soft plume of pink escapes my lips and my magick zips through my veins until I'm lightheaded.

"I'll pick you up at eight." He finishes off his milkshake and stands. Niko digs into his pocket and tosses a twenty on the counter. "Keep the change." He winks and walks out the door with a wave of his hand. As soon as he's on the sidewalk, he jumps onto his longboard and flashes me a wicked grin before rolling down the sidewalk out of sight.

I shake my head and make change with the twenty, stuffing the tip into my pocket. Grabbing his glass, I hand it through the window and spot James emerging from his office. He assess the empty tables of the diner and a pleased smile cuts through his beard.

"Daire, finish cleaning the tables and clock out. Get some rest." He disappears back to his office without waiting for a response.

I speed through cleaning the dirty tables and clock out. I escape out the side entrance and bound up the steps to my apartment. Unlocking the front door, I find Klowbi is sitting in the living room watching TV. She straightens and laughs as I walk in.

"What's got you so smiley?" she teases, lounging on the gray couch with her feet beneath her and a book on her lap. A window is open, sunlight draping across the flowers and herbs hung nearby. Crystals sitting on the ledge glitter in the natural light and the room smells of lavender and jasmine.

"Niko came to visit," I answer, walking into the living room. The tree of life tapestry hanging behind the couch sways in the slight breeze from the open window.

"What did he have to say?" she asks as a conspiratorial grin plasters itself to her face.

"He asked me on a date." My cheeks ache from my smile and my magick buzzes happily within my breast.

"Did you say yes?" She moves so she's leaning over the end of the couch, her arms holding her weight. I nod my head and she laughs, falling backwards onto the cushions cheering wildly. "Yes, about time!"

A laugh bursts from my lips. "He's picking me up at eight."

"It's about time you gave him another chance."

"He caught me off guard."

"A rarity if he got you by surprise. She approved of him."

"Mom?"

"Yeah, she thought he was charming."

"That's because he brought her flowers."

"That's because he wanted to impress her. And you. You two are surprisingly compatible."

"Why is that surprising?"

"You aren't the easiest to get along with," Klowbi admits with a rueful expression. "Desmond's been trying for your heart for years and has gotten nowhere. Niko has known you for less than half that and he's made an impression on you." She pauses and gives me a knowing look. "I see the way you look at him."

I huff and my joyous mood shutters at the mention of Des. "And how do I look at him?"

"Like you either want to murder him or kiss him."

"Most days it's the former," I mutter.

"I think it's the latter."

I wave a hand as if to brush off her comment. "I'm going to get ready."

"Have fun." She turns her attention back to the book on her lap. "You'll have a great time imagining murdering him tonight."

"Shut up," I say and head to my bedroom.

Closing the door behind me, I immediately gravitate towards my Book of Shadows where I'd drawn the image. The original drawing hangs out the book's closed edge. My excitement slips away as I recall Desmond in the hospital and his pleas for help in the Astral. Guilt rakes my insides. I'm going on a date while he lay comatose and stuck in a nightmare. My focus should be on researching the symbol's meaning, not going on a date with Niko.

But I can't back out now, and I'll have ample time to research over the next few days. A few hours for myself is reasonable before diving into this without any distractions.

I pause as I pass my altar on the way to my closet. Ever since Mom died, I've neglected honoring Lilith as often as I used to. When I needed her aid to heal Mom, she did nothing to help me after my years of loyalty. I'm still bitter, but with Desmond in peril and the entity an active threat alongside the Shadows, I need the blessing of a deity to see this through.

Pursing my lips, I continue to my closet and pick out my outfit for tonight. I settle on a gothic crimson dress, a snake ring with black-red eyes, and a silver ring with garnet as its stone. The colors and jewelry are symbols of Lilith, and I pray she's prideful enough to take notice this time.

With an armful of crystal and herb offerings for Lilith, along with my outfit, I pad to the bathroom for a bath ritual. I make quick work of filling the tub with steaming water, lining the lip of the tub with four black candles and three red. I alternate onyx, garnet, and obsidian between the candles, lighting them as I go. As a final touch I pour rose and night queen incense into the bath and sprinkle fresh rose petals on the water's surface.

"Please accept my offerings. Don't let him die, too."

I strip down and sink into the tub as I call on my magick and hover my palms underneath the surface of the water, and I intone.

"Lilith, I invoke you; Lilith, Goddess of darkness, illuminate my temple in black light; Kindle in me the flesh under the domain of the mind; Lilith, Great Mother, offer me the cup of knowledge; Lilith, Timeless abyss, you destroy my fears revealing the secret knowledge; Lilith, Unleash your legions against my enemies; Consume me in your embrace, in the swirling starry horizon.

"*Renich Viasa Avage Lilith Lirach*," I croon. My magick reiterates Lilith's enn, and the vibration in the water increases until it's lapping against the rim of the tub despite me sitting perfectly still.

An otherworldly energy sinks into my flesh, stirring the water into a deepening crimson. The petals atop the water wilt and dry, crisping from a piercing red to deadened black. A feminine whisper brushes my ears, the words indistinct, yet I recognize the dark and mesmerizing energy.

Lilith is here.

"Dark Mother," I whisper and smile. "I feel your essence. I need your help."

The fire flares, but fear does not strike my heart. I sense the difference in her presence to the entity's, and though she is considered a demonic goddess, her energy is pure and ever-knowing, unlike the foreign and heavy press of the entity.

My child. Her voice growls and the water hums.

The candles simmer out and smoke puffs from the wicks. As suddenly as she arrives, she is gone, leaving me in the remnants of her power. Disappointment stiffens my spine. I was hoping for more, a whisper of guidance or a cryptic message. Yet again she has left me with nothing.

The returning swell of abandonment darkens my mood. I exit the tub, drying and dressing quickly while I clean up the ritual remains. I inhale deeply, forcing my bitterness down and think of Niko. His handsome face makes me smile and my heart flutters as I finish plaiting my hair and slip on my swan pendant. I apply a deep silver shadow to my eyelids and a crimson lip stain to match my dress.

I walk into the living room where Klowbi sits watching TV, her feet propped up on the coffee table. She perks up as I enter and smiles so wide her molars are visible.

"You look gorgeous, Daire."

"Thanks, Bambi."

"Niko is going to lose his mind when he sees you."

"Thanks." Prepared to see Niko, my mind wanders back to the previous night when the Shadow intercepted us on the way home. "Klowbi I forgot—"

A knock sounds on the door, and we both glance in the direction.

"I bet that's Niko," she says. "Whatever you want to tell me can wait. Answer it."

Our home is warded and I won't be out all night. I'll tell her when I'm home. The topic of Shadows and death can wait a little longer.

"If you don't answer the door I will," Klowbi teases with a dramatic flip of her hair.

Before Klowbi can make good on her threat, I brush off my dress, and answer the door.

Chapter 11

"Wow."

Niko is staring with his mouth agape and eyes wide as he scans me up and down. After several seconds, he regains his composure and clears his throat, rubbing the back of his neck. "You look beautiful."

I smirk and eye him up. His hair is half tamed with gel and his maroon button-up is a little too big, but his jeans are new without any holes or stains. Leaning in, I place a brush of a kiss to his cheek and smell pine trees and mint. I'm grateful the stench of cigarettes doesn't cling to his skin like it usually does. When I pull away his cheeks are red and his pupils are dilated.

"Hi," Klowbi says from behind me and waves from the couch with a knowing smile.

"H-hey, Klowbi," he stutters, turning to me and offering an arm. "Shall we?"

Taking his arm, I glance over my shoulder and wave goodbye to Klowbi. "Lead the way," I tell him, shutting the door.

"Bring her home at a decent time," I hear her call.

"Before midnight," Niko answers with a grin and a wink.

After locking the front door, Niko leads us down the stairs and exits out the side door of the diner. I glance back in surprise, having half expected the date to be at the diner. He doesn't make a lot of money working at the gas station in town, so I wasn't expecting an expensive traditional date.

"Where are we going?" I ask tentatively as he leads us to a black car parked nearby. "Is that Xuan's car?"

"Yes, I'm borrowing it. For our date," Niko replies as if that were obvious.

"Does she know you borrowed it to see me?"

Niko unlocks the car and opens my door. I raise my brows at him, but oblige as he shuts it and rushes to the driver's side and gets in before answering me. "I didn't give her specifics. It's none of her business what I do in my free time."

"So, what did you tell her?"

"I'm visiting a dear friend."

"And she believed you?"

"I also had to promise I wasn't picking up drugs."

"Ah, so there was a catch."

"If you're the catch, this high tops anything I could buy." Niko grins with a side eye in my direction.

"Aren't you a silver-tongued Casanova? You never answered my other question."

"It's a surprise."

"The answer to my question or the place you're taking me?"

"Taking *us*, this isn't a kidnapping. We're staying in town, but the destination is a surprise." His eyes can't seem to decide if they want to stay on the road or me.

"You know I don't like surprises," I mutter while fidgeting with my silver ring.

"You'll enjoy this one," he promises. A phone chimes and he shifts in his seat while digging it out of his pocket, glancing at the screen and tossing it into the cupholder with his jaw set.

145

Out of curiosity, I sneak a peek at his phone screen. Despite being heavily cracked, I can still read the illuminated text. I look pointedly at him and note the tension in his shoulders as a frown pulls at his handsome features. "Do you need to answer that?"

"No, it's not important."

"Are you sure it's not a family emergency?"

"Did you look at my phone?" he demands and immediately grabs it again.

"I saw that your mother texted you," I confess softly. "Are you still not talking to them?"

Niko shakes his head and throws his phone into the center console so it's out of sight. "No, and I couldn't care less."

"That's a lie. Clearly you're worried about your family. Why are you avoiding them?"

"You wouldn't understand."

"I might."

"You won't."

"Try me."

"Damnit, Daire," he growls, sending goosebumps down my spine. "You're relentless."

"It's one of my defining traits." I pause. "You can trust me."

Niko levels his gaze and my belly heats at the look in his eyes until he turns back to the road. Magick hums in my fingers and a thin pink wisp curls from my palms and floats in his direction. "Fine," Niko concedes and I close my fist before my magick can reach him. "They don't see their son when they see me." His voice is bereft of its usual charm and banter. "What they see is the addict. They see who I was when I used and all the ways I disappointed them."

"But you're clean now. Aren't they proud of you for overcoming it?" I have minimal knowledge of that dark time in Niko's life. It was a taboo topic, but he spoke of his family even less, as if he wanted to forget them entirely.

Niko bursts out laughing, startling me. Magick pops in the air between us with bursts of crimson and red. A small bubble floats towards his hand, popping against his skin and his body jolts, his eyes darting towards me as he readjusts his grip on the wheel.

"For Easter, I went over for dinner because I hadn't seen them in months and Mom kept calling. I smoked a cigarette on the way because I didn't want to go, but I couldn't cancel because Xuan was dropping me off. When Mom hugged me, she caught a whiff of the cigarette and I never thought I could have disappointed someone so much with a stupid stick of nicotine. She wouldn't meet my eyes." Niko shakes his head and his lip curls as he speaks. "Dad wouldn't even shake my hand." He looks at me and sucks in a deep breath. "They're hardline against sinning, and I think the only one I didn't do was murder."

"It was only a cigarette."

"But to them it was still a drug. I might as well have been high on pills with their reactions," Niko growls. "There was wine with dinner and both of them had a glass. They gave me grape juice, the same shit Nadene drinks. When I asked for a glass of wine instead, I thought Mom was going to pass out from shock. Dad didn't say a word to me. He just stared. Like he was waiting for me to fuck up again."

"It's not like you're not old enough to drink."

"Drinking was my gateway to partying, which eventually led me to drugs. To them, drinking is just as bad as getting high." Niko sighs and rubs his eyes. "The only one who gave me a hug when I left was Nadene. She's only six. She's too young to understand why her big brother doesn't visit very often or why Mommy and Daddy were so upset."

"It sounds like they don't understand, so they react the wrong way." I place my hand on Niko's shoulder and give it a brief squeeze. My family is everything to me, I can't imagine not having their love, or at least their sympathy.

"I've accepted my role as fuck-up," Niko admits with a nonchalant shrug.

"What about Nadene?"

"What about her?"

"She might be too young to understand, but it doesn't mean you should punish her the way your parents are punishing you. She clearly loves you, Niko. Give them a chance to understand and try. At least give them the opportunity as they should to you. Not all of us have the chance to try and make amends."

Niko glances at me and there's guilt in his eyes. "I'm sorry," he mutters. "It's not easy being looked at like I'm a monster by my own parents."

"Kids run from monsters," I tell him as he pulls the car over into a deserted parking lot near the hiking grounds. I used to trek them every summer with my parents, and we would hunt for the perfect spot to have our routine picnics. The memory makes me smile despite the strings of grief attached to it.

"What does that make me?" he asks halfheartedly.

"Human. It makes you human." I reach over to grip his hand in mine. "Maybe your parents will never understand, but give Nadene a chance. Give her the guidance you should have had."

"They never let me spend time with her," he confesses and looks out the window, appearing morose. The forest is dark, mirroring Niko's mood, and the only illumination is the car's headlights. The sky is a deep plum purple with the beginning splash of stars.

"Start small." I gesture to the phone stashed between us. "Replying to texts is a good start."

"Tomorrow." He meets my gaze and smiles, bringing my hand to his lips and placing a warm kiss to my skin before gesturing to the forest. My hand tingles and I resist the urge to curl my fingers through his hair and pull him closer. "But tonight, I'm with you. We're here."

"At the hiking trails?" I ask as he shuts off the car and exits. I follow him and take in my surroundings. No one else is here and the trails are too risky to walk in darkness.

I hear the trunk slam behind me and turn to find Niko holding a blanket and two flashlights. He tosses me one and I catch it without fumbling. He smirks in approval and nods to one of the trails ahead. "Follow me."

"If you were anybody else," I grumble, clicking on my flashlight and following him down the dirt path. "I'd have gut punched you and gone home."

Niko chuckles and shines the flashlight in my direction, blinding me before turning back around. "I'm honored you haven't left me puking my guts out on the side of the road."

Leaves crunch beneath my boots as I walk, and I'm grateful for not wearing heels. "Don't thank me yet."

Without the lights from the vehicle, and only the fragile beams from the flashlights, the darkness is heavy within the flora. Soft whispers of thickets and the glisten of eyes from treetops watch us from the safety of branches. In the distance, there's a croon of an owl and a strange, high-pitched shriek from high above. The light bobs with my pace and I have to duck several times, following Niko off the beaten trail to avoid branches scratching at my eyes. My dress snags on a thorn bush and I carefully work it free to not tear the fabric, but my leg catches it from the release and leaves a thin trail of blood. I swipe it away, smearing it, and continue the trek silently as my eyes dart between the trees, searching for faces within the black.

"How much further?" I swipe a stray curl that escaped my braid from my face.

"It's straight ahead," he says and stops in the middle of a small clearing. We are surrounded by woods, everything pitch black.

Stepping into the clearing, my breath hitches when my attention rests on a nest of blankets and pillows with small tea light candles embroidering the edges, emitting a gentle light. Amongst the blankets is a picnic basket and a box of wine. Approaching the nest, I glance up to witness a stunning night sky adorned with infinite sparkling stars.

I stare at him, unable to hide the wonderment of it all. "You did all this?" I ask and bend down to run my fingers across the blanketed nest.

"It took a while to find the perfect spot," he confesses, and I hear his footsteps approach from behind.

"It was well worth the search," I compliment with a shy smile. I fluff a pillow and nestle down on top of it. "I didn't know you could be a romantic."

Niko chuckles and plops down ungracefully beside me, dragging the blanket across both our laps. Now that we aren't walking, the night air nips at my heated skin, and the extra warmth from the blanket, and Niko, is welcome. "I'll take your flashlight." He offers his hand palm up and I hand it over. He clicks them off and sets them aside so we can see only by the stars and the tea lights nearby. "I had a lot of time to think about how a date with you would go."

"Clearly," I say with a hint of sarcasm. "How did you imagine it?"

"I was the smooth, suave gentleman that you couldn't keep your hands off of. You confessed your undying devotion to me and"—Niko pauses and reaches for something beside the picnic basket revealing two beer glasses—"we drank lots of wine."

"Box wine?" I ask, tipping it gently with my fingers.

"Yes, there was a sale at the liquor store." Niko chuckles and begins filling the glasses.

"Very classy with the beer glasses," I tease and take the filled mug from him, cradling it in my hands.

"I thought you'd like my extravagant tastes." Niko grins and lifts his glass. I clink my mug against his and we both take a long gulp. The wine tastes of sweet cherries with a sharp zing afterwards.

"I have to admit, I'm surprised." He's studying me, his eyes flickering to my tattooed fingers that hold the mug filled with wine, to my lips as I speak, to my multi-colored eyes. "It's much better than I could have imagined, especially on such short notice."

"I'm a man of many talents," he says smugly, flashing me a grin. "A romantic connoisseur."

"I wouldn't go that far." I laugh and take another drink. The shadows make Niko's face appear rugged, with sharp angles and hard planes. He looks more intimidating in the light, a harsh attractiveness, and the magnetism of his deep viridian eyes triggers my magick to static and spark. Magick curls around my mug and kaleidoscopes through the wine, creating an outlandish shimmering coral glow throughout.

"You can admit I have exceeded your expectations," Niko croons, reclining back on the pillows slightly.

"Not just yet," I murmur and lean forward to touch the picnic basket centered in front of us. "Did you pack filet mignon in here? I could get past the fact we're drinking box wine if you did."

Niko sits up and snags the basket with a finger and slides it between us. "Unfortunately it's not filet, but I like to think it's the next best thing." Setting the mug of wine aside, Niko lifts the lid of the basket to reveal elegantly wrapped pastries. The sweet aroma makes my mouth water and I lean so close I inhale the mint on his breath. He lifts a pastry nestled in a napkin and offers it to me. I take it and my grin feels the most genuine it has in a while.

"You remembered," I say softly and take a nibble off the scone.

"Blueberry scones, your favorite." Niko beams, clearly proud of himself.

Content, we both sit in the nest of blankets and pillows, sipping our mugs of wine and nibbling on fresh pastries. We watch the distant sparkle of diamond shards scattered amongst the inky black and listen to the sweet whispers of the trees holding the secrets of the wind. I feel at peace, momentarily forgetting the fear of eyes in the dark and the twisted ache in my heart from my mother's absence.

Sucking in a breath of cool air, I glance to Niko who is still watching the stars, the sharp planes of his face deepened by the artificial lighting. "Thank you."

"What?" he says through pastry and looks from the sky to me. His pupils are blown wide, revealing only a ring of emerald.

I swallow as my walls crumble and avert my gaze, swiping crumbs from my lap. "Thank you. For this."

"For taking you out into the middle of the woods at night?" he says sarcastically and smirks. "If I knew that's all it took, I'd have done this years ago."

"Smartass," I grumble and run my nail along the lip of the mug, feeling it catch on the unevenness. "I meant for allowing me time to mourn. I treated you horribly afterwards..." I pause and glance back up at the sky. The stars, for an instant, seem to have dimmed.

"Oh," Niko murmurs and stares out into the forest. We sit silently and I hold my breath, anticipating his response. Finally he returns his attention to me with a wry smile on his face. "Honestly, I didn't want to give this another try. But Klowbi was persistent, saying you needed time. That being alone was how you were coping. I despised you after you abandoned our group. Or I tried to. But even when I tried to forget you, I couldn't. And Klowbi is a good friend. If it weren't for her, I don't know if I'd have done this."

"Klowbi put you up to this?"

"No, she convinced me you were worth another chance." The tension between is heavy, an electric charge building the longer we stay apart. "I'm glad I took her advice."

"I treated her poorly, too. And Dad." There's a heavy weight of guilt pressing on my heart. I was so lost in my grief I ignored the people I still had. Instead of facing it, I hid in the Astral and pushed everyone away.

"You were grieving. You put up your walls to protect yourself. I get it." He shrugs and leans forward again to heft the mug to his mouth. "Just promise you won't do it again. To me or anybody."

"I can try."

"I suppose that's good enough." Niko downs the rest of his wine. He shifts forward and pours himself another glass. I sip from my mug and sputter when I catch sight of the band around his finger. Niko pauses mid-pour, his face filled with worry as I wipe wine from my chin. "Are you alright?"

Once my throat is clear, I nod and gesture to the malachite ring. "You're wearing it."

He grins and lifts it closer, admiring the turquoise glitter embedded in the wooden band. "Figured if tonight is a fresh start, I should commit to the act."

"It's a convincing act."

"That's the point."

We exchange looks and drink from our mugs. My heart pounds in my chest as my magick skates beneath my skin, elated at this discovery. He's letting me back in and the thought terrifies me. Clammy sweat dampens my palms and I wipe them on the blanket.

"You know," Niko begins and his voice is thick, "I despised the fact you wouldn't let anybody help you. I hated that you wanted nothing to do with us. I hated that you pretended everything that happened the past few years never did. You were a stranger."

"Niko—"

"Let me finish before I regret this," he cuts me off and runs his fingers through his hair, mussing it. "Once I realized you wanted nothing to do with us, I tried forgetting about you. Some days that meant getting so high I could barely move and other days it meant getting blackout wasted. I tried going on dates, but none of the chicks were you. I tried going to the bar, but none of them made me feel how you did. I couldn't erase you." His cheeks are flush and his heartbeat is a steady pulse in his jaw. "Klowbi couldn't stand my sulking so she cornered me and said to wait one more day and that you'd be back. I didn't believe her until the night of Beltane. That was the first time since the funeral I saw you."

"What are you trying to say, Niko?"

"I waited one more day for months," he growls and sets the mug aside and leans so close his minty breath teases the stray hairs around my face. "Seeing you again, I witnessed a new version of you. You're distant and cold."

"Then why are you still here?"

"Because I see you. I understand you better than you believe." Heat emanates from his skin and I can almost imagine the taste of his tongue on mine. "But your presence still feels like absence."

"Then make me present," I whisper, and a red wisp exhales from my lips and curls between his. Niko's eyes widen and he inhales the wisp, his jaw twitching in time with his heart.

His lips crash into mine and steal my breath. He cups my face and I feel his fingers thread through my hair, tightening and pulling so my neck is bare. A growl rumbles in his chest as his tongue trails from my mouth, tracing my jaw down to the soft flesh where my heart beats frantically beneath my skin. I grab for his shoulders, my nails sliding along his back

153

beneath his shirt to trace his warm skin. He gasps against my neck and shifts on top, gently leading my head down to the plush blankets.

My magick is raging in my abdomen, an incessant cry begging to be sated. I feel the magick in my fingertips, taste it on my tongue and follow wherever Niko braces against me. My mind is blank and yet bursting with colors. His tongue brushes my lower lip and I take it into mine, tentatively playing my tongue against his. He moans and my magick spurs as I arch involuntarily into his hard hips.

A hand grazes my bare side and shifts up to my breasts as the cloth of my dress rises with his heated touch. I can't catch my breath and my magick is burning my insides. He feels intoxicating, everything black and sharp.

"Niko," I gasp his name into his mouth and he nips at my lip. I place a hand on his chest and push so he is leaning back enough that I can focus my lust filled gaze on his.

"What's wrong?" he asks breathily and leans back into my throat, sending shivers down my spine.

"Niko," I say again, and this time he stops and looks at me. "Not yet."

Disappointment crumbles his handsome features and devastates my heart. He swallows as his thumb pulls at my lower lip and I see the moment he hesitates, and part of me hopes he leans down to kiss me anyway. I wouldn't have stopped him again. Niko sighs and pulls away from me and his presence is replaced by cool night air. Shame heats my cheeks and I fix my dress from riding my thigh.

He lays down next to me, his arms at his sides and we both stare at the stars. Both of us are panting from our exchange, and I still feel the rapid beats in my chest, the searing flame of my magick, and Niko's phantom touches where he had kissed me.

I lower my hand beside his and twine our fingers together. Our gazes lock, the tension between us suffocating, and I wonder if I've made a mistake by not allowing our spark to ignite.

"Not yet," I tell him again, gently, so as not to break his heart. "Maybe one day."

"One more day."

"One more day," I repeat with regret on my tongue.

I close my eyes while still facing him and breathe in his scent, feeling calm and frenzied all at once. When I open them, he is still studying me. His features are softened and innocent, his shimmering emerald eyes a beacon trying to call me home.

We sit like that for what feels like an infinity. Another brief blip of peace. A moment of near perfection.

"I want to help you with whatever you're going through. I don't know exactly what that means and I don't need to, but I want to be there." His grip tightens on mine. "I will be."

"Thank you."

Listening to forest's lullaby, wisps of rose magick float on the air around my face and flutter with our mingled breaths. Stars shine through the haze, fuzzy diamonds in a blanket of black silk. My magick is still seeking Niko. A familiar hollow feeling in the pit of my belly has my fingers tighten on his. I focus on his warmth, on his hand in mine, and force the sharp thoughts in my mind to stay at bay just a little longer.

Before we both drift to sleep, we agree to pack up and head back to town. We each carry a large armload while Niko guides us back to the car with flashlights. The sleep in my eyes fades as we tread back through the dark and the cool night air sends shivers down my arms. I ignore the prickling sensation crawling along my skin that reminds me of being watched.

After throwing the items in the back, we both slip into the front and Niko begins driving down the road. I relax in the passenger seat and watch the dark silhouettes of trees pass us by.

"I'm glad I waited," Niko says, breaking the silence.

"Really?"

"Yes."

Me too. I don't dare say those words aloud. Instead we sit in silence watching the dark road illuminated by the lonely car's headlights.

The tree cover is thick as we drive down the road, still several miles out of town, and movement catches in my peripheral. I glance right, anticipating a deer or raccoon. A human-shaped figure steps from the tree's darkness and my stomach tightens. The Shadow approaches the road as we drive closer.

"What is that?" I hear Niko ask, but my voice is frozen in my throat.

The Shadow extends a hand as we pass and time feels as if it's ground to a halt. Growing terror urges bile up my throat as its obsidian hand presses against the window, talons curling and cracking the glass into hundreds of glittering pieces. A high-pitched ringing pierces my ears, and when I look into the Shadow's face, my heart lurches into my throat.

Flaming red eyes stare into me, the fractured glass between us feeling all too flimsy a barrier to keep the Shadow at bay. Its body is void of color, a darkness in space that destroys all light. Its face twists into a grin filled with razors and a deep rumbling resonates inside my head.

Black Swan.

Its voice is a thundering bass promising death and ruin, an ever echoing reverberation of terror and torment. My blood runs cold and I hear its chuckle inside my head, its eyes reflecting visions of burning civilizations, of mutilated corpses animated to life, a humanity based in Hell.

The moment ends as we pass the Shadow and I hear Niko repeating my name. A dull throbbing stings my hands where a violet orb is cusped in my palms. I clap them together until the magick sizzles out.

I glance back to where the Shadow was standing, but it's gone. I stare out the fractured window and run a finger along it, tracing the deep fissions with my skin.

"Daire, are you okay?" Niko asks with true fear in his voice.

"Yes."

"You don't seem okay. What was that?"

"The Shadow."

"Like from Beltane?"

"Yes. I think it's following me." I feel distant from myself, but it's keeping my terror away. The Shadow knows who I am. Its delight in my fear was evident as it fed me visions of destruction. I shiver and touch the glass, the raised clefts biting into my skin.

"Don't touch it," Niko orders and reaches over to pull my hand away. "What do you mean it's following you? Are you safe?"

"Yes, I use protective magick and sigils at home." Every time I blink, I see the Shadow. The smile that shouldn't exist.

"Do you want me to spend the night?" Niko offers and I notice he's tapping the steering wheel erratically.

"No, Klowbi is home." I still see those ruby fire eyes, a twisted shell of what could have been human.

"Okay," he mumbles, his disappointment obvious. I'm too distracted to pay it much mind.

I don't remember the rest of the drive, or pulling up to the diner. Niko walks me up the stairs to my apartment door. He grabs my hands and holds tight, and knowing he won't leave otherwise, I look into his emerald eyes.

"Call me, Daire." He steps closer. "If anything happens, you call me."

"I will." My words sound unconvincing , but he seems content with my answer. He lets go of my hands as we stare at each other for an awkward breath before he waves and heads back to the car. I unlock the door and enter, surprised to see Klowbi still up. She looks over at me and smiles as she reaches to turn down the movie she's watching.

"You're home late," Klowbi teases. Her face falls as I fumble with the lock. She's up and by my side, leading me to the couch and sitting me down. She clasps my hand. "What did he do?"

My body still feels frozen and I'm desperately trying to keep the fear away, but it's clawing at my insides. My hands tremble and I force myself to inhale deep breaths. Is this what Desmond feels? This unrelenting terror that fills up every second?

"Daire?"

"I saw it again. The Shadow."

"Tonight?"

I nod and recount tonight's events, including after leaving Xuan's when I saw a Shadow then, too.

"It's okay," Klowbi consoles, but it's not. "Do you want me to brew you some tea?"

"Yes." My voice trembles as I stand on unsteady legs. "I'll be right back."

I go from room to room, door to door, window to window, carefully placing protective sigils on each entry and exit. By the time I'm finished, I'm exhausted and fatigued. I change into comfy clothes before making my way back to the living room and falling onto the couch beside Klowbi and we pull the blankets around us as she starts a new movie. She's asleep within the hour, but I lay awake, refusing to close my eyes, jumping at every sound.

For the first time in what feels like years, I have found comfort and solace in someone outside of me, outside of my magick and my misery. But just as quickly as it greets me it shatters, and the darkness reminds me why I can't have such peace. I can't focus on a relationship with Niko regardless of how much I might ache for it. Shadows will drag him down the same path as Desmond. I'm not meant for a simple life. My life contains magick and spells, curses and Shadows, nightmares and death.

I can not love him how he wishes.

The darkness of sleep takes me, pulling me down without a chance for me to fight it.

Chapter 12

Atropa belladonna. Datura. Conium maculatum. Mandragora offici-
narum. Solanaceae.

Standing amongst a garden of poisons, it's hard to believe something so simple and even divine could be so deadly. A cost of existence
for survival. Beauty with lethal consequences.

As I tread through the thinly laid path, I'm careful not to touch
the white trumpet flowers classed as *datura*. Several types of flowering
hemlock sprout nearby, and I duck my head to avoid my hair catching
on the hanging blooms. Thick, dark green leaves with purple stems
and jagged violet petals bud in the center of the leaves that hang across
the path. Mandrake, poisonous if ingested into the body. The plants
surrounding me all belong to the nightshade family. All lethal under
the right circumstances.

Beyond the garden is dense forest. Nothing except thick trees, and
past the first line of woods there is nothing but impenetrable darkness.
It's unnaturally dark, as if light can't pierce the heavy veil. The world is
silent beyond my breaths and careful footsteps. I hear no bird calls nor
insect droning. Everything is quiet, as if the earth is holding its breath.

I survey the poison garden and search for an exit. It seems to stretch endlessly as the forest remains out of reach. I stop to study the plants and am careful of the ones I choose to touch. Brushing my fingers along the wide leaf of a mandrake, the scent of damp soil hits me, and I dig my fingers into the soft ground beside the plant, sifting it through my fingers.

I get to my feet and turn slowly in a circle with my gaze straining to see the obsidian shadows beyond the forest. The feeling of being watched makes my fingers twitch for my magick and my heart rate quickens. It reminds of when the entity interfered during the seance, the same heavy gaze weighing on my shoulders.

I turn back around to continue further down the garden trail, but a wall of roaring flames is consuming the fauna and scorching the ground black as the blaze crawls closer. I hear the screams of mandrakes, high-pitched and deafening beneath the soil, the leaves curling into black shrivels for an instant before being consumed by white flames. I stumble back and turn to run down the path I came. The forest that was once an eerie, lightless black is caught aflame. Sounds of crashing trees and hissing bark pierce the air and I careen down the path with the flames licking at my heels.

The world is blinding from the blaze. I have to squint, and the heat at my back propels me forward, my skin itching from the flames as blisters bubble on my flesh. The smell of burnt hair assaults my nose as I cut my way through the garden, heedless of the possibility of brushing up against the poisonous plants.

Dread clogs my airway alongside the smoke, and whispering panic tightens my throat until all I can manage is a wheeze. I ache to stop to catch my breath, but my magick whispers that if I stop I will burn. If I stop then *it* will catch me.

I gasp in searing hot air, ducking beneath the roaring flames as they tower higher. A stray flare jumps into my path and sears my arm. I scream as agony licks my skin, swatting blindly at the melting flesh and I stumble from the fire's grasping reach onto grass. I whimper as I touch the throbbing wound. I don't have time to examine it and force myself to my feet, bolting into the inferno forest as the fire eats the grass I had taken sanctuary on.

There's crashing to my right followed by a pained, nearly human scream as a tree soaked in flames splits from the ground and falls to the earth. A doe bounds from the path of a fallen tree with raw terror in the whites of her eyes. We run beside each other, the painful wheeze of her lungs the only sound besides the shriek of starving flames.

Her hooves beat the ground alongside me. There's a clearing ahead revealing no sign of billowing smoke or searing brightness from the fire. Something drips down my back, blood or swear I can't tell. My arm throbs with each beat of my heart and tears sting my eyes.

I realize too late that the clearing is not salvation. A cliff looms beyond and I dig my heels into the dirt to stop my descent. The doe bleats as I pitch over the edge, my stomach weightless and my screams are lost to the wind.

I close my eyes and lift my arms to the side in a meager attempt to slow my fall. I jolt and hold my breath, bracing for impact. When nothing happens, I open my eyes and find massive black wings along my arms, carrying me away from danger.

Relief sweeps through me as the cool air soothes my burns and dries the sweat and blood on my skin. I suck in a lungful of fresh air to stop the scorching ache in my breaths. I flap my wings and rise higher into the orange-tinged sky.

A sharp whistle cuts through the drone of the wind and a piercing pain in my abdomen steals my semblance of serenity. An arrow protrudes from my gut with blood blooming fast from the wound. A ringlet of scarlet and the pounding of pain makes my wings falter, and I drop several feet from the air before catching the updraft again. Another arrow whizzes past, then another, and then dozens of arrows are embedded into my flesh. I struggle to keep flying. Pain morphs my vision black, and it crisps long enough for me to watch my wings fray and feathers fall away behind me as they decay to reveal my arms beneath. The wind is coming fast at my face as gravity pulls me down at bone-breaking speed.

I brace for the landing and crash hard, rolling several times before laying still in a mound of dirt my body dragged up with the fall. The arrows in my skin are buried deep inside and several of the shafts have broken off into jagged ends. Immense pain paralyzes my limbs.

Fear encapsulates me as I struggle to breathe. Blood bubbles at my lips and dribbles down my chin. My magick urges me to stand, to run, or *it* will find me which is certainly a fate worse than death. I raise my head, willing myself to rise, but a scream breaks past my lips. I'm covered in blood, arrow shafts protruding from my abdomen like quills from a porcupine.

And then the pain ceases, my breaths coming in swift inhales. I lift my head, finding no resistance, and gape at my body no longer mangled or bloody. Rose petals the color of ink cover every inch where a wound once was with not even the stain of blood to mark my skin. I push to my feet and find only pain from the burn on my arm, my clothes having melted to my skin in a gnarly mesh of thread and flesh.

My child.

I freeze at the feminine whisper, looking up despite the sound having come from everywhere.

"Lilith?"

Snapping branches redirects my attention to the forest and I catch movement deep within. There are no signs that the blaze was an inferno moments ago, no lingering smoke or dead trees. Another branch snaps, loud in the silence, and the outline of a doe emerges, slipping between the thickening darkness. She has a ghastly limp, her body covered in gashes and ash, her front hoof twisted and glistening with blood.

She calls out to me, a broken and forlorn bleat, as she pitches forward and crashes to the ground. I sprint towards her with tears thickening my throat. "I'm here, Bambi." My words surprise me as I kneel beside her, staring into her eyes and finding they're a familiar chestnut brown. "Oh, Klowbi, what did they do to you?"

A few feet away, I note the spark of recognition in her eyes, the hopeful tilt of her head. I reach my hand out to brush her velvet nose when a jagged slash cuts across her throat. Warm blood splatters my face and I taste it on my lips. Terror glazes her eyes, a gurgling plea caught within the wound and falling silent on her bloodied snout.

My scream is frozen in my throat. I lurch forward and catch her head as life leaves her eyes. My magick whispers again, warning me to flee, but staring at the doe leaves me immobile. I can't leave her here. So I stay kneeling in the grass, the doe's head resting in my lap soaked with blood, stroking her face. I press my face to hers with my eyes closed tight, murmuring apologies and false promises.

When I open my eyes again, a black swan rests in place of the doe. The neck is twisted and hanging at a sharp angle, its wings broken with bone shards protruding from the black blood-soaked feathers. Blue and amber eyes stare back at me, the same human eyes as mine.

I scramble backwards and push to my feet. My magick flares again, screaming at me to run, and the press of watchful eyes sends goosebumps down my arms. I dash in the opposite direction of the dead swan and am engulfed by flames of hellfire.

The inferno rages, surrounding me, the heat making it impossible to breathe through the thickening plumes. My skin bubbles and I scream through the searing flames, the blinding light, when a shape takes form in the inferno. Its eyes shift from white hot to blood red, a wicked grin born of flickering flames. I hear nothing besides my scream as it opens wide and lunges.

"No!" I shout, jerking awake on the couch in the living room. The feeling of claustrophobia is overwhelming and my skin feels slick. My hands have a film of sweat, not blood. Sighing, I sag back into the couch, wiping the dampness from my brow.

"Are you okay?" Klowbi asks from the kitchen with a spatula in hand. The smell of bacon and eggs wafts from the skillet on the stovetop. There's a pot of fresh coffee brewing and the earthy scent helps ease the tension in my muscles.

"Yeah," I mumble, sitting up and twisting my black hair away from my neck. "Just a nightmare." Watching Klowbi cook breakfast makes the memory of the dying doe a horrible possibility. I swipe the sweat from my brow and shove the thought deep down.

"Want to talk about it?" Klowbi carries over a mug of coffee with milk and sugar and sets it on the table in front of me.

"Not really." I take the mug and the heat makes me wince with the memory of starving flames. I shake my head to rid the thought and sip the coffee, allowing it to wash the gritty terror from my mouth.

Klowbi returns to the kitchen with a thoughtful expression. "You were pretty restless," she says as she flips eggs in the pan. "And you were talking in your sleep."

"What was I saying?" I take another sip. I don't want to talk about the nightmare. I don't want to remember watching Klowbi die or seeing my swan mutilated in my arms. I don't want to remember the raging fire or face in the flames.

"You said my name." Klowbi offers a sympathetic smile. "Then you started to whimper and gasp. I was worried, but wasn't sure if waking you up was wise. You know what they say about waking people up with night terrors?"

"I'm sorry I scared you." I set the mug down and rub the heat from my hands.

"I'm more scared when you don't talk to me," Klowbi confides and clicks the stove off. "Are you hungry?" she asks, walking over with two plates and setting one down in front of me. She smiles and sits down beside me.

"I wasn't until now," I say, staring at the French toast heavily dusted with powdered sugar and a heaping pile of bacon and eggs.

"Good, cause I would have taken it personally if you didn't eat," she teases and smiles so that her freckles crinkle with the action.

We both start eating, and the second the flavor dances across my tongue any lingering nausea is gone. I finish my eggs and half my French toast when Klowbi speaks up again. "Are you going to tell me about your nightmare?"

Taking a sip of coffee to clear my throat, I shoot her a glare before swallowing. "You don't want to know."

"I wouldn't ask if I didn't."

"Maybe I don't want to talk about it."

"You never want to tell me anything."

164

I frown and am greeted by the same eyes the doe had. I look away to stare intently at my plate, my hunger subsiding. Grumbling, I relent and describe the nightmare in minimal detail.

Silence follows as Klowbi chews thoughtfully on a piece of bacon. "That sounds vivid."

"It felt vivid." I shiver despite the remnants of heat.

"But it wasn't real," she tries to soothe, and though I know she means it to be comforting, it does little to ease the remaining undercurrent of fear.

"No, it wasn't." *But it could be.*

I pick at breakfast, peeling the bacon's hard crust, imagining the nightmarish feel of the flames on my skin. The soft inner layer melding to the charred skin, smoking, seared, dead...

"I'm going to call Thayne."

"You're going to call Thayne?"

I nod. "Yes, Thayne has a massive library that he's been collecting for decades. Maybe he has information on the Shadows or the symbol." He might also have an explanation for my vivid nightmares and if they have any deeper meaning that I'm missing.

"You think Thayne will help us?" she asks and shovels a bite of egg into her mouth.

"Of course, he's practically family. He's known us since we were kids. You know how close he was with Mom." I swallow the ache in the back of my throat and turn to Klowbi. "You're coming with me."

"I am?"

"Yes, you are. Unless you have other plans I wasn't privy to."

She shakes her head. "Nope, my plan was this. Sounds like we are going on a road trip." Klowbi smiles, grabbing our plates and heads back to the kitchen.

"I'll give him a call. Be ready in thirty," I tell her and pat the couch cushions, searching for my phone. I find it in the blanket and unlock the screen. Niko sent several texts asking if I'm alright and if I need anything. A clash of guilt and something sweeter pangs my heart, but I don't respond and instead dial Thayne's number. He picks up on the third ring.

165

"Daire, how are you?" Thayne's familiar baritone voice helps soothe the fear still sticking to my skin.

"I'm alright. I'm sorry to bother you."

"No such thing, though I'm surprised to be hearing from you. Is everything alright?"

"I'd rather explain in person. I was hoping Klowbi and I could come pay you a visit and use your library."

"You never have to ask to use my library. The door is always open for those who seek knowledge." There's a pause. "Are you sure you're okay? You sound frightened."

"I'm fine. Can we visit you? Today?"

"Certainly. I'll admit I wasn't expecting visitors, but I can make the house look presentable." I hear his low chuckle echo through the receiver. "I'll see you two soon."

"Thank you Thayne."

"Blessed be, Daire."

The call ends and I make a mad dash for my bedroom, grabbing somewhat clean clothes and locking myself in the bathroom to shower and change. I strip out of my pajamas soaked in sweat and freeze as I'm staring in the mirror at myself. A scorch mark blisters on my upper arm where flames caught me in the nightmare. I touch the tender flesh and wince at the sharp shot of pain.

Fear drops my stomach into the ground and I force the dread away as I shower and dress in record time. I step into my bedroom, digging for my Book of Shadows and snagging the doodles of the symbol and any stray notes that could be of use.

"Daire, are you ready yet?" Klowbi asks from my doorway.

"Yes, I'll meet you by the car!" I tell her and fold the notes neatly into the Book. I hear her footsteps retreat, the sound of the front door opening and closing tight. I sigh and brush my blister hidden beneath my sleeve.

I grab my Book and start towards the door when a stray thought crosses my mind. I walk forward and kneel beside my bed to peer underneath. The protection jar is shattered into pieces. The quartz has split into multiple fragments, the sea salt scattered finely across the floor boards, rosemary and clove dry and shriveled, and the swan feather looks as if it had been set aflame.

I scoot backwards and shove to my feet. Protection jars only break when they have been used. This one is in pieces.

I take off towards the front door, touching the burn mark on my arm with my Book of Shadows clasped tightly to my breast. Fear hovers in my head like suffocating fog as I realize home is no longer safe.

Excerpt from Daire's BoS
A World of Gray

Lilith has always been a controversial deity. Some say she is a goddess while others preach she is a demonic being. The true first wife of Adam, she was cast aside because she refused to submit to the male half of humanity and pushed to be his equal. Lilith refused to be treated as the lesser, weaker half and instead of wallowing in self-pity and rejection she became the Dark Mother in which she embraced her womanhood, her sexuality, the darkness of the world. Though stories were twisted throughout time placing Lilith as a child murderer and a manipulator of mankind, she is a benevolent goddess who guides and protects her children. Her wrath is one to be feared and her wisdom to be sought after and treasured. She is our Dark Mother, steering us down the Path of Night, through the Path of Thorns, so we can embrace the flower of Black Flame and discover mirth and truth.

There is much to be learned from Lilith and even more to respect. She is not an evil creature nor is she a perfect heroine. She is both, and it is for the individual to decide how to perceive that existence.

If following my witch's heart condemns me to the pyre, I will gladly burn as the villain the world believes me to be.

Chapter 13

Thayne's homestead resides spaciously along a grove of trees. Compared to his neighbors' lavish and mansion-esque houses, his home is modest and homely. He owns several acres of land, including a portion of the grove surrounding his home, and the landscape is well tended. The lawn is a lush vibrant green with a few wildflowers and dandelions poking their blooms from the earth as the true beginnings of summer push their way forward. The neighboring homes are hidden beyond the soft lolling hills, the trees spotted about offering Thayne's home plenty of privacy.

Pulling up the gravel road to Thayne's, a cloud of dust kicks up beneath the wheels behind us and pebbles nip the undercarriage of the car. Klowbi sits restlessly in the passenger seat chewing at her thumbnail.

"That was the longest hour drive ever," Klowbi grouses as I put the car in park.

I huff and gently brush my fingers over the burn mark on my arm. The shirt material is rubbing against it, sending aches and twinges. I feel the phantom heat through the fabric still.

"At least it was only an hour." I grab my Book of Shadows and exit the car. The scent of pine greets me accompanied by the smell of summer, heralding the beginning of June. The next celebrated Wiccan holiday is Litha, the Summer Solstice. Melas puts on a huge festival every year to commemorate the summer and bring in business. It's also where Klowbi and I first met Alko, Xuan, and Niko.

We both start up the gravel walkway to the porch at the front. There's a swinging bench and a rocking chair with a table sat between them. Pots of sage, mint, and lavender stand along the guarded rail. A pair of gardening gloves and a spade sit beside it.

"Thayne gardens?" Klowbi asks and stops to caress the buds of lavender.

"He grows most of his own herbs," I explain, stopping at the front door. "I remember Mom always coming home with bundles whenever she'd help him with his garden. I loved crushing the mint between my fingers." I smile at the memory. Mom would hand me a small portion of the mint she'd gathered so I could crush it in my fingers or chew on the leaves. The flavor was intense and sometimes it would make my eyes water, but it soothed me as a child. She'd often use the mint in tea or making mint lemonade on the summer days where the heat would distort the air.

"It smells so sweet." She smiles as the lavender brushes her nose.

"Come on." I rap my knuckles on the door.

There's a soft thumping of footsteps beyond the threshold that gets louder as it approaches. The door swings wide, revealing Thayne dressed in a red button-up plaid long sleeve that's rolled up to his elbows and old blue jeans. The aroma of freshly baked bread wafts past the threshold and my stomach gurgles despite having eaten breakfast.

"Welcome," Thayne says with a wide grin plastered on his face. His teeth are a stark white against his skin and he towers above both of us. "You two made good time. Come in."

He opens the door wider so we can enter. I lead the way, Klowbi following close behind as we step into the entryway. Shutting the door behind us, Thayne pulls us each into a hug and I try not to wince at the pressure applied to the burn on my arm. When he releases us, I notice a smear of flour on his shirt front.

"Was the drive alright?" Thayne asks, taking several steps back in the direction of the kitchen.

If by alright you mean I didn't see any Shadows following us, then yes, it was great.

"Nothing noteworthy," I reply. The entryway is small, dark, and has a cabin-like feel.

"Great. Let's get you set up in the library." Thayne leads us forward.

On the right is the living room with a brown sofa adorned by blankets and farmhouse pillows. A TV is mounted on the wall and a desk sits along the connecting wall with a standing lamp beside it. Several books splay open with sheets of papers piled on the desk, but it's too dark to make out any scribbled words. Down the wide hall is the kitchen which is one of the house's larger rooms. Fresh loaves of bread cool on the stovetop, a stick of butter and knife beside it. A mug of coffee steams on the kitchenette that's covered in fresh fruits, vegetables and mason jars. Thayne's room and the guest bedroom are down a smaller narrower hall to the left. Straight through the kitchen, past sliding barn doors, is the library.

The library is the largest room in the house, though it looks more like one separate building with living quarters attached to it. The main section of the library is domed with skylights to allow in natural light. Small alcoves along the windows offer cozy reading spots, while a well-loved, sinking couch sits in front of a refashioned long table. Shelves line the walls nearly all the way to the ceiling and hallways of books lead down narrow alleys of novels. The whole place smells of old paper and leather bindings.

We both stare open-mouthed at the expansive room. The library is even larger than I remember. I wouldn't be surprised if we lost our way scrounging through the hundreds, maybe thousands, of levels of shelves. The collection could rival most city libraries. I wonder how many books Thayne owns that are banned or forbidden. Perhaps a secret text lost in the mounds of bound backings.

"Are either of you hungry?" Thayne asks with an amused glint in his eyes at our reactions.

"We ate before we came."

"Of course. Let me grab us something to drink before we get into the thick of it." Thayne turns back towards the sliding barn doors. "Feel free to look around."

"This place is beautiful," Klowbi whispers. Her eyes are still wide and lost.

The barn door slides shut and Klowbi starts in one direction and I go in the opposite. The initial shelves hold newer books, some familiar, but older books swell shelves deeper within. I stop at a unit that is against the wall away from the window's open light and trail my fingers across several spines. These books are older with fraying seams and worn covers. I pull out a maroon cover book with the title *World of Wicca* and skim through the pages. They are thick and crisp between my fingers, and the book still smells new. I put it back and walk further down the aisle, stopping at the sight of a purple spined novel. It's titled *Ancient Astral Projection* with silver lettering. I pull it from the shelf and notice the book is nearly half the size compared to others on the same shelf. I open to the first page that's an introduction with yellow and worn pages. Deciding to hold on to it, I browse the lower shelves and catch sight of a black leather-bound book. I cradle it in my hands, the leather cool to the touch. My magick flares upon contact and my breath hitches.

"*Aberrant Magick: Shadow, Nether, and Ether of the Arcane,*" I read aloud and a shiver steals down my spine. The lettering is pressed into the leather and outlined in gold. Opening the book, the stench of old parchment makes my nose wrinkle and the pages are the color of coffee and milk, tattered along the edges. The first page is blank besides a handwritten note. The writing is strange until I realize it isn't in English. It looks like Latin, but with a more elegant, nearly mystical script. Running my finger lightly over the note, my finger jolts and I snag it away.

My magick is an angry swarm in my abdomen.

"Daire!" Klowbi's voice carries down in my direction, but the shelves lined with books muffle her voice.

Slamming the book shut, I place it in my arms along with the purple bound book and my Book of Shadows and make my way back towards the center of the library. Back at the room's center, I spot Klowbi at the refurbished table, engrossed in a small pile of books. I walk over to her and place my two finds beneath my Book of Shadows so they are hidden. For some reason I can't shake, I feel Thayne won't approve of my choice of books.

Klowbi lifts her head at the sound of my footsteps and smiles, lifting the book she has open in front of her. "Look what I found, it's called *Herbology Without Time*. It's so fascinating. Do you think Thayne would let me borrow it?"

I sit down next to her and meticulously keep the two books hidden from sight. "You can ask, but I doubt he'd mind that much. So long as you don't lose or destroy it."

Before Klowbi can reply, the barn doors slide open again. Thayne heads in our direction with long strides. He places a platter with three glasses and a pitcher of purplish liquid on the table along with bread, butter cubes, and a jar of strawberry mint jam.

"I know you said you weren't hungry, but the bread is fresh and the jam is homemade. Nothing like snacks while reading a good book." He chuckles and pours the contents of the pitcher into the three glasses.

"Thank you," Klowbi says and takes a tentative sip of the drink. "This is amazing. What is it?"

"Lavender lemonade, also homemade," Thayne says proudly and centers the platter in the middle of the table, though he's careful to give the books Klowbi found a wide berth. "Did either of you discover anything of interest?"

Klowbi nods and sets her glass down. "I've never heard of half of these books. Where did you find them?"

"Most were passed down from generations of different people from different walks of life. Some I found myself, others were gifted to me by fellow collectors. It's several centuries' worth of collections. I can guarantee most of the books here don't have many copies floating around out in the world, if any at all." Thayne looks lovingly around the room. A proud collection with knowledge both known and forgotten in one room.

I resist the urge to touch the books I found. Judging by the covers, they are ancient and possibly older than I thought. Especially the leather-bound book with the strange language written in the front. Was it an ancient book written when magick was potent? Surely he would have locked up or hidden away anything that important.

"Incredible," Klowbi says in awe beside me.

"So, why did you two ask to visit on such short notice?" Thayne asks, redirecting the conversation of the topic at hand.

Klowbi and I exchange a glance and I start to explain almost everything that's happened since the night of Beltane. I discuss the Shadow's constant presence and its manifestations. I mention the strange note and experience at Xuan's and grab the slip of paper to show him the copy of the symbol. Thayne studies it, not saying anything, and then returns his gaze to me so I can continue. I finish by explaining that I believe the Shadows are involved with Desmond's coma, and Dad thinks the same, even if he won't say it outright.

Thayne is quiet, and in the silence Klowbi gasps and looks at me apologetically, turning to Thayne again. "Daire had a nightmare last night, too." I shoot her a glare and my lips thin with irritation, but I don't argue either. The nightmare is a development that terrifies me.

"Alright, let's focus on one thing at a time." He sits on the edge of the table as his gaze bounces from Klowbi to me. "The Shadows, let's begin there."

I nod and shift in my seat, my fingers finding the smooth cover of my Book of Shadows. "First off, are you safe? Have you been utilizing your protection spells and protecting your home?" I nod and Thayne continues. "Good. Protecting your space is vital, considering this Shadow sounds stronger and more demonic than what I've heard of."

"I think Desmond mistakenly summoned this entity," I reply, recalling Des's admission of practicing blood magick and the strange vision he kept having, including the symbol. I divulge the information to Thayne, omitting when I saw Desmond in the Astral; he merely raises his eyebrows and nods while tapping his fingers against the table.

"That is interesting," he mutters and pulls the sleeves of his shirt higher. "Can you describe the symbol Desmond mentioned?" I shake my head. "Without knowing what this entity that's following you is, there's not much that can be done. Has it tried communicating with you?"

I hesitate, the lie slipping from my tongue. "No, it follows me. I think it wants to know how easy it is to find me. It feels like it's waiting for something."

"Peculiar," Thayne mumbles and scratches his head. "It sounds as if the Shadow is toying with you, perhaps seeing how much you can take before you snap." His eyes trail towards a bookshelf behind us and nods as if making up his mind. "I think I have a book that might be useful." He goes to the shelf in long easy strides, dragging a finger across the spines before pausing and slipping a book from the shelf. He places it on the table between Klowbi and I. It's a gray book with nothing written on the front. "This book I expect back once you are finished with it. It has no name, but I refer to it as the *Gray Book*. It's one-of-a-kind with decades of studies by first-hand witnesses."

"First-hand witnesses of what?" A list of names with dates from over a hundred years ago emblazon the interior cover.

"Those are all the authors of the book, their experiences with the paranormal of all types, including magickal, and the most authentic information on all types of Shadows," Thayne says and leans back against the table. "Hopefully it will help to identify the Shadow."

"All types?" Klowbi inquires.

"Yes, there are multiple types of Shadows. It will be explained in there." Thayne gestures to it with a half smile. "Do be careful with that book."

"Thank you, we will." I close the cover with a tender swipe of my palm. It appears I'll be doing a lot of reading in the next couple of days.

"Of course. Now, the symbol you showed me. Please tell me you have not done any magick with it."

"Just research, but it hasn't helped much."

"Good. Never practice magick with unfamiliar symbols. That should be common sense," Thayne says, shaking his head. "Desmond should have known better." After a pause, he holds out his hand. "May I see the symbol?" I grab the slip of paper again and hand it over. He stares at it, twisting and turning it, holding it up to the light and in shadow before setting it back on the table and tracing it with his fingers. He glances up and smiles, his teeth a sharp contrast to the rest of his features. "It's your lucky day. I believe I know what this is."

"What is it?" I ask, unable to hide my excitement. Klowbi and I both lean forward.

Thayne turns the paper so it is facing us right-side up. "What does it look like to you?"

Klowbi and I exchange glances and shrug. "A sigil maybe?" Klowbi offers.

"Close." Thayne covers half of the symbol, leaving only the 'n' shape visible. "Now what does it look like?"

Disbelief slams into me. It was so simple the entire time. It wasn't a symbol at all. A part of me is ashamed I didn't see it sooner. "Of course," I say and grab the paper, covering half the symbol, then the other, and then staring at it as one. "It's nordic runes."

"Correct. The same runes we use in spells or rune readings," Thayne clarifies.

"If connected, what do the runes signify?" I ask and Klowbi takes the paper from me.

"You'll have to look into it as runes have multiple meanings. I have another book around here somewhere that goes more in depth about runes and archaic witch teachings."

For the second time, Thayne goes to a bookshelf, this one different from the first, and searches for a moment before pulling out a book with a red cover. The title reads *Symbols and Sigils of the Witch* in small font printed on the cover. Sliding the book to Klowbi, he returns his gaze to me. "This book can answer your questions. It has in-depth information on runes and old witch and Wiccan symbols that were used in rituals or spells. Some of those teachings are old, and for good reason." Thayne turns to me. "Klowbi, start looking into those books I gave you. I'm going to speak to Daire alone."

"Alright." She takes a slice of bread, spreading jam on it, and opens up the red rune book.

"We won't be long. Daire." He gestures and walks away towards a window with a cushioned seat. He sits down and pats the seat beside him. I accept and feel the sunshine against my back through the window, my burn throbbing dully. "I wanted to speak to you privately about the nightmare you had. Based on what you told me previously, I don't believe the nightmare is truly that. I believe it's similar to lucid dreaming, except you are not the one controlling it. An outside source is."

"You think someone else is controlling my dreams?"

"Or something, but yes. Can you provide me some details about the nightmare? I don't mean to pry, but if this is more than a dream, any details are crucial."

I mention the nightmare with flames, poisonous plants, and roses in little detail. I omit the burn part, yet even with minimal explanation, I detect fear in Thayne's eyes. Once I finish, he stares at me with his brows furrowed.

"Which deities do you have the most connection with?" Thayne asks, breaking the silence.

"Why does that matter?"

"I'm trying to help you, Daire."

"I know," I grumble and heave a sigh. "I work with Lilith."

"When did you last perform a spell or ritual for her or seek her aid?"

"The night I saw the Shadow shatter the window." I pause "And when I fell asleep, I had the nightmare."

"How did you honor the goddess?"

"I did a bath ritual. Why does this matter?"

"Because I have a theory," Thayne begins and paces in the light cascading through the window and onto the library floor. "I believe that Lilith was trying to assist you in your nightmare. I think she attempted to show you something, but you said it felt like the dream was a constant back and forth?"

"Yes. There were moments it wasn't so scary, but it didn't last long."

"My theory is that Lilith was trying to give you advice, perhaps a direction to go; I cannot speak for her, but then some*thing* caught wind of your dream and intercepted the connection. I believe Lilith tried to shield you from an unknown interference, causing your dream to shift dramatically." The stress is heavy on Thayne's face, revealing lines of age and worry. "If this being can equal Lilith's power—"

"Then what else can it do?" I whisper and absently touch the burn on my arm before putting my hands in my lap, staring at the tattoos on my fingers. "Damn."

"I'm not sure what it is. It could be a Shadow, though I highly doubt a Shadow could challenge Lilith so placidly. Regardless of what it is, you must be extremely vigilant, Daire. If the entity following you is as powerful as it seems, you must be prepared." Thayne places a hand on my shoulder, squeezing gently. "Don't hesitate to contact me if you ever need anything. You are too brilliant of a witch to be facing this alone."

"Thanks." My tongue is heavy and my fingers are frigid. The entity is taunting me, but its main focus is still on Desmond. But for how long? Even if I manage to save him, wouldn't it just turn its sights on me instead?

"If I were you, I would recommend reaching out to Lilith not only to thank her, but to ask for her guidance and protection. Clearly she favors you, Daire, and that is no light thing."

"I will. It seems that I owe her."

"It seems that you do."

"What should I do about the Shadow, or whatever it is?" I ask, noting the desperation in my voice.

"I hope the books can provide some answers, but quite honestly, I've never seen something like this before. I'll search my library for more books and check if anything else comes up. This library is extensive and finding something might take a few weeks." Thayne scratches his chin in thought. "Besides that, be sure to keep protection sigils on your door. Practice your magick and honor Lilith. We are limited in what we can do until we have more information."

"Thanks Thayne." I brush imaginary dust from my lap, standing.

"Of course." He stops me before I can take another step. "Daire, have you been astral projecting since this has happened?"

I hesitate on whether to answer truthfully, but figure admitting to Thayne that I have won't mean serious repercussions. "Yes, but just once, after I visited Desmond in the hospital. I was at Dad's."

"This is only a suggestion, and I suspect great diligence is in order, but it's possible astral projecting could be beneficial. You may be able to communicate with Lilith in a realm equivocal to hers."

"You think she could help me more there?"

"I can't say definitively, but it would be worth a try as long as your defenses are strong. Ensure your physical body remains secure and avoid prolonged absence. The longer you are away from your physical self, the higher probability the entity stalking could influence you."

I thank him as we start heading back to where Klowbi sits drinking lavender lemonade and scouring over books.

"I'm always here to help," Thayne says and gives me a parental pat on my shoulder. "Have you spoken to your father recently?"

"No, it's been a while."

"You should reach out to him. I bet he could use some company," Thayne suggests, smiling at Klowbi as he approaches. "You two stay and eat up. I have a few tasks to take care of, but I'll be here if you need anything."

Taking a seat beside Klowbi, I take a long drink of lemonade and finish the glass. Klowbi looks at me, then at Thayne as he walks away, and her gaze falls onto the red book. I grab the *Gray Book* and flip it open. "Did you find anything yet?"

"No, there's so much information here, but I think I'm getting close," Klowbi says around a mouthful of bread.

"Keep searching," I encourage, glancing through the long scribble of names. I don't recognize any immediately and some of the fonts have faded from age, making them hard to decipher. I start flipping through the book, scanning pages and paragraphs, looking for anything mentioning Shadows or entities.

Flipping through the *Gray Book*, I try to imagine who else might have imprinted their knowledge onto these pages. Some dates are smudged illegibly, but there has to be a full generation worth of information within the covers. If this book holds vital information that most aren't privy to, then the other two books I found must have secrets hidden within their pages. Maybe even the answer as to what happened to Desmond or Mom.

Sensing the old layers of magick like dust on the pages, my magick trills at the sensation. My fingers quake with the faint memories of magick long ago and my cheeks flush. If magick was stronger that long ago, what was the reason for its fading? What else disappeared among blank pages that humanity's greed swallowed whole?

Thumbing through the pages, I halt my progress when I spot a human silhouette sketched in black ink with white eyes peering from its face. I'm halfway through the book, all of which are handwritten in dozens of different scrawls, but this section appears newer than the beginning. It feels younger too, the magick that seeped through not nearly as potent. Below the sketch is an introduction:

Shadow People, or Shadows, are immaterial beings that have been noted to manipulate their physical form, and in some rare cases, their environment. Negative energies attract them and they can attach to places, things, and even individuals. In my experience, these beings seek to cause mayhem among relationships or the mind, though some argue otherwise, or that their intentions are misconstrued to the human understanding. Regardless, countless eyewitnesses of the Shadows have all described the same intangible beings with similar traits, sometimes being accompanied by temperature differences at the minimum or personality changes at the extreme.

I've condensed all my knowledge and personal experiences with Shadow People onto these pages, but there are likely unnamed beings elsewhere.

Klowbi starts and looks up from her book, a stray breadcrumb clinging to the corner of her lip. "What'd you find?"

"It looks like a guidebook on Shadows," I say, pointing to the first section titled "The Sleepers" and I begin to read.

The Sleepers, though more commonly misdiagnosed as sleep paralysis, are beings that will attack often when you are most vulnerable; asleep. They also have the ability to manipulate dreams and put the victim in a state of temporary paralysis, even upon waking. Sleepers have the ability to physically maim their victim as well, whether that being claw marks, bite marks, choking, or bruising. Some witnesses state that Sleepers will drag victims out of bed or can be felt crawling or sitting on top of them. These Shadows are dangerous and, if experienced, please seek help. If the Sleepers continue their nightly routine of tormenting the victims for too long without disturbance, extreme psychosis and schizophrenia have been diagnosed, in some rare cases leading to death.

"My gods," I blurt and Klowbi inhales harshly beside me. A Shadow that can manipulate nightmares. Was it possible this was the creature stalking me?

"That could be it," Klowbi says, though she sounds more nervous at the possible breakthrough than excited. "It matches what happened to Desmond."

"It's similar, but it doesn't explain his sudden interest in blood magick or the strange visions. Sleepers are only strong during sleep or in the state between consciousness and unconsciousness. Desmond was fully awake when the Shadows appeared and attacked."

"Blood magick may not be relevant," Klowbi counters, dragging a hand across her mouth. A stray crumb falls onto the floor with the motion.

"I doubt that. It seems too coincidental."

"True, but it does seem like a possibility. What else does the book say?" She leans over and flips to the next page.

181

"The Hat Man," I read aloud and exchange glances with Klowbi.

The Hat Man is one of the most common occurrences I've come across for those experiencing themes of paranormal. Regardless of the witness, his description remains constant; a large hulking Shadow with the physique of a man wearing a broad hat, usually a top hat. Upon my own personal experience, he often shows himself in doorways or corners of the room, though this does not limit him. He does not speak or make an attempt to communicate, but I firmly believe he understands our basic underlying thoughts and intentions. I deem him as an observer with minimal malicious or aggressive intents. He is not outwardly imposing, but that doesn't mean he can't be aggressive.

I reread the paragraph several times before sighing. "It's not him."

"Are you sure?" Klowbi asks. I glance over and find her reading her book again with her brows furrowed in concentration.

"Yes." I pull the book back so it is sitting solely in front of me. "Compared to the Sleepers, the Hat Man seems mild."

"At least there is one possibility."

I'm not convinced the Sleepers are the sole culprit for the attack at Beltane or Desmond being in a coma. It doesn't explain the entity in the Otherworld or how I was able to speak to Desmond in the Astral.

The Red Eyed Shadows (RES) make themselves scarce, but when a victim comes into contact with one, there are usually more nearby. RES are extremely aggressive and tend to hunt in packs. They resemble a typical Shadow, except for their otherworldly blood-red eyes. From my firsthand account, the RES first will try to corner the victim and frighten them. The more afraid you are, the larger the Shadows will appear. Without fear, they resort to physical harm, ambushing like starving hyenas. If you manage to escape, you will have the scars to prove it. Protection sigils and certain magick spells can ward them off, or at the very least, give you enough time to run. Avoid RES at all costs.

A cold sweat starts on my brow and my magick tingles in my fingertips. The Shadow that shattered the window while I was with Niko had red eyes, and the creature in the flames had red eyes before it lunged at me. The violent tendencies and feeding from fear aligned with the author's description.

Shadows' aggression and pack-like mentality matched Beltane's night. Except none of the ones I saw had red eyes. And not all were charging forward. I remember there was one Shadow standing on the sidelines watching us. Watching me.

"Daire!" Klowbi shouts, making me jump and a spark of red magick spirals from my pointer finger.

"What? Damnit Klowbi don't shout," I mutter. My heart is pounding in my ears.

"Sorry," she mumbles and slides her book between us. "I found something. The symbols are the Nordic runes *uruz* and *mannaz*. *Uruz* translates to ox, or bull, which has the strength of will and is an animal of endurance, perseverance, health and vigor, along with training due to its capabilities of hard work. *Mannaz* translates to human and represents humanity as a collective like community and relationships, human societal virtues, morality, and values. In reverse, it can mean self-centeredness, loneliness, or manipulation."

"Strength of will and community," I mutter. "What is the entity trying to convey? There's strength in numbers?" I shake my head. Maybe the entity was playing with us the entire time. and trying to distract us so our sights are set on the wrong target.

"I'm not sure, but I found this too." Klowbi flips backwards to a page she bookmarked with a slip of paper.

"The Theban Alphabet," I read while studying the markings. They look ancient and possess a mystical quality to them with sharp lines and swooping curls. Some of the letters remind me of sigils. It's as if someone combined letters with runes, creating an entirely new language.

"Also known as the Witches Alphabet," Thayne's voice booms, making us both jump. He strides into the room, appearing content. "Have you two solved the secrets of the witch yet?"

"It's not solved, but we definitely have some leads," I tell him and gesture to the *Gray Book*. "Have you read this? It has personal encounters with different types of Shadows."

"It has been a long time since I read it and I've read so many books it becomes difficult to remember them all," Thayne admits while staring at the crude sketch of the Shadow. "I quite honestly forgot this was in there until you mentioned it."

"Do you know who wrote it? Or if they are still alive?"

"Look at the book's front, but the more you read, the higher chance the author signed their passage." Thayne flips the book so the list of names is face-up. "This book hasn't been added to in years. I'd be surprised if any of the authors were still alive."

Trying to ignore the breath of disappointment, I close the book entirely. Regardless of the author's existence, numerous pages discuss the Shadows. Not including the other two books I plan on borrowing from Thayne, I'll have plenty of reading content to last me a while.

"You are welcome to stay, but I have errands and won't return for a while. Are you planning on staying the night?" Thayne glances out the window. It must be late afternoon by now. We've been here for a few hours.

Klowbi looks at me expectantly.

"No, we'll stay with Dad. We'll just pack up."

Thayne nods in approval and flashes us a honeyed smile. "Good plan. Feel free to borrow those books or any others you found. If you need anything else, don't hesitate."

I thank Thayne again for his hospitality and we grab our stacks of books. I'm careful to keep my two finds hidden as Thayne escorts us through the house and to our vehicle. He gives us both lung-squeezing hugs before waving at us as I back the car out of his drive and down the road.

"Are we really staying there tonight?" Klowbi pipes up.

"We'll return home tomorrow morning."

I don't want to go home yet, especially after the nightmare of inferno and poison. Staying with Dad is my second home. It feels safe even if it is imaginary.

Chapter 14

Dad has the kitchen window open and he waves us in seeing our approach. As we tread into the entryway, he shoots me a quizzical look; his brows furrow and the wrinkles on his face are prominent. I give him a nonchalant smile, which he returns listlessly, before wandering off into the living room, but not before he holds up a single finger and mouthing the word "wait".

Klowbi and I make our way into the kitchen. The place is tidier than last time. There's no smell of fresh-baked lasagna or grease and sauce stains on the countertops. The kitchen table has nothing besides an unopened bill. I wander around the kitchen while Klowbi sits at the table, and though we both try to look busy, I'm straining to listen to Dad's phone conversation. Klowbi's head tilts in his direction while studying an imaginary speck.

"—deep breaths, there's still a chance he will recover." Dad's voice is hush, but in the silence his words are grating.

"He's still breathing and there's brain activity." Pause. "Don't lose hope." Pause. "I will try to visit soon. Do you have requests for meals?" Pause. "I'll see what I can do. I'll call you tomorrow." Pause. "Stay strong, Aubrie."

A heavy, suffocating sigh escapes the living room and moments later Dad stands in the kitchen entryway. His shoulders are sagging with an invisible burden, his hair has white shot through it, and the crow's feet around his eyes are broad. He smiles at us, but it's lackluster. "I wasn't expecting you two to pop by."

"It was an impromptu decision," I explain, crossing the distance of the kitchen to give him a hug. I hold him tight and bury my head on his chest. His arms are unyielding around me and my ribs tighten from the pressure, but he releases too soon and I step back from the security his hug promises.

"No need to explain. Both of you are a welcomed surprise." Dad pulls Klowbi into a tight hug before releasing her and gesturing to the table. "Sit. I'll get us something to drink. How's coffee sound?"

"Can't say no."

"My favorite," Klowbi says warmly.

Dad walks to the cupboard and grabs three mugs, pouring coffee into each. "Klowbi, you like it black, right?"

"The only way to drink it," she teases, looking at me.

"Shut up," I snort.

"I couldn't agree more." Dad pours three creamer cups into mine and carries the mugs over to us.

"Thanks," Klowbi says, taking a tentative sip.

I swirl my mug gently and watch the hazelnut liquid slosh to the lip of the mug before settling down. "How are you two? Is everything alright?" Dad asks, his concern reminding me of syrup. Thick, sticky, and nearly impossible to be completely rid of.

"We're alright," I affirm, "we wanted to stop by since it's been a while."

Klowbi nods and her auburn curls bounce on her shoulders. "I haven't seen you in so long I wanted to tag along."

"Are you alright? You look exhausted," I cut in before he can reply.

Dad gazes at us, his usually bright eyes now dull and glassy. Finally he sits back, taking a long drink of his coffee and resting it in his lap. "How much of the phone call did you hear?"

"Enough to know it's about Desmond."

A quick nod as his lips tighten into a firm line but he holds his gaze with us, flickering back and forth. "I'm sure you could have guessed, but he's not doing well. There have been no improvements despite his brain activity being high functioning. Do you remember the bruising and nosebleeds?" The question is directed at me. I remember the doctors tossing it up as a delayed trauma response or a blood disorder, but I know that isn't the true ailment. He was in perfect health before he fell into a coma.

Clearing my throat, I search for leaden words that can't articulate what his loss would mean. "Yes, I remember. They've gotten worse, haven't they?"

"Sometimes he breaks out in hives all over, including his face. Nosebleeds can last for half an hour, and when the hives finally start to fade, they morph into hardened bloody sores that are hot to the touch. Doctors have taken samples of the sores, but of course they found nothing." The ire in his eyes reflects my own. The situation is all to familiar, and the tests didn't alter the outcome.

Diagnosis or not, Mom still ended up dead.

"I didn't know it was this bad," Klowbi grieves and shoots me an accusatory look.

"It wasn't that bad when I saw him," I say defensively. "I healed some of his bruises before I left. And there were no sores or hives. When did those show up?"

"About a week ago. Even the bruising has worsened. Aubrie called to tell me that they found fresh bruising on his ribcage and, according to the doctors, the pattern was similar to when someone breaks their ribs. They did a full body scan to make sure nothing was punctured or bleeding internally, but nothing was broken or appeared to be torn. They just appeared."

A burst of pain shoots down my arm where the burn is and I adjust my position in the chair to hide the twinge. This entity is growing more aggressive, coming after me with a vengeance and maiming Desmond with a new ferocity. I'd last seen him with missing digits and the new sores and bruising had to be linked to the trauma he was going through in his nightmare state. My stomach tightens and I stare into my coffee.

What if he never wakes up?

"How's Aubrie doing?" Klowbi's voice shatters my thoughts and I refocus.

A wry laugh escapes past his lips. "As you can imagine, she's not doing well. To be quite honest, if I were in her position, gods forbid, I wouldn't be faring much better. She's strong, but even the strongest people have their breaking points."

"What if I visit? To heal his wounds?" I offer, though a part of me knows deep down even if I did heal his wounds, nothing would stop them from appearing days or hours after I've gone. My magick can only do so much, and as powerful as our bloodline is, it can't wake him from the hold the entity has on him.

"I think the best thing to do is let whatever this is run its course and be there to support Aubrie, regardless of the outcome," Dad says lightly, but I understand the depth of his words.

When Desmond dies, we need to be strong.

I take a sip of coffee to try to dislodge the stone in the column of my throat. It feels tight and swollen, like someone has tried to cut off circulation, and I blink back the shine in my eyes. The mere idea of losing Desmond not even a year after losing Mom is like a hot, jagged blade twisting in my heart. It's as if Dad has already accepted defeat. Maybe that's why the notes and articles disappeared from the table. Dad has lost hope.

"Enough of that," Dad states with forceful exuberance in his voice. "What brought you two here on such short notice?"

"We went to visit Thayne. We wanted to explore his library," I supply with a tight smile. The urge to hide our findings the past couple of weeks since I last saw him is immense, like a huge flashing warning sign. Dad has enough on his plate worrying about Desmond and Aubrie, if he finds out what is happening to me he'd surely short circuit. I have my resources to keep me, and Klowbi, safe for the time being.

"We found these books," Klowbi begins and I kick her under the table. She winces and looks at me, plastering a smile on her face before continuing. "I found these herbology books. I've never seen them in any store before."

I release a sigh, thankful she caught the hint. Dad doesn't need to know. "His collection is astonishing," I add, forcing a fake smile of my own.

Dad watches us and shakes his head, as if dismissing a thought. "That library is Thayne's pride and joy. I bet he'd marry it if he could."

"I think he already has," Klowbi banters. Dad chuckles, a light and airy sound that lifts the weight from his shoulders for a moment. It's the sweetest sound I've heard in a long time.

"I think you're probably right. I've tried playing matchmaker, but he is content with ink on paper." Dad scoots his chair back and stretches with his familiar dad-groan. "Are you two hungry? I haven't eaten yet, but I can whip something up for all of us."

"I could eat. We haven't had a meal since breakfast," Klowbi answers as if she hadn't been eating bread and jam all afternoon.

"Great," Dad says and opens up the fridge, then the freezer, then the cupboards before glancing at us over his shoulder. "How does sloppy joes sound?"

"You're the chef," I say. "Do you need help?"

Dad grabs a pan and hamburger meat along with an array of seasonings and sauces. "No, you two sit. You know I don't mind cooking. Your mother loved my cooking skills. I think that's really the reason I somehow managed to win her over."

"She was rarely in the kitchen," I chuckle. "Unless it involved a simmer pot or the sabbats."

"Remember when she said she wanted to bake homemade Funfetti cupcakes for my birthday?" Klowbi says with a shrill laugh. "She burnt half of them and the others were flat and way too salty."

"We had to open all the windows to air out the house," Dad chuckles, reminiscing. He's adding hamburger to the pan and I smell the garlic cooking into the meat. "Didn't we go to the store to buy you cupcakes instead?"

"Yes, and she felt so bad she got Daire and I our own tubs of ice cream, too." Klowbi grins and I can almost imagine Mom in the kitchen with us, laughing along and reminding us about the massive bellyache that followed the cupcakes and ice cream. The next morning, she made cinnamon rolls from a can, and we dipped them into mugs of hot chocolate despite the fact Klowbi's birthday is in the middle of July. How the four of us sat outside with our feet in a kiddy pool eating slices of watermelon larger than our heads with the sweet juice dripping down our chins and spitting seeds into the lawn. I remembered. I couldn't forget.

"That woman was fierce with her love," Dad says and tosses seasonings onto the beef. "Speaking of, how is that lad, Niko? And your friends?"

"Dad," I groan and Klowbi giggles. "They're all fine."

"I haven't heard from them in a while. I like Niko. He's a smart one. Your mother agreed with me."

"Dad!"

"You can't stay single forever, my little swan." Dad turns to look at us and waves his stirring spoon, sending specks of grease across the floor. "I've always liked the idea of having grandbabies to spoil. I'm not getting any younger."

"Not any time soon," I grumble and cross my arms.

"How are Xuan and Alko?"

"Really good," Klowbi answers.

"What about you, Bambi? Any suitors for your hand?"

"Dad, stop," I groan.

Klowbi blushes and looks away at her nearly empty mug of coffee. Her cheeks brighten with a new tone of red. "Not yet. Maybe one day soon."

"I didn't know there was somebody." I nudge her with my foot.

Klowbi just shrugs and stares intently at her coffee mug. Dad comes forward and sets two plates down in front of us, each one plated with a hamburger bun and a heaping spoonful of meat and sauce. "Dig in."

Dad grabs his own plate and sits down. I let the conversation drop, though I make a mental note to ask Klowbi more later, and take a massive bite of the sandwich. It's juicy and packed with flavor, sweet then spicy with a crunch of onions and a tanginess at the end. It's one of the best meals I've had in a long time.

"How is it?"

"Amazing," Klowbi says through a mouthful.

"I forgot how good your cooking is," I admit, taking another bite.

"I appreciate your compliments, girls," he says. "Daire, I nearly forgot, Aunt Mayve reached out to me a few days ago."

"What did she have to say?" I quip, feigning my tone light.

Dad shoots me a warning glare. "She was checking in and seeing how we are doing. I think Fay's death has been harder on her than she's willing to admit." He takes another bite and chews, making me wait for him to continue. "We should plan a day to see them."

"They aren't like us."

"They are family, Daire, and they are as much like us as we are like them." Dad's voice is firm and unwavering. I can think of a handful of reasons why that's wrong, but I keep my mouth tightly shut to avoid arguing with him. "Being together as a family would benefit us all. You're more than welcome to come, Klowbi. You're practically adopted without the legalities of it all."

"Daire and I would love to go," Klowbi assures, and though we all know I don't want to, I'm grateful she answered for me. If I had spoken, it would have been through gritted teeth.

"Your aunt also said that Sabrina would like to spend more time with you. She was apprehensive about the idea, but you two are mature enough to decide that for yourselves. Don't be surprised to hear from Sabrina in the next few weeks." Dad grabs his plate and stands. "Are you finished?" We both nod and Dad snags the extra plates and rinses them off before leaving them in the sink.

"I'm sure I can give Sabrina some pointers," I grumble. I feel someone kick me beneath the table and Klowbi shakes her head at me. I can't help but smirk.

"I hope you two saved room for dessert," Dad says and pulls out a container from the fridge. "I'll meet you two in the living room. Find something entertaining to watch on the TV."

Together we make our way into the living room and plop down on the couch. Klowbi snags the remote before I can get to it, and I curse at her. "Give that here."

"Nope, mine first," she boasts. I half-ass lunge for the remote in her hands, but she lifts it higher and I miss and fall across her lap. Snagging a pillow, I lob it at her head and she squeals and falls backwards into the couch, refusing to release the remote. "Cheater!"

"Thief!" I counter and sit back beside her, glaring despite the smile creeping across my lips.

Klowbi sticks her tongue out at me and turns the TV onto a reality TV show that I can't stand. I flip her the finger and she returns it with the biggest smile and turns it up a few notches while keeping the remote out of my reach. It was moments like these I find she really is my sister, a pain in the ass one at that.

"What are you two doing?" Dad asks with three bowls balanced in his arms.

"Nothing," we say simultaneously.

"That's reassuring." He chuckles and hands us each a bowl. "Blueberry cobbler and vanilla ice cream."

"Homemade?" Klowbi asks hopefully.

"Store bought," Dad admits. "Next time I'll make it from scratch."

"Deal." Klowbi shovels a spoonful into her mouth.

The three of us eat our dessert and watch the stupid show Klowbi picked and to my dismay, it appears Dad is enjoying it more than any of us. I make a few snide remarks and receive glares from both of them for it which encourages me to continue. During commercial breaks, we talk about the little things in our lives or rehash memories, both with Mom and without her. Before long, the sun has set beyond the horizon, the sky an endless black through the glare of the windows.

"I hate to be the old timer, but I'm heading to bed. You two know the drill." Dad stands, emitting his usual groan with the effort. He gives me a kiss on the head, then Klowbi, and makes his way to his bedroom. "Goodnight."

"G'night."

"Goodnight, sleep tight," Klowbi says drowsily.

The door clicks shut. Klowbi and I turn the TV off and make our way to the spare bedroom. She crawls beneath the soft comforter and pulls the blanket up to her chin, her eyes heavy with sleep. Closing the door, I shut off the light and slide in beside her. We've shared a bed since we were little from countless sleepovers or passing out on the couch from movie nights and drunken late night talks. I barely think twice about sharing a bed, and knowing she is so close eases the small tremor the night induces.

The last time I was in this room, I had astral projected. I had found Desmond, bloody and exhausted, hiding from the entity. The same entity that knows my name and hijacks my dreams into nightmares. Desmond is running out of time. I need to find him again before I lose the chance to save him at all.

"Daire, are you awake?"

"Yes, Bambi."

"Do you think Desmond will be ok?"

You mean, is Desmond going to survive?

"I don't know. I sure hope so."

"I don't understand why this is happening. Why?"

Why us? Because life isn't fair and it's full of demons and the disgraced.

"Luck of the draw and we pulled a shitty hand."

"Daire?"

"Yes, Bambi."

"Are we going to be ok? If the thing that hurt Desmond is now pursuing you... I'm scared."

"We will be ok. I think the answers are somewhere close."

"I don't want you to get hurt. Or Niko or Xuan, or Alko."

"I know. I don't want that either."

"I don't want to lose anyone else."

"We won't. I promise. I'm a Delacroix, remember? I can protect us. My magick will protect us."

"You can't promise that. You can try, but you can't promise."

I'll sure as hell try. Nothing will hurt you, Klowbi. I'll make sure of it.

"You can promise me one thing."

"What's that?"

"Promise me you will be honest with me. No secrets."

"You already made me promise that."

"Well, promise me again."

"Alright. No secrets."

"Good. You don't have to do everything all alone. You've never had to."

"I know."

There's a long stretch of silence before I speak into the darkness again. "Bambi?"

"Yeah?"

"Do you have any suitors?"

"What? No, there's no one."

"But if there was, would you tell me?"

"Of course."

"Alright. We should get some sleep. Goodnight."

"Sleep dreams, Daire."

Listening to Klowbi's breathing even out into long deep breaths, my mind wanders to my nightmare and the hot burn throbbing with my heartbeat. The image of Desmond jumping off a cliff, of frost beading his skin, a permanent mask of terror on his face, and the hopelessness that he's never leaving haunt my mind.

In the darkness and deafening silence, I send out a final thought.

Keep fighting, Des. You can't die. If you die too, then I'll know this world was truly damned from the start.

Chapter 15

Niko has called and texted over a dozen times since our date. I've been too preoccupied to answer, my emotions a haywire of confusion, lust and guilt that have halted me from answering. My magick perks at the sight of his name on my screen and remembering the sensation of his lips on mine sends my heart racing.

Gods, I'm pathetic.

I peek into the hall to ensure I'm truly alone. Klowbi is visiting her mother and won't be back until dark which provides me with long awaited alone time. I close my door out of habit and plop onto my bed with a sigh. Before I can change my mind, I dial Niko's number, placing it on speakerphone while I hold my breath as the rings echo in the silence.

"You *are* still alive. I thought the demons under your bed ate you."

"Hello to you too, asshole," I grumble at his snide remark as my magick sparks defensively against my skin.

"How I yearn for your sweet words. Alas, you were playing hooky."

"I got distracted with other things, Niko."

"But it's common courtesy to reply to your friends, especially your guy friend who last saw you after a Shadow demon broke the car window."

He sighs into the phone, yet I note the humor in it. "I owe Xuan my next few paychecks for that, by the way. Thanks for asking."

"Did you want to talk or did you call solely because you wanted to give me shit for the window?" A ribbon of red flares from my palms and I wend it through my fingers, the magick a static silk against my skin.

"To be fair, you called me." I roll my eyes as he continues. "I haven't heard from you since the date, which went perfectly by the way, until that damn Shadow tried attacking through the window. Then you ghosted me." Niko's tone is sharp and guilt worms its way into my heart. "Again," he adds, as if he needed the finality of the word.

"I'm sorry." Curling my fingers into claws, I slash out at the ribbon of magick and it splits into five threads that spiral lazily in the air. "I haven't slept well since that night and we went to visit Thayne and Dad the next morning—"

"And you couldn't have taken five seconds to call me back and say 'hey, by the way, I'm still alive'?" Niko interjects and even through the phone his words bite. There's bitterness behind them and I imagine the hurt bordering on betrayal in his emerald eyes.

"I'm calling you now."

"You are infuriating," he mutters. "So, are you going to tell me what happened since we last spoke or must I entice you with my charm?"

With a swipe of my hand, the red ribbons flare and disappear, sparkling into dust motes showering down onto my breasts and throat. "Enticement is far more entertaining." I smirk at the idea of Niko on his knees and discard the image before it morphs into something less innocent.

"I was afraid you'd say that."

"You offered."

"Touché," he says with comedic tenor. "Are you going to tell me what happened?"

"There's a lot to explain," I begin, "and over the phone will make it hard to understand—"

"Great!" Niko blurts, cutting me off for the second time. "Then let's meet up, say tomorrow?"

"I have to work tomorrow."

"After your shift, then. We can meet at the beach, a public place, so no creepy Shadows or demons can intervene."

"I doubt that would keep them away." But seeing Niko would be a respite from my constant worry about Desmond and the aching burn that doesn't seem to be healing. It finally scabbed over and the flesh isn't nearly as red, but it's still tender, and when stretched or bumped into it splits and bleeds with a barbed pulsation.

"I didn't hear you agree," Niko teases.

"Yes, I'll meet you after my shift tomorrow."

"And you'll tell me everything."

"As much as I think you'll understand."

"Close enough. You better show up tomorrow or I'm knocking on your front door."

"I'll see you tomorrow, Niko."

"Until tomorrow."

The phone clicks signaling the end of the call. I shove my phone aside and drag my fingers through my thick mass of hair and groan. He's such a pain in the ass. Damn him and my heart.

I search my contacts for one more number and dial with my eyes closed, the warning bells tolling. It rings only twice before he answers, his soft breathing heard through the line.

"Luca? It's Daire."

"Daire!" He sounds surprised, clears his throat. "What's going on?"

"I needed to talk to you. About Desmond."

"Sure, yeah, what do you want to know?"

"Have you heard anything about how he's doing?" I ask, my voice frail.

He sighs. "Yeah, he's still comatose. The tests the doctors are running haven't found anything. They're looking for help from the wrong people. Des doesn't need doctors. He needs—"

"—magick," I finish for him. "Or an apothecary."

Luca snorts. "If only the local apothecary hadn't closed down the year before."

"If only," I jest half-heartedly. "Have you visited?"

"Several times. Roman has too. We're actually going to visit him today. Your dad has been there a lot. If it weren't for him I think Aubrie would have lost her wits."

"I can't blame her." I rub the gloom from my eyes. "One last thing, and it's a weird question."

"Shoot."

"Have you dreamt of Des?"

"Um, I mean I've had nightmares that I get a call saying he's died." Luca's voice thickens and he coughs. "Other than that, no. Why?"

"It's probably nothing," I say quickly, shaking my head as the memory of Des diving off the cliff burns behind my eyes. "If anything happens, you'll call me?"

"Of course," Luca replies, his tone softening. "Daire, are you sure there isn't anything else?"

"Positive. Thanks for answering."

"Sure. Take care, alright?"

"You too. Give Aubrie my love."

"You bet."

Luca hangs up and I let my phone fall from my ear. I should have known he wouldn't have dreamt of Desmond. Des and I were as close as siblings, in tune with each other. It was impossible to determine if Des had somehow connected with me or if the entity wanted me to see him so broken and fearful.

Glancing at the clock, I stand and shift my mattress off its frame and slip my hand in the gap. With Klowbi away for hours, I have free rein over the apartment. My fingers touch the thin spine and I slip it out and let the mattress fall back into place with the book firmly held in my hand. Laying back down on the bed, I run my fingers over the silver lettering and open the book. So far most of what I read in *Ancient Astral Projection* is nothing I didn't already know. A few pages in the book explains astral projection in great detail, including how to do it, and briefly discusses the levels of the Astral Realm. It compares them to a connected staircase, where ascending or descending requires passing through each step. It cannot be skipped or avoided. Each stair is a unique part that makes up the entirety of the Astral Realm.

Skimming several pages, I brush over the basic beginner information with little intrigue and pause when the topic of magick surfaces. Others rarely practice the Craft in the Astral Realm, unlike me. Still I'm cautious with my spell choices. Utilizing magick in the Astral Realm is a delicate balance, and even from my limited experience, it tends to cater towards hazardous rather than advantageous. The last time I had astral projected my magick had reacted defensively on instinct without my prompting which has its perks when in immediate danger.

The book reads how critical it is that the caster in the Astral Realm is not only confident in their abilities, but assertive of their intentions with emotions in check. Magick works instantaneously in the Astral Realm and there can be no hidden intentions or hesitations. The Astral Realm will read the caster openly and without falsifying human motivation, meaning the caster cannot hide their will. If the caster intends harm, then the spell will oblige; if the caster intends to heal, then the spell will restore. Misaligned intentions and emotions can cause spells to backfire, harming the caster or nearby beings. Magick is based on intention, whereas the outcome is based on experience and willpower.

As I turn the page, the book explains how pain works in the Astral Realm. Harm can still occur to the caster even without a physical body. A harmful spell can drain an astral projector's energy, even though the Astral Realm is an infinite source of energy.

Energy healing takes immense amounts of time and rest. The caster's energy weakens and makes projection more arduous. If the projector can no longer stay manifested in their astral form, more times than not they will be called back forcefully to their physical form. Sources claim feeling extreme exhaustion, leading to days of sleep, while others experienced sudden illness followed by a week of recovery. The caster experiences ineffable pain when drained; pain equivalent to your soul being ripped piece by piece from your being, or in physical terms, a fatal wound. Should this feeling arise, quickly depart the Astral Realm and return to the physical world. There have been documented cases where the caster became so weak they could no longer keep themselves manifested in the Astral Realm, but they could not return to their physical beings, either. This results in astral death.

"Astral death," I murmur, sending a cold spike down my spine. My magick stirs and a heavy, slick feeling sinks in my churning belly. A bitter acidic taste coats my tongue.

Astral death, the book reads, is a permanent ending in both the Astral Realm and the physical world. The two worlds co-exist, and one cannot be without the other. Without the soul, the body is an empty shell and is useless otherwise. Astral death is shrouded in secrecy. It is said that the Astral Realm absorbs the projector's energy, offering eternal bliss to the departed. No evidence supports this theory. Avoid astral death at all costs.

Swallowing, I flip through the remaining pages. Most are blank, waiting to be completed, but the author included a brief paragraph on the final page. Wiping my slick palms on my thighs, I read the final page.

Beyond the limitless Astral Plane is the Etheric Plane. Even less is known about the Etheric Realm, but it is claimed this world is not known to mortals. Some label the beings here as demons, angels, gods, or aliens, but claims remain unsupported without evidence. Believing that this realm holds nightmares and monsters beyond human imagination is more plausible. No sources claim what could be there, but theories suggest that all is known and answered in this realm, gifted only to those deemed worthy by the Others. The Etheric Plane resembles the Astral Plane in its boundlessness and constant transformation. However, while the Astral Plane is generally secure, the Etheric Plane is dangerous and inaccessible by anything but chance. It is seen only by the ones who wish it to be seen.

And at the bottom of the very last page, a handwritten scrawl:

Beware the beast that dwells in the depths of the heavens and the abyss of the in-between.

A dozen times I read the scrawl, knowing it's a futile attempt to decipher it. The warning speaks of an archaic nature, a secret split between blood and bone, of sorcery and mystery.

I close the book and brush my fingers along the deep purple cover. I stand to shift my mattress and slide the book back into its resting place and prop myself against the bed.

With an ominous thrill bordering on an adrenaline fueled fear, and the new knowledge in regards to the Astral Realm, I can't resist the craving for it, the beckoning call of the realm and its empowering embrace.

I secure my bedroom door and windows by drawing protective sigils on any exit and pull the curtains to my window. With the lights off, my room takes on a gray hue from the filtered light through the blinds. Reclining on my bed, I close my eyes and imagine flying through the stars in our universe and further, past the millions of suns in the skies and the trillions of planets teeming with gas and iron and acid. My essence peels away and I shoot through the masses, faster, higher, until my bed is far away and yet beneath me.

The world is in hues of crimson, rose, cardinal red, coral, and fuchsia. The grass is a gentle salmon and the dirt a deep maroon. Daire glances at her hands and notices they too are colored within the same palette—her skin a pale pink and nails resembling rust. When she swings her braid around to check the color, it is still the pitch black of space she is accustomed to.

She stands beside a flowing river that eerily reminds her of blood. It looks as if the land is bleeding, unable to clot a gaping gash. Several mud puddles and stones covered in muck and weeds can be seen along the river's edge. From first glance, it appears that the river itself is tearing the earth apart and leaving jagged chunks of flesh behind. Even the trees appear macabre.

Starting towards the nearest tree, Daire brushes her fingers across the translucent bark and pulls back immediately when it gives beneath her touch. Instead of the roughness she expected, it is soft and warm, reminiscent of flesh. Peering closer, she notes the trees seem to sag with an unseen weight. The branches dip like fat hanging from an upraised arm and hold an unnatural curve as if they are joints rather than wood. Leaves and flowers bloom cardinal red with veins. Small, shiny, fist-sized, and circular, they appear wet. They look like human hearts and branches of seeping heartstrings.

Following the river, she glances up through the globose heart-leaves to find the sky a sweet cotton candy pink. A massive white orb with a fuchsia halo hangs in the sky, presumably the mock of a sun in this level of the Astral Realm. There are no clouds, but Daire can imagine that if there were, they'd remind her of globs of fat floating gelatinously in the sky.

Seeing everything the color of flesh-tones sets her on edge. She has never seen a monochromatic world with organ-like structures as the landscape. She's grateful that the grass is not hair or the dirt skin or the sun a beady eye. It still leaves her chilled with her non-existent heart beating frantically in her ribcage.

Movement catches her eye as she winds her way through the forest of flesh. She continues walking, her gaze transfixed by the flash in the river. Seeing anything that isn't close to the surface of the thick red water is strenuous. The surface stirs as a copper tentacle emerges from the river's depths before retreating. The creature the tentacle belongs to is heading the opposite way she's going, swimming upstream and fighting the current. The river, despite the rushing rapids along the embankment, is serene. It appears like stained glass, interrupted only by occasional ripples caused by tentacles or globular masses sinking in the red water.

Besides the few aquatic creatures in the river, there is nothing to keep Daire company save for the fleshy trees. Continuing downstream, uneasiness grows with each step. She is on the third level. From her experience, higher levels have more astral wildlife. But there is nothing in the trees except the pulsing hearts, and there are no playful Fayrie hiding in the bushes like last time. It is eerily quiet.

Peeking through a gap in the trees is a massive blood red lake. Heading down the incline, even from her vantage point, the lake is endless. Unlike the river, which is still and silent besides the beings beneath it, the lake pulses with ripples in even beats, sending waves towards the shore. It looks as if a massacre had happened with how deep and knowing the lake appears, as if it had swallowed up whatever had bled enough to fill it.

Despite how distant the lake is, Daire walks for only a minute before seeing the shore. The waves she glimpsed earlier do not reach the coast, leaving the edges of the lake gleaming like bloodied glass. Shuffling away from the *river, her steps are muffled as she approaches the lake's edge and kneels before it. She dips a finger into the red liquid. It's lukewarm and has the consistency of water rather than blood, and when she pulls the finger out, it isn't stained red like she's expecting. She dips her whole hand in, comforted by the fact it only looks like blood, and calls on her magick to summon an image of Desmond, searching for him through the Astral. Daire concentrates, willing the lake to be used to scry, searching past the ripples emanating from somewhere below, but besides the pink and white-capped waves, nothing shimmers on the surface.*

Daire attempts once more and sends out another burst of magick, focusing on Desmond's terror, the hellfire eyes hunting through the dark. She imagines his pain, his desperation to escape, his screams echoing in her head and the blood-chilling laugh from the entity scraping her bones.

With her hand against the lake's surface, Daire signals again, recalling the details of Desmond cowering behind the chair with leather straps, his missing fingers, the frost eating across his skin, and the low rumbling of the entity's approach. The magickal current has her fingers twitching, and the surface of the water ripples. She sinks into the maroon sand, channeling more of her magick until the water appears to be glowing. There's a flash of a face in the water, a glimpse of diamond eyes.

"Desmond," she gasps, gritting her teeth. "I'm here. Where are you?"

His face appears again. Black and greasy hair takes shape, blood stains his face like war paint that streaks down his throat. The vision wavers, and Daire curses as she pushes more energy into the medium. It strengthens again and she notices where his left ear should be is a gaping hole. His mouth is twisted into a grimace, his eyes bright in the red water.

"Desmond!" Daire cries, her voice breaking. "Can you hear me? Where are you?"

Desmond's features flicker, his eyes darting wildly as if he heard her. She watches as he opens his mouth to speak, but no sound escapes. Daire curses again, her desperation mounting, and pushes her arms deeper into the water. Her magick burns in her chest, a warning headache building in her temple.

"Just a little more," Daire grunts and the glowing water lights like fire.

The joint-like branches shake violently and the ground quivers beneath her feet. The image of Desmond disappears and a jolt of panic has Daire reaching deeper for more magick. The water smooths like glass and the image solidifies. Desmond turns his head, his eyes staring straight at her.

"Des?" She leans closer, her face mere inches from the water's surface.

His lips twitch and they form into a smile. His face tightens, his lips widening and stretching abnormally, his teeth a brilliant white amongst the red. His grin is wider than it should be and his diamond eyes appear distant. Panic settles in Daire's stomach.

The face morphs as Desmond's skin turns black and his smile sharpens into razors. His diamond eyes crumble into black orbs that burst into flames so hot she can feel the heat through the water. A darkness sweeps across the land, decaying the red world into rot and moldering flesh.

"A swan cannot fly without its wings," the entity growls, its voice filled with a cosmic savagery. "And yours have been cut, Daire Delacroix."

An umbrous hand bursts from the depths, wicked claws reaching for Daire's throat. She shrieks and throws herself backwards as a head emerges from the water, fire eyes blazing. A shattering cackle bubbles from its razor maw, its monstrous hands clawing to the surface.

A scream erupts from Daire as she fumbles to her knees, teeth gritted and hands extended. Magick explodes from her palms. Scarlet red and indigo beams slam into the entity. A roar shatters the air, the black decay halting feet from where Daire kneels. The water shivers as the entity steams and sinks into its depths.

Daire stays where she is, gasping for breath, her hands trembling as she watches the water for movement. Nothing else emerges and the earlier calm resumes, but the terror leaves her frozen, too afraid to look away in fear of the entity's return.

After what feels like hours, she stands, her knees shaking with the effort. A tear wells in her eyes, blurring her vision as she sucks in a deep breath. "I'm sorry, Des." Daire bows her head and she wraps her arms around herself.

Static traces her tongue and she lifts her head, searching for the source. The presence is welcoming, a warm blanket after the icy terror the entity left in its wake. She recognizes the sensation, the benevolence and familiarity, from the last time she projected.

"Hello, again." Diare murmurs. "You could have shown up sooner." Her magick stirs beneath her skin with curiosity from the magnetism of the benign power. It feels of home, of safety, and Daire allows the power to settle around her, to soothe the quaking of her limbs.

A low rumble has her flinching, the water rippling as if something is trying to emerge. Daire stumbles backwards further from the shore, shaking her head. "I have to go. I will find you." She isn't sure if she's speaking to Desmond or the calming power. A soft pull comes from her chest, a phantom touch of a connection pulling taut as she closes her eyes and retreats from the bleeding earth and pumping hearts, from the entity dwelling in the depths, and the magick that whispers of home.

Excerpt from the Gray Book

The Mist

This Shadow is unlike any I've encountered before due to its physical form and its disposition. Its physical phenomenon coalesces into what can only be described as an ever-changing black mist. This Shadow is dangerous and tricky to combat, but thankfully its habitat is limited to places of incarceration (such as jails or prisons) and hospitals (often those that hold the mentally unstable). Those that have come into contact with this being all have had physical ailments followed by long-lasting mental conditions. Physical ailments have included dizziness, fatigue, vomiting, headaches, and in some extreme cases unconsciousness and seizures. Psychological distress includes sudden bouts of aggression, increases in anxiety and depression, suicidal thoughts (sometimes leading to actions), and severe personality changes. I theorize that the reason this Shadow Mist is typically only found in locations of incarceration is due to the large masses of mentally unstable people in a controlled environment that would be a reliable feeding ground. It has been noted that once the victims were removed from the infected areas the Mist resided in, they slowly returned to their normal selves, often with signs of improved health.

Chapter 16

A warm breeze brushes a stray lock of hair across my cheek, and when I nibble my lip it tastes of ocean salt, wind, and sand. *Earth, air, and water—nearly all of the elements.* The ocean is calm despite the gusts of sudden wind. Several little ones are running screaming into the cool waters before splashing and clawing their way back to the blazing sand where the young parents sit smiling and laughing. June's hot sun makes the waters barely tolerable while the sand sears soft feet.

Rocking myself softly, I'm grateful the swing I chose doesn't squeak with decades of hard use and rust. Occasionally it groans in protest before falling silent, showing its age through frame stress from uneven weight. My feet are buried in the sand where it is cool beneath and only hot between my toes. It's a welcome sensation with the hint of summer buzzing in the air.

Ever since I returned from the Astral I've been wary of the darkness, fearful that those blazing eyes are following my whereabouts, that razor smile patiently waiting to latch around my throat. I've been terrified to sleep and reluctant to return to the Astral. The entity's words echo in my head, taunting and cruel. Though I'm intrigued by the other calming presence of magick that calls to me, it's not enough to convince me to return any time soon.

Niko is supposed to meet me at the beach like we had discussed. He had yet to show up, so I sat in the swings swaying softly and studying the book *Aberrant Magick: Shadow, Nether and Ether of the Arcane* with the *Gray Book* and *Symbols and Sigils of the Witch* tucked in my bag by my feet.

As I survey the first several pages of *Aberrant Magick*, I realize the book holds the secrets of old magick and the more I read, the darker the magick becomes. It holds forgotten spells of ancient times, dark magick that even I wouldn't dare attempt for fear of karmic retribution, rituals for demon summoning and mind control and perverse manipulation of death. It holds manic hexes and infernal curses that explain how to send hellhounds to tear apart a victim's soul or inflict seven days of agony upon an enemy.

The rituals are worse. They hold the promise of demonic aid with an unnamed cost that will be permanently paid regardless if the witch consents or not. Some rituals demand sacrifices to fulfill the request, specifically human sacrifices. I've read one ritual that requires a sacrifice of a newborn babe fresh from the mother's womb in order to feed the entity being summoned. It makes my mouth dry and gooseflesh prickle over my arms despite the sun beating down from above.

This book was meant to be hidden and forgotten and burned to ash. And yet it sat on Thayne's shelves free for anyone's taking, not even locked away behind glass or sealed in a metal box and thrown into the dark to be forgotten. It made me question if Thayne *knew* he had this book or if it had been misplaced and erased and miraculously found itself sitting amongst hundreds of innocent books on the shelves.

But now it sits in my lap, and I have to wonder if the answer to my mother's death is held somewhere in these ancient pages bound by leather. I feel ashamed that I wanted to keep the book instead of returning it to Thayne. Returning it means never seeing it again. And if the answers are somewhere amongst the old spells and rituals, as long as I don't attempt them, there should be no harm in reading. I know better than to meddle with such ancient beings.

No one knows this book is in my possession; no one will be missing it or scouring for it. I'll return it to Thayne after I find my answer.

For as old as it is, the book itself is in fair condition. It has to be archaic, from the time when magick first emerged, when witches surpassed kings in power and were revered and dreaded, not condemned to the stake. Perhaps it's enchanted to withstand time, unlike all things.

Another chill steals down my spine. Closing the book, I slip it back into my bag and am careful to hide it well. Klowbi wouldn't dare dig amongst my things, and she has no reason to, but the thought of my books being uncovered and stolen from me doesn't sit well. If they fell into the wrong hands, it could be catastrophic.

Hands grab me from behind, gripping my shoulders tight and sending a jolt of pain shooting from the burn. Jumping to my feet, I whirl to face my attacker with my magick curled like vipers in my palms. My racing heart is comforted only slightly at the dizzying hum of magick at my disposal.

Laughter fills my ears before my mind catches up to the man standing in front of me. His laugh is sweet and honest, his cheeks ruddy and eyes flashing brilliant green in the sun. Frowning and embarrassed, I punch his arm and he stumbles in the sifting sand beneath.

"Relax, Daire." Niko chuckles with his famous grin. "It's only me."

"Don't ever do that again." Snagging my bag viciously from the sand and peeking inside to make sure all are accounted for, I secure it tightly. I return my gaze to Niko with my arms crossed. His rust red beanie covers his messy locks and he's wearing a baggy white t-shirt that is miraculously still white and khakis with tears in the knees. A skateboard is leaning against his leg, his nimble fingers propping the board in place.

"I got you good, didn't I?" Niko teases, leaning in and hanging his body weight on one of the chains of the swing. It groans in protest but holds.

"It won't happen twice."

He chuckles and I want to punch him again.

My arm is throbbing from the burn, but it's a manageable pain. No matter what spell or poultice I try, the wound won't heal. Klowbi caught sight of it by accident and I lied and told her I had burned it while working in the kitchen. She accepted my excuse, but it's been harder to hide with each passing day.

"That sounds like a challenge," Niko taunts with a haughty grin. He walks around the swing with the lip of his skateboard trailing in the sand. Further away, seagull screams are heard amidst the lapping of waves on the shore.

"It *is* a threat, and I have no issue in following through." Reaching forward, I snag his beanie and pull it down over his eyes and give him a shove. He stumbles and slips in the sand, desperately grappling for the swing set frame with one hand while futilely holding onto the skateboard with the other.

By the time he regains his balance and his vision, I've already danced away from his reach. He shifts the beanie on his head and several stray locks of hair have tumbled free from beneath. He smirks at me as he devours me with his eyes. "Call it a truce for now. Want to make our way down the beach? As much as I enjoy hearing the screams of children, I'd rather not listen to them all afternoon."

"Lead the way."

"Nice try, you lead. I'm not letting you attack me from behind."

Sand whispers with each of our footfalls. Further up ahead to our right, a group of four around our age are playing volleyball. Several bouts of laughter and curses drift on the warm wind in our direction. Two children are sitting on the shore with their feet buried in wet sand while each wave laps at their pudgy, pale legs. The parents sit in lawn chairs not too far away. Niko and I continue and I can't help but wonder if that's what my family looked like when I was a child. The three of us sitting at the beach laughing and eating watermelon and bathing in the sun without worry of loss or pain; knowing that Mom would kiss me goodnight instead of leaving me lying in the dark trying to remember where the laugh lines are on her face, or how much gray was beginning to show in the midnight black of her hair.

"Did you fix the car window?" I ask as we walk down the shoreline. My bag bumps against my hip reassuringly and my fingers hover protectively over the clasp.

"Yes, but not until Xuan threatened to kill me and bind me to her so I could never escape her wrath." Niko shivers dramatically. "That truly would be my personal hell."

"I suppose you lost car privileges while she was reprimanding you?"

"If she ever saw me driving her car again, I think she'd run me over with it and leave me on the side of the road." Niko pulls at his beanie so the tips of his ears are covered. "But I fixed the window. She was only pissed at me that night. The next day she didn't bring it up once."

"That might be worse."

Niko shrugs and hoists his skateboard higher so it isn't dragging in the sand. "I'm used to her fury, but she's barely left her room since you and Klowbi came over. After Xuan reamed me for allowing damage to her car, she only said to let her know if I feel like I'm being followed or watched."

"Did you tell her it was a Shadow?"

"Yes, I know you didn't want me to, but she needs to know. If it's following you, there could be more following us." His expression hardens, his lips set in an unnatural f.

"You're right," I admit. It wasn't likely anything would be following Niko, but if something found Xuan's powers as interesting as mine it could be catastrophic. "How have they been since that night?"

Niko slows his steps and his eyes are fixed on the ocean. Deep blue crests rise from the horizon and disappear into the dark beneath. "Both have barely left the house. Alko has only now been feeling safe enough to leave his room, but he's casting glamour magick like a madman. I've never seen him so off." He shakes his head as if to rid a memory. "Xuan hasn't said much about it, though I highly doubt she'd tell me if there was something. She knows my feelings towards you..." His words trail off and are swallowed by the clash of waves. "She's been doing a lot of spiritwork, or so she says. I've tried staying out of the way, which clearly hasn't been working."

"Does she still blame me for that night?" I can't mask the vehemence in my voice.

"That is not my place to say, but she isn't nearly as irate, if that's what you mean. You should ask her yourself on Friday."

"Friday?" I sputter, my fingers tightening on the clasp of my bag.

"Damn, I think I spoiled the surprise," Niko teases with an impish grin. "Klowbi is organizing a group night out. If it makes you feel better, I only found out this morning. I bet she'll tell you tonight."

"I hate surprises."

"Good thing it won't be a surprise."

"If it were my choice, I'd stay home," I grumble and Niko gives me a knowing look. "Of course, I won't. If I didn't show up Klowbi would be devastated."

"I'd be left dealing with a terrified Alko, a seething Xuan, and an inconsolable Klowbi. You wouldn't dare leave me to my fate knowing that."

Niko's grin sends my heart rocketing into my throat. I turn to the ocean and taste the salt on my lips and the briny scent drifting from the waters. "I suppose I can't." When I face Niko again, he has kicked his shoes off and stuffed his socks in the heels. He's rolling up his pant legs when he looks up with a cheeky grin. "What are you doing?"

"Rolling my pants up, what's it look like?" He grabs my hand and starts leading me towards the water. I dig my heels in and lean my weight against his, my bag scuffing against the hot sand. "Come on, Daire. The water will feel great."

"My bag." I gesture and he releases my hand. He's backstepping towards the waterline until his feet splash into the ocean ankle deep. His sandy hair is whipping free from beneath the beanie now that he's in the ocean gusts.

"No one will take your bag and we won't be far." When I don't move, he takes several steps backwards until he's knee deep and the water is soaking his khakis. "Trust me, no one will mess with a witch's bag." He tilts his head, plastered with a boyish smile, and waves me closer. He looks so childlike at that moment, so innocent. I wonder how he retained that part of himself when I lost mine so long ago.

I groan and set my bag on top of his skateboard where he left it in the sand. I set my shoes beside it, padding across the sand until the cool water nips my toes. I wade over the slick mud and feel it sticking between my toes. When I'm standing in front of Niko, I cup my hand and send a spray of salt water at his face. His laugh is unfiltered and so authentic my heart flutters. A smile graces my face at the sound.

"And people used to say witches sink." Niko chuckles and sends a massive wave at me with his hands. A laugh escapes me as it soaks my pants and the bottom half of my shirt.

"We float just like you common folk," I say and send another splash of ocean water at him.

I'm unsure how long we splash and dunk in the ocean, but our feet go numb and my skin turns cold by the time we reach the beach. Shivering, we both wring out our sopping clothes and I squeeze saltwater from my hair. Grabbing our things, we follow the shoreline drifting further from any prying ears. The heat radiating off the sand warms my numb toes and sends tingles shooting up my legs.

We both plop down on an empty section of beach and the joyous screams of children are masked by the waves. He sets his skateboard to the side and I prop my bag against my hip again, afraid to leave it too far from reach. Both of our knees are bent, backs hunched, our thighs close to touching, as we watch the hypnotic to and fro of the waves.

"Are you going to make me ask?" Niko's voice breaks the lull of the waves. "Or are you going to make me beg?"

"Begging is more entertaining," I croon, brushing particles of dried sand from my ankles and toes.

"How did I know you were going to say that," Niko mutters. When I don't reply, I feel his stare and I cave and glance at him, dreading the conversation I've been trying to avoid. "You said you'd tell me in person. Well, here I am, in the flesh."

"So it would seem." I return my gaze back to the ocean. The sun is sinking, the sky the color of honey with clouds spun of gold. With a breath of salt, I go over everything Klowbi and I found about the Shadows and the subspecies. I explain the nightmares I've had, but exclude the truth of how I really received my burn. Despite knowing Niko's thoughts about Desmond, I also reveal how dire Desmond's situation is and my hunch that it might be connected to my mother's death, though Niko holds his tongue on the subject. After reviewing everything, I admit my limited knowledge of the symbols, only recognizing them as runes and their associated meanings.

Careful to keep my secret books a secret, I hand the slip of paper with the runes scrawled on it along with the red cover book titled *Symbols and Sigils of the Witch* over to Niko to study. He traces the runes with the book sitting unopened in his lap.

"You don't know what the runes mean?"

"I understand the meaning of the runes, but not the entity's intentions behind them," I clarify and snag the red book from his lap. I flip it open to the marked page with all the runes and their meanings, including in reverse. I point at *uruz* and *mannaz* on the open page of the book. "This is what they mean when doing rune readings, but I can't make sense of it."

Niko stares at it for a quiet moment and his voice startles me when he speaks again. "What else does it mean?"

I look at him, confused. "What do you mean?"

"Magick always seems to be cryptic with more meaning than what meets the eye, right? That's why it's dangerous to practice." Niko hands the slip with runes back to me. "What else does it mean?"

Frantic, I snag the red book from Niko's lap and into mine. I thumb through several pages, recalling when Klowbi said there were charts in the book. I hadn't thought much of it and had spent most of my time scouring my other two books rather than this one after having a sense of defeat when I couldn't solve what the damn runes meant. I stop searching when the charts are visible on the pages.

"My gods."

"Did I solve the mystery of the runes?" Niko leans closer to view the page with his shoulder pressing against mine.

"They are numbers," I say and point to each rune on the chart. "Each rune correlates with a number." It doesn't take long to decipher. "Five. One."

"What does that mean?" Niko asks, his breath tickling my ear.

"You're the smart one, remember? You were the one who said it could have multiple meanings," I remark, disappointment scalding my insides.

"I don't want to take all the glory." Niko grabs the note and my magick buzzes where our skin brushes. "Is this exactly how the entity wrote it in the wax?"

"Mostly. When the entity was writing in the wax, it was a constant flow with no spaces or breaks," I explain trying to recall that night. The chaos afterwards made my writing sloppy while trying to copy the runes and it was possible I had subconsciously written the runes how I recognized them. The wax on the table seamlessly connected the runes, with a dividing slash uniting them into one fluid message.

"A date," I mumble. "It's a date," I repeat, louder this time. "Month and day."

"Five one. That's May first."

"Beltane." A shiver steals down my spine. *When everything started to go wrong.*

"What about Beltane?" Niko asks, shifting backwards on the heels of his hands and straightening his legs.

"I'm not sure," I lie.

Maybe it's my magick or my witch's intuition, but I have a hunch that I need to return to the festival grounds where we celebrated Beltane. I can't ignore the small possibility I missed something at the grounds that can save Desmond.

"I have to do all the work, don't I?" Niko grins and I elbow his ribs in reply. "Not even a thank you?"

"You're insufferable," I grumble, but lean over anyway and plant a light kiss on his cheek.

"That's it?" he asks, but his cheeks are flushed, eyes dilated.

"Don't get greedy."

Feeling lighter than I have in weeks, I press my body into Niko's, careful to keep my burn from too much pressure. He stiffens beneath me for a moment and I feel his muscles relax when he realizes I'm not pulling away. A tentative arm envelops me, gradually becoming a protective hold on my shoulders. I inhale his scent of salt, sand, and herbs along with a slight trace of cigarette smoke.

I focus on the lapping waves morphing gold and orange from the sun, but my mind wanders to the body of water in the Astral Realm, the lake the color of lifeblood where hearts grow on trees. Even now, when I sit on a beach in the physical world, I can still sense the dark magick bleeding into the Astral and the ancient breath of the entity exhaling onto my lips. If I hadn't moved as fast as I did or had my magick spooled to attack, the entity would have me alongside Desmond.

For a split second, the ocean ahead is identical to the one in the Astral Realm, reflecting the same bloody red. A soft pulse tightens in my chest at the memory of the familiar magick. Thayne said Lilith was trying to reach me in my dreams. Is she the familiar magick I've been sensing?

Closing my eyes, I push a tendril of magick and send it outwards across the ocean. I feel a gentle tug against my breastbone, as if a piece of me is slivered and sent out, a minuscule emptiness where the piece should be. After a moment of waiting, I know no one is listening. I call my magick to return and it settles heavy in my belly, my disappointment a stone in my heart.

Niko rubs my arm, drawing lazy circles on my shoulder. "What are you thinking about?" His voice is a breathy whisper against my ear, warm and tender, and I know if I tilt my head backwards our lips would touch.

"Another world."

"What's that mean?" he asks louder. He stops his gentle touch on my arm.

"Nothing," I say quickly. "I was lost daydreaming."

Niko bursts into laughter and he draws his arm away to wipe at nonexistent tears. The absence of warmth where his arm was has me drawing my legs closer to my chest and I wrap my arms around them tightly. "What's so funny?"

"You don't daydream, Daire," Niko says with a quirky tilt to his smile, eyes molten emeralds in the golden light.

"How would you know?"

"Because I know you. Why would you daydream if you could snap your fingers and make it happen?"

"I wish it were that simple."

"So, what were you thinking about?" he asks again. "Don't lie, either. I thought we were past that."

"Damn you." I drag my fingers through my hair.

Lying to Niko twists my gut and I'm unsure if I can convince him to let it go. If I admit to Niko I've astral projected twice, even though we agreed not to, I know he won't be concerned. But if he tells Xuan or Alko, or hell, even Klowbi, it will cause friction between our group again. I already feel guilty keeping secrets from Klowbi. She's the one person I can rely on, but when it comes to secrets, I doubt her alliance. She trusts Xuan nearly as much as she trusts me. Telling Klowbi means Xuan will surely find out sooner than later. Niko came to my aid when Klowbi hadn't, and he had yet to provide a reason to doubt his word.

"If I tell you, you cannot tell anyone else."

"That's not a good thing to start with."

"I'm serious. Swear it."

"I swear." He raises his hand for emphasis.

"I've astral projected twice since Beltane. I know we agreed not to until things began to settle, but I thought I'd find an answer." Words flow from my mouth unbidden. Niko nods along as understanding dawns on his face. "Xuan already isn't happy with me so if she were to find out—"

"She would be livid." Niko finishes for me. "Did you find anything?"

"I saw Desmond," I murmur, combing my fingers through the warm sand. "The first time I spoke to him. He was hiding from the entity. He was missing fingers and covered in blood and grime." I clear the tightness from my throat, glancing at Niko. "He sent me away before I could get any information."

"What about the second time?"

"I saw Des, but I don't think it was truly him." I close my eyes at the memory of Desmond's skin shifting black, his diamond eyes bursting into a blazing fire. "It was the entity. It knows who I am and it wants me." My voice is tiny, barely audible over the crashing waves. "When it's done with Desmond, I'm next."

"Daire." Niko's voice cracks and he reaches for my hand, his fingers overlapping mine. "I won't let it take you."

"Thanks, but I don't think either one of us has much say on that." I squeeze his hand. "There was something else there with me, both times. The energy was very different from the entity's. It felt familiar, like home."

"What do you think it is?"

"I'm not certain, but it could be Lilith. I think she's trying to communicate, but the entity is keeping her from reaching me."

"If it is Lilith, she will find a way to reach you." Niko strokes a thumb along my skin and I lean into his touch. "I'm guessing I'm still sworn to secrecy?"

"Yes, you can't tell anyone, especially Xuan."

"Daire." Niko sighs and pulls his hand from mine. "This is bigger than us both, like you said. Out of anyone, Xuan *should* know because she's in tune with the Otherworld. She can help you."

"So you're going to tell her?"

"No, I'm not a snitch and I made you a promise. Even if it is a stupid decision," he grumbles and I glare. His eyes soften and my heart clenches at his tender expression. "I don't want the entity to come after you again."

"I know."

"I won't say a word, but if something this big happens again, we have to tell the others." Niko brushes a stray lock of hair from my cheek, his gaze gentle. "I'm on your side. They'll be mad at me, too."

I huff a laugh and rest my head on his shoulder, his scent of herb and smoke soothing my rapid heartbeat. "Thank you, Niko."

"You have to promise me something, though."

"That wasn't part of the deal."

"I'm complying with your deal. It's only fair."

"Alright, fine, what is it?" I lift my head and level my stare at him.

"That's the attitude I'm looking for." When I don't smile at his prodding, he rolls his eyes. "Promise me the next time something happens, you *will* tell me."

"Alright, I promise." The lie curdles my tongue.

"That was easy. One more thing," he says and presses closer.

"Two demands? What is it?"

"Don't do anything stupid."

"Now you're really asking a lot."

"Daire, I'm serious. Or at least don't do anything stupid until after our group hangs out. I don't want to be the scapegoat," Niko mumbles and my heart aches at the admission.

"I won't," I promise. At least I can fulfill one wish.

"Does Klowbi know what you told me?"

I shake my head. "No, I was afraid she'd tell Xuan. And I don't want her to worry."

"She's not the only one worrying," Niko says. "I won't tell anyone. I'm no rat."

"Thanks." Niko's arms rest around my shoulders again, his nimble fingers wending my braid between.

I allow myself to sag against him, my head resting in the hollow of his neck. His heart thumps steadily in his chest as I imagine the taste of his lips with his breaths heavy in my ear. But I don't move to kiss him. I stay nestled against him, watching the ocean turn into a kaleidoscope of oranges, pinks, reds, and golds as the sun sets. Despite the overwhelming sense of serenity and comfort, the phantom connection pulls taut in my core, and instead of seeing an ocean of gold, I see an ocean of red.

Chapter 17

The aroma of freshly baked pizza, fried pickles, cheese, and anything else that could be thrown in the fryers wafts through the bar. Through the window, the sky is a purple bruise growing darker by the minute. Some patrons stand outside on the patio smoking cigarettes and sipping mugs of beer. Every so often when the door opens the sickly scent would waft in and mingle charmingly with the taste of fried food before dispersing. A group of young men still wearing their hi-vis apparel stand by the pool table chuckling, betting, and slamming down beers. They appear to be older than me, but it's hard to tell with their scruff of beards and dirt smudged brows.

The crowded bar has few seats available. Usual bar flies buzz around the room, eyeing up any new faces with uncertainty before claiming a stool and demanding to be served with an already drunken grin. The Night Owl is notorious for late night antics, usually involving inebriated scuffles with the rare bar fight thrown in when someone wouldn't pay a bet. It also happens to be the only bar in town with arcade games.

Klowbi and I claim a high top table while we wait for the rest of the group to arrive. I'm sipping a vodka Sprite and Klowbi is on her third glass of root beer since she's just shy of the legal drinking age. Whenever the staff is occupied, I let her sip my drink and laugh each time she grimaces at the flavor. It doesn't stop her from taking more sips, though.

"They burnt your drink," Klowbi chokes out after chugging half of her glass. "All I taste is vodka."

"That's how you know they made the drink right," I tell her and take a long sip. She gags and shakes her head, but not before stealing a quick taste for herself.

"Should we order food?" Klowbi's gaze flitters around the room. The table we're at isn't well lit and her freckles appear much darker, her hair a dark chestnut rather than silky auburn. She wears a quarter sleeve maroon blouse with a jean jacket over top. She's twisting the pink-studded flower bracelet on her left wrist, the scar tissue on her right hand shiny and ferocious in the bar lighting.

"You can, but I'm not hungry." My stomach has been twisting like angry snakes in my belly. I haven't seen Xuan or Alko in weeks and despite Klowbi's reassurance that everything is fine now, I'm hesitant to believe her. "Are you sure there's no bad blood?"

Klowbi's doe eyes are bright when she turns back in my direction. "I spoke with Xuan already, remember? Everything is great." Her smile is loose and giddy as she takes another swallow of my vodka Sprite.

"Are you tipsy?"

"Maybe a little," Klowbi admits, cheeks flushing. "I told you, all I taste is vodka."

"Lightweight," I laugh and finish off my drink.

Klowbi pushes up her jacket sleeves and rests her elbows on the table. "How's your burn? Is it healing?"

I shake my head and push my empty glass to the center of the table. "No, but it isn't getting any worse, either."

"It should be healed by now." Klowbi frowns, her lower lip bright red.

"I'm sure it will be fine. Don't worry, Bambi." I twist around when I hear the front door open. "There they are."

Niko leads the siblings into the bar. He has on a black flat cap with a white bat emblazoned on the front, his sandy hair curling around his ears. Behind him, Alko wears jeans and an oversized jacket. From here, I see a dozen rings on his fingers and a dull glimmer of chain around his throat. Orange mist wafts from the jewelry and Alko appears to be shrouded in glamour magick. I can hardly see his face through the thick fog. Close to his side is Xuan with her deadpan expression and calculating black eyes. She has on a yellow plaid flannel and black jeans with a glint of silver at her wrist. Xuan sees us before the others do and her lips twitch in a semblance of a thin-lipped smile.

Klowbi fumbles and stands precariously on the bottom rungs of the chair, waving an arm wildly to catch their attention. A few extra heads turn with tipsy grins and amusement in their eyes. Klowbi jumps from her chair as our group approaches, oblivious to the other bar patrons, and gives each of them a tight hug. I can't help but notice she lingers longest on Xuan. I don't stand from my seat as I wave in greeting.

"Hey," Alko says and gives me a side hug, surprising me. Being in his presence, I feel magick radiating off of him and my magick stirs in my core. "I'm glad you came."

"I'm happy you all came too. I wasn't sure," I begin and Alko squeezes my shoulder.

"Misunderstanding. Best to leave it where it lies," Alko comforts with a gentle smile.

Nodding, I turn to the rest of the group. "Xuan," I say as she watches me with dark eyes. "First drink is on me."

I barely see it, but she reveals a ghost of a smile. "I'll take you up on that offer."

"I'm going to put in a drink and food order. Usuals for everyone?" Niko says, gesturing to the bar behind.

"Get a pizza," Alko calls.

"And deep fried pickles." Klowbi pipes up.

"We'll find a new table that will fit us all." Xuan gestures to the tiny two-person high top we're sitting at.

"I'll help Niko," I offer, backing towards the bar and snagging Niko by the arm as I go. "We will catch up with you guys."

"We'll be in the back," Klowbi announces, linking an arm with Alko and Xuan and leading the way despite her scuffling steps.

Niko shoves his way to the bar and lets me in beside him. He leans an arm against a pillar to my left to keep unwanted socialization from drunk men and stands closer than he needs to. I don't complain. I lean in closer so my hip is pressing against his and we both try flagging down a bartender. It takes several attempts, but eventually we manage to place our food and drink order.

Niko bends his head so his lips are close to my ear. "Glad to see you and Xuan haven't tried killing each other yet."

"The night is still young and too sober," I mutter back. He chuckles in my ear and it sends gooseflesh down my arms. My magick purrs and tugs, wishing to be closer to him. I clench my fist against the bar top, digging my nails into the wood and focus on calming my magick.

"You might luck out then. Xuan is in a cheery mood today, and I persuaded Alko to shotgun a beer before we came." I hear the grin in Niko's voice and roll my eyes.

When the bartender hands us a platter of drinks, I pay for them and Niko covers the food. The bartender says it'll be a few more minutes before the food is ready so we stay sidled together at the bar.

"You didn't say anything to her." It wasn't a question.

Knowingly, he shakes his head. "I told you I'm no rat. I haven't said anything to her about it. She doesn't know."

"Good." I take a deep swallow of my vodka Sprite. The food is brought out and Niko somehow manages to carry the pizza, deep fried pickles, and two drinks while I carry the remainder. We find the three of them playing darts in the back of the bar and I hear Klowbi's shrill, tipsy laughter and Alko's holler of joy. I set the drinks down on the table nearby and Niko is already inhaling a slice of pizza with cheese dripping down his chin.

"I got a bullseye!" Klowbi laughs and turns to high five Alko and Xuan. Xuan is smiling so wide I can see her incisors. It's a strange sight.

"And we brought drinks." I gesture to the array of flavors.

"And pizza," Niko adds through a mouthful.

"Save some for us," Alko pops a handful of fried pickles into his mouth. "You shouldn't have smoked a joint before we left."

"That would have been boring." Niko grins as he starts on a second piece.

Klowbi walks over as sweat beads on her forehead. "Which drink is mine?"

"I bought you a seltzer. You're welcome." I hand her the can.

She sniffs it and takes a sip, sighing afterwards. "Thanks, this tastes much better." She turns to point at the dartboard again. "Look, I'm almost winning."

"Almost," Alko laughs. "Xuan is winning by a landslide."

"Alright, well I'm not last," Klowbi clarifies, beaming.

"Finish up so I can play," Niko says, taking a long pull from his beer.

Alko snorts. "Shut up and keep stuffing your face."

They finish their game of darts quickly, Xuan throwing only twice more and winning. The five of us crowd around the table, snacking on deep fried pickles and fighting over the last few slices of pizza. Xuan has a slender smile smoothing her features and laughter colors the conversation. We evade any topic that even remotely brushes on Desmond, Shadows, ghosts, or magick. No one bothers us except the bartenders stalking along the walls and asking if we want another round. When they come around for the fourth time, all of us are loose-lipped and easy smiles with laughter bubbling in our throats.

"Shots!" Niko declares, and the bartender walks away to fulfill the request.

"We should play another game," Klowbi hiccups. She's sitting next to me, her cheeks flush and eyes glassy from alcohol.

"Alko and I are playing pool after this," Niko says and Klowbi frowns. "You can shoot a few for Alko."

"You can shoot for Niko," Alko counters and picks at the remaining fried crumbles in the bottom of the basket.

"I'll shoot for you both, to make it fair," Klowbi declares with her hands on her hips.

"Alko will need all the help he can get," Niko teases. "I've seen how he shoots."

Alko frowns as he weighs a pool stick in his hand. "Klowbi and I will kick your ass."

"Yeah we will!" Klowbi cheers and high fives Alko.

Niko shakes his head with a smirk. "I appreciate the confidence. You guys want to bet on it?"

"Drinks, but whoever loses pays me," Klowbi says, breaking her stoic face with a drunken giggle.

"How convenient." Niko pulls his cap over his eyes.

The bartender drops the shots off along with another round of drinks before leaving us again. The five of us each grab a shot glass and lift it in the air to cheers. It's the color of orange juice and smells of pineapple and peach. "To Klowbi, the pool shark," Niko toasts. We repeat the words, clink our glasses, and swallow it down. I take a sip of vodka Sprite to chase the fruity flavor.

"Time to whoop both your asses," Niko gloats, leading the way.

"I'll whoop *your* ass," Klowbi threatens, stumbling after him and nearly knocking her chair over in the process.

"I guess I'll referee," Alko offers, following with smooth movements.

Xuan and I sit alone near the pool table. We watch them for a while as the boys try to show Klowbi how to hold the cue then shoot it. She proceeds to miss entirely and laughs when she nearly catches Alko in the gut with the end. Both of them scramble out of the way when she bends over to try again.

"They'll be at it for a while," I comment with an amused smirk.

"They'll be at it all night with how drunk Klowbi is," Xuan observes.

We sit quietly assessing each other, her eyes gleaming like a cat's studying its prey. I shift in my seat to straighten my spine, refusing to allow her gaze to unsettle me. "How is Farah?"

Xuan tilts her head and takes a drink without breaking her gaze. "She is well." She looks away to watch the others play pool. "I've moved forward from our last encounter."

"As have I." My magick spurs, but I squash it down, ignoring the desire to unfurl my magick around me like a shield.

"I realize my error in my accusation against you. It wasn't just yours, but mine too. I should have prepared for conflict and anonymity when dealing with unknown powers." Xuan's eyes dart towards me. "Forgive my temper when we last spoke."

Her apology makes my blood heat knowing she still places guilt on me for when the entity appeared. As if the fault was mostly mine to bear. "Consider it forgiven," I say through gritted teeth.

"The Shadows are fascinated with you." Xuan lifts her hands to tighten her ponytail, her attention fastened to me. "Klowbi is afraid for you. Even I'm concerned with what they desire from you. Niko told me about the broken window. I'm not upset with you or him, but an angry and powerful Shadow is unusual. Does it still follow?"

"I haven't seen it since," I lie, slightly taken aback by the sudden change of conversation. "Though I doubt it has disappeared."

"And it is a Shadow?" Her voice is quiet, yet it rings loud in my ears even with bouts of laughter and droll of music in the background.

"I'm not sure. It's no demon, if that's what you mean. The Shadows seem to be getting cleverer and more daring." My burn sends a sudden jolt of pain down my arm. I try to hide the wince with a grimace as I sip my drink.

"A dangerous combination," Xuan states and looks to the three attempting to play pool, though Klowbi is rolling the cue between her palms and coaching the boys on the right way to play. "Whatever it may be, Shadow, demon, or other, I do not want it near our group. They cannot come to harm."

"I don't plan to put them in harm's way, Xuan. They are my friends as much as they are yours."

"Wrong, they are my family as much as they are yours." Her tone is ice, unyielding, unflinching. "I will do whatever is necessary to keep them safe."

I stiffen and attempt to keep my tongue in check. My magick feels thick and hot in my belly, sizzling like starved embers. "Then we're on the same side."

"And yet you regard me as if I'm the enemy," Xuan says bluntly. "Klowbi has confided in me about your burn that will not heal. She says it's infected and yet you refuse to care for it." The subject change takes me off guard again and I reach for the burn, seconds later chiding myself for giving it away.

She's baiting me. "Klowbi worries too much. It's healing in its own time."

"But it doesn't heal," Xuan corrects and leans forward as if to tell a secret. "It follows you when you sleep, does it not? That is where the burn has come from. Not from the kitchens, but a nightmare. It follows." Goosebumps scatter over my arms. How the hell does she know my burn is from a nightmare? I haven't confided that to anyone, not even Niko.

"Merely a dream," I say, waving off her accurate accusation.

"A dream is not reality and yet the burn lingers long after the dream has faded." Xuan sits back with her thin cat eyes glittering like black stones.

"What's your point? I'm burned whether it's from dreams or a hot pan on the stove," I snap. My heart is hammering in my chest and all I want to do is wrap my magick around Xuan's throat and stuff her mouth to keep her silent.

"I'm no fool, Daire. I have known you long enough to know how much your word means, and what words you dare not speak aloud. But I hear, I always do. And I know." This time when Xuan leans forward, her face is set in stone and a sudden coldness descends around me. The sickly taste of her magick overflows and sets my stomach churning, my head fuzzy from booze and adrenaline. "You've been to the Astral Realm. I can sense it. A strange essence clings to your aura and it sticks to you."

I keep quiet with my lips thinned in distrust. I've severely underestimated Xuan and her Otherworld abilities. My magick slithers beneath my skin as my frustration rises in my blood.

"I'm not surprised. I suspected you would not follow through with your promise. It's a pattern that you seldom do." Xuan's tone is knowing as her black eyes follow me. "A promise of safety, a promise of trust, a promise of love, and yet it falls short each time. It has affected Alko and I, it has nearly ruined Niko with your hot and cold embrace, and it will surely bring Klowbi to harm if you continue. You distance yourself yet crave attention, but the moment you receive it, you turn cold and throw it back like it's poisoned. You wish to protect us, but you search for secrets and Shadows. Her death has changed you, Daire. Your aura is black and rotten, and I tell you this for the love of our friends that I fear you will rot them too if you do not stop."

My burn throbs with my jagged heartbeat, magick curling into red talons on my fingertips. My first instinct is to lean forward and swipe the talons across her throat, but as soon as the thought crosses my mind it disperses and a sickening shame curdles my belly. "Do not speak about my mother as if you understand the weight of her death," I snarl and lean forward to meet her unwavering gaze across the table. "Don't speak to me as if I don't love them. I'm not the villain your magick paints me to be."

"I don't paint you as anything." Xuan's voice is ice, smooth and harsh. "I tell you this as a friend and as a warning; I will not allow harm to come to them. Not from anyone."

"And I will stop at nothing to protect them. I understand loss just as much as you, and I also understand the sacrifice that comes with it. There is no line I will not cross." Red plumes float from my mouth towards Xuan and her eyes widen until the whites are visible.

"That is what I fear."

"What's going on?" Niko's voice grabs both of our attention. My magick falters at his presence and I feel the sudden press of tears and desperation tightening my throat.

Xuan opens her mouth to answer, but I cut her off, unable to hold my temper or tongue. "I'm taking off. It appears as if I've overstayed my welcome." I push to my feet with my magick whispering beneath my skin. My head swims and I grip the edge of the table for stability.

"Why? Don't leave," Klowbi pipes up from behind. Alko watches with his pool cue white-knuckled in his grip.

"Apparently I'm more foe than friend these days," I spit and shoot an accusing glare at Xuan who sits emotionless. "You guys have fun."

"You can't leave," Klowbi whines.

"But I am. Get a ride from one of *them*," I hiss, stalking towards the exit. The longer I stay, the more I want to rage and let loose my magick swirling inside. I'll say something that I'll regret if I don't leave.

"What happened?" I hear Niko ask.

"I merely spoke the truth," Xuan replies as I force through the exit, ripping towards my car. Klowbi had ridden with me, but at this point I'd prefer being alone all night than dealing with her prying questions while defending Xuan.

The air is cool on my heated face as I stride towards my car. I haven't paid my remaining bar tab, but damn it. The others can cover it or I'll handle it tomorrow.

Unlocking the car, my headlights flash as I rip open the driver's side door. I hear the door to the bar bang shut and hurried steps afterwards. No one can stop me from driving away and escaping Xuan's accusations that I'll rot them if I stay. I don't move though. I stand with my door open and my back turned to the bar, my magick boiling alongside my animosity.

"Daire, wait," a male voice says, panting.

"What?" I snap and turn to see who followed me out.

Lean and sure-footed, Alko stands within reaching distance of me. His obsidian hair is haloed by the lights behind and his almond eyes gleam glassy, but surprisingly, I find no malice written on his face. I expected anger from fighting with his sister, but instead his face is tight and pressed with concern.

"I don't know what my sister said to you, but whatever was said we can discuss later. Don't leave if not for me or Niko, then stay for Klowbi. You are drunk. You can't drive." Alko takes a tentative step closer.

"I won't stay," I state, remaining motionless by the car.

Xuan isn't wrong, that's what irks me. I have broken my word on several occasions besides this one. I have been putting up walls and pitting myself against my friends as if they are the enemies. The rift between them and me is growing, and each time I think I've been mending the rift, it crumbles and fractures from stress. I've been keeping secrets and withholding information. It never used to be this way.

"Then at least let us drive you home," Alko pleads and rests a hand on the car door dividing us. The glamour magick radiates off of him in thick swathes of orange. It's impossible to miss in the darkness. Rings glitter on his nimble fingers arched along the curve of the door. "We're your friends, even if you don't believe it."

I hesitate and look past Alko's shoulder to where the rest of them sit drinking and discussing my disloyalty and lies inside. No, I won't face them with my head hung in shame.

"I'll take my chances," I reply, my tone softening, and slip into the car and start the engine. "Go back inside Alko. I'll see you later."

Alko stands gripping the driver door, his knuckles white in the dark. I know he doesn't want to let me leave. His lips thin, his eyes pleading, but I can tell when he makes his decision. His shoulders slouch and he hangs his head, his fingers slinking from the grasp on the door. "We care for you. Remember that," he says stepping back, first one, then two, then several steps until he's standing closer to the bar than me. Gritting my teeth, I slam the door with a burst of anger and drive out of the parking lot, allowing the briefest glance towards Alko. I turn to watch him head inside, but he's no longer in my line of sight.

I'm far too drunk to drive, but I refuse to turn back around and admit it to them. I'm careful to drive under the speed limit and follow the lines if I start to veer. The drive isn't far, but I'm nervous, with a buzzing head and a tight grip on the wheel.

Already my anger has simmered away and been replaced by gut-wrenching guilt. Perhaps the rift between me and them can be salvaged, but it won't happen tonight. Or tomorrow. They won't understand that I have to see this through. Xuan wants to play it safe to protect the others, but I can't sit aside and watch Desmond die knowing I did the same thing with Mom.

I have a shift in the morning at the diner, but I'll take my chances and call in sick or maybe I'll ask Klowbi to cover for me, though I wouldn't be surprised if she doesn't after tonight.

I'll explain and tell them everything, but I'll have to keep one more secret until after I visit the Beltane festival grounds.

I'll leave early in the morning, before Klowbi will even know I'm gone so she won't be able to stop me. I'll be back by nightfall, hopefully with answers and a fully thought out apology and explanation. Desmond doesn't have much longer. He's been comatose for almost two months, held hostage by the entity, and has no chance of escaping on his own. I have to do this for him.

I don't remember going inside my apartment and lying down. I have no energy to change into fresh clothes. Texting Klowbi, I tell her I won't be going into work, and unless she works the shift, I'm calling in. I never see if she replies or if anyone else texts me as I lie staring at the ceiling in the dark. I hold my breath each time the sound of a car drives by, but Klowbi never comes through the door.

Chapter 18

The sky is alight in an ember orange glow when I finally arrive at the festival grounds spotted with bright green and popping with purple, white, and yellow blooming flowers. Sparse trees bud with fleshy leaves while sweet birdsong fills the forest. Treading further from my car, there are small paw imprints embedded in the soft soil with large prints not too far away leading into the forest.

My temples still throb with each heartbeat, despite having taken a handful of painkillers and slamming water as soon as I woke. It isn't nearly as unbearable as it was this morning, but the brightening sky makes my eyes burn, and I have to squint if I'm not staring at the ground. My appetite is no better, having dry heaved after rolling out of bed and sweating sickly while bent over in the bathroom. Events of the night before came pounding not long after I had finished heaving, guilt and anger warring for prominence. Anger won, but I couldn't say who the anger was directed at.

To my surprise, Klowbi arrived home, though I couldn't pinpoint the exact time, only that it was either late at night or early in the morning. When I left, her door was firmly shut, and I could hear her snores through the frame. I hadn't changed my mind on telling anyone where I was going that morning, and Klowbi would realize once she woke that I was gone. There wasn't service this far in the country, aiding in connecting with nature and our magick. I'd be out of reach until back on the main roads. With a muddled brain, I regretted my stubbornness in concealing my plans, but the fear of losing Desmond was greater.

Even at this distance, I see where tent poles had been erected and the darkened patch of topsoil where the bonfire was, leaving charred remains behind. No trash litters the ground; one of the positives for our festivals is leaving it cleaner than when we first arrived. Staring at it now, the place appears to be the perfect getaway from society, or the worst place to be alone with your thoughts. I could imagine the sounds of laughter and childish squeals, the smell of simmering meats and fruits, the heat from the dancing fires and the pounding of bass drums reverberating through the trees.

The soft whispers of wind through the pines stir a memory from when I was young, back before I had even hit double digits. Mom and I were sitting together after the sun had set and the stars were luminous diamonds blinking in the sky. They looked so massive and bright I had convinced myself that, if I reached a little closer, I could have plucked them from the heavens themselves. I couldn't remember which Wiccan sabbat we were celebrating that night, but I remember sitting in Mom's lap with her arms safely around me, her voice warm and sure against my ear, as she guided my hands with hers, showing me how to use my magick. She'd whisper a word or phrase, I would say it back, and she would gently lead my hands to control it.

I couldn't remember where Dad was, but he was probably with Marc, drinking somewhere else at the festival grounds. I could still recall the heat of Mom's breath against my cheek, the tingling of magick in my fingertips, her soothing tone that often lulled me to sleep; I remembered the honey scent of mead on her breath, her familiar scent of sage and myrrh.

Sudden heartache catches my feet and turns them to lead. I've nearly forgotten her scent, even the sound of her voice is hard to recall. I can still picture her face, but even now as I try to bring her memory forward, it merges with my reflection and I can't tell who I'm imagining. I remember her eyes, an amber and blue, and her midnight black hair thick as rope. I can barely grasp her from memory, and it has been months now since her funeral. Eight months since her death, nearly two years since the beginning of her downfall.

A vile acidic taste coats my tongue and I spit into the dirt. It's difficult to believe how much has changed, yet the festival grounds remain stagnant. The same bonfires will happen years from now, the same tents, the same food, the same love and laughter. The world keeps spinning despite her breath ceasing, though my life feels suspended. The same fires we danced around will flicker with only memories of our time before she died, the same foods will never taste as sweet without her, and the music I used to laugh at will dry in my lungs and turn into a stale cough.

But from her death came my growth. I've mastered the delicate balance of my magick, I can create happiness or illness with a flurry of hands and mutter of words, I can travel to the Astral Realm to a world that exists in parallel with ours and further beyond. I will always be heartsick from her absence and wonder about the unknowns, but I'm a Delacroix, and we do not yield easily. I've sworn to avenge her and I still mean to hold that truth. Saving Desmond comes first, avenging my mother will come soon after.

A shift of black brings my eyes back to focus and the acidic taste fills my mouth again, though this time it tastes more of fear than loss. My magick is thrumming and my palms tingle from calling on it. Ahead of me, no more than several paces away, stands the infamous Hat Man. He looks like the other Shadows, except for the hat outlined on his head. His body is a thick mass of black like all the others. He stands there, watching me, arms at his side with his hat tipped precariously on his head.

Studying his faceless features, I stand still as if that will stop him from advancing. My heart is jackhammering in my ribcage and the pulse is violent in my throat, setting my head to throb and the burn on my arm to ache. The only sound is my harsh breath and the wind flitting through the trees, causing the branches to creak and rub against one another.

The Hat Man does not move. A breeze cuts across the grounds, setting my hair to twist and tangle, but the Hat Man doesn't waver or stir, his hat sitting firmly in place. The sight sends goosebumps to prickle my arms.

When neither of us makes a move, despite the fear caught in my throat and the thin film of sweat coating my hands, I take a step closer. The Hat Man remains motionless. I take another, waiting for a reaction, half expecting him to charge me with hands extended into claws. He doesn't change his pose, nor does he seem to react to my approach. I'm dragging my feet in the dirt, but by the time I'm within touching distance of the Shadow my fear has subsided into a dull roar in my ears.

Compared to the other Shadows I've been in the presence of, he is different. My magick is alert, but I don't feel threatened like I am by the others. He doesn't try hiding or ambushing me, he merely appears in my direct line of vision as if he wants me to take notice.

"Why are you here?"

He doesn't respond.

I try again, but keep my magick cradled in my palms. "Your brethren have been acting out of sorts. They are attacking us. I'm being followed by this entity and they attacked my family. He is my brother without my blood. His name is Desmond." The Hat Man shifts slightly, perhaps the distortion of sunlight, but I think I see his form quiver. "He's in a coma. He's dying. I don't think he will survive much longer." The truth is vile on my tongue and my stomach twists into angry coils at the admission.

This time he tilts his head to the side and I can't help but to believe he's listening to me. From everything I've read about him, most claim that he's more intelligent than the average Shadows, some even categorizing him as a Higher Shadow. Perhaps that means he's above the savage nature of his lesser brethren, or maybe he's smart enough to keep that part of himself under strict control.

"If you know how to save him, show me. You don't want to ignite the wrath of a Delacroix, not even a Shadow such as yourself would be safe." A prickling of magick coats my skin and my core tightens at my surge of magick. The sharp bolt has my fingers flexing as a tendril of red snakes from my fingers.

The Hat Man's head nods so slightly that I barely register the movement. He still hasn't offered a gesture or shown a way of communication. For all I know, maybe he doesn't even understand English and I'm rambling to deaf Shadow ears.

"Useless," I mutter, stalking past him. I'm so close to him when I pass I sense the temperature drop several degrees and a fresh set of gooseflesh prickles my arms. I'm out of his reach in half a dozen steps and the warmth of the sun settles against my skin. Teeth gritted, I start towards the center of the festival grounds to keep searching for clues, still acutely aware of the Hat Man at my back.

Shaking my head in frustration, I rub my temples and close my eyes to ease the pounding. When I open them again, there stands the Hat Man in the same position that I left him. I stop and look back to confirm there's only one of him. The path behind me is untouched except for my faint footprints in the dirt.

"What do you want? If you aren't going to help me, then get out of my fucking way," I snarl at him with fear completely forgotten. Desmond doesn't have much longer to live, and nothing will stop me from searching for clues, not even the damned Hat Man.

The Hat Man keeps his head in my direction and raises his arm, pointing in the direction of the forest bordering along the festival grounds. I furrow my brows, taken aback that he has actually moved more than a twitch of his damn hat.

"What are you trying to tell me? I don't understand."

He vanishes and a brief flush of cold air stirs my hair. It takes me a second to locate him, standing like an inky black sentinel along the border of the forest. Arms back at his side, hat askew, his attention fixed on me. I start to walk further into the clearing, but I look over at him as his sightless face bores into my back.

I sigh, turning on my heels, and head towards him. My feet feel leaden again as I trek across the grounds with the Hat Man at the center of my sight. My tongue is dry and bitter, my stomach churning with a toxic mixture of fear and hope.

It feels as if it takes forever to cross the ground between us, but before long I'm standing in front of him along the edge of the forest. Sun high in the sky and a sheen of sweat on my brow, the forest beyond is portentously dark, even though the sun should be mottling the forest floor.

"Did it happen here?" I ask standing in front of him again. He lifts his arm and points into the forest. My gaze follows the shadowed hand pointing to the inky depths. I swallow the knot in my throat and attempt to calm the pounding in my breastbone, ignoring the throbbing of my incessant burn.

I walk to the edge of the forest where the sun's rays no longer break the shadows between the trees. Unbidden, the memory of my nightmare where the forest burned, the doe died in my arms, and I was shot with arrows, assaults me. I can't shake the feeling now, staring into the black and green depths beside the Hat Man, that maybe the dream is more than that.

But if the answers are in the forest...

Gathering my courage, I lift my face to the sun for the warmth to spur me forward into the dark. Fists clenched and magick coiled, I take the first step and choke down my fear. A glance over my shoulder reveals the Hat Man standing at the edge of sunlight, arms back at his side. Turning forward, I pick my way through the unnatural darkness coalescing through the pines and oaks, pressing another step into the leafy canopy as it swallows me whole.

Excerpt from the Gray Book

The Mimic

Very little is known about the Mimic. The true form of this Shadow being is unknown, preferring the physical form of anything in the physical world to that of the Astral. While it can imitate, it never achieves exactness, often exposing small variations to the unaware. This is usually the only tell when dealing with a mimic; the devil in the details. Known to be a cunning energy, it will pit family against one another, being kind to one member while being cruel to another. Cleanse yourself and your space as soon as the Shadow has been identified.

Chapter 19

Abnormal darkness drapes across the forest, blurring the line between day and night. My stomach is tight and sour with fear, a cold sweat dampening my hairline. Everything about entering the forest feels wrong. No sun glimmers through the canopy, no birds twitter in the branches or squirrels chatter along the base of oaks. It's quiet besides my staccato heart, shallow breaths, and the crunch of twigs and decaying leaves beneath my feet. There's no wind to stir the long reach of branches, and every deepened shadow or shift of little light sets my magick on high alert.

Each second that ticks by presses a cold cloth of fear along my spine, and my throat tightens as if seized speechless. Images of my nightmares flash behind my lids each time I blink. A garden of poisons bursting into ash. Black swan wings stark against a smoky gray sky, soaring before plummeting down, fast and hard, to the earth feathered in arrow spears. Raging fire devouring everything in its path. The dead doe, wheezing and bloodied in my lap, with eyes too human and too similar to Klowbi's.

Deep in the forest, the Hat Man's gaze bores into my back like icy coals, and even out of his sight I still sense the faintness of him lingering at my back. Every time I turn around I expect him to be following in my tracks, but since entering the forest, I haven't seen him reappear. I try not to think about what it could mean that he refused to follow.

From the first step into the forest, my burn has been a persistent ember of pain. I'm wearing a short-sleeve to air the burn, but it's hot with infection and bile pushes at the back of my throat at the slightest pressure, sending stars to dance across my eyes. A few droplets of pus and blood ooze out. I wipe it away, biting my lip to keep from crying out. Even the skin around my burn appears foul, burning a bright red and tender to the touch.

By now I've been walking for a third of an hour with nothing but my disquieted thoughts and the persistent smoldering ache growing along my arm to keep me company. I don't know how far to venture, but instinct tells me I have to trek deeper. Something lingers here, I feel it grate against my magick, warning bells ringing mutely in my head.

A flurry of leaves above and ahead stops me in my tracks. I've grown accustomed to the silence and the sudden shift of noise, normally gone unnoticed, sounds raucous. Perched on a low-hanging branch across my path is a screech owl. Its massive gold eyes watch me from above with quick sharp head movements as I step closer to get a better look. The feathers along the ridge of its eyes remind me of reptilian horns and its razor-blade beak sits centered in its wide face. The owl's feathers are the color of mottled bark, and if it weren't for the deafening silence to give away its movements I wouldn't have noticed it at first glance.

Thayne's voice fills my head. He suggested that external forces manipulated my nightmare, possibly indicating an infiltration by both the entity and a deity. Lilith sits high amongst my chosen deities. During my bath ritual, she had spoken to me, and I believe she had been trying to protect me in my last nightmare with the inferno. One of her symbols is a screech owl. I've seen no living creatures since entering the forest and it seems peculiar to have an owl fly directly into my path and *watch* me.

If it is Lilith, and she is sitting in my path, does that mean I'm on the correct trail or is she sending a warning to turn back? And how can I turn back if there is the slightest chance of finding answers to bring Desmond back from the brink of death? Surely Lilith will understand my reasoning.

I don't wish to disappoint my goddess, but I have to keep going and pray that she'll protect me anyway.

"Lilith, Great Mother, Lady of Darkness, I pray to you and ask only for your guidance and protection, to lead me where I cannot see, to protect where I cannot shield. I will honor you always, Goddess of the Night," I incant to the owl perched above. Its massive gold eyes blink, its head tilts as if considering my words, before the owl opens its wings and takes off into the darkness of the trees beyond.

Alone once more, I continue down the path the owl had roosted above. My first step sends me stumbling and freezes my breath in my lungs at the sudden onslaught of energy shifts. It's as if I've stepped through an invisible barrier barring my world to *this* world.

My magick is screaming, and the intensity of wishing to use it produces an icy trail of sweat along my spine. I have never felt such a craving, an ache, an unrelenting urge to use my magick and let it release unhindered. It feels as if I'm in the Astral Realm with the fluidity of the energy calling to my own.

I've taken no more than a dozen paces when the Shadows appear. They manifest as one. Shadows coalesce all around me and block my path. Their sightless eyes follow me, and the blackness of their bodies commandeers the little light that remains in the forest. The closest Shadows are within reaching distance, and though they look like solid black masses, their bodies roil like a viscous liquid or gas. I wonder if I swipe my fingers through their bellies if it would go straight through or if my hand would catch like a true corporeal form.

Within a stone's throw is a thick roiling mist. It takes no solid shape as it hovers above the ground, sifting between the standing Shadows. I've never seen such a creature and I mentally pull the passage from the *Gray Book* mentioning it. I shiver and decide to keep a wide berth from it, fearing how my psyche will alter should I touch the being.

Turning in a circle, I try to count the surrounding figures. At twenty-one I lose track. There are as many, if not more, than on the night of Beltane when they attacked. I'm severely outnumbered this time, and I doubt my ability to handle so many alone even with the dizzying call of magick. I don't know how to fight them, which magick works or doesn't. Shields can delay their approach, but the sheer number of enemies makes me hesitant regarding their effectiveness. I'll be overwhelmed by this sea of Shadows.

Steeling myself, I step up to the Shadow closest to me, easily within striking distance, and stare into its empty blackness. It's darker than the space between the stars where truly no light lives, an empty pit that somehow holds a semblance of life and intelligence.

"What do you want?" I demand with steel in my tone. Pain crackles from my burn and I gasp at the sharp twist of pain. The Shadow doesn't react. No movement, no words, no breath. Nothing.

I turn to the one beside it. "Why are you here?" There is no answer, but my burn flares and pain lances down my arm and up my shoulder to meet my collarbone.

I turn to a third. "Are you following me?" Again I'm met with silence and a twisting pain sends sparks erupting across my lids.

"Do you remember me?" Nothing but silence and pain.

"Who sent you?"

"Who do you follow?"

"Do you know the Hat Man?"

"Do you understand me?"

"What are your intentions?"

No matter what I ask or which Shadow I confront or if I whisper or scream, they merely watch as I go down the line speaking to each in turn. I can't help but feel the tendrils of insanity seeping in by the time I've questioned over a dozen Shadows with no sign of understanding. My burn is a constant raging fire from my fingertips all the way down my ribcage and creeps into the base of my skull. Several trickles of blood have spiraled down my arm, dripping onto the dirt off my fingertips.

"Damnit," I gasp and wipe my palm onto my jeans stiffened with drying blood.

I grit my teeth and bare them into what I only imagine is an animalistic snarl. "Damn you all. I'll use my magick on you fuckers, if that's what you wish." I raise my palms, ignoring the shot of pain in my arm at the action, and summon my magick. Simultaneously the Shadows take a step back, and though there is no sound with it, I imagine a deep rumble to match their movements.

I can't help myself and laugh before letting my arms fall back to my sides. "Cowards," I spit and continue down the path now lined with Shadow sentinels while I take care to avoid the Mist. With each step, the energy around me feels tighter, sharper, growing more coiled and ready to burst. Magick gnaws away in my belly.

With eyes following every step, I come around a thick mass of trees covered in twisting vines of thorn and stop short. A single Shadow stands directly ahead. It's the same size as all the others with the familiar unearthly obsidian body, but this one has eyes. Bright, vibrant eyes the color of burning rubies and boiling blood. And it's smiling at me with a mouth blacker and deeper than space with fangs lining the bottomless pit of its mouth.

Uncontrollable fear surges through me and I take an automatic step backwards from the Red Eyed Shadow. It tilts its head at me at such an odd and uncomfortable angle it's hard to believe something so alien can exist alongside humanity. It appears larger, gaining bulk the longer I stare into its pulsing, burnt ruby sockets.

Sucking in a breath to calm my heart, I think back to the *Gray Book*, trying to remember what the author had said about the Red Eyed Shadows. *Fear fuels them and makes them look larger,* I recall while keeping my eyes trained on the Red Eyed Shadow. *They have animalistic qualities. They hunt in packs and will corner their victims. Tendencies for ambushes and capable of physical harm.*

I see only one Red Eyed Shadow, but that doesn't mean there aren't more hiding amongst the ranks of the standard Shadows. I'll have to be tactful if I want to escape the horde intact. But if they are as malevolent and unpredictable as the author claims, I doubt I'll have much warning before they decide to launch an attack. I'll have only a slim window for finding an escape route and an even smaller margin for error.

Shifting its head squarely back to center, Red Eyes lifts its arm and gestures at me to approach, similar to the Hat Man's action on the edge of the forest. I swallow a knot of fear and take a step closer. In unison, Red Eyes takes a step towards me. We lock eyes and the shifting redness holds indisputable intelligence. I take another step closer as I'm drawn into the red pools of its eyes.

A growling screech sounds from my right, allowing only seconds of warning before a Red Eyed Shadow, different from the one still standing ahead, bursts from the group surrounding me. All I see at first is its hunched spine and arms extended into claws as it charges. I dodge the attack and feel the icy swish as its claws barely miss my ribs.

Red Eyes grunts and the attacking Shadow stops in its tracks, snarling a few feet away with an oily ichor dripping from its black jowls. Movement from my left peripheral gives away the next sloppy attack as a third Red Eyed Shadow pushes to the front on all fours, its knuckles curled beneath it like thick mutant paws.

It dives at my ankles and I jolt backwards as it gets to its haunches and shrieks, spraying black ichor. Muscles and tendons coil tight beneath the black of its form, the skin shifting like a mirage. Its claws dig gashes into the dirt as it sniffs and salivates no more than a few feet from me. It's much more animal-like than the other two. The first stands observing me, clearly the most intelligent of the group and presumably the pack leader.

The creature on all fours attempts a feeble swipe of its humanoid hands in my direction. This time I'm ready and I conjure a barricade identical to the one the night of Beltane. With a flare of my hands, I mold the purple barricade to form a bubble around me. My core relaxes at the release of tension with the use of magick. The gnawing hunger fades momentarily, only to return with a throttling vengeance.

A sudden urge to use more magick tempts me to lash out at the Shadows, but I stay my hand despite the craving, knowing that only one wrong draw of power could mean allowing my barricade to slip just long enough for one of them to get through. If the Shadows attacked at once, my minimal barricade would provide only a few minutes of protection.

While raising the shield, Red Eyes—the pack leader—grew larger and stood taller than the others with a grin on its inhuman features. I can properly see the fangs now, strange hooks with thorns on each tooth. Being caught by one would be nearly impossible to wrench free from and would shred and tear flesh like razors.

The other two Red Eyed Shadows prowl around the edge of the barricade, heaving and panting. They make weak attempts to swipe at the dirt where the shield digs into the soil. For the first time in a while, I have to admit my carelessness is irreversibly inane. If I had asked for help or had someone with me, it would have improved my chances against the Shadows. But my selfishness and lack of trust has brought me here, and yet I refuse to believe that I can't get myself out. I'm a Delacroix, one of the strongest witch lineages to ever exist. This is a test of my power that I cannot fail.

And if you do, you're dead. Don't screw this up.

My burn pulses and I place my fingers over it to ease the pain, but it only makes it worse. My fingers come back sticky with a film of blood.

Beyond the protective purple bubble, the Shadows have tightened their circle around me as the focal point. Initially there were only three Red Eyed Shadows. Now there are at least a dozen among their ranks. Silence that once filled the forest now resonates with snarls and hisses. Their eyes are an unnatural, burning red through the purple haze with black saliva pooling in the maws of those standing closest to me.

Red Eyes stalks forward, standing tall and triumphant. It's mere inches from the crackling barrier. At least I now know that my magick affects the Shadows enough to make them hesitate. They don't know the rules to this either. If my barrier proves useful, then my attack spells can keep them at bay, at least long enough for me to return to the festival grounds.

"You lead them," I regard the alpha Shadow.

My burn throbs in response and pain shoots down my spine. Red Eyes doesn't speak, but a guttural noise erupts from its throat. One of its lackeys charges forward and screams at me, sending a fresh spray of ichor splattering the barricade. I watch as a thick glob slowly slips down the purple glow. It crackles as if burning from a power source.

"If you leave me be, I won't have to kill you," I warn.

It grins and regards the lackey now slobbering on the bubble. A quick series of hisses and clicks emit from Red Eyes as he watches the lackey. Lackey raises its arm, appearing almost fearful, and glances at Red Eyes before placing a finger on the barricade. There's a hiss, but it pushes its shadow fingers against the purple barricade and gurgles. It hooks its fingers against the shield then drops its hand with a snarl. A thin oily line drips from its jaws to the ground.

They can communicate with each other. Red Eyes shows more intel-ligence than I thought.

"You aren't the entity that's been following me, are you?" Red Eyes goes quiet and shakes its head. *No, you aren't the Shadow. But you understand me.* The others go still, the sea of Shadows quiet.

Red Eyes shifts its gaze to my burn. Quick as a viper, Red Eyes slashes a clawed hand at my protective barrier. For a split second, my magick falters before solidifying again.

As one giant faceless mass, the Shadows closest slink forward with claws slashing and fangs snapping at the barricade. I stumble from the onslaught and my vision darkens long enough for panic to set in. *Fight or die, Daire.* Searching desperately, I call on my magick and the bursting energy I had felt upon entering the forest. The barrier fissures and cracks as claws dig and poke holes in the shield. Black arms and teeth gnash as red eyes glitter through clefts in my magick.

Clenching my fists, I feel the stickiness of blood between my fingers and beneath my nails. Red Eyes catches my gaze as another set of claws pokes through my barricade inches from my face. A spray of spittle manages to sneak through the gap before I can close it, a patch of ichor landing on my wrist, burning cold.

With how fast they're tearing down my magick, I'm not quick enough to patch the holes. It's filled with fissures and larger chunks are shattering with each blow. When I level my gaze at Red Eyes, a grin tears across my face. There's hesitation in its slack mouth and burning ruby sockets.

Summoning my magick and the crackling energy, I shove my hands out and everything explodes.

My protective barricade fragments and shatters into hundreds of pieces, shooting out shards of magick in all directions towards the Shadows. Jagged projectiles hit their mark, sending the Shadows closest shrieking in pain as they sink and dissipate into the ground. A few attempt to fight the culling and drag their melting nails into the soil before morphing into a roiling black mass seeping downwards into the earth. Shadows take off running to avoid the same fate. Red Eyes stands a few feet away with black oily masses bubbling at its feet.

Red Eyes screams. The sound sends my heart palpitating. The ground lurches beneath me, the trees shiver, my blood curdles. It sounds of crunching bones and blood and revenge.

The remaining Shadows lurch forward and fear tightens my throat. Red Eyes grows larger as it watches its brethren charge. I throw out a jagged cut of my hand and a purple scythe slices through the closest Shadows. Their screams rattle my bones.

I force out waves of magick, felling anything in my way. A Shadow is taken in the abdomen, one gets caught in the throat severing its head, another loses half a torso, another its legs. The black mass is endless and as one goes down another rises to take its place.

With a surge of battle cry that tears my throat, I shove behind me and cut a path through the stinking melting bodies, sprinting with their screams and spittle following close behind.

Through luck, magick, or fate, I manage to destroy enough of the Shadows blocking my path and sprint past bubbling claws protruding from the dirt towards the edge of the forest. The forest is a breathing darkness and shapes blur as I bolt through the thick underbrush with tree limbs snagging at my hair and face. It's nearly impossible to tell if the Shadows are catching up to me or if I'm merely passing silhouettes of trees. A cacophony of snarling thunder and a hissing peal echo through the woods. My lungs heave from my burst of exertion and the beginnings of a cramp bite into my side. I'm forced to slow to catch my ragged breaths, tasting iron on my tongue.

Sweat is beading between my shoulder blades and plastering hair to my cheeks and neck. I duck beneath a low-hanging branch, my hair catching before tearing free with a bolt of pain. I imagine the Shadows mere paces behind me, rasping and panting with extended claws.

Pushing through a dense thicket, I risk a glance and my heart jumps to my throat. A swarm of almost one-hundred burnt ruby eyes with obsidian bodies eat the distance between us.

I steady my breaths and clutch down my fear as I call on my magick. A soothing warmth focuses my mind as I form a sizzling orb of magick between my palms while I run. It's awkward having my hands in front, but the burst of power keeps me weaving through the forest. The orb is a mix of violet and purple the size of a baseball. With a quick jerk, I twist and throw the blazing orb at the Shadows.

The ground shudders and I stumble from the impact, catching my weight on a tree, then taking off again. Echoing screams trails gooseflesh along my arms and the overwhelming stench of decay has me gagging. A harsh violet glow lights up the darkness that casts everything in a disorienting hue as the gray settles.

A shape hurdles from my left. It's so close the cold creeps from it and there's rage in the boiling red of its eyes. I swipe my hand at it and a blade of violet buries itself deep in the Shadow's head. It falls with a curdling scream, reeling and twisting as its body dissipates.

I throw thin tendrils of violet and purple magick behind me. I refuse to turn around to check their proximity; my focus stays pinned on the path ahead. I must be nearing the edge of the forest. If I send another blast behind me, it should provide enough time to outrun their thrashing claws. For decades, witches had blessed the festival grounds dissuading stray entities and Shadows from lingering. I pray it's enough to keep the swarm from following.

A shape appears to my right and hot knives pierce my arm where my burn is. The pain is sudden and blinding. I slam into the ground and jar my teeth upon impact. Claws dig deeper into my burn followed by a chilling scream making my ears bleed. Pain racks my body as the Shadow tightens its hold with a demonic grin on its face. The eyes are deep red and endless hellscape.

For a moment I lose myself in them. Then pain spasms through me, my throat raw and ragged from screaming. I force my magick out in a desperate fury. The Shadow on top shatters and those approaching slow when the magick wave hits them. They melt and vanish, but more replace the ones I slay.

I'm struggling to my feet, the pain blinding and my lungs seizing. I taste real blood between my teeth from where I bit my tongue as I fell, and the pain . . . the *pain* from where the Shadow's claws cleaved the wound is pulsing, burning cold. A numbness spreads down my arm, up my neck, and deep into my spine and ribs. If I don't run now, the intense agony and numbness will prevent me from escaping at all.

I'm not sure where my resolve comes from as I get to my knees and the Shadows converge. They approach with careful steps. Those damn beady eyes tear into me with their heads cocked as trills and hisses rend the air.

Raising my good arm, I shoot out small stars of magick in quick succession. Violet stars spin and the Shadows dodge. Some fall screaming to the forest floor, grasping at their brethren in vain. Despite my flash of strength, it fades just as fast and it becomes harder to summon even a sliver of magick. The Shadows must sense my fleeting strength because as one they surge towards me with hungry grins and thirsty eyes.

Desperation chokes me as I stare at the sea of Shadows. "Lilith, Goddess of the Night, I beg for your help. Please." Tears sting my eyes. The numbness is getting worse and the cold burn is sinking deeper, my mind nearly fracturing from the clashing of sensations.

Above is a screeching different from the Shadows and a flurry of feathers descends onto the beings closest. All I see are wild claw swipes, then the Shadow is melting, its scream warbled. Then another Shadow falls, and another. By the fourth attack, I catch sight of an owl attacking them from above.

"Blessed be, Great Mother Lilith." I pull myself to my feet using a low-hanging branch. I start running again and ignore the numbness and bolts of pain in my arm, spine and ribs.

Calling my last grasp of strength, I throw out mini stars of magick all around me, making sure to cover my blindsides this time instead of solely behind me. I'm not going to allow the Shadows to catch me again.

With each step, my body grows heavy and my lungs tighten. Every fiber urges me to yield to the pain, to halt, to rest. I keep pushing, harder, faster, throwing out my magick wildly, hoping the owl is still attacking. I just need a little longer, a little further, one more step, one more breath.

Straight ahead is natural sunlight so blinding from the darkness I've been in I have to squint to allow my eyes to adjust. Only a strong sprint's distance. I'm almost free.

Charging forward, I focus my eyes on the open festival grounds and sunshine only seconds before me. I summon my last bit of stamina, holding my magick in my core, and funnel it towards my palms until I have an orb again. It's smaller than the first, but larger than the stars I've been throwing. Sunlight is only a few more strides. I burst into a sprint and twirl my body as I propel the orb at the Shadows. I don't turn around in time as I trip over my feet and collapse onto the ground, but not before sunlight brushes my face.

I lie on my back with sweat, blood and tears mingling down my chin and throat. I sit up, careful not to press any weight against my right arm. The numbness is so complete I can hardly wiggle my fingers. I only manage a twitch.

Cloaked in darkness, the sea of Shadows looms a mere three meters from the forest's edge. They glare with burnt rubies for eyes and thorns in their smiling mouths. All are silent. No screaming, hissing, snarling, just the whisper of the trees and my ragged pants and whimpers.

But they've stopped chasing.

Slowly, achingly, I stand and wipe sweat off my brow. A few Shadows turn back, venturing further into the forest, while the majority hold fast and observe in absolute silence. The Mist lingers along the edge with wisps reaching in my direction.

The sun is hot and welcoming and a laugh bursts from my lips and I'm unable to stop it. I start laughing so completely that my chest tightens and my stomach clenches as fresh tears start rolling down my cheeks. I suck in slow breaths to calm my nerves.

The Hat Man is nowhere in sight and I'm grateful for his disappearance. I would have attacked him as madly as the Red Eyed Shadows attacked me.

I hiss as I lift my blood-soaked sleeve from my wound. It's burning to the touch, and there's so much blood that it's stiffened the fabric of my shirt. Through the blood and filth are dark veins pulsing beneath my skin as black as the Shadows themselves, oscillating with my heart.

I start limping back to the entrance of the grounds where I parked my car. I walk backwards so I'm facing the wall of Shadows still bordering the edge of the forest. Lifting my good arm, I present them my middle finger, turn around, and don't look back.

Chapter 20

"Where were you? Why weren't you answering my calls?" Klowbi demands, jumping to her feet from where she was sitting in the living room. Her skin is pale in the light of the TV, dark hollows encircling her eyes. Curtains are drawn across the windows that mute the streetlights.

Close to home, the moon appeared and the sky became a blur of blue. I had to stop several times while driving because the pain had caused temporary blindness. Numbness was so awful that I struggled to keep my foot on the pedal and my fingers clenched around the wheel. Each wave of paroxysm lasted no longer than several minutes before it faded enough for me to continue on, but it felt like an eternity while I sat writhing in pain and sweat.

I had done my best to clean and wrap the wound with the mini medkit in the car, but it was burning up and oozing blood darker than it should. Black veins were stemming further from the gash and climbing down my forearm and up my shoulder. I could barely tend to it as the pain was sharp and searing like a hot blade that caused my fingers to tremble uncontrollably; I had to muffle my screams through clenched teeth.

It took twice as long than expected when Klowbi's missed calls and texts finally came through. My sole focus was returning home, and after a pain spell that had lasted nearly half an hour, time was of the essence if I wanted to prevent further festering.

Somehow I manage to close and lock the door behind me before stumbling to the kitchen counter and clinging to it. Sweat beads down my forehead despite the goosebumps prickling my arms. My hair is plastered to my face and I can't stop my hands from shaking.

Klowbi stops halfway to where I stand hunched over. Her face pales and her freckles brighten on her cheeks and nose. Her eyes widen as she stands frozen staring at me. "Daire, what happened?" she whispers and bursts into motion, grabbing me gingerly beneath my arm so I can lean my weight on her.

"Shadows," I gasp and flinch at the shot of fiery pain shooting from my arm down my ribs. "Help me to the bathroom. The burn needs to be cleansed *now*."

Klowbi half hoists, half drags me to the bathroom. I lower myself onto the toilet while she stands dumbfounded in front of me. "Medkit, and grab my healing crystals and herbs."

She goes and grabs the medkit first before bolting into my room for my other tools. I pop the clasp on the kit and grab the medical scissors and cut my shirt completely off so I'm in my undergarments. I grab gauze and hydrogen peroxide as the door creaks open to reveal Klowbi with her arms filled with jars of herbs and handfuls of crystals.

"Set that down," I direct her and turn so she can see the burn. "You need to clean this. My hands are shaking too much." Klowbi gasps and nods, setting her lips into a firm line. "Grab a towel," I add. The last thing we need is being called for a noise complaint because I can't quiet my screams.

With a towel firmly between my teeth, it muffles my cries well enough for Klowbi to douse the burn in peroxide. The liquid pours on clear and bubbles black as if rotten. Pain almost makes me faint twice, but I persevere with only a few tears. She dries the wound and luckily no stitches are need-ed. There's only three tiny holes on the burn where the Shadow snagged me. It's as if part of the Shadow's essence absorbed into my wound, the three gashes the main points of corruption where the black veins emanate from.

Neither the pain nor numbness cease after cleaning the burn. Blood still oozes thick and nearly black with my skin hot with fever. Black veins spiderweb down my arm and my ribs ache with every inhale.

"Why is it black? Why do you look like you're dying?" Klowbi whimpers and dabs a dribble of blood from my arm.

"Because it's Shadow magick," I explain and wipe sweat from my brow. My head feels heavy and I strain my eyes to concentrate. "Grab my mortar and pestle. It should be on my altar. The wound needs to be cleansed with magick." Klowbi obeys and darts out the door. I hear her scrambling and knocking things over before reappearing and offering me the items. "No, I'll tell you what to use."

"How do you know this will work?" Klowbi kneels before me, holding the mortar and pestle.

"I don't." I admit and nod in the direction of the herbs and crystals. "Grab all the yarrow, archangel, and sage—no, grab nettle instead. Make a poultice."

She grabs the jars filled with herbs and carefully searches for the ones I named, placing them in the mortar one by one. "Good. Make it as fine as you can. Grab me cleansed obsidian." I instruct and shake my head in frustration. "No, not obsidian. Hand me clear quartz." She obliges and I run my thumb along the ridges of the crystal before clasping it tightly in my hand. I close my eyes and call on my magick, grateful to feel it stir through exhaustion that has me trembling.

My hands warm and I glance down to see a blue-green glow emanating from between my fingers. "*Sana vulnus meum et tabescendum et putredinem et infectionem ab hoc mundo et ab illis. Sic fiat fiat,*" I chant thrice over while Klowbi mashes the poultice. *Heal my wound and stave rot and infection from this world and theirs. So mote it be.*

After the third chant, I uncurl my fingers to see the quartz swirling with blue and green mists. The crystal is torrid in my grasp from the exchange of magick. I press the cleansed crystal against my burn in hopes of removing the scourge the Shadow transferred to me. It burns for a second before a cooling sensation washes over and I sigh in relief. My wound pulses and bleeds, the blood appearing redder now. Pain has ceased spreading, yet the black veins remain stubbornly unchanged. Hopefully the poultice will expunge the remainder of the Shadow's touch from my flesh. Already the blue-green swirling mists are turning black from the rot in my wound.

"What happened? What's wrong with your arm?" Klowbi pries after seeing the obvious relief on my face. The bathroom smells of strong herbs and iron.

"I returned to the festival grounds in search of answers. I saw the Hat Man and I thought he meant to help me. The damn bastard pointed me directly into *them*. There were so many Shadows, Bambi. At least half a hundred. They weren't the Shadows we normally see either. These ones had red eyes, like what the *Gray Book* explained. They were wild beasts, but some of them showed intelligence. They can communicate with each other and form planned attacks." The flow of words sounds manic as I recite what happened. "They attacked me, but my magick could hurt them. They melted into the ground screaming. I managed to escape, but one of them caught me from behind. I almost didn't make it out, but Lilith heard my pleas and saved me in the form of an owl. She gave me enough time to run back into the sunlight."

"That's from a Shadow?" Klowbi stands and gently touches the burn in examination.

I nod and remove the quartz from my wound, the inside swirling eternally black. "Yes, with red eyes."

She starts slathering the poultice on and I wince and pull back. "Hold still," Klowbi chides and roughly smooths it down until my arm feels heavy and wet. She wraps my arm first in a thin cloth to keep the poultice in place and then finishes off with gauze. The poultice has a bittersweet scent to it and burns upon application, but it's a welcoming sensation. A cleansing burn.

The pounding at the base of my skull is weakening and the grinding against my ribs no longer shoots a constant lance of pain. My arm is swollen with aching heat, but I can apply pressure without crying out in agony.

"That feels better," I mumble and sag against the toilet, blessedly allowing my eyes to flutter closed. My blissful moment is short-lived. I sense Klowbi's accusatory stare boring into me. Opening my eyes, she stands above me with her arms crossed and her mouth strained, a nasty glower in her eyes.

"What the hell, Daire? What were you thinking? You could have been killed by those Shadows and with that wound infected...what if it worsens? What if you fall into a coma like Des? Or worse?" Her eyes widen with fury and a film of tears brims in her chestnut eyes. There's a wobble to her lower lip.

No, please don't cry for me.

"Bambi, I'll be okay. The poultice is removing whatever toxins are left and I'll change it again before I go to sleep." I make an attempt to console, but I have my doubts. I've read accounts about demon attacks, but we know more about them than we do Shadows. This is foreign territory. I have no way of knowing how the toxins will affect my body, mind, or magick.

She's right. I made a reckless gamble following the trail leading back to Beltane. I could have died. Hell, I probably would be dead if it hadn't been for Lilith intervening.

"That was so stupid of you," Klowbi chastises, mashing the poultice with the pestle, making it splatter onto the floor. With a clank, she places the mortar on the counter and glares at me once more. Her face is flushed with anger. "Tell me everything. No secrets."

I recount the story with as much detail as possible, agreeing that secrets would only cause more harm. The story comes out clearer than when I first tried to explain with my pain-infused ramblings. From an outside source I must seem clinically insane speaking of magick and Shadows and deities protecting me in the form of wildlife. Klowbi is used to my insanity and barely batts an eye at the mention of the Hat Man or the Red Eyed Shadows.

"They are much more intelligent than we originally thought. Not all of them, but if enough of them can think and plan like us, then things are going to get a lot worse." I caution after finishing my retelling. "I'm not sure who can see the Shadows, but if they start attacking civilians, if no one can see them but a few, it's only a matter of time before chaos ensues."

"And if they attack the same way they did you..." Klowbi motions to the thick binds of gauze around my arm.

"A lot of people will die. Magick can counteract the toxins, at least it seems to, and it will destroy them, at least for a while." I groan and slowly get to my feet. I grab the towel and wet it with warm water and start wiping down my face, neck, breasts—any place where my skin is slick with sweat and dirt. "Whatever magick is in that forest is potent. As soon as I entered the world grew dark and quiet. There wasn't even the buzzing of insects. The Shadows seemed much stronger than before from the energy in the forest, but so was my magick. It fueled us both."

"Double-edged sword," Klowbi murmurs. "It helps them, but it helps us too." She grabs the towel from my hand and starts wiping the dirt and blood off my back and ribs. I'm grateful for the reprieve and lean against the sink counter with my head slightly hung and watch through the mirror.

"Seems so. My magick has always been reliable, but it was instant in the forest. I barely had to even think about what I wanted, it just happened. It made me hungry to use it," I recall and Klowbi's face twists at my words, but she keeps scrubbing at my spine. "All I wanted was to destroy them. I was reeling off of all that potent energy. It felt so pure."

"Have you ever felt like that before? Has your magick ever reacted like that?" Klowbi tries to catch my gaze in the mirror, but I look away.

"Honestly, it felt like being in the Astral Realm. It was as if any magick were at my disposal with no limitations. If I could conjure it, then it would happen." I adjust so I'm facing Klowbi. She lowers her hand and her eyes flicker to my abdomen before settling on my face. "This is only a theory," I continue. "But what if the Astral Realm is bleeding into our world? Something would have had to trigger it, but the Astral Realm is more or less limitless power. If it's bleeding into our world, then it could be changing the supernatural beings that reside here."

"The Shadows," she mutters and her eyes widen in understanding. "That would explain them being able to interact with our world and becoming more aggressive. They're learning and adapting."

"This could apply to *anything*, Klowbi. Shadows, spirits, demons, anything supernatural could be influenced by this energy surplus." The thought of not only Shadows roaming rampant, but nefarious spirits or insidious demons would be beyond disastrous to our world.

It would be apocalyptic.

There's a moment of silence as my words sink in. Klowbi steps away and the warmth emanating off her fades. "We have to tell the others. Xuan is tied to the Otherworld, so is Alko. They might be equally endangered as you."

"It's only a theory—"

"But it's more than we've had since Desmond went comatose," Klowbi cuts me off and her brows furrow into a deep line. "If these bleedings of power become more common, then we need to be prepared. We need each other and they can help us figure out how to stop it."

I open my mouth to argue, but think better of it and nod in agreement. Klowbi's right. We have to inform them, especially since Xuan is deeply connected to the Otherworld, making her vulnerable like me.

Though a minuscule part of me, buried deep down, relishes the idea of a world truly connected with magick. Witches everywhere would become the ones on top; *we* would have the power; *we* could rule. A world where magick flows freely and only those with it running through their veins would thrive. Covens would be unstoppable. We could rewrite history. Witches would never fear mockery or persecution again.

But the Shadows have the potential to overtake. Spirits who linger could grow more daring, more violent. Demons might no longer be bound to the mortal rules of this world.

"Alright, we'll tell them."

"Tomorrow," Klowbi says firmly.

"Fine, tomorrow," I agree grudgingly.

"Good," she nods, satisfied. Her tone shifts to one of admonishment. "You shouldn't go and do things like that. You could have died. I understand you want to save Desmond, but making brash decisions won't help anybody."

"You're right. I wasn't thinking. I'm sorry." I keep my gaze downcast. "I deserve the lecture."

"You're so stubborn sometimes."

"It's part of my charm."

"Now you sound like Niko," she teases, and I roll my eyes. "Oh, I covered your shift this morning. You're welcome."

"Thanks, I owe you." I make my way out of the bathroom and into my bedroom. Klowbi's soft steps follow behind. I strip off the rest of my dirty clothes and change into baggy sweatpants and a black tank top before collapsing on my bed. Klowbi sets the mortar and pestle on my bedside and sits next to me with her back pressed against the wall, legs extended.

"So, are you going to tell me what happened at the bar last night with you and Xuan?" she says abruptly and I groan and roll over.

"I'm tired. Can we talk about this tomorrow?" I grumble and bury my head into the pillow.

"You might die from your wound tomorrow before you can explain, so no. I think you owe me an explanation, considering."

"Considering," I mutter, and force myself into a sitting position. My eyes are heavy, and had I stayed laying flat I'd have fallen asleep mid-conversation. But once again, she's right, I owe her an explanation, even if it is a brief one. "She said I didn't think things through, couldn't hold true to my word, and my tenacious personality would put others in danger." I pull my hair loose from my braid and comb my fingers through it. I smell dirt and sweat, and beneath that a cloying sweet rot that makes my stomach clench.

"I mean," Klowbi starts softly, "after what you did today, she isn't entirely wrong."

I shoot her a menacing glare and she shrugs. "I don't need another lecture."

"It's merely an observation," Klowbi replies curtly. "Was that all?"

"More or less." Except Xuan had known I'd gone to the Astral Realm and Klowbi hadn't chastised me about breaking the pact. I assume Xuan kept that knowledge to herself. I'm grudgingly grateful for that reprieve, I'd hate for Klowbi to find out about my Astral excursion from someone else's mouth. *Damnit.* "Actually, there's more. I'd rather you hear it from me than anyone else."

And so I confide in Klowbi about my astral projections since our unanimous pact agreeing not to project; I tell her about speaking with Desmond and the hopelessness in his demeanor, all the dread and pain reflecting in his eyes. I tell her about the entity I'd seen hunting Desmond, and the second time it vowing to claim me. I share the truth of my nightmare and the burn's origin, along with the entity bursting from the flames. I reveal everything except for the two books I found; *Ancient Astral Projection* and *Aberrant Magick: Shadow, Nether, and Ether of the Arcane* will stay my secret.

Once I finish retelling most everything I've kept hidden from her, Klowbi sits in silence, staring blankly at her lap. It feels like an eternity as my gut wrenches with anxiety waiting for her to speak. When she does, she doesn't lift her head to acknowledge me, she keeps her eyes downcast. "Now is that all? Or are there more secrets you're keeping quiet about?" Her voice is soft and unwavering, the bitterness of her words sours my tongue with betrayal.

I promise I'll tell you everything, but not yet. Trust me, Bambi. "That's it," I lie and the words stick to my tongue, clinging to the roof of my mouth. *Liar liar liar.*

She nods once, quick. "How did Xuan find out?"

"She says she could tell it from my aura. That it's rotting me," I say and laugh joylessly. *Not to mention she said I would rot everyone around me. You included, Klowbi.*

She nods again and doesn't speak. With a deep inhale, she swings her legs off of the bed and takes one long stride to the threshold. She's so quick to move and my head is pounding with exhaustion. Invisible hands strangle my heart; I barely register the distance between us.

"Where are you going?" She's guarding her features, distancing herself from me by any means possible. It makes my heart sick. There's a tightness in her face as she attempts to hold back tears.

"I'm going to bed. You should get some sleep." Klowbi is already backing into the hallway.

"I'm sorry, Klowbi." I'm sinking down into my bed and I would love nothing more than to sleep and forget everything that's happened the last few weeks.

"Goodnight." Klowbi turns and heads directly into her room without waiting for a reply.

I close my eyes, willing my damned aching heart to quiet. When I open them again, I'm disoriented and realize I had fallen asleep sitting up with the overhead light still on. Still half asleep, I stumble to the bathroom to grab my jars, vials, and crystals that were left on the counter. As I return to my room, I pause outside Klowbi's closed door and listen for her steady breathing. Guilt claws at my insides, but there's nothing for me to do to mend the distrust I sowed tonight.

Shuffling back into my room, I close the door and groggily reorganize my herbs and crystals into the correct location until I'm left with the tainted clear quartz. Without knowing the consequences of the toxins in my body and the crystal, I'm hesitant to dispose of it. I locate an empty jar and place the quartz swirling with inky black inside, sealing it shut and placing it on the windowsill to deal with later.

I shut off the light and crawl into bed, cocooning myself in the blankets and burying my head against the pillow. Even with my exhaustion, it takes time for my brain to settle and quiet. In the darkness, eyes closed or not, all I see are burnt rubies for eyes and thorns that fang a gaping jaw. They follow me into oblivion.

When I wake the next morning, the sun is shining through the blinds casting a golden hue to the room. Everything feels sore and the grime from yesterday is still coating my skin. Sitting up, I groan with effort and tenderly touch the gauze wrapping my arm. I had forgotten to remove the poultice before falling asleep and the remainder in the mortar has hardened. My arm doesn't throb as it once did, but heat still emanates from the wound and I feel a deep burning sensation beneath the skin. Black veins flow from the burn, and they've grown further along my arm, snaking closer to my shoulder and into the bend in my elbow. The pain, still consistent, is at least tolerable now.

Faint sounds of the TV in the living room reach me through the closed door. Klowbi must be up; I smell coffee and it makes my mouth water. Before deciding to face Klowbi, I pad softly to my altar to provide an offering of thanks to Lilith. I center the owl statue on my altar and grab the small blade I use when crafting my blood magick. Nicking the pad of my pointer finger I draw Lilith's sigil onto the owl's head while muttering her prayer. Once finished, I close my eyes and say thanks to her for saving my life and place dried rose petals and chunks of onyx bordering the statue.

I comb my fingers through my hair and exit my bedroom to grab a cup of coffee. Klowbi shifts when I enter and her shoulders tense as she starts biting at her nails. I try not to give notice and make myself a cup of coffee with extra sugar and milk. The ceramic mug is burning the palms of my hands, but it's a comforting warmth. The first sip burns my tongue so sharply that I inhale. It doesn't stop me from going in for another sip and savoring the heat spreading through my chest.

"Good morning," I say, walking into the living room with my mug cradled in my hands.

"Morning," Klowbi mumbles. Her eyes are locked on the TV.

"Did you sleep alright?" I ask and she nods her head while still refusing to look in my direction. Her cold demeanor is sobering. We hardly ever fight, but this feels different. It's like a line is drawn in the sand. One I put there.

"I'm sorry, Bambi. I was trying to protect you."

"Protect me? You were keeping secrets and nearly died because you don't trust anyone!" Klowbi's voice is sharp and shrill, her cheeks brightening with her outburst. "I don't want an apology unless you can prove you trust us. Trust me."

"You're right," I concede, lifting my mug in her direction. "I will prove it when we explain everything to the others."

"I already called them this morning and explained everything to them. They are on their way here to meet us in the diner." Klowbi's tone is clipped and her eyes revert back to the TV.

"You already told them everything?" I take a sip of my coffee and relish the burning on my tongue. I wanted to choose what to tell the group, but Klowbi ensured no secrets stayed hidden. It makes me guiltily grateful I withheld telling her about the two books I borrowed from Thayne.

"Everything you told me last night. We agreed no more secrets," Klowbi scolds, flickering her gaze towards me.

"I thought that was only for us," I mutter and strain to keep the contempt from my tone.

"At my discretion," she corrects. "They should be here soon. We will meet you downstairs after you're cleaned up. You still have blood on your arm." Klowbi shuts off the TV and crosses the living room to the door with barely a glance in my general direction. "I'll see you downstairs." She shuts the door with a finality that leaves me chilled.

The sweetness of the coffee suddenly has lost its appeal. I dump the remains in the sink and decide the sooner I meet with the others, the sooner they will leave. Silently sour, I clean the mortar and pestle, and strip off my clothes and bandages to stand in the seething spray from the shower. A swirl of dirt-riddled water circles the drain tinged with rust. The wound stings from the water and suds. Black veins have deepened the color of my flesh into a mottled gray around the infected area.

I dry and clothe myself in dark jeans and a quarter-sleeve forest green top with a deep neckline. The moon phase tattoo is visible above my breasts and above that my swan pendant. I braid my hair, then ensure the black veins are covered and leave to meet the others. As a last thought, I grab the jar containing the toxic quartz.

I locate the others sitting at a corner booth by the window the furthest from any other customers. Klowbi sits beside Alko and Xuan, leaving Niko sitting by himself. He spots me first as I walk the distance of the diner to where they sit. They each have a coffee cup and a platter of cinnamon rolls with icing. My stomach growls at the sweet scent, yet the idea of eating sets my stomach churning and my mouth tastes like dust.

"Hungry, Daire?" Xuan asks as I approach.

I shake my head and slide in beside Niko who is wearing his flat cap. His malachite ring winks in the sunlight through the panes of glass. "Coffee is fine."

"Let's get to it. Klowbi told us of your errancy and secrets. I am not pleased, but I'm relieved to see you mostly unharmed. How is the wound?" Xuan asks. Her eyes appear as black slits.

"Painful," I confess. Klowbi looks at me and for a moment I see her face slack with sympathy, but when I meet her eyes, she looks away at her half-eaten roll.

"May we see?" Xuan probes. Her vulpine gaze doesn't waver from mine.

"It's not exactly pleasant to look at while at breakfast," I reply with a bitter smile.

"Just show them," Klowbi pleads.

"We're here to help," Niko reminds me. He offers me an encouraging smile, but I want to throw those words back in his face.

You're here because of Klowbi, not me. Without another word, I roughly pull the sleeve up so they see the deep black gouges that are my veins and my colorless flesh and crusty burn. The cloth of my shirt catches the scab and tears as bubbles of blood bead to the surface.

"Holy shit," Niko blurts too loudly. A few heads turn in our direction.

"Shut up," I growl.

"I've never seen anything like that," Alko adds, leaning in with morbid interest.

I pull my sleeve back down and swallow the bolt of pain that follows. "That's encouraging."

"It's gotten worse," Klowbi murmurs. Her eyes have a shine to them and she blinks them frantically.

"That's from a Shadow," Xuan reiterates after a moment of quiet.

I nod and grab the mug of coffee sitting in front of me. I take a sip and grimace at the bite; I hate black coffee. "With red eyes, if that makes any difference."

"How did you cleanse it?" Xuan asks, pulling at her bottom lip, her gaze calculating.

"Hydrogen peroxide and magick." I place the jar with the tainted quartz in the middle of the table. "That's before the poultice was applied."

Alko grabs the jar and lifts it so the quartz is directly in the light. The edges are still clear, but the swirling ink inside isn't penetrated by the light, like clear prison walls showcasing the undulating cloud within. "It looks like it's part of the Shadows." He sets it gingerly back on the table and rubs his hand on his thighs, eyeing it with disdain.

Xuan grabs it this time and studies it, twisting it one way and then the other. "Forget the damn crystal," Niko barks, shaking his head. "Look at her arm. That can't be healthy."

"I'm fine. I think the worst of it was purged already." If it didn't kill me overnight, then I have a chance to remove whatever remains in my bloodstream.

"Keep it cleaned and tell us if it worsens," Xuan advises as her attention shifts from the quartz. Her eyes appear nearly as black as the mist in the crystal. "Can I keep this for research? I can test theories if this is a Shadow sample."

"That makes it easy to dispose of it. Keep the damned thing." I gesture at her and she places the jarred crystal in her bag out of sight.

Klowbi clears her throat. "Before you got here we were talking and decided that since Litha is coming up, and that's where we all met and became friends, we should go together."

The conversation change takes me aback. I force down a steaming swallow of coffee and stifle a shudder. "Is that wise? If the Shadows are a formidable force, shouldn't we avoid festivals centered around magick?"

"Your theory," Xuan pipes in, "about the Astral Realm. If that holds any truth, the festival will be the perfect place to test it. It gives us time to prepare."

"What?" I turn to Niko for guidance. Surely I'm misunderstanding.

Vibrant green eyes meet mine and my breath hitches. "If the Shadows are drawn to magick then they will show up whether we're there or not.

We just know what to expect. Kind of." Niko shakes his head. "I'm not a fan of the idea."

"I agree with Niko," Alko says, surprising me. "It's risky."

"But one we have to take," Xuan insists, dismissing both of their concerns. "If Klowbi and Daire are right, this is an opportunity to learn about the Shadows and defend civilians from potential attacks. We alone possess knowledge about the Shadows and how to stave them off. I can guarantee they aren't pleased that Daire got away. She's already being followed by one Shadow, and now that they marked her, they will be thirsty to finish the job."

"You're going to use me as bait?" The realization heats my blood and fear coats my tongue. I take another swallow of coffee, but it feels as if it clots in my throat.

"A controlled experiment," Xuan corrects. "You will not be alone. One of us will be with you at all times and Farah will patrol the grounds so she can provide warning when something changes."

"When? You sound certain the Shadows will appear. They may not show at all." The thought of willingly walking into the Shadows sends ice down my spine. I'm not ready to face the Shadows again, not so soon after barely escaping them.

"I see it as unlikely. At least one Shadow already follows you, and now possibly a swarm after your stunt yesterday." Her eyes glimmer with warning. "I believe your theory holds some truth. With Litha being one of the most celebrated sabbats, I believe the Shadows will utilize the surge of magick and use it to find you. But if magick is strong for them, it will be for us as well. Alko and I are fluent with magick and will stay within line of sight of you the entire night."

"And if the Shadows attack?" I push and my wound pangs at the mention.

"We will be prepared this time, and we won't be going in blind." Xuan meets my eyes and shifts forward. Even with her petite frame and gentle facial features, the weight of her intensity has me sitting back and holding my tongue. "We must trust one another. If I did not believe the risk wasn't worth the reward, I would not ask this of any of you."

"It's risky, but the crowd will make us harder to target individually," Niko adds in. "What the hell, I'm in. Nothing like a little Shadow hunting to make you feel alive." His grin is prideful and I want to shake him. These aren't just Shadows anymore, they are transcendental. They can attack, they can maim, they can *kill*.

"And what about the civilians? We can't protect them all if they attack. We'd be putting innocent lives at stake." I have enough guilt on my hands, I don't need blood on them too.

"If the Shadows make themselves known they will attack whether we are there or not." Xuan's tone is unwavering, hard. "The reward outweighs the risks. I understand your fear, but you will have friends to guard your back this time instead of empty space. I swear I will do everything in my power to protect you," Xuan vows. It offers little comfort.

"And to protect them as well." I gesture to our table.

"Of course, I figured that goes without saying," Xuan amends, and I remember her words that night at the bar.

"Alright," Alko says reluctantly. "We stand a better chance as a group."

I look at Niko, then Alko, before settling on Klowbi, who stares shyly in return. "What about you? Don't tell me you agreed to this?"

"It was my idea," Klowbi replies. "Xuan merely fleshed it out."

I nod numbly and rub furiously at my eyes. *You volunteered me as bait.* The betrayal is thick in my throat. This is stupid, but it could provide vital information in return and protect innocent lives. Was it worth risking their lives? Or mine?

"It could help save Desmond," Klowbi murmurs, her gaze pleading.

"Damnit," I growl. "Fine, but the moment things go beyond our control, we bail."

There is only an illusion of control. We are at the mercy of the Shadows.

"We are in agreement," Xuan says with a curt nod. "I'll continue making preparations."

We spend the better part of the morning drinking coffee and chatting about lighter topics. For a moment I almost enjoy myself and forget about the Shadows and Desmond. I somehow manage to find my appetite and wolf down two cinnamon rolls, now cold after sitting for so long, and order scrambled eggs and sausage. I haven't eaten since we'd gone to the bar, and didn't realize how weak I felt until finally having a full belly. After finishing my order of eggs, a sudden pang of longing for the Astral Realm sends my magick reeling, and I have to consciously clasp it down. Xuan gives me a curious look, but stays silent. My wound throbs in time with my heart, each pound a warning in my breast.

Liar liar liar.

Chapter 21

It's early afternoon and already the buzz of Litha is choking the center of town. The three-day festivities begin tonight. Several main blocks in town and the surrounding parks are closed off from motor vehicles so tents can be pitched and borderline-stable carnival rides built. Food trailers and tents are set up and selling to those scoping out the grounds early, a few carnies shouting the price for their cheap prizes. Parents are herding their children down the sidewalk, their small fists filled with cotton candy, ice cream, hot dogs, or donuts while the parents follow behind carrying prizes won at the carnival games. Or a screaming child.

After finishing my shift, the idea of fresh air and sunshine was needed to clear my head, so I began walking towards the center of town to recon the celebration. I recognized most of the vendors from previous years. The smell of deep-fried foods made my stomach rumble and seeing the vendor setting up the flower crowns brought a sad smile. Klowbi would want another one this year, as she did every year.

Klowbi and I had barely spoken to one another since I laid out all my secrets. She clearly had her doubts about our impromptu plan, but not enough to voice her concerns. If she felt guilty about using me as bait she didn't say. After all, I had placed the wall between us. She was merely reinforcing what I built.

We agreed to meet and attend Litha together, prioritizing our own safety and protecting nearby families if the Shadows appear. It's impossible to know if they would show, let alone predicting their numbers. If the Shadows showed, we had to bet on the magick strengthening just as it did the night of Beltane and back in the forest when the Red Eyes attacked. If the magick was stronger, then it gave us the surprise advantage since I doubted the Shadows knew to expect a counterattack, yet they'd still have the edge in numbers and aggression. If they made an appearance, there's no way of knowing if our magick combined would keep the Shadows at bay, or if they would melt and stay gone upon impact, or if they were targeting me, or if this was a damned heroic death wish from the start.

If, if, if....

So many ifs, so much uncertainty. We are going into this blind, and the few facts we do know are barely enough to keep our heads above water, let alone turn the tides if things go wrong. Celebrating Litha this year is met with dread instead of excitement. The first year Mom won't be celebrating with us. With me. Dad decided to be with Aubrie and a few coven members instead of being in town, another first. It's a blessing in disguise, knowing Dad will be far away from whatever hell happens this weekend.

The clamor of vendors and children grows softer as I distance myself. I'm not aware of where I'm going until I'm walking beneath the granite arches of the wrought-iron gated cemetery, treading silently past dozens of headstones. Some are newer, still gleaming with fresh vases of various colors. Others are old and weathered with missing chunks of stone and barely legible engravings. A few withered flowers lie by a headstone and most of the graves are too old for anyone to bother gifting them.

After Mom was buried, I went with Dad to visit her grave the first few times. But each time we walked down the dirt path together, my feet became lead and it was nearly impossible to breathe. It felt too real going to visit her headstone and being welcomed by cold unfeeling rock instead of her warm embrace, her skin perfumed with sage and myrrh.

When we last visited, I couldn't maintain composure and ended up lashing out at Dad, Mom's gravestone, the deities I prayed to, the doctors who failed us, the world, and anyone who would listen. I've refused to come back since, and though the guilt of ignoring Mom's resting place made me ashamed, the prospect of facing her ashamed me more.

I see her gravestone. No flowers lay at the grave. The headstone remains clean and retains its new sheen, the inscription legible. Seeing the bare grass feels wrong. She was always warm and bright when she was alive, always wanting more flowers or plants in the house or garden, and she and Klowbi would bond over gardening techniques or sharing how best to use certain herbs.

A lone dandelion sprouts just off the path. Smiling, the memory of drinking dandelion tea on a cool day while munching on dandelion cookies stops me in my tracks. As a child, Mom would encourage me to collect as many dandelions as I could carry for cooking purposes. If leftovers allowed, we would attempt creating a new dessert or drink. The result usually lacked the sweetness of her familiar recipes. As I grew older, picking dandelions lost its joy, but baking and talking for hours remained just as satisfying. Where others saw a weed, Mom saw a flower, a cookie, balms and soap, jelly and honey, brightness and wishes. When a flower was picked because of its beauty, it would dry and die days later, but if a dandelion was picked, it didn't matter because the seeds would live and create more. A resilient flower. A useful resource.

A reminder of what I lost.

Bending down, I pluck the dandelion from its roots and cross the rest of the way to her gravestone. As if made of glass, I kiss the dandelion and place it in front of her headstone, brushing my palm across the engraving.

Fay Delacroix. Daughter. Sister. Wife. Mother. Witch.

I sit down within arm's reach of the stone. Already the invisible hands are squeezing my heart, my throat tight, and a warm pressure pushes at the backs of my eyes. I remember now why I refused to come since the last time. If I can't see what remains of her, I can almost pretend it's just a nightmare. But almost isn't reality. She's still dead.

"Everything is different without you here." I swallow the painful press of tears in the back of my throat. I inhale slowly to steady the tremor in my voice and hands. "Nothing is as it was. Desmond is dying, Dad is lost without you beside him. Aubrie is broken with the thought of losing her only child. I look at my friends and see only strangers. The Shadows are following us, hunting me. I'm wounded and marked by their foreign touch. They seem to be growing stronger, more intelligent, hungry." I rub furiously at my eyes and warm tears smear against my cheeks. "Something calls to me from the Astral Realm. I think somehow the realm is bleeding into our world. Some moments I think I can feel the energy brushing against my skin and calling to my magick."

I lift my gaze to stare at my mother's name engraved upon the stone. I trace my fingers along the indents and my tears darken the marker. "Nothing is the same since you got sick, and it's only gotten worse since you died. Food still tastes bland and gray. The sun holds no warmth, and even the moon fails to inspire me. Most days I can only focus on my anger or nothing at all, otherwise the sadness would devour me. I'm afraid for my life. I'm afraid tonight the Shadows will attack again and we are too ill-prepared and outnumbered for a confrontation. I'm afraid my friends will get hurt." Sniffling, I rise to my feet and calm my aching heart. "You promised you'd be there for me always. You said you would always be there to guide me, to protect me, to mentor me. But I need you now and you're not here."

My eyes are dry and the only trace of having cried is in the congestion of my nose. Placing a hand on the top of the headstone, I bow my head. "I know it was not your choice to leave us. Every night I go to sleep hoping I'll wake up to you cooking breakfast and humming in the kitchen." My words are a gentle murmur, hardly audible even to my ears. "Guide me, Mom. I still need your wisdom. Lend me your strength. Guide my heart as you did my hand when I was young." I put two fingers to my lips and kiss them, pressing against her name etched on the stone. "I miss you more than you know. I promise I will visit again after whatever happens tonight. Maybe next time I see you, I can give you a hug." The thought induces a smile and eases the grief in my heart. Even though it would mean leaving

Klowbi and Dad behind, it would mean Mom wouldn't be alone anymore. "I love you."

The walk back to my apartment is uneventful. My heart and mind lighter and clearer after visiting Mom, but fear still slithers and twines in my belly. Passing the countless food vendors has my stomach clenching and I want to heave. I suck down a lungful of air and keep walking with my mind focused on getting home.

Only a few more blocks from home, my phone rings, startling me from my thoughts. I glance and barely make out the name before answering the call. A cold stone sinks into the pit of my stomach and bile coats the back of my throat. Any other day, the call would be welcome. Not today.

"Hey, Thayne," I answer while continuing down the sidewalk.

"Daire, I'm glad you answered. Are you alright?"

"Yes, why wouldn't I be? Did something happen?" As I walk past the massive throng of people, I hiss when my arm is jostled and a bolt of pain shoots through my shoulder and into my back. The flash of pain blinds me, but it recedes as fast as it came, leaving only a dull throb.

"Of sorts. Don't worry, it has nothing to do with Desmond," Thayne explains. "I was cleaning my library, sorting out books and mending those that are well worn. I found a box I think you'd be interested in. I'll hold on to it for you, but I'd rather you visit soon."

"What is it?" I ask with my interest piqued. I'm nearly home now and am grateful for the lessening of the press of bodies and chaotic sounds of the fair.

"It belonged to your mother," Thayne's voice is gentle when he replies. My heartbeat quickens and my fingers cling to the pendant around my throat.

"I can't come today, but soon. I'll be sure of it." Anything that was Mom's should have been handled by either Dad or I and I don't recall ever giving anything of hers to Thayne. "What is it?"

"I think it best you see for yourself. I don't want to delve deeper into what I found than I already have," Thayne admits. "Come whenever you wish, but I think you'll want to see this."

"Thank you, Thayne."

"Of course. Be careful, Daire."

"Always," I say before ending the call.

Once back in my apartment, my arm is aching and swollen. The base of my skull smarts with each throb, sending spirals of dizzying stars across my vision. For a brief moment, I stumble and lose all sight as the pain increases and I curl my hands into fists, my nails cutting crescent moons into my palms. The distinct pain keeps me focused until the dizziness fades and I reach my room.

I haven't cleansed my wound since waking before my shift. I realized early on that mundane techniques for healing the wound did little to nothing to ease the pain, swelling, or fever festering. Black veins expand across my arm making it increasingly difficult to hide. The veins snake entirely up to my shoulder and down to my elbow and faint traces of it spread along my forearm. I have to use concealer to hide it or deal with concerned glances and questions. I'm sure to an outsider it looks awfully like drug abuse with my blackened veins, strange puncture marks, and swelling. The magick doesn't permanently stave off the ache, but it dampens it enough for me to ignore it.

I'm afraid of what will happen once the veins spread up my neck and into my brain. It's a morbid thought to think that perhaps the Shadow left a fragment of itself inside me, utilizing me as its host to strengthen and feed off of my energy. Besides the damnable pain and inky lines that are my veins, I haven't noticed a change. I tried scouring the *Gray Book* for any similarities between my wound and the other Shadows, but there's nothing remotely close to my situation. If it continues to grow worse, I'll have to reach out to other practices of magick before the damage becomes irreversible.

But until then...

Resetting and organizing my altar, I grab a silver handheld mirror and place it in the center, lighting four red candles and one black one to create a pentagram with the black candle at the top and the mirror completing the pentacle as the circle. I kneel before my altar, grab a razor blade, and stare into the mirror while watching the flames flicker on the outside. Closing my eyes, I call on my magick.

"Renich Viasa Avage Lilith Lirach," I chant. There's a pull in my core and something whispers against my ear, rustling my hair. My eyes fly open, but I'm alone in my room besides my reflection and the flickering candle light.

Tightening the grip of the razor blade between my fingers, I shift my sleeve off my shoulder and gently press a fingertip against the reddened flesh and the black snakes coiling beneath my skin. The pain sends a fresh wave of dizziness to my head. Steadying my hand, I slice the blade into my burn and a thick swell of black blood wells. Dipping my fingers in the blood and holding back swears from the insistent jolt of pain, I inscribe Lilith's sigil in the center of the mirror that creates the pentacle. The blood looks even darker against the reflected surface and gold glimmer of the candles.

"Lilith, Dark Goddess, Great Mother, hear my call. I offer my blood to you in an offering of thanks. Guide my heart as it is yours. Guide my hand to protect those who are worthy of your illumination. Guide my mind so I may drink from the cup of knowledge. Goddess of the Night, heal my wounds and protect me from the legions of darkness against your domain. Timeless Abyss, Mother of Darkness, consume me in your embrace, in the swirling starry horizon."

A foreign wind stirs my hair and the candles flicker and whimper in reply. Lilith has heard my prayer. I almost imagine her presence residing around me, within me, her voice giving me strength and her hands guiding and expunging the infection from my wound.

A strange violet glow emanates from the mirror with her sigil written in blood. The ache lessens and even the swelling and redness recedes, though the oily black is stark against my pale complexion.

"Thank you," I murmur and close my eyes. "Blessed be, Great Mother." When I open them again, the candles are smoking from the fire having gone out and I know Lilith has left to return to her domain. The mirror still reflects a violet glow.

I don't dare touch the mirror. I stand and recite Lilith's enn thrice more in thanks and step back. I leave the offering for her, planning to clean it up before leaving tonight. I grab the razor blade and go about cleansing it and my wound, firmly wrapping it in case the bleeding doesn't clot. I'm careful not to slice too deep or too wide, but if the toxins somehow affect bleeding, I want to make sure I have it wrapped tightly.

I'm finishing wrapping my wound with a fresh roll of gauze when a pull towards my magick stills my hands. The thick taste of static coats my tongue, and when I stare at my palms and summon a tendril of blue healing magick, it responds sharply, as easy as flipping on a light-switch. If I focus I can almost hear the humming of the magick in the air, a heavy press against my skin, a familiar sensation from when the Shadows attacked me in the festival grounds. My magick craves to be released despite just crafting a blood spell, an insatiable hunger hovering just beneath the skin. The Astral Realm is bleeding again. I taste it on my tongue, feel the pull from the realm whispering to me, waving me forward.

Come home, it says, *come home.*

Excerpt from Daire's BoS

Simple Warning Spell for Adversaries

Light a black candle and chant the following:

Blood turn black and flesh turn blue
I will curse you if you force my due
By bones to break and mind put under
I'll curse your eyes, a heart asunder
I'll call down a plague of flies
Blood go black and flesh go blue
Evil from me rounds back to you
My soul clean and yours on fire
You fuck with a witch you get burned, liar

Chapter 22

Sipping a glass of vodka cran, I plait my hair to hang heavy along my spine before doing a once over in the mirror. Already the humidity of the night can be felt through the window pane, and as much as I'd prefer to wear a dress for comfort, I decide on ripped gray jeans and a quarter-sleeve gray blouse. It won't hinder my movement, and it will protect my wound with its ever growing black roots. As always, my swan pendant hangs at the base of my throat. Several of my tattoos are peeking out from hair and cloth, and my eyes are lined and winged in black with thick lashes framing my blue-amber mismatched eyes.

Klowbi pops her head in and nods approvingly at my attire. "You look like a badass!"

"I look better than I feel."

Klowbi smiles sympathetically while adjusting her rose-colored blouse.

Everyone will meet at our place and walk together to the festivities. We argued over driving versus walking, but driving through thick crowds when trying to escape a nearly invisible foe sounds more difficult than fighting the crowds on foot. In the worst-case scenario, we'll clear the festival's perimeter and use my vehicle to leave town. I hope it won't come to that.

"This shirt is too tight. It makes me look frumpy and washed out." Klowbi yanks on the shirt, her lips thinned in disgruntlement.

"It suits you. It makes your hair look redder," I compliment and twirl one of her auburn curls around my finger teasingly. She frowns and swats my hand away. I huff in amusement.

"Finish your drink. They should be here any minute," Klowbi grumbles, stalking back out to the kitchen.

The wall between us is still up. Our conversations no longer flow, and a heavy tension exists in its stead. My heart shatters each time she dismisses me, every time she refuses to meet my eyes.

By trying to protect her I only managed to push her away.

I follow and take a long swallow of my beverage. My stomach is in nervous knots and a thin film of sweat coats my skin. The vodka is warming my belly and settling my jitters, though I'm careful not to drink so much that it will affect my intuition or reflexes. I need my wits about me tonight and my magick at full strength.

"Hey, Bambi," I say and catch her arm before she walks too far. She pulls her arm from my grasp, my stomach tightening as she eyes me. I swore I'd keep her safe tonight, and I find myself wishing she wouldn't come at all. I want her to stay here behind sigils and spells.

"What's wrong, Daire? You look pale." Her voice is laced with concern but she doesn't cross the distance.

"I don't like the idea of you coming to the festival," I contend for the dozenth time tonight.

Her gaze softens as she studies my features. Her hand lifts towards me, but she hesitates and threads her fingers through her hair. "I told you I'm coming with you. I'll be fine. If anything, I'm worried about you. You're the one they attacked."

"I know," I grumble, my eyes darting away with guilt thinning my lips. I grab my drink and take a long gulp. The vodka burns as it goes down. A fire grows in my chest and a pleasant heat spreads all the way to my fingertips. "I just have this feeling they will show up tonight."

"You don't know that, but we're prepared if they do," Klowbi says, already turning away.

We are hardly prepared.

I take a step towards her and block her path. "Listen to me, I'm warning you tonight is going to be dangerous. I did blood magick while you were at work to ease the pain in my wound. It worked, but not long after I could feel the magick spike. I can taste it on my tongue, I can feel it against my skin. I can hear it, Klowbi." I stare at my hands as if expecting my magick to spiral free from whim. "It's been getting stronger as the day's gone on. It's as close to tangible as magick can get. It's stronger than the night of Beltane, or when the Shadows attacked me. *Stronger* than both those days." I wipe my palms on my hands and meet Klowbi's gaze, finally appearing concerned. *All she sees tonight is hanging out with friends and celebrating Litha as the day we became a group.*

And tonight will be anything but that.

"Alko is bringing glamour," Klowbi insists with an imperceptible shake of her head.

"Barely enough to conceal one of us, let alone five. The Shadows have grown more cunning since your last encounter. They can communicate with each other; they show strategy."

"You mentioned most Shadows still acted animalistic and obeyed only the intelligent." Her eyes glimmer with innocence so pure my chest tightens. She won't take no for an answer, yet she doesn't comprehend the danger she's walking willingly towards.

"Not exclusively. Most still showed venereal tendencies. The scent of carnage and blood would send any animal into a craze." I grab the nearly empty glass and stare at my inked hands covered in runes. "Imagine feeding into the bestial nature of a being we know little to nothing about."

"Daire, you aren't—" Klowbi pauses when the sound of voices float from beyond the front door. Knuckles rasping on wood snaps the silence, and Klowbi offers a chastened smile. "Strength in numbers," she reiterates, turning her back and opening the door to greet our friends.

In one smooth motion, I down the remnants of my drink, hoping in the action the grievance bearing heavy on my shoulders washes down with it. It doesn't. I smile grimly and face the others as they file into our entryway. Xuan leads first, her eyes pinning me, her head tilting at my downtrodden posture. Alko is close behind, his hands filled with jewels and pendants and a tentative smile pulling at his lips, though his wide eyes reveal the skittishness he's trying hard to placate.

And last comes Niko with his signature grin and ebullient emerald eyes latching onto me. His eyes are magnetic and my magick stirs at the sight of him as a film of pink wafts past my lips. He appraises me and lifts an eyebrow in a query at my stiff form. Rather than questioning me, he slides forward and lifts an arm around my shoulders. When I go to shrug him off, he reveals his hand, which is holding my now empty glass stained with cranberry juice.

"This is a problem," he says as an introduction. A flimsy smile pulls at the corner of my lips.

"Alko, the glamour," Xuan directs. He lays out the trinkets on the countertop, splaying them with his fingers so they aren't as tangled. Xuan looks at us and gestures to the jewelry glittering in the kitchen lighting. "Everyone, grab at least one. Daire, I'd recommend grabbing two. Masking your energy is vital tonight."

The jewelry glows orange. I can tell which ones are heavily glamoured to mask our trails. Those seem to be wafting waves of glamour magick. When I hover my hand over them, my magick stirs in my core and a prickling sensation covers my fingertips tracing down to my palm. I taste the glamour, thick and viscous, grating against my tongue, and the heightened magick in the atmosphere only increases the magnitude of the spells Alko crafted.

Klowbi grabs a flower brooch and pins it to her hair, the gold rose blinking in the light. A mist of orange oscillates around her face, partially obscuring her features. Ideally, any magick users would see the same effect, including the Shadows.

Alko already wears his usual jewelry, permanently glamoured. An even thicker mist swarms his figure; it's the most distracting I've ever seen his magick. It looks like an orange strobe light is on him, nearly blinding with the intensity of it.

Xuan layers a necklace around her throat, the crystal pressing close to her collarbone. Niko wears his newly glamoured malachite ring with a glamoured chain barely distinguishable around his neck being mostly hidden by the collar on his shirt.

I grab the remaining glamoured baubles; an obsidian ring which I place on my right middle finger. The magick is so strong a wave of dizziness washes over me, the additional magick sending a warm current up my arm. The second piece is an evil eye bracelet thickly coated in glamour that I slip over my left wrist. A second, more dominating wave of vertigo overcomes me, absorbing into my skin when my magick accepts the strength it offers.

"These are powerful," I mutter, swiveling the bracelet between my fingers.

"I glamoured them every hour," Alko explains. "The evil eye seemed like it would offer more protection than a typical bracelet. I figured it couldn't hurt to have a little extra defense."

"Thank you." The glamour magick parts around our group as if sensing they are not the threat we're hiding from.

"The sun will set soon," Xuan states. "I'll explain as we walk."

Filing out, I lock the front door and walk down to the sidewalk. We fall into rhythm with Xuan in the center of our group, Klowbi and Alko walking slightly ahead, Niko and I slightly behind. The cool air feels heavenly against my face and my eyes dart wildly at each shadow we pass and hooded stranger that bustles by.

"Firstly, never wander off alone. We must always be paired. Since we are an odd number, we must stay in groups of two or three. No one is allowed to be left alone," Xuan begins, voice gentle yet firm as she speaks. "Farah will scout the crowds and report any Otherworldly sightings to me. She is scanning the path we're walking to the festival. While her talents aren't foolproof, please report any suspicions, no matter how minor, if you observe or sense anything out of the ordinary. It might mean the difference between life and death tonight." Xuan glances over her shoulder at me, her slanted eyes black glinting like a feline's. "Have you sensed a shift?"

I nod once. "Yes, since this morning. It's been getting stronger as the day has gone on. It's as if the energy is building against a solid force, and any change against whatever is holding the energy force back will explode."

Her mouth flattens into a thin line as if displeased by my comment. "I've sensed it as well, as has Farah."

"I feel it, too," Alko says from ahead. "My skin feels sticky, itchy."

"You know," Niko starts beside me, "now that you mention it, I sense it, too. I thought maybe it was all in my head, but it's like a static is pressed against my skin, making it prickle. Like a constant itch."

"Oh," Klowbi pipes up. "I thought I was just anxious, but I feel it too. It's like an electrical current."

Xuan and I exchange a look. "The magic might be powerful enough to appear to other civilians. They may not understand the anomaly, but the magick aims to appeal to their familiar senses; prickling sensations, dizziness, static, even nervousness or an unexplained jitter."

"That's bad, isn't it?" Niko asks.

"Not entirely," Xuan answers. "It means the energy is extremely potent, so we must be careful. It also means it will be easier to tap into for those who are familiar with magick."

"Like Daire." Niko glances at me and offers me a smile full of teeth.

"Yes, like Daire. I might have more control of it as well, if it's as strong as I believe it to be. Alko should too, perhaps even you and Klowbi. You are familiar with the basic tells of magick energy, in which case you might be able to sway the power and utilize it."

"I'll be able to use magick?" Niko asks with the giddiness of a child. "Hell yeah!"

Xuan ignores his comment and I roll my eyes. At least we agree on something.

"Lastly, if things become above our control, we leave. Do not play hero. Do not be a martyr. It doesn't matter who is in trouble, unless it is one of us we do not risk our lives for strangers. We find each other and we get to safety. We protect our own." Xuan's tone is unyielding and an icy shiver shoots down my spine.

People might die tonight. A warmth brushes my hand, then entwines it, and for once I don't shake free of Niko's grasp in mine. Tonight his touch is welcome.

"Are we all in understanding?" Xuan asks, and each of us pipes up in agreement.

"What do we do until then?" Niko asks, squeezing my fingers.

"We hope they don't show and enjoy the night like everyone else," I say grimly.

A thickening crowd envelops us as we walk, forcing us to move shoulder to shoulder. Tents and walkways are lit up and lights have been strung in the tops of trees, creating a hypnagogic reality. The sky is awash in violets and indigos with splatters of sparkling constellations. Even the full moon can be seen, cast in an unnatural crimson that sends goosebumps down my arms.

Sounds of laughter and children screaming joyously pierce the air. On any normal occasion, the shrill voices would bring a smile to my face, but tonight my stomach knots in apprehension and inconsolable fear. So many children, so many families, and all grievously unaware of the danger they are in.

People will die tonight.

A forceful shove sends me stumbling into Niko, stepping on his foot in the process. He helps right me, the rest of our group continuing with the swarm of the crowd towards the heart of the festival and unaware of our lagging. He clasps my hand in his and leads us in the general direction our group went while casting sidelong glances at me. Concern is written on his face and a small part of me whispers to kiss him to wipe it from his features.

"You seem distracted," he remarks as a way of conversation.

"I've got a lot on my mind."

"You're not the only one." He doesn't push the subject, so I remain silent.

As we walk the general path the others followed, we pass dozens of different food vendors selling everything from hot dogs and chicken strips to deep fried Twinkie's and Oreos. The combination of smells is a disorienting aroma, discouraging my hunger more than encouraging. A designated beer tent is positioned far from children while the line meanders through makeshift vendor alleys. On the opposite side are the carnies shouting their prices for rigged carnival games; little kids with bright eyes staring in wonder at the oversized stuffies while the parents reluctantly grab their wallets. In the distance, live music is playing and there's a shifting wave of bodies undulating to the music, couples and kids alike dancing in the colorful strobe lights. Picnic tables are placed at random for seating. A young couple sits together, sharing an array of fried foods while staring lovingly at one another and casting shy smiles.

They might die tonight.

Niko pulls me along until we're standing at a picnic table our group has claimed. Relief is palpable on their faces when we emerge from the crowd. Klowbi grabs my other hand as we approach and pulls me forward. Once out of the crowd she releases her hold, chewing on her thumbnail.

"I thought something had happened already," Klowbi whispers, her gaze bouncing to everyone but mine.

"Only the crowds," Niko assures her with an easy grin. "Lucky she has me."

All three of them look at our clasped hands and embarrassment has me pulling free and crossing them over my chest. The last thing I needed was Niko doting on me. And if anything did happen, I'd need my hands.

I ignore Niko's blatant disappointment when I release his grip. "Don't let me stop you from enjoying yourselves."

"It feels wrong," Klowbi admits.

"It's not," I assure her. "Nothing might happen." I don't believe this for a second, but I don't dare admit my false reassurance.

"I saw a flower crown vendor along the way," Xuan suggests.

"Don't let Niko anywhere near them," Alko teases, forcing lightness.

"It was one time," he mumbles, but a smile still plays on his lips.

"But it was such a memorable time," Xuan reiterates, staring at Klowbi. I think I see a hint of a smile before her face falls flat.

"Let's go," she affirms, grabbing Xuan's hand.

"I'll stay here," Alko says to their backs.

The three of us sit on the bench, Niko beside me and Alko across. My stomach clenches as the static of magick bristles against my skin. I taste it on my tongue, flavorless yet full of body. It sends my head swimming from the rush of power and I draw a simple protective rune on my thigh to ease the increase of pressure from the energy.

"Did you feel that?" Niko asks and for once there's no humor in his tone.

Alko nods, his umber eyes wide with fear. He shifts uncomfortably in his seat. His gaze bounces along the crowd as he pulls at his hair with one hand, then forces it into his lap only for his hand to reach for it again moments later. "It's getting stronger. Maybe this was a bad idea." Alko's attention darts in the direction his sister and Klowbi wandered off to.

"A little late for that now," Niko comments.

"Give me your hand," I tell them. Niko shrugs but places his hand on the table for my inspection. Alko freezes, momentarily distracted by my request.

"Why?"

"Do you trust me?"

He hesitates only for a breath and places his hand between us. Calling on my magick, I trace a protective rune on the back of Alko's hand. His eyes widen and breath hitches. His fingers twitch at the warmth of the magick flowing from my hand into his, but he doesn't pull away. When I finish and turn to Niko, Alko stares at his hand as if it's the first time he's seeing it.

"I could feel it," he whispers. "I can faintly see the outline."

"Damn," Niko says, "you really do have the magick touch."

"Shut up," Alko and I say in unison.

The three of us dissolve into nervous laughter, forgetting the scythe hanging over our heads. Klowbi and Xuan appear moments later, a flower crown upon both their heads and one held delicately in Klowbi's good hand. She smiles as they approach and prances to where I sit, placing the flower crown amongst my black curls; a tentative peace offering. The flowers are a deep red, appearing black in the muted lighting. Klowbi's crown is an array of pinks and purples, while Xuan's is gold and peach.

I catch Niko staring and he nods approvingly. "Don't trample this one," I tease while tilting the crown at an angle for emphasis.

Niko throws his hands up in exasperation. "It was one damn time!" He stands and brushes himself off. "I'm going to try my luck with some carnival games," he announces with an easy grin. His eyes are flickering emerald flames in the fantastical shimmer of light. My core tightens when his gaze brushes to mine. "Anyone care to join?"

Alko stands and looks at Xuan with a flash of fear and concern in his eyes, though fear for him or for her I can't say. "I'll join."

Niko gestures while walking backwards. "Great. Be prepared to be overwhelmed with prizes."

"Good luck," Klowbi calls and sits where Niko had been. "I might find you guys later to try the carnival games."

"I'll show you all the secrets," Niko promises as he and Alko make their way through the crowd. Even from this distance, Alko's shoulders relax and he throws his head back with laughter, presumably from a comment Niko made.

"How much do you want to bet they come back empty-handed?" I muse as their forms disappear into the massing crowds.

"You don't think they'll win any?" Klowbi asks.

"Niko won't," Xuan replies, "he's overconfident. Alko might, but Niko will claim it was him."

"Classic Niko move," I mutter, shaking my head.

A sudden surge of energy slams into me, sending my vision into a flurry of dancing spots and my magick flares. Shooting pain stems from my burn down to my ribs, and I cover my side and arm where the pain blazes. I hear Klowbi and Xuan saying my name, but it takes several moments for the disorientation to subside before I can decipher their words.

"Daire, are you okay?" Klowbi's grasping my good arm, the pressure feeling close to pain and I flinch away.

"Just a flare up," I reply and wipe sweat from my brow despite the cool night air pressing against my skin. The pain is constant with each thump of my heart, sending dulled flashes of agony down the entirety of my arm and branching into my shoulder-blade and spine. I grit my teeth and shove the pain down, but Klowbi's gentle touches and questioning has me jittery.

"No," Xuan says from across the table where she sits, her voice barely audible over the deafening sounds of the crowd. "It's growing stronger. It feels alive."

Klowbi fidgets in her seat. "Why can't I feel it?"

"You do," Xuan answers. "The jitters you're feeling are more than likely the magick. I've been watching the crowds and it's affecting them too." She nods behind us, and as subtly as we can, we both turn to look over our shoulders. "The parents and their three boys, I've been watching them. The parents appear anxious, but the youngest child keeps looking around as if he senses something. He'll stare at his hands and scratch at his arms. The other two can't stand still, and I've seen one of the kids cry twice within the last half hour. They can feel it, but they don't understand it."

"They're scared." Klowbi's voice is gentle, empathetic.

They might die tonight. That's the only thought that enters my mind watching the family. The boys might not witness tomorrow's sunrise. Or they may go to sleep as orphans tonight.

"As they should be," I mutter.

"How much danger are we in?" Klowbi asks and turns back around so she's staring at Xuan and I. "Maybe we are in over our heads. What are we trying to accomplish?"

Xuan and I exchange looks. We both acknowledge the answer and our lack of preparation, but confessing this to Klowbi, Alko, and Niko will only heighten their terror. Xuan and I are the strongest magick wielders of our group, Alko being middle ground will be fine temporarily on his own, but Klowbi and Niko are as defenseless as infants. We don't know if they'll even be able to *see* the Shadows like us. If they can't, my focus will be on protecting them and getting us out of harm's way. Though I doubt having my friends swarm around me is a brilliant idea either. If the Shadows want to finish what they started, then they'll be hunting me, and keeping Klowbi nearby is one of the worst things I can do.

For once, I'm grateful that Xuan is with us. There isn't a doubt in my mind Xuan will protect Klowbi if I can't. I know I can rely on her for that.

"Enough to justify why we're here," I say after a pause. "But Xuan and I have sufficient magick to protect you and the boys. We're here to protect the innocent and learn what we can." *At least I hope we do.*

"It's good to be afraid," Xuan assures, "it means you're still alive."

Again, Xuan and I share knowing looks, and she offers the slightest nod. My heart relaxes at the gesture because I know she sees the doubt in my eyes that my smile can't hide. *Protect her if I can't, Xuan, you must do that much.*

"Alright." Klowbi sighs and her posture appears less tense, though she's tearing at her nails with her teeth.

"That was quick," I hear Xuan comment, nodding in the direction over our shoulders again.

It takes a moment to locate them, but once I do, it's hard to tear my gaze away. Alko and Niko are walking shoulder to shoulder, both with bright smiles and their laughter floats above the ruckus of the crowds. The vibrant green of Niko's eyes stand out. I turn away and pull my sleeve down over my wound with a wince.

"You came back empty-handed." Klowbi observes with amusement.

"Well, you see, what actually happened is we won several prizes, but there were these kids who looked so sad and prize-less, so we were kind enough to give them ours," Niko explains in faux chivalry.

"Isn't that convenient?" Xuan remarks, unable to keep the sarcasm out of her tone.

"I'd say it was rather generous of us," Niko says, coming to my side of the table and leaning a hip against the edge. The stench of cigarettes clings to his skin.

"So, how much money did you lose?" I ask, staring up at Niko through my lashes.

His Adam's apple bobs as he swallows, his gaze refusing to stray from mine. "I have enough to get some food."

"I'm hungry," Klowbi says sweetly. "Will you buy me some food?"

"Am I allowed to say no?" Niko asks the group, yet he's staring directly at me. I smile and shake my head.

"You walked right into that," Alko chuckles.

"Shut it," Niko grumbles, sighing. "Alright, fine. Come on, let's go get some food."

Klowbi jumps to her feet and stands beside Niko with a ridiculous grin plastered to her freckled face. "Is everyone coming?"

I glance at the crowds thickening around us and my stomach seizes. The idea of walking into the crowd with so much pent up energy in the air is nauseating. And being jostled unnecessarily will only increase the ache in my wound. "I'll keep the table for us."

"Someone has to stay with you then," Alko states.

"I'll stay," Xuan volunteers, ignoring my glower in her direction.

"We won't be long," Klowbi says, oblivious to my discomfort at being left alone with Xuan. She takes Niko and Alko by the arm and walks with one on each side of her to the desired food vendor.

We sit in silence and watch the crowd. My skin feels tight, like I've grown out of it, and I find myself scratching my wrists and arms, pulling at the skin as if that would release the tension. My arm is throbbing with my heart and there's a sharp stab behind each beat that has me gritting my teeth. Everything is too loud, too tight, too painful—too much. The static in the air makes my tongue feel thick and heavy, yet my head feels light and airy. The energy is spiking again. Xuan is pulling at her bottom lip and her dark eyes are darting to the faces in the crowd, her shoulders rigid.

"Another spike," Xuan confirms when I lift a brow.

"They still haven't shown yet."

"But they will."

"Get them out of here." I lean forward across the picnic table so I don't have to shout over the crowd. She leans forward as well and our eyes lock, mine filled with color and hers as black as pitch. "Promise me you'll take them far from here, regardless of the circumstances."

"Daire, I'm sorry for my false accusations towards you. I hold no ill will against you." She offers me the smallest tremble of a smile, her lips thin as thread, but a smile all the same. "I promise to protect them. They are family. But we will not leave you behind if the worst should come."

"If the worst should come, there will be nothing *to* leave behind." I sit back and wrap my braid around my fist, giving it a tug, and letting it fall against my shoulder. "But thank you."

Xuan sits back and her eyes are fluttering amongst the crowds again. "Farah has been wandering the crowds."

I'm grateful for the change of subject. "Can she sense the change too?"

"She does. She cannot pinpoint where the energy is bleeding from. She says it is disorienting, and the raucousness of the crowds doesn't help." She tilts her head, reminding me of a feline with clever eyes and a cunning mouth. "For lack of a better term, it's sensory overload. It's all too loud, too bright—"

"Too much," I finish for her. "I can agree with that."

"As can I. The energy is potent. It tastes bitter." Xuan grimaces and adjusts the flower crown on her head. The gold and peach flowers compliment her tawny skin and dark eyes. It makes her appear years younger than she is, though she already looks underage due to her petite frame and unblemished skin. "How is your arm?"

"Ghastly," I reply with a wry chuckle. "If it worsens, I'll have to use magick on it. The pain is hardly bearable as is, but with each spike, it's been getting worse."

"Withhold for as long as you can," Xuan advises. "Too much magick in such a high concentration can be dangerous. It will either act as a beacon and draw the Shadows directly to us, or it will act as a match to ignite the flames."

"Great options," I huff. "Either we use magick and give the Shadows a flashing sign of where we are, or we don't use it, the pressure keeps building, and it causes mass destruction from the sudden onslaught of pure energy." I summarize with a sinister smile. "What great odds those are."

Xuan shrugs as if this is nothing new to her. "The chances of true annihilation are finite. I would not worry about that."

"And the beacon?"

"Highly probable. I'd recommend staying our hand until they show themselves."

"And once they do?"

"Make sure you have a clear shot or escape route."

"Lovely."

I hear them approach before I see them, despite the screams of kids and adults alike. Alko and Niko have beers clutched in their hands and Klowbi has a seltzer. The boys must have bought her one since she's underage. Alko is carrying a corndog, Klowbi has a bag of mini donuts, and Niko is eating a pork-chop on a stick, though it's half consumed already.

"I told you that you were taking us the wrong way," Klowbi chides over her shoulder to Niko and offers us the bag of donuts. Xuan sniffs it and pinches a greasy donut from the bag. When she offers it to me, my stomach roils and I lean away from the smell of sugar-coated grease before I heave.

"I got turned around," Niko grumbles and takes a long draught of his beer.

"I can't believe you guys are drinking right now," I mutter.

"It's to ease the nerves." Niko shrugs. "I've been drunkered in worse situations."

Perhaps, but this is an entirely foreign danger, even for you, Niko. Instead I say, "Drunkered isn't a word."

Niko scoffs and takes a savage bite of his pork-chop.

"The fireworks will be starting soon," Klowbi announces. "Let's find our seats."

"Not too deep into the crowd," Alko warns.

"And keep some distance between our group and others," Xuan adds.

"Got it." Klowbi salutes and leads the way.

The sky is a deep bruise with fleshy strips of red along the horizon. Xuan walks beside Klowbi with Alko trailing close behind. Niko keeps pace with me and once he devours his pork-chop, he brushes his knuckles against mine. The touch is reassuring until the fear twists in my belly from the deepening darkness growing along the edges of the illuminated festival grounds.

We manage to find a fairly deserted section of grass to stake as ours. Klowbi is in the center, her head pillowed in Xuan's lap, an arm on Alko, a leg on me. Niko is sitting on the edge and I can't help but think he did it on purpose, making sure he is the barricade between us and any fair-goers. On the opposite side lies Alko, engulfed in darkness.

I'm too anxious to make conversation, so I listen to Klowbi chatter with the others. People gather, waiting with bubbling excitement for the start of the fireworks. An announcement is made stating the fireworks will start soon.

Five minutes later, the excited chatter turns into satisfied oohs and ahhs as colors burst into the bruising sky. Deafening booms rattle my heart. Dozens of mini falling stars bludgeon the heavens.

Chapter 23

The sky is wrought in vibrant colors of reds, pinks, blues, and oranges, and deafening blasts from deflagrate are hypnotizing paired with the bright and disorienting flashes of light and darkness with each airborne explosion.

Yet the next spike of energy hardly compares to the light show in the sky. My head swims, the world is blind and deaf, and I feel nothing except the devastating onslaught of power. Once my vision and hearing returns, I glance at the ring and bracelet blessed with glamour and find it burning with magick, a thick orange viscosity. My heart is a jackhammer in my breast, and I look to the others to gauge if they felt the shift too. Klowbi is no longer laying down, but sitting up and grasping my leg with an iron grip only associated with terror. Alko is staring wide-eyed at the forest draped in velvet black while Xuan has her eyes closed, her lips muttering as if conjuring a spell. Niko's hand is gripping my wrist protectively.

It's a sensation that I could never mistake or forget. The infinite power thrumming in the air around me and brushing my skin is akin to being in the Astral Realm. My magick is growling and aching to be released. I recognize the insatiable hunger to access my magick as I did in the forest when I was ambushed by the Red Eyed Shadows.

My wound feels hot and festering with infection. I wonder if the lightheadedness is from the sudden pour of energy or from the Shadow-infested wound. The pain is similar to when I first received it, and it takes all my control to imagine my magick flowing through my bloodstream and sectioning off the area of corruption and numbing my nerves. It's a method of magick use I'm unfamiliar with, but with the extra boost of energy around me I manage to cordon off the malady, the pain somewhat tolerable.

"There's another surge," I tell them. Through the shrill wails of fireworks I'm not sure they hear me.

Klowbi leans over to Xuan when she opens her eyes. She says something to her, though I hear nothing besides the drumfire surging in the sky and the rattle of my heart in my ears. Klowbi then leans over to me and presses her lips to my ear, tickling the stray hairs. "They're here," are her only words and dread thickens my tongue. It takes me a moment later to realize Xuan was speaking to Farah, who has been patrolling the grounds. The massive energy spike must have been when the Shadows decided to make their entrance, and Farah was at least able to warn us before we were taken by surprise.

I try to avoid thinking about all the families and couples sitting unaware at the festival. Of those three boys and their parents sensing something is off but unable to explain why. *People are going to die tonight.*

Without another word yet in synchronized movement, the five of us get to our feet, drinks and food half-consumed and completely forgotten on the grass. Alko leads the way out of the mass of families observing the fireworks. Klowbi is gripping Xuan's shirt to avoid separation and Niko has an arm protectively around my waist.

We barely make it several paces before the first scream pierces the air like gunfire, shattering the lull of silence from the fireworks. The screech of explosions drowns out the scream completely. The sound is anything but joyful. It holds true pain and anguish, bloodcurdling in nature that makes my hair stand on edge.

One person has died tonight.

We keep shuffling our feet slowly back to the whimsical lights of the carnival. Our progress is slow going in muted lighting while trying to avoid ankles and fingers and cans. Trekking becomes challenging through the throng, our heads on a swivel where darkness lurks.

Then I see it along the embankment of trees. It's watching us. The Shadow's eyes flicker an unholy white with a thorny smile to match before everything descends into pandemonium.

And the screams worsen tenfold.

Within seconds, the enthrallment of the fireworks celebrating Litha turns into a mob of terrified families screaming, shoving, and stampeding to get to safety. Screams pierce the air, and it's impossible to tell if they are from fear, pain, or loss. Flashes of lights and resounding thunder from the sky merely adds to the disorientation, casting the entire grounds into a strobe light of colors and obsidian. Gunpowder stings my nose leaving a metallic residue on my tongue.

In the mad scramble of running from the darkness I lose sight of Klowbi and the others, and the comforting press of Niko's arm around my waist is now empty space. An inhale and they are there, exhale and they are gone.

A toddler screams somewhere to my right within the mesh of feet and legs. I attempt to rescue the child from the mayhem, but the crowd's force carries me along, and my flower crown is tramped into the dirt. I search desperately for the child, glimpsing a small figure curled up, soaked in what appears to be beer or soda. When the light flashes again, I realize the liquid is blood. The child's fair skin is sticky with it. Sobs are no longer rising from the toddler.

People are going to die tonight, so make sure you aren't one of them.

I start in the direction I last saw my friends, catching sight of a thick roiling black mist converging with the crowd. The victims slam into one another, throwing elbows to faces as the Mist claims them. I've barely made it several paces, the crowd surging and seething with a mind of its own, when I dig my heels in, coming face to face with a stranger.

She's female and blocking my path. My instinct is to charge forward and keep going, but something makes me hesitate, and I take a closer look when the lights flash above again, rendering her in a sickly red glow. Her face is gaunt and her eyes are empty, as if seeing without understanding, and a strange milky film covers them. Even her face seems wrong, appearing empty, deranged, animalistic. At first glance she appears feeble and thin, but the straining of muscles against her skin says otherwise.

And the blood, so much of it. A deep maroon dripping steadily, her shirt is sopping with it. Gloves made of gore cover her up to her elbow and spatter her biceps. Another flash reveals freckles of blood on her cheeks, chin, and nose. And the butcher knife fisted in one hand is lathered in the slaughter of civilians.

Behind the bloodied husk of the girl is a Red Eyed Shadow. People stampede and when they spot the girl with the knife they keep their distance. A shove from behind forces me into the girl's path. No one acknowledges the Shadow.

Steeling myself and clenching my fists, I summon my magick and my courage. "Release the girl and return to your domain," I warn and lift my hands with palms open. A flare of purple laced with indigo flickers in my palm like fire.

The Shadow smiles with a thorny grin and raises a hand with one finger extended in my direction. The girl lunges forward. Balanced on the balls of my feet, I manage to sidestep left and feel the fury of her swinging the knife and the guttural scream that follows. I swipe my hands in the direction of the Shadow and purple flames snarl along its arm. The Shadow doesn't shatter nor melt into the ground like they did when I was ambushed. A splintering hiss emanates from it and its eyes alight like molten lava. Besides appearing more enraged, its form does not waver.

I've barely a moment to catch my balance when the girl turns and swings her barren fist into the side of my skull. Covering my head, I grimace at the burst of pain and the dark spots that dot my vision. She comes barreling at me again, snarling like a rabid animal, and her fingers sink deep into my hair and scalp. I scream, more from rage than pain, and throw my hands at her face, groping for her hair, her eyes, her throat, anything I can dig my fingers into in order to make her release.

I manage to hook one thumb into an eye. The other grasps her wrist clutching the blade. My nail digs into the soft, gummy tissue and her screams follow close behind. My stomach churns, but I keep adding pressure, nearly popping her eye until finally she wrenches free.

One hand covers half her face in a futile attempt to aid her wound. She advances with her fist clasped tightly around the butcher knife, taking wild slashes with each step. Her perception must be off from the damage I did to her eye since she's slashing air more than she's slashing me.

As her arm flails, her face sets into a snarl, and the blade catches on a few unlucky people fleeing towards the streets. Several times I feel a fine spray mist my arms or lips along with a gasp of pain; the victims don't stay long to argue. The fireworks above have mostly ceased besides a few stragglers, but the chaos has only heightened from the knife-wielding girl.

She catches my palm with the blade's edge and I rear back from the flickering blade, the pain welling with each pulse of my heart. She cackles and behind her the Shadow is still smiling, watching with burnt ruby eyes. In my peripheral, with the crowd thinning, more Shadows observe from the outskirts as their mouths salivate with ichor.

The screams haven't lessened, nor has the magick humming in the air. I throw another burst of magick at the Shadow and lunge towards the girl. The Shadow howls, but remains standing, angry and unwavering.

No one else seems to see it. My magick is struggling to make an impact. Is it possible the Shadows have somehow bypassed their realm completely into ours? Manifesting into it yet not seen by those who exist here?

My gaze catches on the brilliant flashing of the blade dimmed with blood clutched in her hand. Whatever corrupt magick the Shadow is wielding against the girl, whatever person she once was, is gone. She's their puppet, her sights locked on me, my eyes locked on the blade. My magick against her blade are poor odds, but if I can get the blade from her, my chances of escaping increase along with everyone else's.

Swallowing a lump of fear, I clench my fingers and call on my magick. The feeling is intense and my skin itches with the vibration and ache to release, but I hold on tighter as the power siphons into me. The girl's face is void of emotion, except for the deranged smile plastered on her face and the voracious gleam in her inhuman gaze. We stalk each other in a circle, the Shadow following within several feet of her.

"Hiding behind a human now," I taunt with a laugh void of humor. "And to think that I once thought Shadows were something to be feared."

The Shadow's eyes flare brighter and it hisses in response. The girl's lips tremble into a feral snarl foreign to a human expression with a strangled sound mimicking the Shadows. We continue to side step, our gazes glued to the other, and I watch her drag her back foot with a slight limp to it. She appears about my height and a sickness seems to have claimed her body, giving her a cadaverous look. The magick the Shadow is using provides her supernatural strength, but she's still human. Her weaknesses are the same as mine.

The girl lunges with a guttural scream as spittle flies from her lips. I brace myself a breath before her arm holding the blade stabs downwards at my chest. I'm ready this time and manage to counter her weight with my own, clasping my fist around her wrist to keep the serrated blade from my skin. My other hand has an iron grip on her forearm. With our faces so close, I smell decay on her breath. She screams and tries snapping at my throat. I throw my head back out of her reach and focus my magick in my hands to transfer to her skin.

I revel in the itch on my palms, her skin blazing. Her eyes widen and I see the tainted whites of her eyes and the milky film coating them. She thrashes as my magick enters her body, purging her of the Shadow's wicked magick. The Shadow behind her is seizing and whispering in and out of our reality, appearing as a ghostly outline one moment and corporeal the next. The Shadow's eyes burn bright as it lurches towards me with outstretched claws.

But instead of touching me the Shadow touches the girl. Her screams cease and she stops moving entirely, her milky gaze latching onto me as her strength returns. She wrenches her forearm from my grip and it lessens my hold on her arm clutching the blade long enough for her to pull free. She charges and swipes at my face while my equilibrium is off center. Whipping my head back I stumble away, but not quick enough. I feel the decisive cut of the blade against my face before I hit the ground. Blood blinds my right eye, but I have enough sense to kick my legs up as she jumps on top of me. Foam is spitting from her lips. The Shadow somehow keeps a hold on her and her knife slashes violently in the air to reach me.

Hands grip her shoulders and she's flung backwards, severing the connection between her and the Shadow. She's crumpled on the ground, the blade no longer clasped in her hand but still within reach. The Red Eyed Shadow snarls and stalks towards the girl. Above me stands Niko with sweat on his brow and a wild gleam in his emerald eyes.

"The knife!" I shout at him and scramble to my feet.

The wound is throbbing with my heart, though it must have missed my eye since I can make out blurry shapes. I swipe furiously at the blood sticking my eyelids together and watch as Niko turns his back to me as I struggle for breath.

Already with the knife back in the girl's possession, she slashes at Niko and my heart stutters. It misses him, but when her other fist collides with his nose, he fumbles backwards and hunches over. Blood oozes where he clutches between his fingers. He straightens as both the girl and the Shadow cackle in unison. Niko shakes blood from his fingertips.

"You fucking bitch," Niko spits and charges the girl. Her face slackens as she tries to throw the blade between them, but she's too slow and Niko lands a solid blow to her face. Blood gushes and it's a torrent of grunts and swears, of fists of flesh and dense thumps from collision.

I focus my attention on the Shadow now that Niko is fighting the girl. Widening my stance, I shove my hands forward and a flaming torrent of red bursts from my hands, strangling and tightening around the Shadow. Its scream has me flinching, and I glance at Niko to find more blood on his arms and torso, though whether it's his or hers I can't tell. For now, he holds his own and banishing the Shadow should bring down the girl.

Pouring more into the onslaught, the magick cascades over Red Eyes. Shadows stalk closer to our battle, hissing and trilling with vehemence. Keeping one hand focused on Red Eyes controlling the girl, I throw my spare hand out at the advancing Shadows. Spikes of red magick shoot from my palm and embed in the closest one. It slows but doesn't stop its approach.

Fear fills my mouth as bitter as bile. They aren't stopping, and I can't hold them all by myself. Niko grunts as the knife slices through his bicep. A second later it catches his side. A third time his forearm while trying to block the blade.

One of the encroaching Shadows falters and shimmers. Another one closer to it fades for a moment and both turn their backs to us. From over their shoulders, three forms run towards us. A laugh of disbelief passes my lips and I want to sag with relief.

Xuan is somehow wielding magick, a faint flickering spark with a hint of red. It lands its mark each time. Klowbi and Alko are following along, Klowbi speaking to them and pointing out any Shadows coming closer while Alko uses his own magick to create a path to us. Never have I been so happy to see them.

I blast my magick at the Red Eyed Shadow controlling the girl until it hisses and stumbles backwards. The haunting red of its eyes is only several shades darker than that of my magick spooling around its obsidian frame. The new audience of Shadows has halted their approach as Xuan and Alko's magick takes them from behind, surrounding them as they surround me. A foreign flitter of glee sputters in my heart that we could still win this battle.

Xuan is standing closest to me with her eyes narrowed into slits of concentration. In the darkness there's a gleam of sweat on her brow. Wiping away my own sweat and blood from my eyes, I sneak a glance at Niko and find he's still struggling against the possessed girl and soaked in blood.

"Xuan," I shout to her and she glances in my direction. Beyond the growing swarm of Shadows, Alko and Klowbi are making their way closer to Niko. "Focus your magick on the Shadow controlling the girl. If we break the Shadow we break her."

Xuan nods sharply, unfazed by the thick layer of blood crusting my skin, and redirects her sparks of magick to the other Shadow. It takes only a few breaths before the Shadow starts screaming and rearing its head back. The sound sends goosebumps down my arms and a dull ringing starts deep in my ears. Several Shadows have shrunk away and are fleeing from our group.

"Niko," I scream, his head twitching at the sound. His gaze doesn't waver from the girl. "Go for her ankle." He does, kicking out a well-directed foot that snaps against her joint. She stumbles and an inhuman shriek of pain erupts from her mouth. "Xuan, now!" I shout and both of our magick flows increase. Alko is chasing off the remaining Shadows with Klowbi keeping her eyes where he can't see, protecting his blindside.

Red Eyes is splintering and shattering from Xuan and mine's combined magick, the suffocating presence of the energy around us leaving my limbs quivering. One foot melts into the ground and a hand explodes into fragments, disintegrating with the wind. Its red eyes flash brilliantly and the cry of distress sounds almost fearful. I keep pushing despite the exhaustion nibbling at my energy and ignore the tremble in my hands.

With an entire arm gone and a leg melted up to the knee, the Shadow screams, baring its thorny fangs with weeping red eyes, and lunges in the direction of the girl and Niko. I charge forward to block its path, but the Shadow is too fast. It snarls as it passes Niko and he hesitates at the aggression. But it's all the Shadow needs as it clings, melts, and merges into the girl.

There's a moment of silence amongst our group. Then the girl stiffens and her lips twist into a barbaric snarl. She lifts her head and her eyes are no longer milky white, merely two voids in her skull. She jumps Niko and her knife falls into him so hard and fast the spray of blood is unmistakable. I hear the sucking wet sounds of the blade being wrenched free of his flesh with each swing.

Alko shouts and runs to his friend. Klowbi screams and falls to her knees. Xuan and I bolt forward to pry the psychotic bitch off of him. She's standing over him with the butcher knife clutched in her hand and Niko's blood coating her entire front. Niko is lying on the ground at her feet and I can't count the wounds he has sustained with how thick the gore coats his skin.

The possessed girl looks up with a savage grin on her face as Xuan and I approach. She stiffens and collapses to the ground. Her body twitches and contorts, her limbs tucked awkwardly beneath her weight as she convulses. A dribble of drool pools from the corner of her mouth and turns into a pinkish foam as her eyes roll up into her head. Seconds later she stops moving and her breaths halt.

"She's dead," I confirm and dive the rest of the way to where Niko collapsed on the ground. The dirt underneath is soaked with his blood. I vaguely sense Xuan kneeling beside me, Alko and Klowbi standing on his other side while keeping a wary berth of the dead girl. The knife is glinting a few feet from her prone form.

"Niko." My voice trembles as I gently touch his abdomen where a deep crimson is bubbling from the gash. His head slowly turns to me and his skin is deathly pale. "We need an ambulance."

"I'll find one," Alko blurts and takes off running, his voice hoarse as he calls for help.

"You think it'll scar?" he asks, weakly nodding to a stab wound by his collarbone and shoulder.

"Yes, it will scar," I murmur, sucking in a shaky breath. Brushing a hand over his cheek to wipe away blood, his lips twitch into a smile. "Why did you do that?"

"To protect you," he whispers, and his emerald eyes flutter, unable to focus on anything.

Klowbi is standing still, clearly in shock and so pale I'm afraid she'll faint. I look at Xuan and am grateful to see she's keeping her fear under control. "I'm going to try to use some of my magick to staunch the bleeding," I tell her. "Keep him awake and his heart beating."

"Save him," she orders and clasps her delicate fingers over my wrist.

I feel her flow of energy and magick mingle with mine. I sense the dark presence of her connection with the Otherworld and for a moment my magick recoils until I accept the power and place my hands over his heart. I'm careful on how much pressure I'm placing, but he winces anyway.

I start a slow trickle of healing magick and watch a faint glow of blue and green beneath his skin, rolling into each vein close to the surface, steadily increasing my magick until my fingers are tingling and growing numb. I've healed aches and pains before with my magick, but never to this extent. His wounds are fatal, but if I can stop the bleeding, then perhaps the paramedics have a chance to save Niko.

He's hurt because of me. The Shadow wants me and his stubborn ass had to play hero. Niko doesn't deserve this ending, not after fighting and defeating his own demons just to die by mine.

I can't lose you too.

"Your face," Niko mumbles, attempting to raise his hand before falling back to his side. "You're bleeding."

"I'll have a scar too," I say breathily. I swallow my tears, refusing to let any of them see me break.

"That's sexy," he slurs and his eyes roll into his head.

"Stay awake, Niko," Xuan declares and pats his cheek. He groans and his eyes flutter open again.

"I'm so tired," he mumbles. A bubble of blood pops against his lips.

His blood is thick and warm against my palms. It's sticking to me like syrup, and the sickly sweet scent of blood is churning my stomach. I can't tell if my magick is doing much, but the bleeding is seeming to slow the longer I urge my magick through his bloodstream. I feel his heartbeat beneath his chest, though it's faint, I swear I feel it strengthen every few beats.

"You can rest soon," Xuan tells him.

"Am I...going to...the hospital?" Niko manages with a thick blood clot dripping down his chin.

"Yes," I tell him, "they are going to help you."

He chuckles, but winces and gasps with the effort. "Please promise me."

"Promise you what?"

"You'll break me out of that hell," Niko sputters with a grimace. "I hate the hospital."

Despite the situation, a smile cracks my lips. "I promise."

"Good." He sighs and I think he's fallen unconscious, but he stirs again and his eyes snap open as he tries to focus on me. "It's okay if I die."

"You aren't going to die."

"I might."

"You won't."

"But if I do, it's okay."

"Niko, please..."

"I protected you guys. I'm fine with dying. I'm not afraid." Niko flashes me a smile coated in blood.

A tear rolls down my cheek, but I swipe it away with my shoulder, refusing to release my magick from his broken body. "You won't die. I swear it." My voice is so solid and unwavering I almost believe it.

"Daire." Klowbi's voice startles me. Her eyes are red and puffy, but she maintains composure. "Alko is coming back. He has medics with him."

"One final push," Xuan urges.

Shuttering my eyes, I send out one final wave of magick coursing through Niko. His breath hitches and his fingers spasm into the dirt as his chest heaves with a gurgle. His skin appears to be glowing from beneath and it fades quickly. I hear voices behind me and I lift my hands from his chest, severing the magickal current. Xuan releases her hold on me and Niko and stands to her feet.

I'm slower to do the same. I wipe away more blood from his chin and cheeks, smearing it away from his dazed eyes. Recognition flickers in his emerald gaze when I lean into his vision, and I lean down and press a kiss to his lips. When I pull away, I feel the blood dancing on my tongue and tingling my lips, tasting magick. "If you die, I'll kill you." Niko smiles before his face goes slack and his eyes close.

"Step away."

Stumbling to my feet, I watch numbly as the paramedics swarm Niko. They place tourniquets and bandages to stop the bleeding and hoist him onto a gurney. It happens so fast. One minute he's there, the next they are wheeling him away, leaving nothing of him behind but his blood staining the earth.

One of the male medics turns to us and then the girl on the ground who they confirmed dead. I knew she was no longer a threat. A Shadow possessed her completely, and she was already frail and sick to begin with. No one could survive a possession like that. She was merely a pawn in a larger game, discarded after her usefulness was spent.

"That looks like it requires stitches," the medic says, gesturing to the slash over my eye. "Are you all alright besides that?"

We all nod. "I can wait for medical attention," I say to the medic.

"Don't wait too long. There's a medic tent set up in that direction," he says, pointing. "You can't miss it. All four of you stop there before going home." He turns and gestures to the girl. "Do you know her?"

"No, she attacked us," Xuan answers and I'm grateful for her speaking up.

"And the boy?" he asks. "Is he your friend?"

"Yes," Xuan says, "he's our roommate."

"I have to be honest, his wounds are deep. If you have his family's contact information, I would give them a call," the medic concedes with an apologetic glimmer in his eyes. I can tell he's danced with death tonight. "We will do all we can for your friend. Stay safe." He offers us one more sympathetic look before jogging after his comrades.

Sluggishly, the four of us make our way up the hill, our feet dragging against the dirt, our arms encircling each other as though our worlds would fall apart if we let go. Klowbi keeps her head down, but I won't avert my gaze as we pass through the festival to the entrance. Tents are toppled over and ripped to shreds. I see one smoldering with a few flames licking the sides of it while firefighters douse it with water.

Medics flood the fields. Bodies are lying unattended on the ground. I don't look at their faces, imagining that it could be Niko. People are huddled along the edges, crying, shrieking, sobbing. A mother is holding her dead child in her hands, screaming and rocking the limp form in her arms. A teenager is stumbling with the help of her friend towards aid, her face painted in blood. Surrounding us are screams of loss, cries of death, and whimpers of the wounded.

How many people died tonight? It's pure hell. The Summer Solstice began with sunshine and fireworks, but ended with the screams of mothers and Shadows.

Any adrenaline I felt earlier is now fading, and the ache of my wounds are prominent. My hand is pulsing from where the blade caught me, my forehead and brow burning. My Shadow-touched wound feels on fire.

Everything hurts, my muscles are sore, and my mind feels bent. Even with magick still oscillating around us, I sense it fading and weakening, and in its place is exhaustion and fatigue filling the empty spaces. The static I felt earlier is less disorienting now that I've grown accustomed to it and fed from the surge. With it lessening, I feel a growing abyss inside me, aching for more, my magick unsated.

We finally manage to crest the hill and slow at the top to survey the carnage. The festival is in ruins with not a breath of laughter to fill the empty space. Klowbi tugs at my hand, but I shake my head and turn to watch. I know I couldn't have stopped the onslaught, but I can't help but feel responsible for the chaos. The Shadows wanted me, they marked me, and this is what they brought with them. Carnage. Even with our futile efforts, how many lives did we really save? How many did we damn instead?

Guilt seizes my stomach, but anger is quick to replace it. Several light-less forms wander the grounds like lost souls. The Mist slinks amongst the victims, thick tendrils wrapping around their skulls. Some Shadows still stalk those who remain, mingling close, feeding off the heartbreak and distress. Several have red rubies in their faces, but most are solid black with nothing but thorny smiles. Victims are clueless to how close they stand.

"I see them too," Klowbi whispers beside me, her hand clasped in mine.

"We saw them the moment they appeared," Alko confirms, an arm slung around his sister's shoulder. "Once we realized you and Niko were separated, we tried fighting against the crowd to find you."

"You came just in time," I admit. "If Niko didn't find me when he did, I'd be in his place right now." Guilt crushes my heart, but I force it back with the anger in my fists, in the tightness in my jaw. "If you guys didn't find us when you did, things would have ended up differently."

No one says another word. We leave it at that.

As I watch the remaining Shadows, my gaze catches on one as it turns to stare up at our group on the hill. Its eyes are bright embers with an unnaturally wide smile of thorns. A fury storms my blood and my teeth grit so harshly I hear the bone grind. A wrath so pure and violent overtakes me as the Shadow grins. It knows how many lives they took, how many lives they destroyed. It knows I failed to protect my own.

A surge of power feeds my hysteria, and my wrath boils into unbridled vengeance. I siphon my magick and release my hold on Klowbi. A wave of uncontrolled power and a guttural cry leaves my body as a dome of violet with me as the epicenter bursts outwards towards the festival grounds. The dome grows higher as it gains momentum, pushing past the fallen and mourning families, and shattering any Shadows it comes in contact with. I watch with pride as the Shadows burst into onyx shards, melting into the earth. The Red Eyed Shadow doesn't break eye contact with me until the violet veil crashes into it, shattering it like the others. The dome fades and only once it's dispersed do I turn back to my friends.

They're staring at me, all three of them, with terror in their eyes. Even Klowbi who is accustomed to my magick looks uncomfortable. My narrowed eyes survey the crowd as bystanders stand and search for an unseen presence, then return to their tasks.

"Did you...?" Alko asks before going silent when I turn to address him.

The look on my face answers enough as he falls silent. Somehow, perhaps because of the remaining magick surges, they felt my outburst and saw me disintegrate the Shadows with one last show of vengeful power. If only I could have done that sooner, though perhaps it was the anger that fueled my final bout of strength. I don't dwell on the how or why. I relish the fact that I *did*.

Klowbi grips my hand and we stand in silence watching the grounds now empty of Shadows, but still filled with the cries of the wounded. I think of Niko. And the glare of red eyes.

Chapter 24

The halls of the hospital reek of the ill and dying. A delicious scent, one promising of a feast. Soon. Today I am here for someone specifically, a prize patiently waiting to be won.

My movements are fluid and quick as I glide through a maze of passages. The night shift is quiet, distracted by the unusual quantity of moribund burdening the rooms. Tonight the hospital will be a charnel house.

A dark grin twists my faceless features and I catch sight of my arms, not human, but obsidian and Otherworldly. I exist through the eyes of a Shadow. My fear mingles with its excitement, egging it on quicker as it feeds through our momentary connection.

We—it—passes through the corridors with little hesitation. Whenever a night nurse barrels down the hall, we melt into the darkness or slink into a nearby room or broom closet with little issue. They stink of desperation, and I can sense their hearts fluttering in their breasts, a tantalizing temptation.

Twice I stop to follow a nurse descending to a room where death lies waiting. The urge is too great, but clarity surfaces and my direction changes, slipping through a new corridor with renewed speed and hunger gnawing at my insides.

The hunger is bottomless, a teething thing that sets my fangs gnashing and growls rumbling my throat. None are near enough to hear my frustrations, the cravings spurring me closer to the prey. Its mother is vacant, a rarity in the night, and my window of opportunity is closing.

*I cannot wait one more moment. To taste the fear on my tongue, the surprise and relief, a sharp tang, a blip in time to sate the infinite hunger. Always craving more. More. **More.***

I stop abruptly in front of a door like all the others. Lifting my head, I sniff and find none but the prey waiting for me inside. I push through the gap, shutting the door firmly behind as I glide to the bed.

The prey looks much like it does in the hellscape I've designed, except he appears more frail. Less afraid. No matter, it will still taste divine.

The prey lays broken and unmoving in the hospital bed. It's almost unfair how easy it is, but alas, not all can be fighters like her. He will suffice.

Salivating with a starving snarl savaging my larynx, my clawed hands reach for the prey's throat. Its skin is soft and supple, dimpling beneath caliginous claws. I hover my maw over it, breathing in what remains of its life, of its soul. It tastes of cinder and frost, a delectable combination.

My fangs sink over its lips, my grip tightening around its jugular. The machines begin to beep and fret, sounding the alarm. It will not matter. The prey is mine now.

The prey struggles meekly beneath my grasp, its head twitching, but caught between my fangs it has nowhere to go. The blaring of the machines is heinous to my ears as the beeps grow closer together, less and less time apart.

It gives one final gasp, one futile pitch at life, before the bray of machines is a continuous sound. Bruises form along its throat, blood dribbles from its nose and mouth, and I suckle the sweet taste from its flesh, savoring the flavor of its final breath—

Jolting awake, I swipe at my eyes to remove the sweat stinging them. My clothes are plastered to my skin and my hair sticks to my face in clumps. An ache throbs around my jaw and my stomach heaves with unfathomable hunger.

I saw him again. Desmond, frail and prone in the hospital. The creature, a Shadow, feeding from him while he couldn't fight back. I stare at my hands, imagining his skin beneath my touch, my nails digging into his throat. But no, that wasn't me. I'm in my apartment, far from Desmond.

I shift to stare out the window of our living room. The sun is blinding in the sky and I can make out the vibrant blue beyond the glass and partially closed curtains. I sit up with a throbbing ache in my head. My fingers brush against a patch of gauze taped to my forehead where the knife had caught me along with the palm of my hand.

My forehead required five stitches from the laceration by the knife-wielding girl. It would leave a scar starting just above the ridge of my brow and slicing my right eyebrow in uneven halves and marring the tender flesh at the corner of my eye, barely missing my eye itself.

My left palm will have a scar as well, and my Shadow wound seems to be a permanent resident on my skin. Thankfully Klowbi came out unscathed physically, though mentally she seems debilitated. Neither of us could fathom sleeping alone. Our rooms felt too dark and quiet for thoughts to fester. Sleeping in the living room was our best option, and her presence and the buzz of the TV were comforting enough to lull me to sleep.

Alko and Xuan had minimal wounds, a few scrapes and bruises, but they avoided the worst of the damage. Niko didn't. After the paramedics carted him away and the shrill of chaos had ebbed, we parted ways. Alko and Xuan left to contact Niko's parents and try to gain entrance to the hospital while Klowbi and I went home. Xuan promised to give us updates throughout the night. The last update I heard before sleeping mentioned his critical condition, with him in and out of consciousness due to severe lacerations. His parents were in a panic state despite Niko preening that they wanted nothing to do with him.

It always takes the worst to see the truth.

Beside me, Klowbi stirs and her eyelids flutter before opening into slits. She groans and scrubs at her eyes. "Is it morning already?"

I huff in amusement and glance at the clock. "It's afternoon, actually."

"It feels like I could sleep for another full day," Klowbi mumbles, shifting into a seated position. She looks at me with a pout on her face. "You look like hell."

"Thanks. So do you," I mutter and rub at the gauze on my brow. The pull of the stitches paired with the material of the gauze makes my skin itch.

"You need to wash your cut. It bled through last night," she amends, narrowing her chestnut eyes. "Did you sleep last night? You were really restless."

I shrug and a shiver steals down my spine at the sudden image of Desmond in the hospital. The taste of his blood on my tongue, of cinder and frost as I press my fangs to his lips. The futile twitches of his body fighting for life.

It couldn't be real. Dreams aren't reality.

"Coffee sounds good," I answer with a nod towards the kitchen.

Klowbi glares at my redirection, but concedes and slowly gets to her feet with the blanket cocooned around her shoulders and dragging along the floor. "I'm on it. Are you hungry?"

I shake my head even though her back is turned. "Just coffee is good for me." The back of her head is a snarl of auburn knots, a few locks of hair sticking out at odd angles.

While Klowbi is shuffling in the kitchen, I dig for the TV remote that's wedged between the couch cushions. I flip it out of sleep mode and turn on the local news station. While waiting for the commercial to end, I wrap a spare blanket across my lap and call on my magick. It responds and a warm thrum resonates in my core, washing away the remainder of the icy remnants of the dream. Today's energy isn't as potent as it was yesterday during the attacks. Yet there's still a foreign static to the air I'm unaccustomed to.

The coffee pot gurgles to life at the same time the local news station comes back on. The first story, unsurprisingly, is about Litha, the Summer Solstice festival from last night. My heart sinks as the reporter narrates over clips of the carnage, and even with the video sound muted, the screams still singe my ears.

Though the clips are short and clearly handpicked to avoid the worst of the damage and bloodshed, the aftermath videos show a desolate fairground covered in handmade crosses, balloons, and flowers to mark the injured and dead. There are people lined up along the quarantine area with picket signs demanding justice while others stand solemn with tear-stained eyes and vacant looks. A reporter interviews a handful of people that had attended during the attack and each interviewee shares their trauma and heartbreak.

Klowbi is standing at the edge of the couch and her eyes are shining, her bottom lip trembling. I don't want her reliving last night, but I need to know the count of injuries and deaths. Our presence felt inconsequential in the grand scheme of the carnage. Maybe I wanted to torture myself with the statistics. Or hope that those kids' photos weren't displayed on national television.

When the last video clip is played, the screen transitions to the stats. At least two attackers were present, including the girl who attacked and died. Some theories propose there may have been up to four. I wondered if the Shadows had somehow managed to possess that many individuals, or if some were strong enough to attack in their semi-corporeal state. Regardless, the only one accounted for was the dead girl who had attacked us. If there were any others, they managed to evade authorities.

More than thirty people were injured, with roughly a quarter in critical condition. My gut twists at the memory of Niko being carted away. Klowbi shuffles into the kitchen and pours two cups of coffee. She's quiet and unnaturally still with her back to me.

A numbness squeezes my heart at the death toll. Seven people died, two of whom were children while the rest spanned from teenagers to middle-aged. Their faces, names, and ages flash across the screen in quick succession. It's hardly enough time for the amount of loss of life to view their perfectly chosen photos with wide grins or flattering poses.

Klowbi passes me my mug, sweetened how I like it, and she slowly lowers down next to me. "Please turn this off. I can't think about this right now." she whispers and the break in her voice aches into my quivering fingers. Without another word, I change the channel to the cooking network.

"I'm going to clean my wound. You're on movie duty," I tell her, standing with my coffee in hand. She offers me a superficial smile as I walk down the hall. Klowbi needs me to be her anchor, to give her a sense of control and comfortability, of normality. She needs to pretend everything is fine to cope with such a traumatic experience. Hell, I need someone to be the same for me.

I wish you were here, Mom. I sigh as I close the bathroom door and stare into the mirror. *I wish I could hear your voice. To have one more hug from you while you tell me everything will be okay even if it won't. I need you here.*

I grab everything I need to cleanse and bandage my wounds. I start by eyeing my Shadow wound and douse it with alcohol. I suck in a breath at the dizzying pain before dabbing it dry and lathering it with ointment. I don't know why I bother since nothing has healed the wound, but the pain is grounding. Unwrapping the bandage on my palm, I follow the same procedure, hissing at the burning pain and slathering the ointment on and wrapping it back up in gauze.

Staring into the mirror, I carefully peel off the bandage on my face and toss it aside. Small, nasty stitches mar my pale face. My stomach plummets seeing the damage. My eyes warm and my vision blurs when I know I no longer look like Mom as much as I used to. The cut will scar, and though it will be thin, it will be noticeable.

I steady my hands and dab a mix of water and alcohol on the incision, nearly crying out from the pain shooting behind my eye and into my temple. Keeping my lips pressed tight, I dab an antibiotic ointment over it and leave the wound exposed since the bleeding has stopped.

After rinsing my hands of ointment and blood, I take a long sip of coffee. It burns my tongue and throat, but the warmth eases the aching in my chest. I tenderly hold the cup in my hands, relishing the warmth, and jolt when my phone starts blaring on the bathroom counter.

Clasping the mug in one hand, I check my phone. It's Dad. Guilt churns my insides when I see he has been trying to get a hold of me since the chaos of last night. There are countless missed calls, texts and voicemails all pertaining to our wellbeing.

Exiting the bathroom, I head into the living room where Klowbi is flickering through different movies, her brows furrowed in concentration. I take a seat next to her and burrow beneath the blankets with my coffee resting in my lap before answering the call.

"Thank gods," Dad says breathily into the phone. "Are you alright, Daire? I've been trying to reach you since I got word."

"I'm sorry, I should have texted you back. Everything was so chaotic last night I hardly looked at my phone once we got home," I say as Klowbi arches her brows in question. I mouth "Dad" before returning my gaze to my steaming mug. "We actually just woke up."

"No need to apologize, little swan. I'm just happy you're alright," Dad replies and I hear the oomph as he sits down. "Is Klowbi with you? Your friends? Are they safe?"

Tenderness squeezes my heart and a ghost of a smile flickers over my lips. "Klowbi is next to me. She's fine, just exhausted." I suck in a breath to steel myself before continuing. "Alko and Xuan have a few cuts and bruises, but they're fine otherwise."

"And Niko?"

I wince at the name and take another scalding sip of coffee before answering. The heat does little to ease my aches. "Niko is in the hospital," I answer quietly and ignore Klowbi's stiffening posture. Nestled in the blankets, she shifts and burrows into the couch nest. "He saved me from the girl, the attacker." Before Dad can interrupt, I go into depth of everything that happened last night; the increase of magick and the Shadows, the Shadow possession of the girl who attacked civilians at the festival, the new scar on my face from her murderous attempts, and Niko charging to my rescue only to be charged into the hospital. "I haven't heard anything from Alko or Xuan since last night."

"I'm sorry, Daire."

Invisible hands twist my heart and I have to close my eyes and suck in a deep breath to compose myself. When I open them again my vision is slightly blurred. "I'll let you know the minute I know more." I'm grateful my voice doesn't betray my heartache.

"I saw the news. It's being broadcast nationwide. They are saying it was a cultist act of terrorism, but if you say it's the work of the Shadows…" he trails off and clears his throat. "We can theorize all we like, but it's a conversation for another time. I'm happy you and Klowbi are safe. And your friends. I will ask my deities to watch over you and ask for a quick recovery for Niko."

"Thanks." I set my mug on the table next to me.

"Unfortunately, I am calling with other news. I hate to put more on your plate, especially after the night you've had. You're too young for all this heartbreak," Dad rambles and my stomach tightens the longer he speaks.

"What happened?" I interject. Klowbi turns to look at me. Her chestnut eyes mirror the fear from last night.

"I'm sorry, Daire," he begins and his voice cracks. "Desmond passed away early this morning."

It takes longer than it should for his words to register. My mind is unnaturally quiet and my heartbeat is too loud. I clear my throat and struggle to find words. "What?"

"I'm sorry," he repeats, his voice thick with tears. "Aubrie called as soon as he flatlined. He started convulsing and wasn't getting oxygen to his brain. His nose had been bleeding incessantly, his bruises were getting worse, he wasn't healing." Dad takes a moment to compose himself. "I know you two were close. I'm sorry, little swan."

"Daire?" Klowbi whispers and I shake my head. Heavy droplets slink down my cheeks and I'm too frozen to wipe them away.

"He's gone?" I whisper.

"I'm going to help Aubrie with the funeral arrangements, but I would feel more comfortable having you under my roof, at least for a few days. Klowbi is welcome to come," Dad says, ignoring my rhetorical question.

"I'll be there tonight."

"No, I don't want you driving in the dark. Not after last night. Get some rest and make the drive tomorrow. One more night won't hurt." Dad's voice is forcefully light.

I nod before clearing my throat from the sticky pressure. "Sure, yeah, I'll leave tomorrow morning."

"I'm here for you both. Tell Klowbi I love her," Dad says softly. His voice sounds like it's so far away.

"Okay."

"I love you, Daire. Be safe. I'll see you tomorrow."

"Okay. Love you too."

He hangs up the phone. I stare at it before chucking it across the living room only for it to slam into the wall and clatter to the floor. Tears come unbidden no matter how hard I rub at my eyes. The tears smear into my gaping wound and sting from the salt. The sobs come next, followed by the invisible hands wringing my heart to pieces. It's agony, and if there were a spell to quell the pain, I wouldn't hesitate to use it, no matter the cost.

Desmond is dead.

The memories of my dream flash behind my burning eyes and cold realization sends me spiraling. Sobs wrack my shoulders as I heave for breaths that are too small, my cries loud and barren. I knew something wasn't right with those dreams. *It* showed me Desmond's death. Whatever hellscape he had been stuck in during the coma had killed him. The demon hanging onto him had killed him, but only after weeks of endless torture.

He started convulsing and wasn't getting oxygen to his brain.

The dream ended when Desmond was strangled.

"Fuck!" I scream and bury my face in my hands, scrunching into the smallest form I can. I start rocking back and forth, sucking in straws of air and wheezing with the effort. My heart is bleeding in my chest. I feel it sloughing away from the inside.

Arms wrap around me and my sobs worsen at Klowbi's embrace. I scream and swear and sob into my arms, ignoring the shooting pain from my stitches. He is dead. Dead. *Dead.*

First Mom, now Desmond, and Niko might be next.

I saw Desmond die. I killed him.

No, I saw the monster kill him. It wasn't me.

"Damnit," I sob and curl into Klowbi's arms. She rubs my back in slow circles and her grip is so tight she almost manages to bring me back to reality.

After what feels like hours, I finally manage to calm my screams and tears to a trickle. I sniffle and wipe the tears from my swollen face. My head is pounding and a tendril of blood drips into my eye. Klowbi grabs a tissue and gently dabs it away, her eyes just as puffy as mine.

She doesn't say anything, she just holds my hand in hers as we sit in silence. I'm grateful I don't have to explain. She knows. It's not everyday I lose my mind.

Last time I acted like this Mom had died.

"I'm going to lie down in bed," I mumble thickly.

"Do you want company?" she asks with a gentle squeeze of her hand.

I shake my head. "Not right now. Just give me a moment. Find us a lot of movies to watch."

She nods and watches me leave. I don't bother with my half-empty cup of coffee. I already want to vomit the little I did drink.

Shutting the door, I drop to my knees and hold my head in my hands as a fresh wave of tears burn my face. I gasp in a breath of air and look upwards towards the ceiling. The monster stalking Desmond wanted me to see his death, it wanted me to know what it's capable of. Now that Desmond is dead, it will pursue new prey.

And I'm next.

My grief morphs into cold anger. I crawl into bed and lie flat to avoid falling or knocking something over which will inevitably bring Klowbi into my room. This is my last ditch effort for answers. And, guiltily, my way of coping.

Steadying my breaths, I close my eyes and ignore the throbbing in my stitches. I push past the aching in my heart and use it as fuel. My body relaxes and I fall into bliss with the taste of magick potent on my tongue.

Excerpt from Daire's BoS

Book Entry After Fay Delacroix's Funeral

Do not stand at my grave and weep
I am not there; I do not sleep
I am a thousand winds that blow
I am the diamond glints on snow
I am the sunlight on ripened grain
I am the gentle autumn rain
When you awake in the morning's hush
I am the swift uplifting rush
Of quiet birds in circled flight
I am the soft star shine at night
Do not stand at my grave and cry
I am not there; I did not die

Clare Harner

Chapter 25

It doesn't take long for Daire to realize something feels wrong. She has astral projected countless times to the point it feels like second nature, a different way of breathing. But the second her body begins to relax and her mind shoots off to another dimension, she knows she is being pulled and guided rather than controlling the level she coalesces to.

Her essence is bounding through each level in nonexistent heartbeats. The higher the level she goes, the more she realizes the danger she's willingly placing herself in. It's dangerous pulling out of an astral projection before forming, unless adept in manipulating that form. Daire doesn't trust her skillset despite her wide berth of knowledge. A part of her wants to discover what is beckoning her. Remembering the energy that called to her the past two times, she seeks its true identity. After what happened with Desmond and the Shadows, she knows caution would be the smarter move, but her heart is too sick with grief and her mind tunnel-visioned on revenge to ignore curiosity.

Feet hitting the ground, Daire gasps when the thrum of power sends her skin humming. The potency of the magick is making her bones and blood vibrate. She feels high from the pure energy enveloping her. Head dizzy and clear, muscles wired and solid; magick cool and unwinding with barely a thought.

It's the best she's felt in years.

Without the physical limitations of her senses, she observes her surroundings effortlessly. From the intensity of the energy, she knows she is beyond any level she's ever astral projected to on her own accord. Perhaps level twenty, she speculates. Her knowledge suggests she's deep in the Astral Realm. Anything can reside this far into the unknown.

Standing deep within the bowels of a cave system, a gold and silver glow is cast throughout the entirety of the tunnel. Had she been in her physical form, her eyes would have needed to adjust to the darkness. The entire tunnel has diaphanous veins of glowing gems lacing through the flooring, climbing the walls, but stopping at the ceiling that twinkles with the cave system's personal galaxy.

Gold and silver light do nothing to detract from the glimmer of the gemstone stars above or dampen the roiling mists of shifting star clusters. It's impossible to tell the distance between the golden rivers of the floor to the florid galaxy above. Stalagmites rise adorned with silver and gold, reaching high but not quite scraping the ceiling. The stalactites hang from galaxy clouds and nebulas, impossible to see their beginning but appearing to be dripping silver from stars.

Daire brushes a tip of a finger against a stalactite's silver glow. It's frigid to the touch, but her being jolts from the pure essence of magick, her tongue turning into static, skin buzzing with a numbing high. A breathy laugh escapes her and silver beads her breath. Her magick itches beneath her skin from the contact.

With a flick of her wrist, her fingers curl and pull on a thread of magick. A thread is all that's needed. Purple bursts amalgamates with an indigo ribbon which easily molds with the slightest twitch of a muscle or thought. She forms it into a flower of incredible detail before twisting it into a miniature stalactite with its own purple and indigo threads.

The gold and silver glow heightens as she manipulates the magick, feeling not an ounce of exhaustion but rather an increase in power as if the cave is fueling her own energy with its own.

The cave system continues with filaments of luminescent gems veining further inside. Overhead the galaxy shifts and distorts, forever changing and glimmering. Daire treads deeper, brushing her fingers against the veins and reaching up to touch the breathing universe despite knowing she will never reach.

The familiarity of energy sends her insides coiling, recognizing the invisible pull from before. It's even stronger now, an invisible tether blindingly guiding her to the other end. Whatever is calling to her, she isn't afraid to face it. Daire knows she hadn't been ready before, but after Desmond's death and the Shadows' attack, waiting would prove fruitless. If this tether is calling to her it has to mean something. If someone means to harm her, she trusts her ability to escape. Yet her gut feeling says they would have already done so.

Whatever is calling her forward, it is here on this plane with her. It feels close. A large cavern opening yawns ahead, and her gut tightens at the change. The tether is growing stronger as she approaches the cave. It's in there somewhere, waiting.

The entrance of the cave glows and swirls like the aurora borealis, dotted with diamonds for stars. Daire touches the edge of rough stone and it's searing to the touch. Had she been in her physical form, her hand would have blistered and bled, but there is no pain to greet her despite the uncomfortable itch of heat. She walks through and stops at the gaping threshold, slack jawed.

A tree of ethereal beauty grows in the center of the cave system. It's larger than a redwood, larger than anything in the physical realm. Looking at the ceiling, Daire breathes with the cosmos, unable to see the top of the tree. It's growing forever up into the cavern and hasn't breached the top. The tunnel's gold and silver glow fades, replaced by the massive tree's radiance.

Threads of gems from the tunnel have woven into the larger cave system, veining around the tree but never intercepting, and forms a circle around the base. The tree seems to have molded with the cavern, growing with it and utilizing it in all its forms. She can almost imagine the veins on the floor representing the roots of the ethereal tree.

Whispers of silver vein from the base of the tree and up towards the trunk before shifting to colors of the rainbow with prevalence of purples and pinks. Its leaves, though they appear feathery, shift like iridescent scales, never holding their color for long. They hold an undertone of silver, similar to the base, and the feathered leaves seem to reflect the celestial kaleidoscope above.

Daire walks closer, unafraid and unseeing of anything except the elysian astral creation ahead. As the distance dissipates, she notices the silver veining crawling along the trunk are runes, though none she is familiar with. They pulse with age and of knowledge no human can understand, of truths and lies better left unknown. They aren't from Earth. Symbols glow brighter with each tree pulse as if it has a heartbeat. Despite there being no wind, the feathered leaves above whisper and shift. A shiver steals down her spine and her magick stirs within.

The tether is taut as if the other end is within the tree. Daire extends an inked hand and places it firmly against the silver glow of the trunk. The bark is rough and warm, and a calmness washes over her. Even the grief held within her heart lessens. Her flesh sings from the touch and her skin glows with the colors of the bark. Her skin tingles, her magick stirs, and an indigo glow from her fingers feeds back into the divine being, glowing in time with the bark and wanting more.

There's a shift in the surrounding energy, enough to stir her hair and the whispers of the feathered leaves above. Daire retracts her hand and the welcoming warmth and calmness drains. Her skin no longer glows, but there's a phantom tingle where her magick was interacting with the celestial tree. Something sets her shoulders rigid and Daire swivels on her heel.

An iridescent mist the same shifting color as the feathered leaves forms a few feet away. The glow of the rocky tree roots and the tree itself reflect off the mist until a shape takes form. Within a breath, a woman is standing where the mist coalesced.

Her skin is pale and her hair is an unending black, thickly braided over a shoulder. Her dress is simple, showing off her generous curves with a deep cut revealing much of her breasts. There's a fine line at the hem and the long sleeves of her dress similar to spider silk. The material appears black, yet reflects the shimmer and vibrancy in the cave. Her dress is like the ceiling, the cosmos cut into clothing.

When her eyes open, the stutter in Daire's heart has her stumbling closer. Her eyes are a brilliant flash of amber and blue. Hair the color of space between the stars. Her physique is so familiar and foreign Daire can't stop herself from reaching out and stepping closer.

"Mom?" Daire whispers, her voice is loud in the silence of the cavern.

The woman smiles and opens her arms wide. "Black Swan." Her voice is sweet and warm, reminiscent of the celestial tree when she had made contact.

When Daire is standing an arm's reach away, her hope plummets. The woman's voice sounds deeper, raspier than her mother's. Her hair is the same as Daire's, but her mother always let it fly free instead of keeping it wrapped in a braid. While they had similar body types, this woman is more endowed on top. But it's her eyes that give it away. Unlike Daire's, along with her mother's, amber and blue eyes, this woman's is gold and plum.

Anger floods where hope once was. Daire takes a step back, her eyes narrowing and her fists clenching by her sides. Deception has her magick sizzling, and already Daire is debating how to hurt the stranger standing so close. It isn't until she realizes the tether is to this mysterious woman, not the ethereal tree behind her, that she slightly relaxes her standoff stance.

"Who the hell are you?" Daire demands acridly. She raises her palms in her familiar fighting stance with thick swathes of red magick pooling around her palms. The glow in the cavern ignites and the tingle of increased power chases down her spine.

The woman smiles knowingly, baring her teeth, and shakes her head dismissively as if disappointed. Her arms slowly fall to her sides and she takes one step closer. The cosmos of her dress rustles. "Child, that is no way to speak to your elder."

"Do not call me child," Daire retorts and manipulates the swathes of red magick to surround the mystery woman. The woman smiles wryly, her plum gold eyes locked onto Daire. "Don't fuck with me. Answer the question."

The woman chuckles and glances lazily at the magick swarming and blocking her path. "You have a mouth on you," she comments. "There's no need for such brashness. I'm here to help you, Daire. Please, send your magick away." She bats a hand at the flaring red teeming around her.

"How do you know my name?" Daire increases her magick flow. With a flick, the swarm engulfs the woman, leaving only her face visible.

The woman's smile quickly shifts, irritation evident in her eyes. "I will explain, but first, this must go," she scolds and with an adroit twirl of her fingers, the magick disperses with a sigh and dissipates into the air. Lights from the cavern dim after the magick has settled. "Much better. Now, come closer. I'm sure you have questions."

Fear prickles the back of her neck. This woman is able to manipulate her magick like it's nothing. Clearly she is adept at magick and controlling it in the Astral Realm. A formidable foe. Though her fear is hovering, it can't hide the tether calling her closer to the stranger. Her magick isn't perturbed by the woman's presence, and it helps that she looks like Daire's mother.

Daire stalks forward the remaining distance. She doesn't want to submit to the request, but she's curious about this lady she feels inexplicably bound to. Once standing directly in front of her, she crosses her arms and grits her teeth.

"I'm grateful that we are finally able to meet. I've been trying to contact you these past weeks and I found I made the most progress when we were both in the Astral Realm. I know you still feel my energy calling to yours. Do not reject it. The sooner you embrace it, the easier it will be to talk in the future." The woman smiles warmly and clasps her hands in front of her with a slight bow of her head. "My name is Adeline Delacroix. I'm your grandmother with many greats in front. And as I said before, I'm here to help you, Daire."

"How do I know you aren't lying?" Daire asks and takes a step back. "It's not unknown that some projectors can shift their appearance."

"You wish for proof?" Adeline asks, arching a thin black brow. She huffs, clearly irritated, and Daire recognizes the habit as her own. "My presence here should suffice as proof. Fine. I appreciate the skepticism." Adeline's gaze is fierce as she watches Daire. "I know of our entire lineage. I know that you only have one true born Delacroix cousin, a girl of twenty named Sabrina, fathered by Aiden Stone and born by Mayve Delacroix. They have forbidden their daughter to utilize her gifts, quite foolish I must say. Mayve is the youngest of two, her elder sister being the late Fay Delacroix who passed on Halloween. But, this is all public records, is it not? I'll go deeper then. I see the doubt on your face.

"*Fay was your mentor, guiding you the moment you took your first breath. You were born with near a full head of hair and you rarely cried as a child. As you got older, you realized you weren't normal like the rest. You could see things others couldn't, like magick and Shadows.*" *Adeline sighs and brushes a stray strand of hair behind her ear.* "*At nine years old, you came home from school terrified of Shadows that mocked you, unseen by others. Your friends thought you were peculiar and crazy because of this, so you learned to keep quiet. But they kept getting closer because you kept feeding them your fear. Fay taught you how to be rid of them, didn't she? With a lock of hair, a candle, essential oil, and a few words, the Shadows disappeared. It didn't take long for you to latch onto your power. You knew you were better than the kids at school. You were gifted. So when one of the kids tried threatening you, once you returned home, you decided to teach them a lesson. At the age of ten, you attempted baneful magick for the first time. Quite remarkable. They left you alone after that, partly because they were in the hospital after falling ill overnight. To further prove, I can elaborate on your third instance of baneful magic. That was a feat, though the aftermath—*"

"*Alright!*" *Daire shouts, raising her hands.* "*I believe you.*"

Adeline smiles and Daire returns the favor bitterly. "*Good, then we can get to the real reason I'm here.*" *Her nimble fingers smooth the shifting cosmos of her gown, sending ripples down its length.* "*I've been watching everything that's been happening in the physical realm from the Astral Realm. And when I can, I've been trying to protect you. The Shadows pose a greater threat than I could have anticipated. They are growing too smart too fast, and their latest attack is evidence of this.*" *She pauses and her youthful features crinkle into regret and sympathy as creases form around her mouth and eyes.* "*Your friend, Niko, he is brave. I'm sorry I was unable to help him that night.*"

"*Get to the point,*" *Daire snaps, her voice leaden with chagrin.*

"*Shadows are only part of the whole. Something has been following you.*" *Adeline's gold plum eyes flash to the Shadow wound on Daire's arm, though unseen in the Astral Realm.* "*It has marked you. I tried to prevent it, but it was stronger than I could foresee.*"

"*What marked me? This happened in a dream,*" *Daire remarks with a guarded tone. Her eyes widen in understanding as they flutter from the glowing ribbons of the cavern back to Adeline's tight features. "It was you. You were in my dream with the fires."*

"Yes, I tried protecting you in the only form I could. Unfortunately, my efforts were for naught." Adeline reaches forward and gently presses a hand to where Daire's Shadow wound would be. Her touch is gentle, delicate, and Daire has the urge to lean into it. She doesn't. "I'm grateful I was able to manifest the day you foolishly decided to brave the festival grounds alone. Even you wouldn't have been able to fight all those Shadows."

"That was you?" Daire whispers. "But I thought it was Lilith as the owl."

"It was the best way for you to understand you were being protected. I followed Lilith's guidance when I was a young witch. Same as you. I hoped you would catch on that something was watching over you. A guardian angel, if you will."

"Thank you," Daire mumbles.

Adeline drops her hand before folding them in front of her abdomen. "Do not thank me, child. I have come to help you erase a mistake I created."

"What mistake?" Her eyes flitter behind her to the magnanimous astral tree. It appears to be pulsing with a heartbeat and the feathered leaves shudder.

"There is a reason why Delacroixs do not live to their full lives. Why most only birth one child under the Delacroix name. And why I have been stuck in limbo." Adeline grimaces and her shoulders tense. Her eyes appear to glow before dimming in the gleaming cavern. "Centuries ago, back when I was still alive, a few close friends and I would practice the Craft. Engaging in such abhorrent acts was strictly prohibited, leading to a falsified trial and execution."

"Witch trials," Daire murmurs.

Adeline nods in acknowledgement. "Yes, witch trials. One night, we fell on poor chance, and a dear friend of mine was caught. Somehow I evaded being seen, but my friend did not. She was taken into custody and tried for witchcraft and devil worship. Despite the fact we never once used our magick for ill, her pleas fell on deaf ears. She was burned alive." Adeline's features twist into a cruel mask before softening once more, her gaze refocusing. "I wished for revenge, and so I began my journey into the darker arts of magick.

The spells and rituals that should be forgotten and buried deep I dug up and practiced relentlessly. I'm sure you can imagine the transformation. Magick of this kind corrupts the soul and toxifies the magick of the wielder. I realized too late the damage to my own person could not be rectified, but I still sought revenge."

"Did you get it?" Daire asks. "Did you avenge your friend?"

Her smile is cold and her head dips once. "Yes. Not only did I murder those who murdered my friend, but I destroyed the entire town in the process. I did not regret it. A part of me still doesn't." She levels her gaze on Daire. "But I regret bringing this burden onto my descendants. Onto you."

"What's the burden? I don't understand what all this has to do with me." Daire tenses at the peering stare of Adeline. If what Adeline says is true, then it explains why she's so powerful. But it leaves more unanswered questions than it does answer them.

"I perished in that town. Magick killed me, but something was born from my death and it latched onto my daughter, Serina. She bore the burden, the first of many." Adeline finally turns her gaze to the tree, her features limned in silver and hues of elysian life. "I believe I created a curse that's passed down from one generation of Delacroix to the next. The magick in our blood bonds with the curse. We cannot hide from it. It cannot be avoided." Adeline goes to stand beside Daire. She shifts to study the cavern and the astral tree.

"Have you ever wondered why you never met your grandmother on the Delacroix side? Why most don't live past fifty? Why your mother suddenly sickened and nothing could prevent it, not even magick?" Adeline pauses as her words sink in. Daire turns to face her with an accusatory glare. "It is the curse. You are next, Daire. You are the eldest Delacroix and you may have another decade or so before it catches you. But it will catch up and you will die, just like my beautiful daughter, just like all the daughters descended, and just like your mother."

Daire keeps her gaze glued to the feathered leaves shifting like scales. Her heart is hammering so hard in her chest she can feel the throbbing in her temple from her stitches in her physical form. The dread that clutches her insides urges her to scream and lash out.

"Are you fucking serious?" she growls, clutching at her head.

"Unfortunately, yes," Adeline says, pursing her lips. "Watch your tongue. It's filthy."

Daire shoots her a glare to match her filthy tongue. "I'd say my response is adequate, considering you damned the entire Delacroix lineage. Thanks for that by the way."

Adeline smiles again and a surge of animosity crinkles Daire's face. "I told you to not thank me," she replies, turning to address Daire. The expression on her face paired with the brilliance in her gold plum eyes defies her expectations of defeat. There's a glimmer of cunning and perhaps even madness. "I found a way to not only halt the curse, but to destroy it. I cannot achieve this goal as I only exist here. I need someone in the physical realm. I need someone who can wield magick as easily as they can breathe. Someone who can learn quickly and will not shy away from what needs to be done. And they must be a Delacroix."

"And you think that's me?"

"I know it must be you. You are one of the most brilliant witches ever born, Daire. You trust your magick and you learn faster than most I've ever seen. Your will and gift are undeniable, but the sacrifice will be excessive. If this works, never again will a Delacroix fear growing old and bearing children. And you will live." Adeline lifts a hand and gently brushes a thumb over Daire's jaw. Despite the urge to pull away, she holds still. Adeline smiles at the acceptance of her touch. "This is an ask you are welcome to deny, but know you have lived half your life already if you wish not to proceed."

Daire pulls her head from Adeline's touch. She turns to face the tree again, willing for an answer to become apparent. Her options are limited already, but this new information leaves her cornered. If she refuses to end the curse, her life will end by fifty and her children will share the same fate. However, the threat of the Shadows remains, and their intertwined nature will grant them an opportunity to grow stronger in mind, strength, and military strategy. They have the potential to wipe out the human race, if not turn it into an apocalyptic nightmare.

"What about my aunt or my cousin? Wouldn't this affect them?" Sabrina embodied the essence of a Delacroix. Wasn't this her burden, too?

"I believe the curse will reach them as well. They are not safe. Though the fact they do not actively practice bodes in their favor. They are not in tune with the magick in their blood, leaving it dormant, therefore leaving the curse temporarily dormant. They may gain a few extra years, but in the end, it will claim them too."

"So it's me or no one."

"Yes, so it seems."

"What is the connection between the Shadows and the curse? I understand where I come into play, but not how they do." Daire crosses her arms as Adeline purses her lips again.

Another huff of annoyance escapes past Adeline's lips. "The magick I used to destroy the town and its residents was darker than anything you could conjure today. It corrupted me. As I was learning the secrets, I received help from a Shadow, though I don't believe it was the typical Shadows you've been dealing with. This one was different. It held itself differently, had higher intelligence, and it could interact with my dreams, and eventually it could guide me while I was awake. It couldn't harm me, but it could feed off of my energy and, in turn, fuel my power. I believe whatever it was, it manifested as the curse, and over the years it has increased its individual power. With the flux of power it was able to manifest itself into different realms and became able to communicate with like-minded beings, though of lesser status.

"I believe the Shadow that aided me is using the Delacroixs as a means to an end, and the Shadows you are dealing with are the army it's creating." Adeline glances at Daire before continuing. "I know this is a lot and I'm sorry to pass this burden onto you. If we can stop the curse from progressing, in theory, it would stop the Shadows as well. You have the potential for great things. I can mentor and guide you. I'll share all my knowledge, making you one of the most powerful witches to have ever lived. But there will be sacrifice, and once we start down this journey, you cannot turn back. You must commit and you must not flinch."

"But I can stop it? I can save my family?"

"Yes, I believe it is possible."

"Alright," she says and turns back to face the unnerving gold plum eyes. "I believe you. I'll do whatever I can if it means I can protect them."

Adeline's features are strained and her pale skin appears ashen. "As long as this is your choice. You must commit entirely."

"It is and I will."

"Then it is done. Our connection you feel will only grow with time now that we have spoken and you have accepted my guidance." Adeline brushes a thumb along her jaw again, a tentative smile on her red lips. "I will reach out to you within the next few days. I have many preparations to make, so please rest until then." She smiles again and her eyes have a weary sheen to them. "My condolences for your loss. Desmond was taken too soon. Such a powerful soul."

Daire starts and takes a tentative step back. "How did you...?"

"I told you, I've been watching for a while." Adeline takes a step back, holding her gaze. "We will speak soon, Black Swan."

And just as she first appeared, an iridescent mist coalesces where Adeline once stood, hiding her form until it dissipates, and leaving behind nothing but empty space.

Chapter 26

Relief floods through me as I pull into Thayne's gravel drive. My eyes ache from exhaustion and tears and my stitches itch furiously. Painkillers and magick fail to soothe the discomfort, leaving me to futilely rub the throbbing skin.

Klowbi wanted to come, but I refused her. She didn't know Desmond like I did, and I know she meant to be my support like when Mom passed yet I couldn't agree. The only reason I managed to convince her was because of Niko. He needed her more than me when he woke up. She agreed to stay home, but promised to call me every day for updates on both our ends. I told her I'd be home after Desmond's funeral, assuming nothing else happened.

As soon as I made it out of town and onto mostly empty roads, I tried focusing on the tether pulling at my center. Even now I feel Adeline's faint call whispering to me. When I tried feeding into it and calling it closer, the tether seemed to strain and grow faint. I stopped as soon as the feeling surfaced, and once the feeling returned to how it was, I attempted once more. Again I received the same result. After three unsuccessful tries, I abandoned my efforts and turned my attention to the lengthy journey ahead. I would have to ask Adeline the next time we spoke how to strengthen our bond.

Perhaps against my better judgment, I decided to keep Adeline my secret for now. No need for the others to get involved. They had too much to deal with. And they wouldn't understand that this wasn't me trying to satisfy my curiosity anymore, this was personal.

This had turned into a vendetta.

Trusting what Adeline had described regarding the Delacroix curse and the explanation for the sudden and violent death of my mother proved my own theory was correct. I knew her death wasn't normal. As much as I love Dad and Klowbi, they didn't want to hear about my theory on Mom's supernatural death. But I was right. If they didn't believe me then, I doubt they'd believe me now, even with the uproar of what we've been dealing with the Shadows. They'd more than likely try to brush it off as a misled trauma response, desperation of organizing chaos, and looking for answers where there weren't any.

After the dust settles, I exit the vehicle and approach the front door. Most of the herbs along the porch have bloomed and been placed in larger pots, the smell of lavender near overwhelming. A dirty spade lies on the porch floor while the front door remains open. It's a warm day, the sun dappling the lush grass through the clouds.

Guilt seizes me as I rap on the open door. The last time I was here, Klowbi was with me and we had requested Thayne's guidance before seeing Dad. I borrowed two books which should have been locked away but are now hidden in my car. Guilt isn't enough for me to confess; there is still so much I have yet to learn from them. I will return them eventually, but only after I read everything. He couldn't miss what he doesn't know he had.

"Come in," Thayne calls from inside.

Entering, I follow his voice to the kitchen. Thayne is washing vegetables in the sink, and he turns to me with a grieving smile as he towels his hands dry. "It's a relief to see you Daire," he says as his eyes flicker over my face and the line of stitches across my brow. He opens his arms wide and I comply, grasping him in a hug. His arms are solid and warm, and for a moment I feel my walls begin to melt. Steeling myself, I pull away before my emotions wash away my resolve.

"I can't stay long," I say and pinch my pendant between my fingers.

"No rush on my end, you can stay as long as you'd like. I'll be heading that direction tomorrow to help Aubrie and give your father a break." Thayne's smile twists my heart. "How are your friends?"

I shrug, looking past him towards the closed barn doors that lead to the library. "Rattled, but breathing," I reply. "How's Aubrie?"

Thayne rubs the back of his neck and shakes his head. "Not well, as you can imagine. She's lost her only child a second time. The coma scare was bad, but now she's entirely disconnected from reality. She goes through the motions, hardly eats, she's empty." He tilts his head, offering a knowing smile. "Not that I have to explain this to you."

No, I understand Aubrie's situation better than most. "What did you want to show me?" I ask, gesturing to the barn doors.

"I was reorganizing and cataloging the literature when I came across a box with Fay's name." Thayne doesn't miss a beat while he explains and leads the way through the barn doors and towards a darker alcove. The curtains are drawn but a slash of sunshine cuts across the table with a cardboard box filled with stacked tomes. He comes to a stop in the score of light and the books in shadow.

"As you're aware, I have hundreds to thousands of books in my library, some gifted while others were found or handed off to me for safekeeping. Dallan asked me to hold onto these items after Fay passed. Naturally I agreed, and I had stashed them in the backroom to go through when the time was right." Thayne glances at the books and his eyes appear even glossier from the rays slipping through. "I only just rediscovered the contents, and I hate to admit curiosity got the better of me as I leafed through them. They were not meant for my eyes, so I called you. I glimpsed enough to find they originated from a Delacroix. Dallan may not have been aware of the box's contents when he gave it to me."

"Why didn't he offer it to me?" I mumble and brush my thumb over the spine of the top book. It made my heart quicken and ache knowing my mother was one of the last ones to have held it.

"Death makes memories painful," Thayne answers solemnly. "Grief replaces our logic. I'm sure sorting through her belongings and years of life together was difficult. They had loved each other since they met." He chuckles with pained amusement. "I imagine Dallan was sorting quickly which is why he handed it off to me and not to a dumpster. I'd suggest asking him if you're uncertain."

It's sound logic. Dad ran on autopilot, fulfilling all obligations while taking precious little time to mourn until later. The house was sold not long after and suddenly my childhood was uprooted and twisted, mottled with grief and despair. Within seconds, my life was thrown off its axis and had never resumed to normal.

Stemming the tremor in my hands, I lift the first book from the box and tenderly turn the pages, glancing at a few to decipher the topic. I place it down and take the next one, thinner than the first, and quickly flip through its pages. The cover is smooth and silky with very little dust littered on the pages.

"I cleaned them as best I could before you came. While sorting I found most of them were old spell books and past teachings passed down from generations. There's decades of teachings there. From the little bit I read, some appeared to be of the old way, traditions long since modernized." Thayne steps back and the slash of sunlight reaches over my inked hands and onto the books piling beside the box. The covers shine in the light, smoothed from generations of use.

Thayne's insistence on my visit for old spell books puzzles me. While the books are intriguing, the urgency lacks significance. Then I find the final book at the bottom of the stack. The binding is old and frays along the ridges of the spine and corners. The cover is gray leather, appearing mottled like the color was darker but diluted with time. As if made of glass, I lay it out in front of me and smooth the cover with my palm. My chest tightens, my heartbeat rapid in my throat, when I comprehend what I'm staring at.

"I admit I read a few pages, but nothing sensitive. I haven't touched them since besides tending to the tears and mending what I can," Thayne says, his voice a smooth rumble.

"Does Dad know?" I ask and flip through a few pages. My heart is beating faster as I scan the smooth scrawl with curling loops and whorls. Fine penmanship.

"No, I doubted he wanted it returned with how quickly he handed it off. I know you would have wanted this in your possession."

"Thank you."

I have never seen this book before, nor did Mom ever mention this hidden stash. At first glance, the gray-leather bound book could easily be overlooked, but not with a witch's eye. It's clear that this book was well-tended to despite the slight wear and filled with pages of handwritten scrawl.

It's a Book of Shadows.

The further into the book I scour, the more unfamiliar the magick becomes. There are countless spells, rituals, potions, and symbols scribbled across the yellowed pages. The ink, despite the decades of age, shimmers in the sunlight. I go through it faster, scanning the loads of information at my disposal.

"Who owns it?" My voice is breathless and I glance up at Thayne to find his dark eyes studying me before turning back to the pages. The smell of musty paper clogs my nose.

He leans over to point at an initial at the bottom of the page. The ink is smudged, but readable after a moment.

"MD?" I mumble and flip through several more pages before stopping at a section where a handful of pages were torn from the spine leaving only flayed shreds in its place. "Do you happen to know about the missing pages?"

"No, but they appear to have been ripped from the book long ago." Thayne shifts and a shadow flits over the pages. "Everything Dallan gave me was in those boxes. I'll let you know if I find any spare pages floating around, but I presume they are long gone."

"Thank you," I say again and meet his gaze. "I wanted to see this."

"I knew you would. They are yours to take. You stake more claim to them than I do." Thayne begins to retreat so I have a space in the cordoned off alcove. "I'll be in the kitchen if you need anything."

I nod in acknowledgment but I don't notice his absence. I'm too focused on reading the neat script. I trace my finger over the edge of the sheared paper centered in the spine of the book, scanning the pages before and after the missing text. I reread pages and pause when a phrase, ritual instruction, or symbol catches my eye from familiarity. Then I move to the next paragraph, questioning what vital information has been ripped free.

A strange pull from the center of my chest sends warmth tingling through my lungs and ribs, warming the cavity around my heart. Adeline's tether is calling to me. I send out magick feelers through the bond and this time they reach her.

Seven days... her voice whispers in my head before falling silent.

Excerpt from MD's BoS

Lucid dreaming has been my preferred method of meditation. For weeks I have struggled maintaining mastery of my mind. Where once I found peace and solace, now dread and paranoia fill the void.

My dreams are no longer mine. They feel tainted, foreign, bastardized. Neurosis ascending control.

When I wake I recall little. Blurry images, muffled sounds, sour smells. Something hides in the deep recess, yet upon waking there is no recollection beyond fear.

The spell is near complete. If successful, my recordings will remove the haze of my consciousness. The third eye will open.

MD

Thank you for joining me on this journey. Whether you were here from the very beginning or discovered the magick along the way, your support has turned a dream into a reality.

Each time I meet one of you it reminds me why I love what I do. Your belief in these pages, in this world, and in me means the world to me.

If the characters made you laugh, cry, or gasp in horror, please leave a review or rate the book. Your support helps more than you realize.

Thank you for reading and taking a chance on this story.

Much love,

A. R. Stern